Since I Last Saw You

a novel by
Alice Ann Kuder

With gratitude
Alice Ann Kuder

The Telltale Scribe
Seattle, Washington

Published by The Telltale Scribe, Seattle, WA
ISBN: 978-0-615-92523-3

Grateful acknowledgement is made for permission to use the following copyrighted materials: "Joy is Like the Rain." Words and music by Miriam Therese Winter. © copyright: Medical Mission Sisters, 1965. All rights reserved. Used with permission. "Lessons." Words and music by Shari Kruse. © copyright 2013. All rights reserved. Used with permission. "Since." Words and music by Shari Kruse. © copyright 2013. All rights reserved. Used with permission. "Waiting for the Rain." Words and music by Shari Kruse. © copyright 2013. All rights reserved. Used with permission. "Thanksgiving Song." Words and music by Shari Kruse. © copyright 2013. All rights reserved. Used with permission. "What Thou Givest." Rabbi Morris Adler. © copyright 1967. Reprinted from B'nai B'rith International.

Dedication

This book is dedicated to the legion of extraordinary teachers I have been fortunate enough to encounter in my lifetime, some in traditional classrooms, and many more outside of academia.

I want to express my deep appreciation to my very first teachers, my parents, Marge and Al Kuder, and my sisters, Susan Kuder Dunn, Joan Kuder Bell, Mary Kuder Pong, and Lori Kuder Bento.

I share my protagonist's dilemma of having a list of Georges too long to publish, so I will single out one of my teachers and let her represent all the others: Noreen Higgins.

Mrs. Higgins was one of my English teachers at Centralia High School. As I recall, I only took one class from her and we didn't get to know each other well. The reason she stands out is because she is the first person who ever pulled me aside and commended me on my writing abilities. I have never forgotten her praise and encouragement, and I credit her with setting my feet on the yellow brick road that led directly to the publication of this novel.

Prologue
November 21, 2012

Ali sat looking out the window at the driving rain, one hand propping up her chin and the other absentmindedly stroking the cracked leather upholstery of the well-worn couch. She loved this little hideaway where she could be alone without being lonely.

She and Isaac had stumbled upon the cabin while hiking the backwoods of Mount Baker in the North Cascades. *How many years ago was that? Ten? Fifteen? No, it must have been fourteen years ago,* she thought, *because it was the year we got engaged.* It was about this time of year—late November—but the weather then was dry and crisp. The trees were dropping the last of their leaves, carpeting the ground with a mosaic of gold and red and orange. It was a magical autumn.

Today, however, Mother Nature was showing her more dramatic side. The wind and rain had already been pummeling the area for hours and the weather forecast was for more of the same throughout the night, possibly all weekend.

If Ali were less familiar with this place, she might have been more concerned about being alone on a mountaintop during such a violent storm. But she had arrived a few hours earlier in her ancient-yet-dependable Jeep Cherokee, fully intending to stay put for several days. Despite her family's protestations, this is where she wanted to spend her first Thanksgiving since the death of her husband and daughter ten months earlier.

"And it's going to be a day. There is really no way to say 'no' to the morning." ~ Dan Fogelberg

Chapter 1
February 13, 2012

Ali was slow to wake this morning. The clock claimed it was 7:13 a.m., but the room was still dark. *Why*, she wondered, *were the shades drawn?* She always left them open when she went to bed so she would wake with the morning sun. Isaac had long ago acquiesced to her preference for morning light, even though he preferred to delay his own waking as long as possible.

Isaac. Zoe. For those first few merciful moments after waking, she had forgotten that Isaac and Zoe were gone. Forgotten that her life was irrevocably changed. Forgotten that the future she and Isaac had so carefully planned was now an unattainable wish.

How, she wondered, *could we both have taken for granted how fragile life is?* A wave of physical and emotional pain enveloped her, sending her back under the down comforter, where she gratefully fell back to sleep.

An hour later, as she slowly reawakened to her new reality, it seemed to Ali as if every emotion she had ever felt and every experience she had ever had, had become like colored shards of memory forming a kaleidoscope in her brain. The pieces, though vivid in her mind, collided and changed so rapidly that she wasn't able to make sense of the patterns they formed. She felt dizzy, off-balance, and nauseous.

Reluctantly, Ali sat up, pulled back the covers and set her feet on the floor. Looking across the room, she saw her reflection in the vanity mirror. The beguiling, Cheshire grin that was Ali's hallmark, was nowhere to be found, but her dark, thick mane brushed her shoulders as usual. She was glad to see that her bangs camouflaged the creases that seemed to have appeared on her forehead overnight. *I guess this is what a forty-two year old widow looks like*, she thought to herself. Then she burrowed back down under her comforter, praying that it would live up to its name.

She wondered again about who had drawn the bedroom curtains. Hearing the familiar rattle of teacups coming from her kitchen, Ali knew she wasn't alone. Several friends and relatives had offered to stay and keep her company in this home she no longer shared with anyone, but who had actually spent the night? Ali tried to remember the previous evening, but she couldn't think clearly.

A moment later, she heard a light knock on the bedroom door. "Come in," she responded, more out of habit than any real desire to see anyone.

"I didn't wake you, did I? I thought I heard you stirring." Of course it was Gwen who spent the night. How could Ali not have guessed that?

"Would you like some coffee or something to eat?"

Ali's stomach convulsed at the thought of eating, but she was also conscious of feeling weakened by a lack food. Eating had not been a priority, or even a desire, since the accident three days earlier.

Had it really been just three days? Hadn't Isaac and Zoe already been gone for a lifetime?

"Thanks, Gwen, but I don't want anything just now. I'll eat something after I shower and get dressed." *If I shower and get dressed*, she thought to herself.

Gwen entered the room, sat on the edge of the bed, and took Ali's hand in her own. "How are you feeling this morning? I know that's kind of a lame question, but I don't know what else to say. I guess that's pretty ironic since I write greeting cards for a living."

Ali didn't answer right away. She was grateful that Gwen was the kind of friend who could tolerate silence, because answers to even the simplest of questions didn't come quickly or easily now.

How are you feeling? How many times had she already been asked that question since the accident, by well-meaning friends and family, not to mention medical personnel and police officers? *Gwen was right to ask it*, Ali thought. It is the requisite question at times like this, and although probably less perfunctory than when asked during the course of an ordinary day, she always felt unable to come up with an accurately descriptive answer. And today was no exception.

"I'm fine. I'm okay." Those answers weren't exactly lies, but they weren't exactly the truth either—at least, not the whole truth. It seemed strange to Ali that it should take so much effort to answer a simple question, especially when the answer didn't really matter. *I am how I am*, she thought.

"I feel . . ." she began slowly, "I feel as if I am drifting through time and space, like the pictures you see of astronauts floating around their spaceships in zero gravity."

It's true, she thought to herself, *the law of gravity no longer applies to me. Isaac and Zoe kept me grounded. Without them, I expect that I may just float away.*

"Is that a good feeling or a bad feeling?" Gwen asked.

"I'm not sure," Ali confessed. "More good than bad, I guess. It's like the out-of-body experiences people describe when they die on the operating table. Like I'm watching myself, but I can't really feel anything."

Ali fell silent again for a minute, before continuing. "Numb. I guess 'numb' is the best way to describe how I feel. Does *numb* count as a feeling? I mean, isn't it the antithesis of a feeling?"

"It counts," Gwen affirmed, "but I don't know how long it will last. I hate to state the obvious, my friend, but there is a lot of pain ahead of you, and once it hits, I suspect you'll wish you could feel numb again."

∮∰

Gwen's prediction was devastatingly accurate. In the days and weeks that followed, Ali suffered one painful emotion after another—sadness, anger, confusion, disbelief, and despair. Sometimes a single feeling lingered for days, until she knew it intimately. More often, several different facets of pain combined, forming an emotional cyclone that gathered strength and speed until she was mercifully thrown clear for a while. Sometimes, the respite came from activity—physically putting herself in motion as Isaac had so often done. More often, it came in the form of sleep. She was grateful that sleep had always been her mind and body's natural coping mechanism during times of stress.

How awful it would be, she thought, *to have insomnia when all you want to do is escape from your own thoughts.*

Naps, Ali contended, *are wasted on the young.* She remembered how she used to hate them as a child. When her sister and brother were both old enough to go to school, and it was just Ali and her mother left at home during the day, Ali insisted that she was "too old" for naps. However, by midafternoon each day, it was obvious that she was not.

Mom allowed her youngest daughter to save face by declaring 1 p.m. to be "story hour." Every Monday morning, the two of them made a trip to the library and brought home a week's worth of books. Every afternoon, Ali would choose one of the books and climb onto her mom's lap, where she would inevitably fall asleep during the story telling.

Ali carried on the tradition with her own daughter, Zoe, and now was so grateful that she had. Oh, what she wouldn't give for the solace of feeling Zoe curled up in her lap once again—or to curl up in her own mother's lap today.

℥℥

Ali realized how fortunate she was to have so many caring friends and family volunteering their help. *"If there's anything you need . . ."* was a genuine, if vague, offer she had heard many, many times since the accident. It was the same offer she had often made to countless friends in similar unhappy circumstances. Rarely did anyone take her up on it, even though she had also been sincere. Now she understood why.

Opening the drawer of her bedside table, Ali pulled out her leather-bound journal and pen, and began to write.

13 February 2012

Everyone keeps asking me if I need anything. What I need is for someone to tell me what I need. I can't focus long enough to figure out what I

Alice Ann Kuder

ought to be doing. I'm sure there are all kinds of things to take care of, but I can't seem to think of what they are. Isaac used to tease me about the endless lists I make to keep myself organized and feeling in control. Now, I can't even come up with a list, let alone check things off. Being organized just doesn't seem important anymore. And being in control . . . well, that was always an illusion, wasn't it?

Ali had purchased this particular journal more than a year earlier. Until recently, it contained only a smattering of innocuous entries. Now, over half the pages were filled with rants, ramblings, questions, and grievances. More than a few pages were stained by her tears.

Just then, the doorbell rang, bringing her out of her reverie and back to the present. *Am I expecting someone?* She couldn't remember. She peeked out through the etched-glass side window to see her mother standing on the front porch. Shaking her head in an attempt to clear the fog that so often enveloped her mind these days, she chastised herself, *how could I have forgotten that Mom was coming over?*

Ali's entire body relaxed at the sight of her mother, knowing that the only thing separating her from sheer comfort and affection was a few inches of wood.

Chapter 2
1976-1982

"It's Lassie! Mommy, Daddy, look! Gramma and Grandpa Donker sent me a Lassie dog for my birthday, just like the one on TV!" Six-year-old Ali was beside herself with joy! Jumping up and down while clutching the stuffed animal to her chest, she declared, "Oh, I love you, Lassie!"

"That's wonderful, Sweetheart! She's just beautiful," said her mother. "Gramma and Grandpa really wanted to be here, Honey, but they just couldn't make the trip this year. Gramma's not feeling very well."

"I wish they were here. I like it when they come to visit. Grandpa always gives us gum even though he's not 'sposed to," eight-year-old Nathan said with a giggle.

"Tattletale!" Chloe admonished.

Turning everyone's attention back to the birthday girl, her father said, "Looks like you have one last present, Ali Oop. Let's see what it is."

Ali held the stuffed animal tightly with one arm while reaching for the unopened gift. She somehow managed to rip the paper off without letting go of her new best friend.

"It's a coloring book! And it's full of pictures of horses!"

"That's from me!" big sister Chloe said with pride. "And I got you some new crayons, too. The *big* box with sixty-four colors!"

Temporarily releasing her hold on Lassie, Ali greedily leafed through the pages, trying to decide which picture was her favorite.

"The big box? Really? All my own? Oh, thank you, Chloe!" After giving her sister a quick hug around the neck, Ali went right back to the coloring book. "I want to color one right now!"

"Not so fast, Pumpkin Pie," said her father. "You know the rule. You have to write a thank you note for the gift before you can play with it. Your sister will help you."

"Okay, but can I use my new crayons to write the thank you note?"

Her parents exchanged an amused look before her mom said, "Sure, Sweetheart. I think we can bend the rule a little bit this time."

Bent, but never broken, it was a rule that took deep root in Ali, and just one of the many ways in which her parents taught her the importance of saying thank you.

છ૭૯ર

Mount Vernon is an inconspicuous little town sixty miles north of Seattle. The locals will assure you of three points: first, that their city is close, but not too close, to Seattle; second, it's rural, but not too rural for city lovers; and third, it's small, but not too small to have all the important amenities.

Anchored by the historic Lincoln Theater on South First Street, downtown Mount Vernon consists mainly of small, locally owned businesses, typically quartered in vintage brick buildings. Its wide, brick boulevards encourage strolling and create a friendly, small-town atmosphere.

Beyond the city's commercial business district, acres and acres of lush, rich earth are still host to farmlands, berry fields, and horse-boarding barns.

છ૭૯ર

Ali Benevento considered herself fortunate to have grown up on her family's berry farm in Mount Vernon, alongside her older siblings, Chloe and Nathan. Ali had fond memories of playing among the rows and rows of berries with her brother and sister. The low-lying strawberry plants were perfect for hurdling, while the raspberry bushes provided exceptional cover for hide-and-seek.

When not tending to the strawberry, raspberry, and blueberry bushes, their father, Martin, moonlighted as a tractor mechanic and their mother, Peggy, taught fifth grade at Lincoln Elementary School.

Every June, soon after school let out for the summer,

busloads of local teenagers came to the family's farm to earn money by picking berries. The most handsome fruits were sold to grocery stores, while the less perfect were reserved for making jams and jellies.

Ali loved to hop out of bed in the early morning and watch as the buses rolled in and the twelve-, thirteen-, and fourteen-year-old kids piled out. After stowing their lunch bags and picking up fruit carriers, they were each assigned a row to harvest. Martin and Peggy were savvy enough to know that forbidding the young pickers to eat the succulent berries would be a fruitless battle, so instead, they allowed them to eat as many berries as they wanted while they worked. The amount of fruit consumed was about the same either way, but giving permission meant that the field supervisors didn't need to waste time and energy being watchdogs.

Pickers were issued punch cards to keep track of the number of boxes they filled each day and the number of days they worked. Those who missed no more than two harvesting days during the brief three-to-four-week season were rewarded with an end-of-harvest picnic in addition to receiving a bonus for each box they had filled.

There were always a few kids who got fired for excessive berry-throwing or generally goofing off, but most were hard workers who were grateful for the opportunity to earn some spending money before they were old enough to get "real jobs."

Ali was jealous of Chloe and Nathan when they got to pick alongside the other kids in the fields, but she learned the meaning of backbreaking work the first year she joined their ranks. It taught her a lesson about the duplicity of envy that she never forgot. As an adult, she equated it with the admonition, "Be careful what you wish for; you might get it."

∞)(∞

Along with the profit-producing berry fields, Mr. Benevento nurtured a few grapevines in the family's backyard. The vines didn't grow as well as they did in arid Eastern Washington where he was raised—and certainly not as well as they did in Palermo, Italy, where his father and grandfather grew up—but they supplied enough decent grapes to allow him to indulge his passion for winemaking. Unfortunately, his knowledge of wine and winemaking far exceeded his time and resources for producing it.

As she got older, Ali became more interested in the grapes than the berries, in part because she loved watching her father cajole the clusters of delicate fruit into wine. Her fascination was further fueled by her grandfather's romanticized stories about "the old country."

Every Sunday, Martin drove to Rest Haven Nursing Home at Fir and 8th Streets, to pick up Grampa "Papa" Gesepi, and bring him to the house for the afternoon. While Peggy was preparing dinner—ably assisted by either Chloe or Nathan— Ali would climb up on Papa's lap, begging him to tell her again about life on the Benevento family vineyard in Italy. She never tired of hearing stories about her deceased grandmother, and all of her Italian aunts, uncles, and cousins, whom she longed to meet. Her not-so-secret wish was to explore the Italian wine country for herself when she grew up.

ଈଠ

Peggy and Martin shared the opinion that Europeans had a much healthier attitude towards the consumption of wine than their American counterparts, so the Benevento children were allowed to drink wine at dinner, when in their parents' presence. They often made a game of identifying the various varietals, describing the bouquets and guessing the vintages.

Eventually, Ali's interest in wine and winemaking grew to be as fervent as her father's. As a teenager, she spent countless hours at his side in their tiny vineyard, asking questions and learning all she could about making fine wine. She imagined owning and operating her own winery some day, perhaps in partnership with her dad.

First, however, she wanted to spread her wings and break away from the familiar, if beloved, surroundings of her hometown. In her family, education held high value, so going to college was a given. After that, she was open to whatever kind of adventure presented itself.

But those things were still far in the future, whereas the Silver Star Stables, just down the road, provided a much more immediate allure.

When Ali was growing up, one of her family's favorite activities was attending horse shows and competitions at various nearby stables, like Silver Star. Mom, Dad, and Chloe were satisfied just to watch, but Nathan and Ali both caught the fever and begged for riding lessons. Owning one horse, let alone two, was beyond the reach of the family's budget, but Peggy and Martin decided that the cost of lessons was manageable.

Of all the horses boarded at Silver Star Stables, Tsunami, a chestnut-colored quarter horse-Arabian mix with a distinctive white muzzle, was Ali's admitted favorite. The diminutive mare weighed nine hundred forty-eight pounds and stood fourteen and a half hands at the withers. She combined the speed and gentleness of her Arab ancestry with the energy and balance of her quarter horse forbears. In Ali's eyes, she was perfect.

Ali's infatuation with Tsunami began when she saw her performing in a key pole race at an equine games-day competition. She couldn't explain why she felt so drawn to "Tsu" as opposed to the others, but there it was. After the games were over, Martin took her to the stables to meet Tsunami and her owner. He was surprised to find Ali suddenly taken shy, grasping his hand tightly, and hiding behind him as they approached the stall and greeted the horse's owner.

"Hi there, my name is Martin Benevento, and this is my daughter, Ali. We were in the stands today watching you and your horse compete. You were both wonderful."

The woman turned toward them and smiled. "Nice to meet you both," she said. "I'm Susan Schuster, and this is Tsunami. We certainly didn't win any ribbons this time, but we had some fun. She was pretty hot today, which is my fault. I haven't been able to make the time to ride her much recently."

"Hot?" Ali asked meekly as she peeked out from behind her father.

"Yes, that's horse talk for 'wound up.' She just had a lot of pent-up energy," Susan explained.

"How did she get the name Tsunami?" Martin asked.

"Well, that's my sneaky way of naming her after myself. I introduced myself to you as Susan, but my family always called me Sue. I'm fascinated by tsunami waves as well as horses, so when a friend suggested that name and I realized I could call her Tsu, for short, it seemed like a perfect fit!

Crouching down to address Ali, Susan asked, "Do you ride?"

Gaining courage, Ali stepped out and responded, "I want to, but I don't know how. My brother, Nathan, is taking lessons now. When he finishes, I get to."

"I see. Then will you lease a horse to ride?"

Ali looked up at her father imploringly, anxious to hear what he would say. "We're hoping to find someone who's willing to do a partial lease until we see how much time the kids actually devote to a horse."

"Well, you might just have found that person," Susan told them.

ಔಂಡ

Nolan Shafer loved teaching beginners how to ride horseback—especially children. The young students invariably exhibited a sense of awe, respect, and enthusiasm that reminded him of how fortunate he was to work with the horses and people at Silver Star Stables.

Martin and Peggy did their research before choosing a riding school and instructor for Nathan and Ali. They were happy to discover that Silver Star Stables had a superior reputation among local horse owners. The barns were clean and well maintained with a dry, organized tack room; the horses were calm, healthy, and well shod. All the instructors were amiable, self-confident, experienced professionals. Nathan Benevento was Nolan's 161st student and Ali would become his 169th, so Martin and Peggy felt confident that their children were in good hands.

The night before her first lesson, Ali was so excited she couldn't sleep. She had been dreaming of this day ever since she got the horse-themed coloring book from Chloe on her sixth birthday. After she saw the movie classic *National Velvet*, and later, *The Black Stallion*, her affection for all things equine was undeniable and insatiable.

ഇൻഗ

"I don't get to learn on Tsunami?" Ali was crestfallen.

"I'm afraid not, Ali. Tsunami is a bit too high-spirited for a beginner," Nolan explained. "It's important to train on a horse that is alert, yet calm and not overly sensitive. All horses pick up on the emotions of their riders, but some are more forgiving than others. As a beginner, you'll probably feel nervous and unsure at first—everyone does. You need to practice on a horse that's used to beginners so you have time to learn the basics without being afraid of your mount."

"But I love Tsunami. I really want to ride her." Ali's pleading bordered on whining.

"Did you hear the quality of your voice just now, Ali?" Nolan asked. "One of the first things you have to learn about being around horses is to always speak in a calm, confident, quiet tone of voice. Does whining get you what you want from your parents?"

"Sometimes . . . but not usually," Ali admitted reluctantly. "They don't like it when I whine."

"Neither does your horse," said Nolan.

"I understand that you're anxious to ride Tsunami, but do you really want to subject her to your natural nervousness? Wouldn't you rather start off your riding relationship with her as a confident, self-possessed horsewoman? After all, horses have long memories, Ali, and just like with people, you only get one chance to make a good first impression."

Ali's only response was to frown and look down at the ground. She could tell she wasn't going to win this argument.

"How about if you let me introduce you to Merry? She's a wonderful horse, too. I'm sure you'll like her. You'll get to ride Tsunami soon enough."

Ali was unconvinced until she actually saw Merry. She was a beautiful palomino, impeccably groomed and exuding serenity. And Ali could have sworn—though she knew it was silly—that Merry actually smiled at her when they met! She was sure then that learning to ride was going to be every bit as wonderful as she had imagined.

ღოღ

When the grapes and the horses weren't luring Ali outside, the family piano made her a willing captive indoors. Playing the piano filled her with a joy so deep and consuming that her family often teased her about preferring it to them. Happily, she was quite talented, so even her endless hours of practice created a pleasant soundtrack for her family's daily life.

From the time Ali was tall enough to reach the keyboard and plink her first tentative notes, piano music became like the lure of a siren to her. In fact, one of her earliest memories was of sitting on the piano stool, trying in vain to make her feet reach the pedals.

Hunting and pecking, she eventually found the keys that produced the notes of the tunes she heard in her head. "Mary Had a Little Lamb," played with one hand, eventually gave way to "Twinkle, Twinkle, Little Star," which lead to "Happy Birthday," played with both hands. By the time she was nine, she had mastered a dozen different Christmas carols, all played by ear.

At some point in her childhood—she couldn't remember exactly when—Ali began creating her own elementary tunes. Or, as she put it, recording songs in her head. Not knowing how to read or write music, she committed some of her compositions to memory for her own pleasure, but she never shared them with anyone.

Family finances—already stretched thin by the cost of riding lessons—were such that Ali didn't start taking piano lessons until she was twelve years old. Talented as she was, the lack of formal training earlier in life limited her horizons as a performer. Fortunately, that was never her ambition. Nor did it diminish the euphoria she experienced when she played.

Because she was so young when she became infatuated with the family piano, it was years before she realized that it was a bit of an antique; or more precisely, a relic. The battered, cherrywood upright had endured three generations of grimy fingers, damp environs, and infrequent tuning. Even so, Ali managed to coax some beautiful music from its overtaxed strings.

Sunday afternoons at the Benevento house evoked scenes reminiscent of those in Norman Rockwell paintings, as the family gathered around the piano and sang songs that spanned decades and genres.

While Ali's fingers beguiled sweet melodies from the decrepit piano, the notes produced by her vocal chords were not equally as pleasant. Her older sister, Chloe, on the other hand, sang as divinely as Ali played. When the two girls accompanied one another, everyone within earshot felt compelled to stop whatever they were doing and listen. Their shared love of music created an unbreakable bond between the sisters that only grew stronger as they grew older.

"Gratitude is happiness doubled by wonder." ~ G.K. Chesterton

Chapter 3
November 23, 1978

Peggy Benevento loved Thanksgiving, and her holiday table reflected that love. It was always splendid to behold.

First, there was the table itself. It was not an antique yet, but it was built in a time when furniture was intended to be handed down from one generation to the next. Made of heavy dark oak, it weighed nearly two hundred pounds. The ornately carved legs showed that it was made by craftsmen who regarded their work as an art form. Its top measured five feet by forty-four inches, even before Thanksgiving morning, when the insertion of the five leaves expanded its breadth considerably.

Once adorned with Peggy's white lace tablecloth, freshly polished, sterling silver utensils, cloth napkins, and china dishware, the transformation from family dinner table to royal banquet table was complete.

Poised in the center of the table was the truest symbol of Thanksgiving, the cornucopia. The decorative horn of plenty spilled its contents of fruits, vegetables, and nuts from one end of the table to the other as a reminder of God's graciousness and generosity.

Although it entailed considerable work, Peggy loved all the holiday preparation—especially the last minute tasks required on Thanksgiving morning. Looking down the length of her holiday table, she felt a thrill of anticipation knowing that that very evening, three generations of Beneventos would gather around it for a traditional Thanksgiving dinner.

Not satisfied to limit the celebration to immediate family, every year the Beneventos hosted an open house on Thanksgiving Day. Friends and neighbors were invited to drop by throughout the afternoon to visit, greet one another, and toast their good fortune with a glass of Martin's homemade wine.

The open house became a quintessential community event

as definitive of the holiday as Thanksgiving dinner itself. In fact, while the Benevento children were growing up, they assumed that everyone celebrated Thanksgiving in this same fashion. When they got older, they were disappointed to discover that this was not the case, and each of them eventually made the holiday open house a tradition in their own home.

℘℘℘

"Mom, why do you like Thanksgiving so much?" eight-year-old Ali asked as she helped her mother arrange the cornucopia.

"Oh, there are so many reasons, Sweetheart. For one thing, I love the weather this time of year, especially the days when the air is cool and crisp. I like pulling out my heavy sweaters and snuggling up under the down comforters. I love sitting in front of the fireplace, watching the flickering flames. I enjoy the falling leaves and the gusty winds that blow them every which way. Life seems to slow down just a bit in the autumn; it's like we get a breather between the non-stop activity of the summer and all the Christmas preparations ahead in December."

"But all the plants die this time of year," said Ali.

"Yes, that's true, their leaves and blossoms die off, but most of them will come back in the spring. It's more like they are going to sleep—like when you used to take your afternoon nap."

"Why else do you like Thanksgiving?"

Peggy thought for a moment. "I like Thanksgiving because it's a 'reminder' holiday. It reminds us to be thankful for what we have. It reminds us to appreciate the people we love. And it reminds us of our connection to the earth. I like that it's a quiet, peaceful holiday. It isn't about presents or candy or games."

Ali shrugged. "I like some parts of it—like eating breakfast in our pajamas and watching the parade on TV—but I think Thanksgiving's kinda boring after all the grown-ups get here."

"I know. I thought it was boring, too, when I was young. It's a holiday that you will appreciate more as you get older, though."

"Why?"

"Well, because when you get older, you realize that just being around people you love and care about makes you feel good, even if it's not always exciting. And that's what Thanksgiving is all about—gathering with people you love and stopping to recognize your blessings.

"It's so easy to take things and people for granted, Ali. Appreciating what we've been given is very important. I love the fact that Thanksgiving is a whole day dedicated to just that . . . giving thanks."

Satisfied that the horn of plenty in the center of their table was fulfilling its role as a symbol of abundance, Peggy turned her full attention to her youngest daughter. Moving over to the couch, they sat and snuggled close together.

"Ali, I'm going to tell you a very important secret and I want you to promise me that you will always, *always* remember it, because it's the key to happiness."

"You're going to give me a key? I love keys!" Ali said excitedly. "Can I wear it on a chain around my neck like some of the kids at school do?"

"No, this isn't the kind of key you hold in your hand. It's the kind of key you keep in your head and your heart."

"Huh?"

"You know how sometimes a word can have more than one meaning? Well, there's more than one kind of key. In this case, the word 'key' means 'the way to find something.' When I say I'm going to give you the key to happiness, I mean that I'm going to tell you how to find happiness. Do you understand?"

"I think so."

"Ali, here's what I want you to remember: The key to happiness is *gratitude*."

"What's gratitude?"

"Gratitude means being thankful. Like when we say grace before dinner, we tell God that we are thankful for our food."

"That doesn't sound like a very good secret," Ali said with a note of disappointment.

"It's the kind of secret that becomes more important when you are older, but I want you to learn it now so you can always be happy.

"You know how you get sad sometimes? Like when your brother takes a toy away from you? Or when your dad and I tell you that you can't have something you really want? Well, if you stop thinking about what you *don't* have and start thinking about what you *do* have, you'll stop being sad."

"I will?"

"Uh-huh. Every time. Maybe not right away, but it's the fastest way to feel better. So remember, the more gratitude you feel for all your blessings, the happier you will be.

"And Ali, this is a secret that it's alright to share."

৪০গু

Chloe, Nathan, and Ali awoke early Thanksgiving morning to the enticing aroma of fresh baked cinnamon rolls. It was just one of the traditions they could always count on.

The day before, they had watched their mother prepare the dough. Twice during the course of the day, they saw the dough rise, as if it were trying to escape the confines of the huge ceramic mixing bowl that was reserved just for making bread. Each time it rose above the top of the bowl, their mother would appear and punch it down again. The third time it rose, the real fun began!

First, Peggy overturned the bowl and dropped the big fluffy ball onto the counter. With a heavy rolling pin she shaped the dough into a rectangle, then brushed on melted butter, and sprinkled it with sugar, followed by cinnamon and raisins. (Ali would have preferred the rolls to be raisin-free, but she was outvoted.)

Next, Peggy enveloped those luscious ingredients inside by rolling the adorned dough into a log. Finally, she coaxed the roll into a circular shape with end meeting end, and deftly sliced through the dough—not quite all the way—at three-inch intervals, causing the dough to separate just enough to suggest individual rolls. Then she covered her tantalizing masterpiece with a damp towel and placed it in the fridge.

In the morning, when the sweet bread came out of the oven, Peggy topped each roll with icing and maraschino

Alice Ann Kuder

cherries alternated with walnut halves. This special preparation, their mother told them, transformed ordinary cinnamon rolls into a Swedish Tea Ring. The kids didn't care whether it was Swedish, Italian, or American. The tea ring was a thing of beauty and a keenly anticipated treat.

⁊

"Donald Duck is my favorite."

"Not me. I love Snoopy."

"No way. Superman is the best!"

"What do you think, Dad? Which balloon do you think is the best?" asked Nathan, hoping to draw support for Superman.

"I really like the marching bands more than the balloons," Martin said.

Still hoping for a tiebreaker, all eyes turned to their mother.

"Mom, don't you like Donald Duck the best?" asked Ali.

"The balloons are all wonderful, but the floats are my favorite part of the parade," Peggy said diplomatically.

"I like those, too!" said Ali. "I want to ride on one someday. I wish they still used horses to pull the floats. Tsunami could pull the float and I could ride on it. That would be so cool!"

"Could we go to the Macy's Thanksgiving Day Parade for real next year? Wouldn't that be awesome?" Nathan suggested, looking to Ali and Chloe for support.

Peggy and Martin looked at one another and smiled, but didn't answer right away. Inwardly, they were both pleased that their three half-grown kids would even consider taking a cross-country trip together. They knew it wouldn't be long before twelve-year-old Chloe and ten-year-old Nathan would chafe at the idea of even being in a room together with their family, let alone a car or a plane. At eight years of age, they still had some cuddle time left with Ali, but that would be gone before they knew it.

"Would you really want to be away from home on Thanksgiving?" Peggy asked. "Your grandparents wouldn't be with us, and we couldn't host our Thanksgiving open house."

"Not to mention we'd miss out on your mom's spectacular Thanksgiving dinner!" added Martin.

The kids protested a bit, insisting it would be okay to break tradition just one year for the sake of a trip to New York, then they settled back down in their warm, comfortable family room to watch the rest of the parade on TV.

Just as the final float with Santa Claus came on the screen, the lights in the house flickered and the power went out.

There they sat, all five Beneventos still in their pajamas on Thanksgiving morning with no electricity. No lights, no furnace, no TV . . . and no oven.

The power outage didn't come as a complete surprise. The wind and rain had been steadily gaining intensity since the night before and the weather forecasters had predicted a major storm. Even so, no one really expected the weather to interfere with the holiday festivities. Now they would have to reexamine their clearly false assumptions and formulate a "Plan B."

Since it was only 10 a.m., the lack of lights wasn't really a problem. The temperature outside was in the low forties, so they knew they wouldn't freeze to death without heat. An extra layer or two of clothing would keep everyone warm enough—layers and two wood-burning fireplaces.

They were all still full from their breakfast of cinnamon rolls, bacon and eggs, so the big question was what to do about dinner? Peggy, always thinking ahead, had wisely held off putting the turkey in the oven, just in case they lost power. She knew that if she put it back in the freezer now, it would stay plenty cold enough to avoid spoiling—but Thanksgiving dinner with no turkey or ham?

And what about their annual open house? Would their friends and neighbors brave the storm to come and visit? Just as Peggy wondered about this out loud, the first knock came at the front door. Five minutes later, another knock, and a few minutes after that, a third knock. By noon, the Benevento living room was overflowing with family, friends, and neighbors. Somehow, the foul weather seemed to draw people in rather than keep them away. Not only did they come, but they brought food to share, games to play, and musical instruments to provide entertainment.

Before long, the dining room table was overflowing with a feast that mimicked the cornucopia and put the usual Thanksgiving dinner to shame.

ಐღ

The storm continued, unabated, through the early evening hours, giving the guests reason to linger much longer than usual. The power remained out all over the county, so neighbors who would have gone home to a cold house were especially grateful to stay in the warmth and comfort of the Benevento's home.

As the sun went down and the house grew darker, Peggy and Martin lit the candles they had strategically placed throughout the house earlier and stoked the fires in both fireplaces. Then they gave Nathan, Chloe, and Ali the task of making sure all their guests had glasses filled with age-appropriate beverages for toasting.

Everyone looked to Martin as he raised his glass. "Friends," he began, "we feel so blessed to have you all here with us today. It's been an unusual holiday to say the least. The storm forced us to forego some traditions, but there's one we refuse to abandon, and that's saying what we are thankful for."

"Before we start," Peggy interjected, "I'd like to add a new twist to that tradition. As many of you know, my mother passed away this year. In the course of my grieving, I realized that I was sad not only because I had lost someone I loved, but also because I had lost someone who loved me.

"This is the first Thanksgiving I have spent without my mother in many, many years. Although she can no longer be here in body, I want her to be here in spirit, so here's the twist I propose. From this year forward, let's not only name some*thing* we are grateful for, but also some*one* we *wish* could be with us. Maybe it's someone who has died, or maybe it's someone who just can't be here in person for one reason or another. In other words, let's call to mind the special people who love, and have loved us and include them in our celebration by remembering their names out loud. I'll start."

Peggy raised her glass and said, "Happy Thanksgiving, Grammy Marge!"

The room fell silent for a minute as each person privately reflected on who and what they were grateful for. One by one, each guest spoke up and soon the air was perfumed with the names of loved ones, past and present; people too special to be forgotten.

After the last guest reverently uttered their loved one's name, the soothing sound of a strumming guitar emerged from the back of the room. Everyone turned to see who was playing. Martin recognized her as, Evie, the woman who had recently moved into the old Druffle place a mile or so down the road, and thought it wonderful that she would come to the open house her very first year in the neighborhood.

Evie simply said, "I call this "Thanksgiving Song.""

Then she began singing softly:

When I'm living in the city and the fast life gets me down,
I'll think of this old table and the times we sat around.
Of the days of easy living and the music that we made
Where the cedar grows and the rooster crows and evenings are homemade.
In this cabin near the river where we laughed and where we grew
Trading long forgotten stories of people we once new.
Where we came to know each other learned to call each other friend
Every visit is a treasure and the pleasure never ends.
Some snowy evening in the winter when you're reading round the lamp
When the garden's under cover and the forest trails too damp.
When you've tired yourselves with talking and you've nothing much to do
Sing a song and think about me I'll be singing one for you.
In this cabin near the river where we laughed and where we grew
Trading long forgotten stories of people we once new.
Where we came to know each other learned to call each other friend
Every visit is a treasure and the pleasure never ends.
Every visit is a treasure and the pleasure never ends.

ଚଡ଼ଔ

Whether because of the storm or in spite of it, that Thanksgiving turned out to be the most memorable open

Alice Ann Kuder

house the Beneventos ever hosted. For years to come, neighbors would say to one another with a nostalgic tone of voice, "Remember the Thanksgiving Day storm in '78? *That* was a great Thanksgiving."

"It takes courage to grow up and turn out to be who you really are."
~ *E.E. Cummings*

Chapter 4
1967-1990

"No! Not again!" Karl groaned and shook his head. "I guess your old man will never learn not to leave you uncovered between diapers. You've got great aim, kid, I'll give you that."

Karl wasn't new to the task of diapering a baby; he had changed his share with their daughter, Jackie, who was now four years old. Truth be told, he enjoyed being a hands-on father, especially when his children were this young—a time when they grew and changed so rapidly. Still, his baby boy seemed to require much more attention than Jackie had at that age. Whereas she was observant and quiet, Isaac was physical and chatty.

Just as Karl reached for a fresh diaper from the pile to his right, his six-month-old son chose that moment to roll over for the first time . . . right over the edge of the changing table. It was some superhuman combination of instinct, intuition, and peripheral vision that made Karl turn back just in time to catch Isaac, mere inches from the floor.

Karl's heart was racing as he clutched his son, forbidding his imagination to fill in the blanks of the alternative outcome just averted. He reluctantly loosened his grasp when he realized that baby Isaac was laughing with delight! Far from being frightened, Isaac reacted as if he had just discovered he could fly!

That was the moment that Karl first knew he and Elizabeth would have their hands full with this little guy; Isaac's initial death-defying barrel roll and his ensuing glee were just the first indication that he would grow up to be an adrenaline junky. Indeed, throughout his life, the faster and more dangerous the sport, the more Isaac loved it.

His addiction truly kicked in on his ninth birthday, when his parents gave him the skateboard he'd begged for. In no time at all, Isaac mastered classic boarding maneuvers such as the Caballerial, the FS 540, the Fakie, the Varial Kickflip and a half dozen other tricks, usually performed at top speed. He told his friends that he was humoring his parents by wearing pads and a helmet, but there was more than one occasion when safety gear protected him from serious injury, even if he didn't know it. Like most kids his age, Isaac thought himself to be indestructible and had very little fear of physical risk, but he was careful anyway because he knew that broken bones would prevent him from doing the things he loved to do.

Skateboarding satisfied Isaac's desire for excitement during his preteen years, growing up in tiny Xenia, Ohio. Once he turned fifteen, however, he fixed his sights on cars and international racetracks. His bedroom walls were covered with posters of his racing idols: Mario Andretti, Dale Earnhardt, Sr., Richard Petty, and Johnny Rutherford. His shelves were crowded with model cars that he built with his father. Formula 1, Grand Prix, Sprint, Indycar, and NASCAR—he loved them all.

For his seventeenth birthday, his parents took him to the Indianapolis 500, a two-hour drive from their home in Xenia. After watching the first race he vowed to himself that he would one day have his own racecar. He wasn't sure he had what it took to compete in events like the 500, but he was determined to find out. Knowing that this wasn't a cheap ambition, he was glad he had made the effort to earn good grades in high school because he'd need a college degree that would help launch him into a well-paying career.

ஐௌ

When it came time to choose a college, Isaac looked for one that combined a reputable academic program with a location conducive to extra-curricular sports. He decided on a degree in Business Administration at the University of Colorado, in Denver. Although Denver wasn't a hotbed for auto-racing, the Rocky Mountains provided an excellent playground for skiing, snowboarding, and mountain climbing—all of which fed his never ending quest for excitement. He believed in always having a "Plan B" and reasoned that earning a general business degree would effectively prepare him for a variety of career options.

Now twenty-two, freshly graduated from CU and recovering from a recently broken heart, Isaac saw no reason to limit his job search to Colorado. Although moving back to Ohio would have made more sense for pursuing an auto-racing career, he looked to the Pacific Northwest instead. His sister, Jackie, was working for Microsoft as a software developer at their headquarters in Redmond, Washington. He and Jackie had always been close, so that provided a strong pull. Plus, his years in Colorado had fostered in him a love for all things mountainous, and Washington state boasted not *one*, but *two* mountain ranges—the Cascades and the Olympics—to feed his passion.

Though he hated to admit it, his youthful desire to become a professional racecar driver, was beginning to wane. He still loved the cars and the speed, but the nomadic lifestyle was less attractive to him now. Even though his last relationship had ended badly, it taught him that he wanted to eventually get married and have a family. He realized that family life and auto-racing weren't totally incompatible, but he knew from reading about the big-time pros that the two weren't often successfully combined. Reluctantly, he decided to let racing take a backseat to his ambitions for his personal life, and he considered other professions.

Even so, Isaac hoped to somehow stay on the periphery of the sport. He was thankful that Jackie, years earlier, had suggested he look for a job in an auto parts store. At first he had balked, finding the idea of such menial work offensive to his teenage self-esteem, but when he expressed that point of view to his father, Karl gave him a dressing down. "Who are you to think you're too good to start at the bottom? If you really want to own an auto parts store some day," he told his son, "you'd better learn the business from the ground up." Isaac spent the last two summers of his high school years stocking shelves and waiting on customers at Dayton Xenia Auto Parts.

Now, together with his college degree, he was ready to cash in on that experience. Foregoing the usual help-wanted-

Alice Ann Kuder

ads method of job hunting, he paid a professional writer to help him create a killer resume and cover letter, then proceeded to hand deliver it to every auto parts store in the metropolitan Seattle area.

Many of the store managers Isaac spoke to told him he was overqualified for the clerking positions they had open. They felt sure he would be bored and move on within a few months time. Others—recognizing that Isaac was management material and secretly afraid he might take their jobs—turned him away with similar excuses.

After twenty-two rejections, Isaac walked nonetheless confidently into the twenty-third store on his list, Sterns' Auto Parts, in south Seattle's industrial Georgetown neighborhood, and struck gold.

ℰↃﾒↂ

At sixty-three years of age, Austin Sterns was looking for someone to take over the business he had started out of his garage forty years earlier. Although he and his partner, Robert, regarded Sterns' Auto Parts as a family business, they had no children of their own, so there was no heir apparent. They had put the business up for sale two years earlier, but the only bids came from big corporations. Since making a huge profit was not their main objective, they turned down the offers and decided to look for a buyer who would love the business and the Georgetown neighborhood as much as they did.

They had considered their current employees as potential buyers, and even contacted some former employees, but no one seemed like a good fit. Still a few years from retirement, they decided to bide their time. When Isaac walked in and introduced himself, both Austin and Robert recognized his potential right away.

ℰↃﾒↂ

When Isaac drove up to Sterns' Auto Parts, he noticed the reader board out front, which read: WE INSTALL WIPER BLADES. *A simple, and effective way*, he thought, *to get across the message that customers should expect service "above and beyond."*

Isaac climbed out of his copper-colored 1976 Pontiac Firebird—his way of paying homage to Jim Rockford in *The Rockford Files*—and stood for a minute, looking at the store and the surrounding buildings. When he walked in the front door of Sterns, he felt like he'd come home. It was just the kind of place he was looking for—small, privately owned, and well stocked. He took a breath. Six other privately owned places and sixteen corporate stores had already turned him down. *I only need one person to say "yes,"* he reminded himself.

"Hi, is there a manager available that I could talk to?" Isaac asked the young man behind the counter.

"Yeah, one of the owners is in the back. I'll get him for you."

Now, taking a closer look around, Isaac confirmed to himself that the store was clean, well organized, and carried quality merchandise. The prices seemed reasonable as well. The owner obviously understood the importance of creating a welcoming environment and providing value.

A minute later, Austin came striding out from the back, extending his hand to Isaac.

"Hi, I'm Austin Sterns. I'm told you asked to speak to a manager. What can I do for you?"

"Mr. Sterns, you have a very impressive store here and I'd like to work for you in any capacity that will benefit your business. When can I start?"

Once he found a place to live and got settled into his new job, Isaac started looking for another outlet for his daredevil instincts. He found it in skydiving.

Skydive Snohomish was a small family-owned business that catered to first-time skydivers. Headquartered at Harvey Field, about twenty miles north of Seattle, it was also a home base for experienced jumpers.

While driving along Highway 9 on his way to explore the area around Lake Stevens, Isaac spotted a billboard promoting Skydive Snohomish. It triggered a Pavlovian response in him.

He immediately abandoned his plans for the rest of the day, followed the directions to the airfield, and signed up for the next available class.

As he was filling out the necessary and exhaustive legal liability paperwork, Isaac looked up and discovered a second reason to appreciate skydiving. She was blond, five foot six, slender, and answered to the name of Valerie. Turning on his considerable charm, he successfully drew her into a conversation, and quickly discovered that her sense of adventure came close to matching his own—which made her seem even more attractive.

ຂ

"We offer two types of jumps for first-timers," explained the guy behind the counter. "There's the tandem jump, where you're literally strapped to your instructor when you jump out of the plane. Then there's the static line jump, where we attach the ripcord on your parachute to a clip inside the plane. The ripcord is pulled when you jump, deploying the parachute five seconds after you exit the plane."

"Is there an advantage to one type of jump over the other?" Valerie asked.

"Well, the tandem style is sort of a 'training wheels' approach," the clerk explained. "It's less dangerous because you have an experienced skydiver controlling your flight, but you get to experience free fall and you only need thirty minutes of instruction. Of course, some people don't like the idea of being strapped to an instructor they barely know.

"If you go the static line route, you get to jump solo. It's obviously more dangerous, so it requires several hours of training. Most first-timers choose the tandem style."

Isaac and Valerie, of course, chose the static line option.

ຂ

Since I Last Saw You   29

In addition to Valerie, there were six others in the first-jump class with Isaac: an eighteen-year-old girl whose grandfather paid her way as a birthday present; a forty-seven-year-old pharmacist who was looking for a way to add some excitement to his life; a sixty-three-year-old man who had wanted to skydive ever since watching the TV series *Ripcord* as a kid; a fifty-four-year-old widow whose deceased husband had forbidden her to even think about trying it while he was alive; a twenty-four-year-old female taxi driver from New York who was in town on vacation; and a thirty-six-year-old construction worker who couldn't back down on a dare from his poker buddies.

Their instructor, Kevin, had made over eight hundred jumps in the three years since he took up the sport. "It changed my life," he told them. Without expounding on this simple statement, he paused for a moment, then launched right into the course content.

"Skydiving is a dangerous sport. Don't let anyone tell you it isn't," Kevin said. "That's one reason we have you read and sign the liability waiver before you even take the class, and it's why I'll have you initial this training checklist as we go along. We want you to be fully informed about the risks and fully trained about how to minimize those risks so you can appreciate the whole experience."

The next instruction Kevin gave them appealed directly to Isaac's "Plan B" mentality.

"The most important safety procedure you need to know is how to deploy your reserve chute if your main chute doesn't work properly, so I'm going to show you that now and we'll practice it practice it over and over throughout the class. We want this procedure to become second nature to you."

Kevin went on to show them a demonstration pack, giving special attention to the emergency handle.

"If you get in a jam—and we'll talk later about how to know when you're in a jam—here's what you need to do: Look. Reach. Pull. Clear. Arch." After thoroughly demonstrating each step, he repeated them again. "Look. Reach. Pull. Clear. Arch. I want you to practice saying the steps out loud and making the motions because it will help you

Alice Ann Kuder

remember in the event of an emergency. Everybody do it with me. Ready?"

For the next four hours, the group learned about rules and regulations, skydiving equipment, the aircraft, exiting the plane, steering the parachute, landing, and post-jump procedures. Kevin showed them how a parachute is packed and what happens when it deploys. Then he described the sights, sounds, and sensations they could expect to experience during their jump.

"I know I've given you tons of information this morning," he said. "It's a lot to take in. I always say it's a little like trying to get a drink of water from a fire hose. I don't want you to worry about not being able to remember everything I tell you. I repeat the really important stuff several times and we're going to spend the second two hours of the class going over the emergency procedures. I don't want to scare you, but I want you to be completely prepared in case something goes wrong. If you know how to identify a potential problem and know what to do about it, you can relax and enjoy the ride. Sound good? Okay, let's take a short break. I'll see you back here in fifteen minutes."

During the break, Isaac approached Kevin privately. "Hey, Kevin, great class so far. I wanted to ask you, what did you mean when you said that skydiving changed your life?"

"It's kind of hard to explain," Kevin replied. "I think most skydivers feel that way, but it's such a personal experience. If you ask five different jumpers why they love the sport, you're likely to get five different answers, but you'll probably hear commonalities like 'excitement, adventure, challenge, pushing limits and adrenaline rush.' When I jump, it's like time stops. I get to the airfield, get out of my car and leave all my cares behind. I just concentrate on the jump. Afterwards, when I get back on the ground, my worries seem so much less significant. When I first experienced it, that new perspective made a really big and positive change in my outlook on life.

"Then there's the whole social aspect of the sport. The people you jump with regularly become like a second family. I think it's because skydiving is such a great equalizer. It puts everyone on the same plane—I know, bad pun. It doesn't matter who you are or what you do. When you get up there, you're just the same as everyone else. And when you share your passion for the sport with other skydivers, you come to care about each other. I get together socially with other jumpers at least twice a month. We have barbeques, potlucks, wine parties . . . any excuse to get together."

"That surprises me," said Isaac. "When I look at the people in this class and how diverse our backgrounds and experiences are, it's hard to imagine we could all become good friends."

"I know, but it happens all the time," Kevin assured him. "Like I said, skydiving is a great equalizer."

ဆာ

Isaac would never forget his first jump. His excitement and anticipation grew throughout the training. The more he learned, the more fascinated he became. He couldn't wait to get up in the air.

The Cessna 182 carried just three passengers at a time, plus the instructor and pilot. Isaac was slated to go up with the second group. Everyone had suited up together, so he sat anxiously awaiting his turn as he watched the plane take off with the first group.

Trevor, the pharmacist, was the first to jump. As far as Isaac could tell, it went off without a hitch. His chute deployed five seconds after he exited the plane and he looked to be in full control as he banked left, then right, and soared through a clear sky for several minutes before landing.

Cynthia, the taxi driver, was next. She had been full of questions during the class and seemed quite nervous about the whole thing. Isaac wondered if she would actually jump, but jump she did, and in great style.

The third student to jump was Stan, the sixty-three-year-old *Ripcord* fan. As Isaac watched Stan exit the plane, he recalled the conversation they had earlier in the day during one of the breaks. Stan confessed to Isaac the reason he had waited so long to fulfill this dream.

Thirty years earlier, at an airfield in California, Stan had

Alice Ann Kuder

trained for his first jump, just like today. By luck of the draw, he was to be in the second group to go up that day, so he and the others watched as the first in line in the first group positioned herself to exit the plane. They all counted aloud in unison as she jumped: One-one-thousand. Two-one-thousand. Three-one-thousand. Four-one-thousand. Five-one-thousand . . . then watched the parachute deploy right on cue. She soared for several minutes and landed uneventfully on the ground, not far from her target.

Then, the second student got in position to jump. He stepped out and grabbed the strut just as they had all been trained to do. When he let go, the static line deployed the chute as expected, but the wind caught him in such a way that he did a back loop through the lines of the chute, causing it to malfunction. Instead of seeing the chute unfurl, the crowd on the ground saw streamers—the cords and the uninflated fabric of the canopy— flapping uselessly above the jumper. In his head, Stan was screaming, "CUT AWAY YOUR CHUTE! USE THE RESERVE! NOW!" Instead, the jumper pulled the emergency handle on the reserve chute without first ejecting the main chute. The reserve got tangled up with the streamers, which prevented it from inflating, too. He was out of time and out of options. He died on impact.

"I couldn't believe what I had seen," Stan said. "I was too shaken to consider jumping after that. Two of the other students in the second jump group backed out that day, too. One woman went up on the next flight a few hours later— after the coroner came and cleared the field—and made her jump.

"I should have gotten right back up on the horse. If I had, I probably would have been enjoying the sport all these years instead of wishing I had."

"What finally got you to come back and try again?" asked Isaac.

"I was reading a magazine article recently that cited statistics about accidental deaths. Did you know that the top five causes of accidental death in this country are auto accidents, poisonings—which includes drug overdoses—falls, fires, and choking? The number of fatalities attributed to skydiving in the United States averages about thirty per year. That's out of roughly two *million* jumps per year! According to the article, you're much more likely to die from a bee sting or a lightning strike than from skydiving! Besides, skydiving equipment has gotten safer every year. Nowadays, in a situation like the one that killed that jumper, there is just one handle to pull; it cuts away the main chute for you, then deploys the reserve.

"Anyway, when I read that article, I realized that I do things every day that put me at much more risk of getting seriously hurt or dying than skydiving does. So, I decided I'd waited long enough to face my fears, and here I am."

ಬಂಡ

During the pre-flight practice session, Kevin had shown everyone the hand signals he would use to prompt them during the flight. Their helmets and the noise from the plane, he told them, would make it difficult to hear once they were in the air.

Just before they climbed into the plane, Kevin pointed at each one of his students individually and had them demonstrate the emergency sequence again: *Look! Reach! Pull! Clear! Arch!*

The pilot took the group up to the jumping altitude of three thousand feet and nodded to Kevin.

Lydia, the eighteen-year-old, was the first of their group to jump. She performed flawlessly.

Now, it was Isaac's turn. As the pilot circled back around toward the jump zone, Isaac watched Kevin for the signal to scoot forward and position himself near the door. The eager anticipation he felt this morning didn't come close to matching the thrill and excitement he was experiencing now. All his senses seemed to be on fire and he thought to himself: *This is how it feels to be really alive!*

He waited for the thumbs-up from Kevin to step out and reach for the strut. Slowly, he inched his hands further out until his feet left the platform step and he was suspended from the wing by his hands alone, with his legs flying freely. When Kevin gave the final thumbs up, Isaac fearlessly let go of the wing strut. He felt the expected and satisfying tug as the static line engaged the ripcord. He arched his back and stretched out his arms to get in the proper symmetrical flying position. Then, he looked up in anticipation of the chute opening, and began to count down the five seconds that would change his life. One-one-thousand. Two-one-thousand. Three-one-thousand. Four-one-thousand. Five-one-thousand.

Whump! Isaac felt a sudden upward jerk as his chute caught the air and inflated. He reached up to grab the steering toggles and immediately did the controllability check he learned in class, pulling down on the toggles to flare the parachute, then turning right and left. *Yes! Yes! Yes!* He was flying!

The first thing he noticed was the quiet. The only sound was the air whooshing by, and even that seemed noiseless. Then he looked out to the horizon and banked to turn a full 360 degrees. Overcome with a sense of awe, he felt as if he were suspended not only in air, but in time. At this moment, only he existed, and he hadn't a care in the world. *This must have been what it was like for God on the first day, looking down on His creation and declaring it good,* he thought.

ဆာ

After that first jump, Isaac was hooked. Valerie, on the other hand, was not. She decided that one jump was quite enough, as was her one date with Isaac.

Rather than dwell on the rejection, Isaac concluded that Valerie's attention span was about as long as the ripcord attached to a static line. No real loss. He had found a truer love in skydiving.

Having deftly sidestepped a potential broken heart, he couldn't wait to get back in a plane and jump again. Determined to give his total attention to skydiving, he eagerly pulled out his credit card and signed up for the full training program. Three months later, Isaac had twenty-five jumps under his belt, earning his Level A license with the United States Parachute Association.

Chapter 5
February 13, 2012

Ali opened the door and practically fainted into her mother's outstretched arms. To her own surprise, Ali immediately broke into tears, which turned into sobs that coursed through her whole body. The two women stood in the doorway, silently embracing, then together slowly sank to the doorstep. Still, Ali's sobbing continued. It broke Peggy's heart to know that there were no words to console her daughter. Losing her granddaughter and son-in-law was devastating enough for *her*; she could not imagine the pain Ali must be feeling. Peggy sent a silent prayer of gratitude to the heavens for thus far sparing her the pain of burying a child.

Ali had lost an argument with her family two days earlier. She insisted that she was fine in the house by herself. They insisted that she needed emotional support in the days leading up to the funeral—and they were determined to provide it.

Martin, luggage in tow, walked up to find the two women in a heap on the stoop, still entwined in each other's arms. They seemed totally unaware of his presence. He told himself he was just being practical when he detoured to the back door and let himself in. After all, he couldn't very well jump over them with suitcases in hand. But the truth was that when he saw them, he felt very near to crying himself, and that wouldn't help anyone.

Chloe and Nathan were scheduled to arrive in time to join Ali and their parents for a family dinner. Chloe and her husband, Roger, thought it best if he stayed home with their infant twins.

Eventually, Peggy and Ali made their way to the sofa in the living room. Martin built a fire in the fireplace and put on a pot of water for tea. When he opened the refrigerator, he found it overflowing with casseroles, desserts, fruit, and beverages that friends had obviously brought over. Part of him had been hoping the fridge would be empty so he would have an excuse to escape to the grocery store if the evening got to be too painful for him to bear. As much as he loved his daughter and wanted to help comfort her, he was not particularly adept at showing the tenderness he felt. Peggy, on the other hand, seemed able to channel Mother Teresa in these situations.

Martin silently served the tea along with some crackers and cheese, knowing that it would likely all go untouched. He thought about excusing himself but realized it wasn't necessary—the women were too preoccupied to notice whether he was there or not. Relieved, Martin slipped out the back door and disappeared into the garage. He might not be good at hand-holding, but he was a passable auto mechanic. If he couldn't console his daughter emotionally, he could at least ensure that she was safe physically—at least while driving—by giving her car a once-over.

⊱⊰

Ali let out an audible sigh and squeezed her mother's hand. Neither of them had said a word since Peggy arrived. She knew her daughter well enough to know that she would talk when she was ready. Until then, silence was more powerful and comforting than any words she might offer. Besides, once Nathan and Chloe arrived, the opportunity for quiet solace would be lost.

Finally, Ali stood up and wandered around the room that had been the hub of her small family's life. She fingered the framed photos on the mantle, re-shelved the novel that Isaac had been reading, took Zoe's iPod from its dock and scrolled through the playlist. The titles made her smile.

1. **Fireflies** - Owl City
2. **Some Nights** - Fun
3. **Moves Like Jagger** - Maroon 5
4. **Paradise** – Coldplay
5. **Chattanooga Choo Choo** – Glenn Miller Orchestra
6. **You Belong to Me** - Taylor Swift
7. **Hall of Fame** - The Script

8. **Thrift Shop** - Macklemore
9. **I've Got the Magic in Me** - B.o.B.
10. **Fireworks** - Katy Perry
11. **Dog Days Are Over** - Florence and the Machine

There were no sad songs in this list; they were all fun and full of life—just like Zoe had been. Ali noticed there were even a few big band numbers in there, thanks to an accidental family viewing of an old movie, *The Glenn Miller Story*, starring Jimmy Stewart and June Allison. Ali, Isaac, and Zoe had stumbled across it while channel surfing one night. When it was over, Zoe immediately uploaded some of the songs from iTunes and insisted that her parents show her how to Swing Dance. They pushed the furniture out of the way and turned the living room into a dance floor for the next hour, all the while laughing hysterically over the abnormally high number of left feet they had among them.

When they weren't goofing around, Zoe was actually quite agile and moved with surprising grace for a young girl. Her long, dark, wavy hair flowed freely around her cherubic face, seeming to accentuate her apple cheeks, and giving her a perpetually happy appearance.

Smiling at the memories, Ali sat down at the piano and began to play "In the Mood." Just then, Chloe walked in and said, "How about playing something I can sing to, Ali Oop?"

Ali looked up in surprise, leaped to her feet, and ran into her sister's open arms. The two held each other, rocking back and forth slowly, tears flowing. After a few moments, as if through telepathy, the sisters released each other and dried their eyes in silent agreement that there would be plenty of time for crying later. Tonight was about relishing the comfort of family.

Chloe opened the piano bench and pulled out several well-worn songbooks dating back to the days of their family sing-a-longs. Their contents ran the gamut from church music, to pop tunes, to Christmas carols.

Thumbing through the books, Chloe's intention was to find some fun, upbeat music to lighten the mood, but her plan took a detour when she happened upon "Amazing Grace."

Alice Ann Kuder

That particular hymn never failed to move her, and she knew it was a favorite of Ali's as well. When she placed the sheet music on the piano, Ali nodded her head appreciatively and began to play as Chloe and their mother stood by the piano and joined her in singing.

"Amazing Grace"

Amazing Grace, how sweet the sound,
That saved a wretch like me;
I once was lost but now am found,
Was blind, but now, I see.
T'was Grace that taught
My heart to fear,
And Grace, my fears relieved.
How precious did that Grace appear
The hour I first believed.
Through many dangers, toils and snares
We have already come.
T'was Grace that brought us safe thus far
And Grace will lead us home.
The Lord has promised good to me.
His word my hope secures.
He will my shield and portion be
As long as life endures.
When we've been here ten thousand years
Bright shining as the sun,
We've no less days to sing God's praise
Then when we've first begun.
Amazing Grace, how sweet the sound
That saved a wretch like me.
I once was lost but now am found,
Was blind, but now, I see.

When the last note faded away, Chloe smiled at her sister, sat down next to her on the piano bench and resumed flipping through the songbooks, trying to find something uplifting. While she was looking, Ali began playing a tune her family didn't recognize. It was a pleasantly haunting melody that seemed to teeter on the razor's edge between cheerful and melancholy.

"Ali, that's lovely. What is it?" her mother asked.

Ali kept playing, but didn't answer right away. Finally, she said, "It doesn't have a name. It's not even a whole song, really. It's just the start of a tune that popped into my head one day and stuck with me. Every once in a while I add a few bars. Someday I hope to finish the music and add lyrics, but I'm in no hurry. The inspiration will come to me when the time is right."

Nathan looked at his little sister and shook his head gently from side to side. "Just when I thought I knew everything there is to know about our Ali Oop, she up and surprises me!"

Suddenly, Chloe cried out excitedly, "Ah-ha! I found it!" And she propped a songbook up in front of Ali. It was the theme from *Rocky*, "Eye of the Tiger", which provided the perfect segue to change the tone of the evening.

The next hour was like a showcase of the pop hits of the '80s and '90s. "Physical," "Billie Jean," "I Love a Rainy Night," "Jump," "Broken Wings," "We Got the Beat," "It's Still Rock 'n Roll to Me," and "All I Wanna Do."

Nathan walked through the front door, dragging Martin with him, just as Ali started playing "The Macarena." Despite loud groans of feigned distress from the entire group, Chloe pulled them all to their feet and coached them through the half-remembered-half-forgotten dance steps.

Emotionally sated by the music, physical hunger took center stage, and the family followed their rumbling stomachs to the kitchen. Everyone foraged through the over-stuffed fridge to find their own particular favorites—lasagne for Martin, tuna casserole for Chloe, rice and beans for Peggy, ham for Nathan, and mac and cheese for Ali—then they all sat down together as Martin poured the homemade wine he had decanted earlier.

Nathan stood and raised his glass, as did the others. "To Isaac and Zoe: Forever in our hearts."

"The best thing about the future is that it comes one day at a time."
~ Abraham Lincoln

Chapter 6

16 February 2012

The funeral is tomorrow . . . is it considered one funeral or two when two people are being eulogized and buried? As if it really matters. My mind seems to conjure up all sorts of silly, inconsequential thoughts and questions like that these days. Then again, everything seems silly and inconsequential without Isaac and Zoe.

17 February

I feel humbled, but not surprised, by the number of people who came to the funeral. I expected to see some of the managers from Sterns' Auto Parts, but so many of the regular employees showed up, too. A lot of them reintroduced themselves to me at the reception and told me how much they appreciated that Isaac ran his company with such integrity.

I recognized people from Skagit Speedway and Skydive Snohomish, too. I don't know whether they saw the obituary or read about the accident in the paper. Maybe Gwen contacted them?

And all of Zoe's classmates and many of the teachers from her school showed up. I can't imagine what it must be like for a ten-year-old to go to a classmate's funeral.

I'm grateful that so many people came—it was more comforting to see them all than I expected it to be—but I'm glad they're gone, too. I never would have suspected that being comforted could be so exhausting.

18 February

I keep thinking about something farmer Jay said to me yesterday after the funeral. Ha! How funny that I would call him that. I just realized that I don't know Jay's last name! Isaac always referred to him as 'farmer Jay'. He'd say, 'I feel the need for speed. I'm taking #76 to farmer Jay's track.' And off he'd go with his sprint car in tow to work off some stress. Anyway, yesterday Jay pulled me aside to express his sympathy. Then he told me not to worry about #76. He said I had enough to deal with and he'd take care of it. Just as I started to ask him what he was talking about, we got interrupted, and before I knew it, I'd been whisked away to another corner of the room by some friends from work. I never got the chance to talk with Jay again before he left. I guess there will be plenty of time to follow up with him later. It didn't sound like anything urgent. I'm just curious as to what he could have meant.

19 February

I didn't go to Mass today. I knew there would be so many well-meaning people expressing their sympathy and asking me about the funeral. How do you answer someone who asks you if it was a "nice" service? I wonder what a "bad" funeral service would look like

Alice Ann Kuder

20 February

The house is so quiet now. Everyone has gone home—back to their own lives—lives that haven't changed as mine has. If only I could go back . . .

I guess I should get out of bed. There are probably things I ought to do—I can't think what they might be though. Nothing seems important enough to deserve my attention or energy.

23 February

I should probably throw out all the dead flowers, but then what to do with all the vases? I don't have the mental energy to make such decisions.

27 February

Principal Brumsickle called today to tell me that Zoe's classmates have all chipped in to buy a maple tree to plant on the school grounds in her honor. What a lovely thing to do. Zoe loved trees. When she was five years old, she took her dad and me by the hand and walked us all around the yard telling us the names she'd given each tree and bush. I still remember them all.

1 March

Mom came over today. She stocked my freezer with meals she made for me. She must have been pretty appalled by the state of my house because she arranged for a housecleaner to come tomorrow. I don't know how the house gets dirty.

Most days I just sit on the couch.

6 March

I finally left the house today for something other than groceries. I drove out to Issaquah Commons because we used to love going there as a family, and I miss that. We each had our favorite stores. Isaac practically drooled whenever he went into REI. Wandering through there today, I half expected to find him swooning over the latest ski equipment or trying on a new pair of hiking boots. Instead, I saw a young girl who looked so much like Zoe that for a split second, I thought it *was* her. My heart nearly stopped. When I realized my mistake, I felt as if I'd been sucker-punched. I sank to my knees in the middle of the footwear aisle and my whole body started to shake. There was a bench a few feet away from me so I pulled myself up onto it and just sat there for the longest time. I was so grateful that no one noticed me. I didn't want to have to explain myself to anyone. When I was finally able to stand up again, all I wanted to do was go home, curl up on the couch, and hide under the chenille throw. That was around 11 a.m. It's now 6 p.m. I don't remember driving home, and I have no idea where those seven hours went.

11 March

I was supposed to go back to work today. It didn't happen. I'm so fortunate to work with such wonderful, caring people. John called from the office last night to ask how I'm doing and what time I expected to be in today. That's all it took for

Alice Ann Kuder

me to break down. He could hear me sobbing from the other end of the line. I couldn't even say anything intelligible or coherent. Finally, he found a diplomatic way to say that I'm clearly still a mess and it's apparently too soon for me to come back to work. I hate the fact that my staff has to pick up the slack and cover for me after so long, but I'm grateful that they are.

31 March

Gwen came over again this morning and convinced me to go to church with her. I looked around at all the people in the pews and wondered how it is that they can go on with their lives as if nothing has happened?

I can tell that Gwen is worried about me. I see the concern in her eyes. She says I'm too thin. I stepped on the scale after she left and was shocked to see that I've lost ten pounds since the accident. A year ago, that would have been cause for celebration, even though I wasn't much overweight. Now, my weight seems inconsequential at best.

1 April

April Fools' Day. Zoe used to get such a kick out of coming up with ideas to fool her dad. He always played along, pretending to be caught totally off guard. Sometimes he really was. Last year, Isaac offered to give Zoe a ride to school, which she happily accepted. When they went out to the car, she walked around to the passenger side and said dramatically, "Oh no, Dad, you've *got a flat tire!" Isaac groaned loudly and walked over to take a look as Zoe giggled and shouted, "April Fool!"*

We always laughed a lot, the three of us. I miss the sound of our laughter.

෨෭

"Come in," Ali shouted listlessly without getting up from the living room couch.

Gwen opened the door and entered. In place of a greeting, however, she chastised Ali mildly. "You left the door unlocked again?"

"Obviously a rhetorical question."

Gwen frowned at the all-too-familiar sight of her dear friend curled up on the sofa, dressed in old, oversized sweats that had obviously been Isaac's. She was concerned about Ali's continuing lethargy, so she had come today with a plan in mind.

"Get up, change your clothes, and get in the car," Gwen said. "We're going for a ride."

෨෭

"It was a pretty ugly divorce," Gwen admitted as they crossed over Lake Washington from Issaquah by way of the I-90 floating bridge. It wasn't necessarily the most cheerful topic, but Gwen was happy to discuss her own emotional history if it distracted her downcast friend.

"That surprises me," said Ali. "You're such a kind and generous spirit—I can't imagine you in a contentious relationship."

"I appreciate your flattering analysis of my character, but as my marriage was breaking up, I said and did more than a few things I'm pretty ashamed of now.

"Breaking up," Gwen continued. "Why do they call it 'breaking up'? Breaking *down* is more like it. My marriage broke down." Ali noted the tinge of muted pain in Gwen's comment.

It was the kind of crisp, clear April afternoon that all Seattleites treasure—and none take for granted—after abiding the gray, gloomy days of winter. As Gwen drove through the brick-pillared entry gate and onto the narrow, wooded lane leading to Dunn Gardens, she felt the familiar yet always magical sensation of stepping through a looking glass. One minute she was in the city, and the next she was in the country. Over the years she had come to regard the gardens as her own urban oasis. She hoped that Ali would find it a peaceful, personal refuge, too.

Tentatively pulling into the tiny visitor parking lot in her whisper-quiet Nissan Leaf, Gwen knew she would be fortunate to find a spot. As they got out of the car, she was gratified to see Ali looking around appreciatively at the lush, green surroundings. The two hooked arms and Gwen led the way to the E. B. Dunn classroom. Knowing that the gardens were open to guided tours by appointment only, Gwen had called to find out if there were any scheduled that day. As luck would have it, there was, and she was able to persuade the group's leader to allow her and Ali to join them. Although she probably could have called in a favor to gain permission for a private stroll through the gardens, Gwen thought that having a guide might be a more effective method of distracting Ali from her heartache for a while.

As they were waiting for the tour to begin, Gwen said, "Thanks for letting me vent about my relationship with Steve. You'd think that after eight years, I would have run out of things to say about my marriage *and* my divorce. Apparently, that's not the case. How did we get on that subject anyway?"

"I don't remember," Ali said, "but it's not as if you talk about your ex constantly. In fact, in the years I've known you, you've rarely mentioned Steve. If you need to talk more, though, I don't mind listening. God knows it takes my mind off my own troubles," Ali assured her.

"Well, then, that sounds like a win-win proposition. Right now though, let's concentrate on enjoying the garden tour. The rest of these nice folks probably don't care to hear my story," Gwen said, tipping her head toward the others gathering nearby.

œ∞Œ

After thanking the docent for the enjoyable and informative guided tour, Gwen turned to Ali and asked, "Well, what do you think of Dunn Gardens?"

"They are beyond lovely," Ali said with genuine enthusiasm. "I can't believe I didn't know this place existed! I picked up one of the brochures telling about the history of the grounds and was surprised to find that they were designed by the Olmsted Brothers back in 1915! I'm not a gardening enthusiast, but even *I've* heard of them. I can see why they were so well-regarded."

Gwen was inwardly pleased that her plan to coax Ali out of her somber mood seemed to be working. "Agreed," she said. "Every time I drive onto the grounds I'm blown away by the contrast between the towering Douglas firs and the delicate trillium groundcover—not to mention everything in between. And aren't these rhodies spectacular?"

"They really are. I mean, it's common to see them practically everywhere in Washington—I guess that's why it's the state flower—but I didn't realize they could grow so large!" Ali said. "How did you hear about this place, anyway?"

The two had been wandering along the woodland trail on the north edge of the property when they came across a bench that seemed to be calling their names. They sat and rested as Gwen recounted her introduction to Dunn Gardens.

"I first heard about the gardens back in 2005, when I was in the thick of my divorce. There was an article in the *Seattle Times* about a private grant they had received to help restore and renovate the grounds for public enjoyment. On a whim, I signed up for one of their garden classes and just fell in love with the place. I've always loved the *idea* of gardening—I've just never had much of a talent for it. So when I saw they needed volunteers, I decided it would be a great distraction from all the drama I was going through. It got me out of the

Alice Ann Kuder

house, made me feel useful, and introduced me to a whole new group of people; it was just what I needed. I've been volunteering here as a docent ever since."

"You work here as a docent? No wonder you know so much about this place and its history. I don't remember you ever mentioning it before."

"No, I guess I haven't. I don't know why," Gwen admitted.

She continued, "The Dunn Gardens Trust is a non-profit organization. With the exception of the curators, gardeners and part-time office staff, it depends on volunteers to do everything from organizing tours and fundraisers to running the website. And I've got to say, they hold some of the most creative fundraisers I've ever seen. This summer, for instance, they're hosting an event they're calling 'Mallets in Wonderland.' It's going to be a colossal croquet competition on the great lawn. We should go!"

"That does sound like fun," Ali agreed. Changing the subject ever so slightly, she said, "Okay, so now I know all about The Dunn Gardens, and I've really enjoyed it—thank you very much—but what I don't know is why you really brought me here today."

"I just thought you might find it as comforting and peaceful as I do. I realize that my divorce doesn't come anywhere close to the kind of tragedy you've suffered—I don't mean to insinuate that it does—but it was a real low point in my life and this was a place that helped me regain my sense of self. I can't say that the gardens will necessarily do that for you, but I want to help you find something or someplace that will.

"I'm not telling you to 'get over it'—my God, it's only been a few months! I just want to encourage you to find a new interest, or maybe re-engage with an old one that'll give you a reason to get off the couch and start to breathe a little more deeply again."

Ali bowed her head, covered her eyes with her hands and sighed deeply.

"I'm so tired, Gwen. I just feel so incredibly tired all the time."

Gwen reached over and rubbed her friend's back. "I know.

I know," she said. "I suppose this was a silly idea. I don't mean to be offering a Band-Aid when you need a tourniquet."

"No, no, I know that's not what you're doing. You're a good friend, Gwen—a really good and thoughtful friend. I don't know what I would have done without you these past months. I'm glad you brought me here; your point's well made. I'm just not sure I'm there yet. I suspect I still have quite a few more hours to log on my couch before the sunrise."

"If there is such a thing as magic, it is our ability to change our emotional and physical state simply by changing our thoughts."
~ *Charlotte Davis Kasl*

Chapter 7
Autumn 2000

Having worked her way up through the ranks from a part-time stocker for PCC Natural Markets during her high school years, to her current role as a wine buyer, Ali knew every facet of the company and was proud to be associated with it.

In accordance with PCC's philosophy that good wine should be accessible even to those of modest means, Ali's job was to discover and procure fine, affordable wines exclusive to PCC as well as those carried by other stores. Her position both allowed and required her to travel extensively through Europe and the United States to accomplish her mission, and she considered it both a professional and a personal victory when she succeeded.

A few months earlier, at a manager's meeting, Ali had proposed hosting a food and wine-pairing class at Seattle Central Community College on Capitol Hill to promote PCC's newly expanded wine selection. She was more than qualified to teach the eight-week class and thought it would be great fun. So when PCC needed a unique give-away to pull people into their booth at the annual University Street Fair, paid tuition for the class seemed like an ideal prize.

&)(&

Little did Gwen Gotshall know when she filled out an entry form at the PCC booth that it would lead not only to a free wine class, but to a lifelong friendship as well.

"I won? Well, how great is that?"

Gwen was pleased, but not surprised that she had won the drawing. She was accustomed to winning prizes—she swore it was because of her attitude toward contests, she simply expected to win—and was excited about this opportunity to learn more about wine. She arrived early on the first night of class so she could introduce herself to the instructor. Before the evening was through, Ali and Gwen were well on their way to becoming good friends.

Both women had traveled throughout much of Europe, giving them an immediate connection. Since her traveling was mainly for her job, Ali spent much of her time in the Old World at various vineyards in the major wine regions.

Gwen's job writing greeting cards allowed her to work from anywhere, so her trips to Europe were purely for pleasure. She spent a great deal of time doing the usual touristy things and indulging her passion for shopping. She loved hunting for antiques most of all, but was smart enough to avoid falling in love with anything that couldn't easily be shipped back to the States.

On the last night of class, the two women decided to go out afterward for a celebratory latte, having had quite enough wine for one night. Being in Seattle, they had their choice of half a dozen different espresso cafes within a three-block radius. Although it was a little further away, they chose the legendary B & O Espresso on Belmont, because they could relate to the owners, two women who, in 1976, had pioneered Seattle's love affair with espresso—for that reason, and because B & O served incredible desserts.

Thankfully, the coffee line was short by that time of the evening. Ali ordered a decaf hazelnut latte and Gwen got a decaf mocha. They decided they could justify sharing a piece of carrot cake, since they had walked, rather than driven, the six blocks from the college.

After commandeering a table by the window—people-watching was always a unique experience on Capitol Hill—Ali asked a question that had been on her mind for a while.

"Gwen, the first night of class you said that you're used to winning contests because you expect to. What did you mean by that?"

"Oh, wow," she said. "I don't really have a short answer to that question. It's all tied up with my whole belief system. Are you sure you want me to get up on that pulpit right now? How late is this place open? We could be here for a while."

"Okay, I consider myself warned. And yes, I still want to hear all about it. You have such a positive outlook on life, even though you've hinted about some tough times in your past. I'd like to know how you achieve the kind of serenity and contentment you seem to have."

Gwen felt flattered. "It's nice to hear that you perceive me that way. I *do* feel pretty content with my life, even though it's far from perfect. I'm probably not going to tell you anything you haven't heard before, but I suppose it can be helpful to see how someone else has arranged all the pieces; kind of like a magical jigsaw puzzle where more than one possible picture can emerge.

"Anyway, I told you I don't have a short answer, but I guess it all boils down to this: I believe that we each create our own reality," Gwen began. "My world, my life, is whatever I believe it to be. My thoughts have tremendous power—as do yours—and I'm learning how to make those thoughts work for me. I suppose it starts with positive thinking, but it's so much more than that. For instance, my luck at winning contests; I visualize myself winning, and more often than not, I do."

She continued, "You know how once you become aware of something, like a song or a product or an idea, and suddenly it's as if you see it everywhere? Well, that's kind of how I came to this conclusion about creating reality. It's from a lifetime of connecting the dots that keep appearing before me: some come from experience, some from books, some from other people. I'm sure there are a lot more dots ahead of me, and I'm happy that the picture I have of how to live my life keeps getting clearer."

"Hey, if the dots are creating pictures, maybe they're really pixels," Ali joked.

Gwen chuckled as she rolled her eyes at Ali and continued. "The roots of my beliefs are in Christianity. I'm careful about what I share, though, because fundamentalist Christians seem to feel threatened by some of my views. I don't see a conflict, but sometimes others do.

"Anyway, I went to church with my family every Sunday when I was growing up. I learned about God and Jesus and Scripture and the power of prayer. And it worked for me for a long time. It gave me a great foundation, but more dots kept showing up!

"I love the Scripture passage about being made in God's image. I'm enamored with the concept of the Holy Trinity and Jesus as God's son. I think we're really blessed to have Christ as an example, a teacher, and a conduit to show us the way to live.

"Then I learned about other great teachers like Buddha and Mohammad and I wondered: Why are they seen by some as lesser sons of God than Jesus is?

"When I learned what a small portion of our brains we humans actually use and develop, I wondered if perhaps Jesus was the exception to the rule. Perhaps he utilized his *entire* brain and *that's* what elevated him to the level of the Divine.

"The next 'dot' I remember discovering has to do with abundance. I don't recall how the topic came up, but a friend of mine pointed out to me that greed can usually be attributed to the belief that there's not enough of some things for everyone. This leads us to compete with one another for what we perceive as limited resources—whether it's money, food, love, or anything else we value. In reality, there's plenty of everything for everyone, and when we come to understand and believe that, we can let go of a lot of fear that might otherwise lead us to do crazy things. I realize that the notion of 'plenty of everything for everyone' sounds like a paradox, and I suppose it is, but that's a whole other discussion, so I'm going to leave it at that for now.

"Another 'dot' came in the form of a book by Charlotte Davis Kasl, titled *Finding Joy*. The most powerful concept for me in that book, was that we are entitled, as children of God, to feel joy. "It is our natural birthright," as she puts it.

"Another dot was the movie, *What the Bleep Do We Know?* You've probably never heard of it because it came and went pretty quickly, but it was a major motion picture starring Oscar winner, Marlee Matlin.

"Unfortunately, it's not a particularly great movie. The storyline is contrived and much of the dialogue is pretty dreadful, but it does a good job of melding scientific and nonscientific evidence showing that our thoughts can actually

Alice Ann Kuder

bring about physical changes in people and things.

"Still another dot was the book, *Ask and It Is Given*, which was referenced in the credits of *What the Bleep Do We Know?* I found a copy in a used bookstore. When I discovered that the authors claim to be channeling the spirit of Abraham, my first reaction was to reject it outright as the work of kooks, but for whatever reason, I kept reading. The more I read, the more impressed I became by the wisdom of the message. That's when I concluded that truth is truth, no matter what the source. In other words, whether the authors were really channeling Abraham or were off their rockers, the things they were saying rang true. I knew I could learn some valuable lessons from them if I could keep from judging the source. And I have. I've now read the book several times, and each time a different part speaks to me, because each time I'm in a different place spiritually and emotionally.

"Perhaps the most well known 'dot,' to the general public at least, is *The Secret*. You probably remember what a phenomenon it was from about 2004-2006. It seemed as if *everyone* had read the book, listened to the CD, or seen the movie. Its authors implied that *The Secret*—which they also referred to as the law of attraction—was a panacea to whatever ailed you, and the public ate it up. It was so popular that it eventually doubled back on itself and became the butt of a lot of jokes. Critics emerged from every corner to pull back the curtain and expose *The Secret* as just another hoax perpetrated on a gullible public. Even less effective than positive thinking, they said, *The Secret* was just *wishful* thinking.

"In my opinion, though, it was the critics who perpetrated the hoax. In the end, the authors probably did everyone an injustice by making it sound too easy. That gave the naysayers the ammunition they needed to shoot it down. In matter of fact, the message contained in *The Secret*—in my opinion—has the power to change lives for the better for those who take it to heart and are willing to do the work.

"So, from all those dots, here are some of the primary beliefs that have emerged for me. I use them as affirmations."

"First, negative thoughts serve no useful purpose.

Second, I am on this earth to create and experience joy.

Third, every event produces positive manifestations.

Fourth, I deserve to be happy, healthy, wealthy, and loved.

Fifth, there are no mistakes; there are no accidents. Everything happens as it should.

"When I remember these things—when I let myself really *feel* the truth of these affirmations—I feel content."

Ali looked across the table at her friend with fascination. "Wow. You've given me a lot to chew on. Thanks for sharing all that with me."

Ali paused for a moment while she finished her latte, then asked, "Do you really believe that *every* event produces positive manifestations?"

"I really do, but I can understand why you'd question that statement in particular. It's easy to buy into the idea of pure evil and the devil. When I finally thought long and hard about all the 'bad' things that have happened to me in my life, I couldn't name one that didn't have some kind of positive after-effect. That's not to say that the ratio of good to bad is always equal; lots of events produce more bad than good results, and vice versa. However, if you accept the premise that every event produces at least *some* positive results, then you have to conclude that there is no such thing as 'pure evil' and probably no such thing as the devil."

"No devil?" Ali asked.

"Well, I suspect that the concept of the devil comes from our need to personify evil. We like to believe there's a devil because we need a scapegoat for our evil acts. The devil—if he even exists— isn't the source of evil. Fear is the source of evil. Acts of evil are committed by ordinary people—not devils—who are afraid of something. The surest way to rid our world of evil is to shine a light on our fears. When we do that, the darkness—aka evil—disappears."

" 'A light shines in the darkness and the darkness shall not overcome it,' " Ali recited. "I don't pretend to know a lot of Scripture—especially not by heart—but that's a bible citation that has always stuck with me. I find it very reassuring."

"Me, too."

"Any other words of wisdom you'd like to share with me before we call it a night?" Ali teased.

Gwen chuckled. "Yes! It's all about joy—so laugh every chance you get!"

Chapter 8
April 2012 to November 2012

10 April

Everyone seems to think I should see a therapist to help me get through this. I think so, too. Maybe tomorrow.

20 April

I had my first appointment with Dr. Bolles today. I didn't know quite what to expect. I think it went okay. I liked her and felt comfortable with her. I'm not a big fan of medication, so I'm glad she didn't try to convince me to take "happy pills." She did review a list of the symptoms of clinical depression with me. I'm experiencing 8 of the 13 most common ones. How could I <u>not</u> be depressed after what happened? I guess the real question is whether I need drugs to help me get over it. The doctor said it's up to me. I'm going to sleep on it . . . probably for about 12 hours.

27 April

After doing some online research and thinking about it some more, I decided to ask Dr. Bolles for more information about antidepressants and how they work. She explained that <u>clinical</u> depression is actually an imbalance of the chemicals in the brain that normally regulate our emotions. If those chemicals are out of whack, no amount of

Alice Ann Kuder

trying to "pull yourself up by your bootstraps" is going to do the trick. Emotional trauma like I've experienced can cause that imbalance. Sometimes the body restores the balance on its own, sometimes it doesn't. Anti-depressants aren't really "happy pills" at all; they simply help to restore the proper chemical balance. That makes a lot of sense to me. I think it's time I tried some.

20 May

The antidepressants are finally kicking in. The doctor warned me it could take several weeks, and it did. Now I'm getting back some of my energy and even a little enthusiasm for living. I'm sleeping less and eating more—which is good because I lost another 5 pounds in the last 6 or 7 weeks. I was glad to lose the first 7 or 8, but not 15. Nathan says that I've gotten too thin—that I don't look healthy. Only a brother can get away with telling a girl that! I know he's right, but I just hadn't been able to convince myself to eat. Now I'm getting my appetite back. I think I'm feeling better not just because of the medication, but also because of the therapy sessions with Dr. Bolles. It really does help to tell my thoughts and feelings to someone who doesn't judge me or try to solve my problems for me. She understands my anger toward Isaac and the guilt I feel about letting people think we had the perfect marriage. I don't have to pretend anything when I'm in her office. Hopefully I can learn to be that way outside her office as well.

18 June

It feels good to finally be back at work full time. Everyone at PCC has been incredibly understanding and supportive all these months. I know that my coworkers have picked up a lot of my slack, and I'm really grateful. A lot of employers would have cut me loose by now. I hope I can repay my boss' kindness someday and live up to the faith they have in me.

4 July—Independence Day

Another holiday so different than in the past. When I close my eyes I swear I can see Zoe wielding a sparkler, spelling her name in the air and singing "bibbidi, bobbidi, boo." And Isaac, standing at the barbeque striking a macho pose as he grills our hamburgers.

My sadness has a different quality to it these days. Happy memories are almost that again, not so bittersweet. I guess time really does dull the pain. I can finally imagine a day when my memories will bring more comfort than sorrow, and when I won't feel guilty about feeling happy.

15 August

I went riding again today. Getting back in the saddle—literally—has been my saving grace these past few months. When I sit astride Palermo, the connection I feel with her is almost spiritual. It's as if I absorb her strength and serenity, just as I used to with Tsunami.

Alice Ann Kuder

3 September

Today would have been Zoe's eleventh birthday. This year it lands on Labor Day.

I miss being a mother. I didn't realize before how much of my identity was tied up with being Zoe's mom. I often felt inadequate for the job. She deserved the perfect mother, and I certainly wasn't it. Lucky for me, she loved me anyway.

To my darling Zoe,

The day you were born you recreated my world in your image. It is that image that sustains me. Death cannot erode it.

I miss you so much. I miss your smile, I miss your laugh, I miss hearing you call me mom. I miss the things you did that made me crazy and sometimes angry.

How I would love to have to pick up your dirty clothes from your bedroom floor or wipe down the kitchen counter after you make a sandwich. Nothing would make me happier than to have to remind you to brush your teeth or make your bed. I wish you were here so I could yell at you to turn down the volume on your iPod. I'd give anything to see you roll your eyes at me or pout because you didn't get your way.

I'm sure I didn't tell you often enough that you were—that you are—the greatest source of joy I've ever known. Even now, when I can no longer hold your hand or kiss your cheek, thinking of you gives me the courage to breathe, the will to endure, and the ability to desire a future for myself.

Love never dies, neither yours for me, nor

mine for you. You will live in my heart until forever.

Your Loving Mom

15 September

Halloween stuff has already been on the store shelves for weeks now. Zoe always had such fun deciding what she would be. Invariably, she changed her mind at least 3 times before settling on just the right outfit. We never bought her costumes; we always made them together. My favorite was the year she announced that she wanted to be a jellyfish! We put our heads together and came up with a pretty ingenious idea, if I do say so myself. We bought a clear plastic umbrella—the dome-shaped kind—and lined it with a battery-operated string of clear Christmas lights. Then we attached blue and white streamers for the tentacles. She looked amazing! Isaac always dressed up to take her out trick-or-treating. He loved wearing his classic pirate costume. Every year he added another special touch—a new sword, gold medallions, or a latex facial scar. Thank God I never missed a single Halloween with Zoe.

28 September

Today was hard. I don't know why. I just felt like crying over every little thing. I haven't had a bad day like this for quite a while. I guess it's the bad days that help you to recognize and appreciate the good ones.

Alice Ann Kuder

17 October

Our Indian summer is slipping away. The holidays will be here before I know it—the first without Zoe and Isaac. I've always been an early holiday gift shopper. The other day, I was walking through Target and saw a sweater that Zoe would have loved. My first instinct was to buy it and stash it away for Christmas. Then I remembered. It's an awful feeling, not having anyone to shop for.

18 October

I went back to Target today and bought the sweater. I'm going to contact YouthCare, in Seattle, and adopt a teenage girl for the holidays. I can give her the sweater and some of the other things I would like to have given Zoe. YouthCare does such great work helping homeless teens. Who knows? Maybe having Zoe as a sort of spiritual Secret Santa will make a difference in another girl's life.

5 November

Thanksgiving is just three weeks away. Over the years, I have grown to love the holiday as much as Mom does. Even so, being grateful for what I have, rather than dwelling on what I've lost will be a challenge this year. I've been thinking a lot about how and where I want to spend the holiday. I would have thought that I'd want to cocoon myself in familiar traditions with a houseful of people, but I find that, instead, I'm craving solitude. I haven't been up to our cabin on Mount Baker since the accident. Maybe I could spend the holiday weekend there? That won't go over big with Chloe and Nathan, not to mention Mom and Dad. I'll need to be really sure it's what I want to do before I even mention the possibility to them.

Alice Ann Kuder

> *"Life can only be understood backwards;*
> *but it must be lived forwards." ~ Søren Kierkegaard*

Chapter 9

Once Ali was all settled in, she stood silently in the middle of the cozy log cabin and felt a sense of mild panic surge through her body. Before her fears could get a firm hold of her, she pulled out her journal and began to write.

21 November

What was I thinking? Why on earth did I think that being alone in an isolated mountain cabin on Thanksgiving weekend, especially this year, would be a healing experience? I have no one to talk to, no one to support me, no one to distract me from the grief that still ambushes me when I least expect it.

Maybe Mom and Gwen were right. It might be too soon for me to be alone. It felt so right when I was planning it. I swear I could hear the cabin calling to me. If I just have the courage to embrace the silence rather than run from it, there is something here for me to learn. I can feel it.

The sound of the rain pounding on the roof and window temporarily pulled Ali's attention from her journal. *How did I ever survive those first few months after the accident?* If not for the proof offered by the calendar, she would have sworn that time had stopped. She hadn't consciously created any new routines that didn't include Zoe and Isaac. On the contrary, her life, which had seemed so orderly and predictable before the accident, had become as scattered and unrecognizable as an ill-constructed jigsaw puzzle. *When and how did I find the faith, hope, forgiveness, and acceptance required to get through this devastating loss?*

After several minutes of listening to the wind and rain punish the cabin's exterior, Ali picked up her pen again and resumed her writing, continuing to ponder the seeming miracle of her emotional survival.

It's been 10 months since the accident. I have survived 10 months of the worst pain I can imagine. I know I still have a lot of healing to do, but I need a break from the grief. I don't know if that's even possible, but I need to find a way to stand still for a minute and assure myself that at least the worst is over. I've made it this far without imploding. God knows I didn't think I could or would. All those days when I couldn't get out of bed, all those times I broke down crying for no obvious reason, yet somewhere I found the inner strength to keep living. There were so many times when I didn't want to. So many times when I wanted to give up, but that's just not an option for me. I have too much faith and too much hope that I will eventually be happy again and love again. I still feel like I'm betraying Isaac and Zoe by even wanting to be happy without them, but I know that staying miserable is no tribute to them. I want to love and be loved again because of what they taught me about love.

Writing always calmed Ali; she had already filled three journals since the accident. Some of what she wrote she also shared with friends and her therapist, but the pages also contained thoughts and feelings so dark and painful that she hardly recognized them as her own. Those, she kept to herself.

In the days immediately following the accident, Ali had received dozens of cards from thoughtful friends doing their best to provide some solace. Although most of the cards contained little more than a few poetic words of sympathy, it

Alice Ann Kuder

was comforting to have tactile evidence that so many people cared about Isaac, Zoe, and her. One card also contained a page of prose that spoke to her deeply, so she tucked it in her journal. Now, ensconced at the cabin, she pulled out the well-worn piece of paper and read it yet again.

What Thou Givest, O Lord, Thou Takest Not Away
by Rabbi Morris Adler

Shall I cry out in anger, O God,
Because thy gifts are mine but for a while?
Shall I forget the blessing of health
The moment it gives way to illness and pain?
Shall I be ungrateful for the moments of laughter,
The seasons of joy, the days of gladness and festivity?
When tears cloud my eyes and darken the world
And my heart is heavy within me,
Shall I blot from the mind, the love I have known
And in which I have rejoiced?
When a fate beyond my understanding takes from me
Friends and kin whom I have cherished, and leaves me
Bereft of shining presences that have lit my way
Through years of companionship and affection.
Shall I grieve for a youth that has gone
Once my hair is gray and my shoulders bent,
And forget days of vibrancy and power?
Shall I in days of adversity fail to recall
The hours of joy and glory Thou once had granted me?
Shall I in turmoil of need and anxiety
Cease blessing Thee for the peace of former days?
Shall the time of darkness put out forever
The glow of the light in which I once walked?
Give me the vision, O God, to see and feel
That imbedded deep in each of Thy gifts,
Is a core of eternity, undiminished and bright;
An eternity that survives the dread hours of affliction and misery.
The youth that once was mine
Continues to course in memory and thought
And remains unspent even in age.

It lingers in the brightness still cast
Upon the dimmer landscape age unfolds.
It gives vitality to the compassion,
And strength to the greater understanding
Which many years of living and feeling
Have brought as their enriching gifts.
Those that I have loved, though now beyond my view,
Have given form and quality to my being
And they live on, unfailingly feeding
My heart and mind and imagination.
They have led me into the wide universe
I continue to inhabit, and their presence
Is more vital to me than their absence.
What Thou givest, O Lord,
Thou takest not away
And bounties once granted
Shed their radiance evermore.
Within me, your love and vision,
Now woven deep into the texture,
Live and will be mine, till Thou callest me hence
To another realm, where these moments of eternity
Shall be joined together
In unbroken sequence
To form eternal life.

෨෬

After preparing herself a simple dinner of vegetable soup, Tuscan bread, and cheese, Ali was a bit dismayed when she looked at her watch and discovered that it was only 6:37 p.m. The sun had gone down nearly two hours ago, and a long, quiet evening still lay ahead. She was certainly getting her wish for time to be alone and reflect.

As she sat at the kitchen table gazing at the familiar surroundings of the cabin she and Isaac bought so long ago, she felt overcome by memory and emotion.

She remembered the trip to Worldly Treasures, the furniture store in nearby Blaine, where they bought the rough-

Alice Ann Kuder

hewn desk that now stood in the corner. It was there that five-month-old Zoe pulled herself up for the first time. The cabin's aromatic cedar closet was Zoe's favorite destination when playing hide-and-go-seek. The faux antique bell jar clock on the mantle was a third anniversary gift from Isaac to Ali. And the wall of framed photos recalled blissful days of building snowmen, birdhouses, and woodpiles together as a family.

Grateful as she was for these memories, their sweetness was poisoned by the bitterness she still felt. Would she ever be able to stop blaming Isaac for causing the accident that put an end to their future? She really wanted to—needed to—she just didn't know how. She sensed that finding a way to forgive Isaac was the linchpin to her own healing.

Ali shook her head, wishing she could clear her mind of these unrelenting questions as she used to shake and clear the sand in her childhood Etch-a-Sketch.

When that didn't work, she decided to enlist the aid of the bottle of Merlot she'd brought with her. She poured herself a glass and turned her attention to the collection of DVDs by the television set. She had done enough thinking for one night; it was time for some mindless distraction.

Thumbing through the stack, she ran across *It's a Wonderful Life* and chuckled. *How ironic,* she thought, as she popped the disc in the player and settled back for her annual visit with George and Mary.

A second glass of wine, together with the soft, flickering light of the television, quieted Ali's mind and body. She felt calm and relaxed to a degree she hadn't felt in some time.

Unconcerned about missing significant plot points to this story she knew so well, Ali allowed herself to drift in and out of consciousness. The last ten minutes of the movie were her favorite part, so she was glad that she roused again for the scene on the bridge where Clarence points out, "You see, George, you've really had a wonderful life."

When it came to the part where George finally declares, "I want to live again!" Ali suddenly sat bolt upright. Once again, she reached for her journal and began writing.

That's how I feel! I want to live again! Thanks to all the friends and family in my life, I finally feel as if I want to live again!

If I were to write a sequel to this movie, it would begin with George seeking out and individually thanking all the people who made his life worthwhile. He would sit down with each of them and tell them everything he appreciated about them and what they had taught him. He would tell them how <u>his</u> life would have been lesser if <u>they</u> had never been born.

Maybe that's what I should do. When I think about it, there have been so many special people in my life who have taught me about loving and living. How many of them have I thanked with the earnestness and deliberation they deserve?

Curious about the answer to her own question, Ali pulled a legal pad and pen from her briefcase and started recalling the significant relationships in her life. The list began with her sister, brother, and parents, but after that the names weren't so obvious. Deciding to go in chronological order, the next persons she thought of were her kindergarten and first grade teachers, her favorite babysitter, her camp counselor, her BFF from high school, her first boyfriend, a coworker, her youth minister, and on and on. By the time she'd finished, she'd filled two pages with names of people who now, or had at one time, played a significant role in her life—more than sixty individuals whose lives had touched hers in a way that had made her a better person. So many! And surely more would come to mind.

As she reviewed her list, Ali felt overcome with love and gratitude. How appropriate, she thought, that I would think of these special people on Thanksgiving. I have so much to be thankful for materially, but without these people, the physical comforts wouldn't mean anything.

Alice Ann Kuder

With that, she flipped to a new page on her pad and began writing a letter to the first person on her list. Her mother.

Dear Mom,

You have taught me so many invaluable lessons during my lifetime that I scarcely know where to start. Most were just a by-product of day-to-day life, barely noticed at the time. Those are the moments that have become significant in hindsight. Here's one.

When I was a senior in college, my ego took a severe blow from my calculus teacher, who awarded me a "D" for my efforts in his class. The only other "D" I ever got was in my high school geometry class. (Yes, math was the common factor here.) It's not as if the low grade came as a surprise to me. I was fully aware that I didn't understand calculus, I was just hoping I had clued into enough of it to scrape by with a "C". No such luck.

When I got back to my dorm room, I picked up the phone and called you to confess my failure. Through my tears, I told you of my shame and humiliation. You patiently allowed me to ramble on with my 'woe is me' sentiments for several minutes, then said, "Well, I hope that's the worst thing that happens to you today."

That stopped me dead in my tracks and immediately put things into perspective! I'd been living with this fear of failing calculus from the first day of class three months earlier. During that time, the dreaded outcome grew in my imagination until it was the size of Mount Rainier! In a matter of moments, your words showed it to be just a speed bump on the road of my life. There was no real tragedy here, only a disappointment—a minor setback in the grand scheme of things.

I have always known that you are proud of me, no matter what. I know you believe I can do and be anything I set my mind to. I feel it. And so I believe it of myself. Your unflinching faith in me has given me the self-confidence to achieve so much more than I might otherwise have accomplished.

Now, at this time of genuine tragedy, your faith in me helps me believe that I can survive even this. I may not want to, but I can. I will.

Some days, simple survival still feels like a formidable goal for me. And I might be satisfied to merely survive, if you hadn't also taught me the key to achieving genuine happiness.

Although I couldn't have been more than seven or eight years old,

I remember vividly, a conversation we had about the merits of Thanksgiving. You told me it's your favorite holiday because it's all about gratitude, and being grateful is the key to creating a happy life.

That truth is the inspiration for this first letter, in a series of letters I intend to write. Each missive will express my gratitude to an individual in my life—either past or present—that I credit with making me a better person.

You have all my love . . .

Until forever,

Ali

Alice Ann Kuder

P.S. Of course, having given birth to me, you have the distinction of actually "making" me a person. The others merely helped to improve upon your initial handiwork. ;-)

ೱೲೲ

Two hours and three letters later, Ali felt both gratified and exhausted. She finally abandoned the paper and pen in favor of her bed and immediately fell into a deep sleep.

A few hours later, she awoke suddenly, turned on the light and reached for the pen and dream journal she always kept next to her bed. Ali often remembered her dreams after she awoke, and tonight's dream was particularly vivid and stirring so she wanted to write it down before she forgot it.

I am sitting at a huge dinner table in the middle of a forest eating Thanksgiving dinner. Zoe is there. So are my second grade teacher, Mrs. Saureault, my college roommate, Brenda; my piano teacher, Mrs. Andouille; as well as Abraham Lincoln, Oprah Winfrey, and several other people who I don't recognize. I don't know who the host is, but everybody seems to know one another and be on an equal footing. The mood is very jovial and serene. Everyone is talking at once on subjects both profound and mundane. Several different languages are being spoken; nevertheless, I can understand them all and follow the multiple conversations with ease.

The table is set with fine china, sterling silver, linen napkins, and crystal goblets, but no one is using any of these things. They are all feeding one another by hand from the feast that continually flows from the cornucopia in the middle of the table.

As I reach for some bread I feel a gentle tug at

my chest. When I look down, I see a shimmering, silken thread of energy—nearly invisible—which passes through a small golden ring attached painlessly to my breastbone. It extends across the table in one direction, connecting me to one of the guests I don't recognize, and in another direction, to Zoe. The same thread connects Zoe back to me as well as to another unknown guest. Looking closely, I see that the thread crisscrosses back and forth across the table, time and again, connecting each person to every other person at the table. The result is a translucent web of energy that seems to hover several inches above the tabletop.

Each movement by anyone at the table results in a subtle, almost sensual tug, which radiates positive energy along the thread and is felt by every other person.

I look back toward Zoe, but she's disappeared. Everyone has disappeared. I'm alone at the table, but oddly, I don't feel lonely. I can no longer see the web, but I know it's there because I can still feel the tugging. I am left feeling incredibly serene and well fed in every way.

Ali put the pen down and fell back into a deep, satisfying slumber. When she woke up several hours later on Thanksgiving morning, the dream was still fresh in her mind, evoking wonderful feelings of intimacy and connectedness. It also made her wish that she could share Thanksgiving with some of the special people she had been remembering. For a moment, she considered driving back to Mount Vernon to join her parents for their traditional dinner and annual open house. However, the storm had continued through the night and Ali knew the mountain roads would be impassable, if not nearly washed away. Like it or not, this is where she would spend the holiday.

Alice Ann Kuder

Ali's dream convinced her of the importance of the letter-writing project she'd started the night before. She continued writing throughout the morning, and each letter made her long to spend time with that person again. *How wonderful it would be to bring all of them together in one room to share their wisdom and their love,* she thought.

Inspired by her dream and with no one else around to tell her she was crazy, Ali decided to host a virtual Thanksgiving gathering. She chose a dozen of the people on her list and set places for them at her Thanksgiving dinner table, complete with place cards. She even had photos of a few of them from albums she kept at the cabin, so she taped their pictures onto the chairs. On their dinner plates, she placed the letters she had written to them. But there were so many more people she wanted to invite. She needed a way to represent them at this feast as well. Looking around, she saw the garland of leaves Zoe had made of construction paper and taped together to decorate the cabin several years ago. *That's perfect!* She thought.

Ali carefully took the garland down from the wall and separated the paper leaves. Then, she took a Sharpie, wrote a name on each leaf, and scattered the leaves in the center of the dinner table around the horn of plenty. *Now the table is complete and the party can begin,* she thought with satisfaction.

Ali raised a glass of wine and toasted her virtual guests before serving herself the simple, yet sumptuous Thanksgiving dinner she had brought with her from home. *Yes,* she said aloud, *this is where I was meant to spend this special holiday.*

Chapter 10
1991 and 1983

"Isaac, you're barely twenty-three, you just moved to Washington, and you've got a promising new job. Why would you choose now to start jumping out of perfectly good airplanes?" Jackie teased her younger brother.

She knew very well that Isaac loved any activity that spiked his adrenaline level. He always had. In this regard, they were total opposites. Jackie was fearful of any undertaking that might possibly cause her bodily harm. Her brother's latest plan to take up skydiving was, she supposed, just the latest in a predictable progression of death-defying pastimes.

Growing up in Xenia, Jackie loved the miles and miles of flat Ohio terrain; Isaac longed to climb some real mountains. Jackie liked to swim in the shallow end of the pool; Isaac was doing backflips off the high dive by the time he was five. Jackie resisted having the training wheels removed from her bike until friends starting teasing her; Isaac started begging for a skateboard when he was seven.

Despite her inability to understand her brother's attraction to all things dangerous, she could see that it made him happy, so she supported him in whatever he wanted to do. Strangely enough, Jackie never really worried about Isaac hurting himself. Between his exceptional physical coordination and his self-confidence, both siblings believed Isaac to be invincible. And big sister was satisfied to get her thrills vicariously through baby brother.

If Isaac had enough physical courage for both of them, Jackie had business acumen to spare. She had an innate ability to organize, manage, and supervise people and projects, and she did it with such tact and diplomacy that they scarcely noticed she was telling them what to do and how to do it.

When she was in the fifth grade, Jackie successfully established and published a school newspaper. As a high school freshman, she organized a campaign to get Dell to donate computers to the Xenia Community Center and then she taught free computer classes to the public. When she turned eighteen, she ran for the elected position of Precinct Executive in Greene County, and won. Her list of accomplishments grew longer and more impressive every year.

Confident that he was an intellectual match for his sister, Isaac was content to play worker bee to Jackie's queen bee. There was not one drop of competitiveness or resentment between the two siblings. On the contrary, Isaac admired his sister's abilities and benefited from them often—especially when he needed to earn money to finance his daredevil activities.

Six months after she got her first job as a cashier at the local Kroger, Jackie convinced her manager that fourteen-year-old Isaac would be a great bagger. Her boss was so impressed with Jackie's maturity and performance that he happily took her recommendation. Isaac lived up to his sister's hype and proved to be a hard worker. Before long, he was promoted from bagger to stocker and gaining valuable experience in retail sales.

ଓୖଔ

It was a beautiful September Saturday for Xenia's annual Old Fashioned Days. Jackie and Isaac had made a pact when they were very young that they would always go to the event together. Despite the teasing they endured from friends— "You're going with your *sister*?"—even now that they were in high school they still held true to their pledge. It was just too much fun to miss.

Despite its name, Old Fashioned Days seemed to reinvent itself every year. Rather than rely on the same old exhibits and events, the planning committees showed endless creativity, offering activities and events as varied as antique car shows, puppet shows, art exhibits, cake walks, and dunk tanks. Musical options included barbershop quartets, country- and western bands, and gospel singers, along with rock 'n' roll performers. For the more competitive fair-goers there were beauty contests, pizza eating contests, and hog calling contests. Tours of the Greene County Airport and historical homes appealed to the more sedate persons in the crowd. And, of course, there was always a carnival area with game booths and rides for the kids.

As they strolled through the center of the festival burying their faces in huge clouds of cotton candy, Jackie turned to her brother and said, "Isaac, you need a plan."

"I do? A plan for what?" he asked, knowing that his sister would not disappoint.

"A plan for making money doing something you love to do."

"Knowing you, you already have a plan in mind, so why don't you save me some time and just tell me what it is?"

"Okay, Smarty-Pants, I will. Instead of stocking grocery shelves at Kroger, I think you should apply for a job stocking auto parts somewhere like Dayton Xenia Auto Parts or NAPA. You're crazy about racecars; you hang out at Kil-Kare Speedway every chance you get. I'll bet that a job at the auto parts store would give you an opportunity to rub shoulders with a lot of the racecar drivers. Knowing them would probably open some doors for you in the racing world. Plus, it would give you practical work experience in a business that's at least *related* to racing."

"Huh. That's a pretty good plan except for one small detail; I don't want to stock auto parts for someone else."

"Oh," Jackie said, feeling her spirit deflate.

"No, if I'm going to work at an auto-parts store, I want to *own* it!"

Alice Ann Kuder

"Reality is merely an illusion, albeit a very persistent one."
~ Albert Einstein

Chapter 11
November 25, 2012

When Ali drove up to the house, she saw that Gwen's car was in the driveway. She knew that her good friend would be waiting inside, anxious to hear all about her weekend in the woods. Ali didn't mind; she'd had quite enough alone time, and talking to Gwen was always therapeutic and comforting.

Gwen was relieved to have Ali safely back home and seemingly at peace. Although Gwen had lived alone ever since her divorce fifteen years earlier, she couldn't imagine spending an entire weekend all by herself at an isolated mountain cabin.

After unloading the car, Ali lit a fire in the fireplace, then joined Gwen in the kitchen while her friend brewed a pot of tea. This was a ritual they had shared many times over the years, in both good times and bad.

Once they were comfortable, Gwen probed for details. "What did you do with yourself all that time? I'm sure I would have been bored and lonely—and maybe a little scared."

"Believe it or not, I mostly visited with old friends."

Gwen listened intently as Ali described her experience. When Ali got to the part about compiling the list of special people, Gwen asked to see it. She was surprised to discover how many of the people she knew, even though she and Ali had only been friends for the past dozen years.

"Who's Ben Gainor?" Gwen asked. "The name is familiar, but I can't put a face to it."

"I don't think you knew him. He was my boss when I first started at PCC, but I considered him to be more of a mentor. I really admired him, though I wouldn't say we were close friends. He taught me a lot about finding serenity through service to others. He died suddenly of an aneurism a couple of years ago. He was only fifty-eight years old."

"Oh. So your list *does* include people who've passed away?"

"Yes . . . you seem surprised."

"Well, there seems to be one glaring exclusion from your list, and I thought maybe it was because he's gone."

Ali had hoped that Gwen wouldn't notice that Isaac wasn't on the list.

"No," Ali said. "I didn't exclude Isaac because he died; I excluded him because I'm still so angry with him that I can't always feel the love."

"Well, it's about time you admitted it!"

"What? You *knew*? Why didn't you say anything?" asked Ali.

"Of course I knew. I just figured you'd bring it up when you were ready to talk about it. I've gotta say, I'm surprised it took you so long. It must be eating you up inside."

A deep sigh predicated Ali's explanation. "You're right, it is. I couldn't say it out loud before now because I'm ashamed of feeling this way, but I blame Isaac for the accident. I do. I blame him for dying and for taking Zoe with him. *He killed our daughter*, Gwen! He took away the only child I will ever have. How do I forgive him for that? He might as well have taken my life, too."

With that confession, Ali dissolved into tears. Gwen reached for her hand, pulled her close, and rubbed her back. Once her sobbing subsided, Ali explained, "The first few days after the accident, I was in such shock that all I felt for Isaac was love. I felt like all the goodness had suddenly been sucked from my life—the laughter, the companionship, the intimacy, our family, the future we had planned. But once my head started to clear, I remembered that things hadn't been good between us for quite a while. I don't think Zoe had caught on yet. I think Nathan sensed something was wrong, but I hadn't confided in anyone about our problems. I suspect that Isaac talked to his sister, Jackie, about it, because she seems rather cool toward me since he died, but she's never said anything directly.

"Because no one knew we were having problems, everyone assumes that I'm grieving the tragic ending of a happy marriage. I don't want to disrespect Isaac's memory so I just let people believe what they want to believe, but I feel like a liar and a hypocrite pretending that Isaac was perfect and our marriage was perfect.

"Maybe we *would* have worked through our problems. Maybe we would have been happy again. Now, I'll never know. I was already angry with him about that. The fact that he caused the accident, and died before we could resolve our problems just added a whole other layer of acrimony."

"Okay, I understand why you're mad, but why do you blame him? It was an accident."

Ali's voice became colder, harsher, and louder now. "It *wasn't* an accident—it was a *crash*. An *accident* is when something bad happens that you can't avoid. An *accident* is when you're following the rules and something unexpected results. Isaac wasn't following the rules. If he hadn't been texting while he was driving, the crash never would have happened. It wasn't an accident; at best, it was an unintended outcome. But unintended or not, his carelessness killed our daughter and it killed him. He died the way he lived: ignoring danger and inviting tragedy. The irony is that with all his daredevil antics— skydiving, racing, skiing, mountain climbing—he died in a common, ordinary car crash. But it didn't have to happen. He knew better.

"I can't forgive him, Gwen. I just can't forgive him. I can't forgive myself either. The text he was answering was from me. My last communication with him was a cryptic message: 'When will you be home? We need to talk.' "

"Oh, Ali, you didn't know. You couldn't have known he would be driving when he got your text. Even if you *had* known, it's not your fault that he chose to respond while he was driving. You have to give yourself a break."

"I don't know, Gwen. Maybe. That's what Dr. Bolles says, too.

"Every time I think I have a handle on all this, every time I think I've accepted what's happened, the anger comes bubbling back to the surface and it feels as if I'm right back there on the day it happened."

"You're going to have to find a way to forgive him, Ali. Don't ask me how, but staying angry is only going to hurt *you*. I can't see any benefit to it. Can you?"

"No, I can't. I know you're right, but I'm just not there

yet."

The two friends sat silently for a while as they contemplated Ali's quest for resolution.

Gwen got up and poured them each another cup of tea, then picked up the list again.

"Who's Eric Wicks?"

"He was a classmate of mine at Western in Bellingham. We were both business majors so we had a few classes together, but mostly I got to know him through Campus Christian Ministry. That's what they called the nondenominational worship community that met on campus.

"Eric was a strong believer. He played guitar and wrote a lot of his own Christian music. He used to lead a sing-along in front of the fountain in Red Square every morning. Rain, shine, or snow, there was always a good-sized group gathered around to sing with him. It was like a quick little worship service; a non-threatening way for people to give witness to their faith in a public place. I really enjoyed it.

"Of course, I developed a huge crush on him, but he was in a serious relationship with a girl he'd been with since high school. He was very upfront about his commitment to her. I never stood a chance, so even though we got to be pretty good friends, I never confessed my crush.

"When I started dating a guy from my dorm—geez, I can't even remember his last name—the four of us started hanging out together. You know, we went to the movies, and concerts, and an occasional dance.

"Even though I grew up going to church every Sunday, by the time I got to college I was really questioning my faith. Eric and I had quite a few deep conversations about God and religion and how faith translates into daily life. He really helped me crystallize my beliefs and my commitment to living a moral life based on the teachings of Christ.

"Until this weekend, I hadn't thought about Eric for years. I have no idea what happened to him. Even though he was a business major, he talked about going to seminary and becoming a pastor. I'm pretty sure he had secret ambitions to get some of his music published, too. He and Nancy—his girlfriend—probably got married, had a bunch of kids, and settled into small-town life somewhere."

Satisfied that Eric was just a sweet memory, Gwen picked up the stack of envelopes and asked, "So what are you going to do with all these letters you wrote?"

"You know, I've been thinking about that. You're probably going to say I'm crazy, but I'm thinking about using the money from Isaac's life insurance to take a year off work."

"Really?" Gwen's eyebrows shot up in surprise. "I hope you don't mind me pointing out the irony in that, given that Isaac was always pushing for you to work fewer hours."

"Yeah, I know, and believe me, I feel a good amount of regret over not listening to him. I wasted a lot of time working when I could have been spending it with my family. I'd give anything to be able to turn back time and make different choices, but that's not an option."

"And what do you intend to do with all this time off?"

"Well," Ali admitted, "that's the crazy part. I want to track down the people on my list and deliver the letters to them in person. It would be a year-long road trip of sorts."

"By yourself?"

"Uh-huh. I'm thinking about leasing a car—or maybe taking Isaac's, though that would feel a little strange—since my Jeep isn't really up to a cross-country trip. I'll be traveling alone between stops, but I anticipate some awesome reunions."

"Wow. That's quite a plan. Are you sure you've thought it through all the way?" Gwen asked with a touch of concern.

"Frankly, no. But I'm sure you'll help me," Ali said with a wink.

"We were together, I have forgotten the rest." ~ Walt Whitman

Chapter 12
1996

When her brother, Nathan, first introduced Ali to Isaac, she thought her heart would stop. He wasn't classically handsome, though she did find him unbearably attractive. Six feet tall with an athletic build, Isaac had an easy smile and pastel blue eyes that radiated sincerity.

Ali was immediately and utterly charmed. Later, she would come to appreciate Isaac's intelligence and wit, but what initially drew her in was more basic than that. It was the way he smelled. Never in her life had she noticed a man's natural scent before, but Isaac seemed to emit a musky fragrance that she could only describe as entirely masculine. She felt slightly embarrassed by her pheromonal attraction; it would be years before she confessed it to this man who would be her husband.

ℬℭ

Nathan had always been the quintessential athlete. Although he had intellectual interests, he only felt truly alive when he was physically active, so it was no surprise to his family that he found a way to turn sports into a career. Preferring the less mainstream sports, he showed strong abilities in swimming, golf, track, and tennis. When the winter snow arrived each year, he grabbed his skis and his snowboard and headed for the Cascade Mountain Range. Crystal Mountain, White Pass, Snoqualmie Pass, Mission Ridge—he knew them all intimately.

Never having the ambition to play sports professionally, Nathan combined his love of physical fitness with his ability to teach and opened up his own Pilates studio in Bothell. In the winter, he scaled back the Pilates classes and worked as a ski instructor at Stevens Pass, which is where Nathan and Isaac met. They hit it off immediately.

Isaac craved activity, too, but while Nathan focused on skills, Isaac thrived on thrills. The faster and more dangerous the sport, the more he loved it.

ℴℙ

Having grown up in Ohio, where molehills were considered mountains, Isaac didn't learn to ski until he moved to Denver for college. What he lacked in years of experience, he made up for in fearlessness and passion. By the time he met Nathan—a natural athlete who practically grew up on skis—Isaac, who had only been skiing for five years, nearly matched Nathan's skill level. Neither Isaac nor Nathan ever met a mountain they didn't like, but they both favored Stevens Pass because of the diversity of challenging runs and the night skiing.

ℴℙ

Ali and Chloe were driving back to Seattle after visiting their cousins in Yakima, in Central Washington, when they decided to pay a surprise visit to Nathan at Stevens. It was nearly noon, so their chances of catching him on a break from giving ski lessons were fairly good. Sure enough, they found him in Pacific Crest Lodge and convinced him to join them for lunch at Iron Goat Pizza.

The server had just delivered their food when Isaac walked in. Nathan spotted him from across the room and waved him over.

"Iceberg! Hey, it's good to see you. How're you doing?"

"Couldn't be better! There's nothing like a couple of really great runs to start a day off right."

"Isaac, I'd like you to meet my sisters. This is Chloe and Ali."

"Your sisters? I wondered how you got so lucky as to have the two most attractive women in the room sitting at your table. Do you mind if I join you?"

"You're here alone? That's surprising. You usually have at least one ski bunny trailing after you," Nathan teased.

"Ski bunny? Really, Nathan, what century are you from?"

Chloe said, making a pretense of sounding indignant.

"I guess that did sound rather sexist and condescending, didn't it, sis? *Mea culpa, mea culpa, mea maxima culpa*," Nathan said, pounding his chest in feigned contrition.

After giving the server his order, Isaac turned his attention back to the group and observed, "You two aren't exactly dressed for a day on the slopes."

"No, we were just driving over the pass on our way back home, so we thought we'd stop and make our brother buy us lunch," said Chloe.

Ali hadn't yet said a single word. She was still waiting for her heart to start beating again. *Maybe if I exhale I might be able to join the conversation*, she thought. Who *was* this fabulous guy, and why hadn't Nathan introduced them sooner? She looked skyward and sent up a silent prayer that she wouldn't say or do anything stupid in front of him.

Apparently, her prayer was answered, because the next day Isaac called her and asked if she'd like to meet him for coffee.

ℴℙ

"Skagit Speedway? You want me to go with you to Skagit Speedway?" she asked.

"Yeah. So you've heard of it?" Isaac asked.

"Heard of it? I grew up five miles from the track, in Mount Vernon. How do *you* know about it?"

"I discovered it when I moved to Seattle in 1990. I was really happy to find a sprint car track so close to the city."

"So you're a racing fan?" Ali asked.

"That's an understatement. I've been in love with auto-racing since I was a kid. When I was a Cub Scout, I won my first pinewood derby race; I must have been about seven or eight years old. Then I graduated to soap box derby cars. When I got old enough, my dad bought an old jalopy and we used to spend hours tinkering around on it. It drove my mom and my sister nuts when we talked about it at the dinner table.

"Growing up here, you must have been to the speedway a million times. It's probably old hat to you." Isaac guessed.

"Actually," Ali admitted, "I've never been there."

"*Never?* Not even once? Why not?" Isaac sounded genuinely shocked and bewildered.

"As far as I'm concerned, cars are just a convenient mode of transportation. Auto-racing never really appealed to me. In fact, I should probably be embarrassed to admit this, but I don't even know what a sprint car is. I mean, I know what it *is*—it's a racecar—but I don't know why it's called a sprint car or what makes it different from other kinds of racecars."

"No need to feel embarrassed. I prefer someone who admits when they don't know something to someone who pretends they do.

"They're called sprint cars because they're designed to go a short distance at a very fast pace, similar to track-and-field sprint runners. They're usually run on an oval, dirt track. The track here at Skagit is three-tenths of a mile. I don't want to get too technical on you, but sprint cars have a very high power-to-weight ratio so they can really fly—up to 140 miles per hour."

"You lost me with the power-to-weight ratio stuff," Ali admitted.

"All that means is that the cars are designed with high horsepower engines and light-weight bodies. That's how they get their speed."

"How can sprint cars be lighter weight than other racecars?"

"Easy. They take out all the unnecessary stuff—like the starter and the flywheel."

"The starter? Gee, call me silly, but I would have thought a starter was pretty important in a car!"

"Okay, you're silly, because you'd be wrong. To eliminate the need for starters, sprint cars use 'push cars' to get them going."

"Alright, enough of the mechanical info. What is it about racing that you love so much?"

Although Ali asked the question with genuine interest, she also felt her hopes for romance deflate. She just couldn't see herself getting serious about a guy who was passionate about racing. *Is this relationship doomed before it even gets off the ground?* She wondered.

"What do I love about it? Wow, where do I start? Well, for one thing, it's exciting! The speed, the competition, the adrenaline . . . when you're racing around that track, you know you're alive! You can't take anything for granted—not your car, not your body, not the other drivers, not even the dirt on the track. You're totally consumed by the moment. It's incredibly intense—in a good way."

"What about the danger of getting hurt? Aren't you scared?"

"Sure, there's some danger and some fear, but that's part of the excitement. You're challenging yourself on so many levels—mentally, physically, spiritually."

"Spiritually?" Ali sounded both surprised and skeptical. "What kind of spiritual challenge is there to auto-racing?"

"Well, I don't know if other drivers feel it, but it makes me think about my life and how I want to live it. It makes me appreciate what I have and the people I love. It reminds me that it could all disappear in the blink of an eye. Some people might call it 'living dangerously'; I call it 'living.'

"It's too easy to get complacent about life. I never want to be a person who coasts through life, always taking the safe and easy route. I *like* feeling excited! I think that excitement is one of the things that makes life worthwhile. Don't you?"

"Hmmm. I don't think my need for excitement is on the same level as yours. There are a lot of other things—safer things—that make me feel life is worthwhile."

"Such as?" Isaac asked.

Ali liked the fact that despite his obvious enthusiasm for his own point of view, he also wanted to hear hers. How many dates had she been on where the guy was so self-involved that he talked on and on about himself and his interests without ever asking about hers?

"People, mostly. It's the people in my life that give it meaning." As Ali said this, she thought to herself, *Oh, geez, he's going to think I'm really boring.*

So she tried to redeem herself. "It's not that I don't like to be active, it's just that who I'm with is usually more important to me than what I'm doing.

"That's why I'm really careful about who I spend time

with. I choose to surround myself with positive, caring people. Negative people suck the life out of you. They aren't worth the energy they demand. Especially the drama queens."

Isaac was a little worried now, because he really liked Ali, so he felt compelled to ask, "Does my love of excitement make me a drama queen in your eyes?"

Ali paused for a moment before answering. "You know, on first glance, it would seem like drama and excitement are synonymous, but maybe they're not. I'll have to give that some thought."

"Well, here's something more to think about. It's not just the excitement that makes me love racing—there's the social aspect, too. Like you said, it's people that make the difference."

"Are you talking about the other drivers?" Ali asked.

"Yes, but not *just* the other drivers. There's the pit crew and the racetrack staff, and the families."

"The families?" Ali asked.

"Believe it or not, going to the races is really a family activity. Fans come in all ages and sizes, but they don't usually come alone. Even if they don't always come with traditional, blood family members, they make families among themselves. Most fans come weekend after weekend for the entire five-month season. Granted, the drivers don't get to participate in that side of things so much, but we see it happen and it feels good to know that we contribute to it. So, yes, I agree with you. It's our relationships with people that give life a lot of its meaning."

Ali took a deep breath and thought to herself, *maybe this could work after all?*

"Okay," she said, "let's go to the races."

§◯◯℞

Ali had a hard time getting to sleep that night. It wasn't the caffeine that kept her awake—coffee to a Seattleite is like wine to a European—rather, it was her date with Isaac. She was attracted to him in so many ways and for so many reasons, but his affinity for dangerous pastimes made her more than a little uncomfortable. Before she had a chance to process the information about his love for sprint car racing he started talking about his passion for skydiving. And she already had firsthand knowledge of his skiing exploits.

Racing eleven hundred pounds of metal around a dirt track at speeds of a hundred or more miles per hour. Swooping down mountainsides, dodging trees and avoiding cliffs with strips of fiberglass strapped to his feet. Dropping out of the sky from twelve thousand feet up in the air and trusting a sheet of nylon to break his fall. *How is it,* she wondered, *that this man is still in one piece?*

Then again, horseback riding wasn't totally devoid of danger. Her parents had been hesitant to let her learn to ride for fear that she might get hurt, but her obvious love of horses eventually persuaded them to give in. Though she'd fallen from her horse a few times over the years, she'd never been seriously injured. If anyone ever tried to convince her to give up horseback riding because of the potential for injury, she knew she wouldn't. *Shouldn't I give Isaac the same latitude, or is this part of his personality a deal breaker?* She knew she needed to give this serious consideration . . . while she could still retreat with her heart intact.

∞℃∾

When they first drove through the front gates of the speedway, Ali was surprised to feel right at home. She had attended her share of Mariners and Seahawks games over the years, but this had a very different feel to it.

"I'm already beginning to think I really missed something all these years," she said. "I grew up so close to here, and I never even gave the speedway a second thought. To be honest, I always thought racing was a sport for rednecks." Ali cringed a bit when she heard herself make that confession. "I hope that doesn't offend you," she said apologetically.

"No, it's nothing I haven't heard before. I don't know why that's such a common misconception. I think you'd be hard pressed to find ten thousand people in Western Washington who qualify as rednecks."

"Ten thousand spectators? Every week? Where do they all

come from?"

"Being from just across the river in Mount Vernon, you know that Burlington, where the track is, is halfway between Seattle and Vancouver, B.C., so the track is really well located. Enthusiasts come from all up and down the I-5 corridor."

"And where do the racers come from?"

"About ninety percent of the drivers are local hobbyists, but some are professionals who come from all around the country. It's a *really* expensive sport, but the prize money can be pretty substantial . . . anywhere from twelve hundred to twenty-five thousand dollars per race."

"How expensive is 'expensive'?" Ali asked.

"I'd say the average sprint car costs between thirteen and fifteen thousand dollars to build. After that initial expense, the engine and the tires are the things that need replacing the most often. Tires run about two hundred dollars each and usually need to be replaced every two to three nights. A good used engine costs between ten and twenty thousand. A brand new engine costs anywhere from twenty-five to forty thousand, and lasts for about fifteen to twenty races. Like I said, it's an expensive sport, even if you have sponsors. That's one reason I don't race full time. It's also one of the reasons I went into the auto parts business!" he said, with a wink.

"What are the other reasons . . . for not racing full time, I mean."

"Well, really dedicated, or maybe I should say *addicted* racers, spend two or three nights a week working on their car. Then, the races themselves are pretty much every weekend for five to six months out of the year. I love racing, but not so much that I want it to be my whole life. There was a time— from about age fifteen to twenty—that I really wanted to go pro, but I took a good hard look at the kind of life that the pros live and I decided it wasn't for me. I want a more balanced life than that. Eventually, I want to get married and have a family. It's not impossible to do that as a professional racer, but the odds are against it."

"Why's that?"

"The huge commitment of time and money are at the top of the list. Then there's the fact that the pros have to travel all over the country and their spouses—yes, there are professional women drivers, too—can't always go along. These guys get treated like rock stars by the fans, and that can lead to a lot of temptations on the road. It's pretty hard to resist after a while . . . I'm told."

"You didn't mention the reason I thought would top the list."

"What's that?"

"The danger of getting hurt or even killed!"

"Yeah. That can cause some tension in a marriage, too, but it's really not as dangerous a sport as you might think. Accidents are common, but serious injuries aren't. Deaths are even more rare," Isaac assured her.

"Even so," Ali insisted, "I can see how the fear and worry could cause some serious stress that would be hard on a relationship."

"Like I said, I decided it's not the lifestyle for me."

∞♋

Since this was more or less their first real date, Isaac had considered trying to impress Ali by taking her to a fancy restaurant for dinner before going to the speedway. Instead, he planned it so they would arrive at the track about an hour before the first race. He wanted a chance to show her around and introduce her to some of his friends who worked at the track.

To prove to Ali that chivalry was alive and well in the racing world, Isaac took her to the souvenir stand to buy her a memento.

"Choose anything you'd like," he said with a dramatic voice and a flourish of his arm. Then, in mock secrecy, he leaned over and whispered loudly to the girl behind the counter, "There's nothing over twenty bucks, right?"

Ali laughed and played along. "Where do you keep the diamond studded racing goggles?"

Despite the joking, she really did want something tangible to help her remember this date—in case she didn't get invited on a second one. She decided on a sequined sweatshirt with the year "1996" printed beneath a picture of a sprint car.

Isaac held Ali's fanny pack while she put on her new sweatshirt, then took her hand and led the way to the stands.

As their fingers intertwined, Ali felt a shiver run through her. She thought to herself, *here I am, a grown woman, and just holding hands with this guy makes me weak in the knees! I could be in real trouble here.*

At the same time, Isaac was thinking, *handholding is really underrated. How can something that looks so innocent be so sensual? It's like publicly sanctioned foreplay.*

∞⚮∝

When it was time for the first race to begin, they settled into their seats and Ali turned to Isaac. "Isn't it a little strange for you to be sitting in the stands instead of racing?" she asked.

"It is, a little, but I was a fan before I was a driver, so this feels very familiar and it's still fun for me. I love being a part of the crowd. Remember when you asked me what I love about racing and I said part of it is the social aspect? Well, a lot of these people come every weekend and sit in the same seats next to the same people, so they get to know and care about each other. It's more fun to watch the races surrounded by people you know and like. Some fans even take it a step further. On Friday evenings, after work, they pile into their campers—usually with their kids in tow—drive to the speedway and stay all weekend! They park in the same spot, next to the same people every week. It's like a giant tailgate party. There's definitely a community feeling to the whole experience."

"What's a race day like for you as a driver?"

"You know, even after years of racing, I still get butterflies on race day, so I'm usually up and at 'em by about eight in the morning. There's a lot of ritual to the day. First, I meet up with my pit crew for breakfast. We each have our favorite place nearby so we rotate locations. Mine is Bob's Burgers and Brew—they have a great Sunday brunch, by the way. Ted, one of my crew guys, prefers Farmhouse Restaurant out on La Conner- Whitney Road. He says it's because they make their pancakes from scratch, but I think it's because they make a killer Bloody Mary.

"By nine-thirty or ten we're giving the car an initial once-over and getting it loaded in the trailer. Then I pack my racing bag. I always do it myself because if anything I need is missing I don't want to be able to blame anyone else for the screw up."

"Your racing bag? What all do you keep in there?" Ali asked.

"It's a combination of practical and personal stuff. A driver's racing bag is pretty sacred, even though it's really just a glorified duffle bag. Mainly it holds our racing suit, gloves, goggles, shoes, socks, and helmet. The bags usually have inside pockets where we store extras like protein bars, water bottles, eyeglasses, and that kind of stuff. Plus, every sportsman has their superstitions and good luck charms, so most of us keep some sentimental items like pictures of loved ones, rosary beads, award ribbons—that kind of thing."

"It sounds like the inside pockets are where the real treasures are kept."

"That's probably true, but it's a lot easier to race without a rabbit's foot than without your driving shoes."

Isaac continued describing the race-day schedule, trying to give Ali a complete picture.

"The pits open at four in the afternoon, so we usually head for the track around three. That gives us time to unload the car from the trailer, check the tire pressure, check the track conditions, and get suited up before the five o'clock drivers' meeting. That's when the officials announce anything new and important, and remind us to play nice. At six, the qualifying time trials begin and at seven o'clock, the main event starts. The whole thing wraps up around ten. Of course, after that, we break out the beer and sit around telling tales of our victories and defeats until the wee hours."

As if on cue, the announcer's voice came over the PA declaring the start of the first race. "Welcome race fans to Skagit Speedway! You're in for a thrill tonight so sit back and enjoy a great show! Tonight's events will be . . ."

"Love is a friendship set to music."
~ E. Joseph Cossman

Chapter 13
1996-1998

"Oooh noooo, Isaac, I absolutely will not jump out of an airplane with you. Get that idea out of your head," Ali said.

"You didn't want to go to the speedway with me either, and look how much fun you had there. You even admitted that you wish you had gone years ago."

"Okay, yes, I had a great time at the sprint races, but there's a big difference—a HUGE difference—between watching other people risk their lives on a racetrack and risking my own by skydiving.

"You really are the embodiment of a daredevil, aren't you?" Ali asked.

"You're not the first person to call me that. I don't deny the "devil" part," Isaac said with a grin, "but my motivation has nothing to do with being dared. I just love the adrenaline rush I get from activities that involve speed and physical risk. It's exciting to me; it makes me feel alive!"

"Why does this conversation sound familiar?" Ali asked.

"Probably because the reasons I love skydiving are pretty much the same reasons I love racing and skiing and mountain climbing.

"Didn't you tell me that you own a horse? Horseback riding involves some physical risk, doesn't it?" Isaac asked.

"Some." Ali admitted. She had wondered if he would ever pick up on this seeming contradiction and point out that 'what's good for the goose is good for the gander.' "It depends on the style of riding you choose—English or Western—and the events you participate in. It's not unusual to fall off a horse every once in a while, but most people never get seriously injured."

"Still, I'd think that would give you a better understanding of my passion for auto-racing and skydiving. You asked me what I love about those sports. So what is it you love about riding?"

"Gosh, I guess I fell in love with horses first, and that just naturally led to riding. I remember, as a young girl, being in awe of them. They're such beautiful, graceful creatures; so proud and powerful . . . almost regal. I've always been fascinated by the way they move. I can watch them for hours and never be bored.

"Mom and Dad used to take us kids to local horse shows; it was one of our favorite family activities. I noticed how some of the horses and riders seemed as if they were almost one being . . . or an extension of each other. I wanted, more than anything, to experience that kind of bonding and connection.

"I started riding lessons when I was about eight. I was so little, and there I was sitting atop this twelve-hundred-pound gentle giant, feeling perfectly safe and totally excited. When she started to move beneath me, it was the most amazing feeling. Horses are incredibly intuitive and sensitive to their rider's disposition. The more you ride together, the more challenged you feel to find that perfect rhythm that allows you both to perform flawlessly, jump after jump."

"Wow," said Isaac, "I've rarely heard you talk at such length about anything."

"Oh, no," she said with a small degree of embarrassment. "Was I rambling?"

"No! It's just obvious that you're very passionate about horseback riding."

"That's true. Maybe more than I realized. I guess I've been doing it for so long that I just take the reasons for granted. Now that you asked me why, I'd have to say it's the challenge of creating a partnership with your horse that allows you to perform together in perfect synchronicity. And you're right, when that happens, it does give me the same kind of rush you describe. There's something about harnessing that power that's addictive."

"What about the physical risk?" asked Isaac.

"I guess I've come to take that for granted, too. I don't even think about it anymore, but it probably does add to the excitement," she admitted.

"Maybe the difference for me is that I trust people and

animals more than I trust machines. I guess I think of a horse as a partner and a car as more of a . . . a weapon. It's like horseback riding is a collaboration and auto-racing is a competition. Now that I say that out loud, it seems kind of absurd, but there it is."

"That's an interesting point of view. I don't necessarily agree with it, but it's interesting.

"By the way, did you ever come to any conclusion about whether excitement and drama are the same thing? Do you think I'm a drama queen to be avoided?" Isaac was almost afraid to ask, but his feelings for Ali were getting stronger at an alarming rate, so he needed to know.

Ali *had* given that question serious thought. She knew that if she was going to keep seeing Isaac, she needed to come to terms with the drastic difference in their definitions of excitement.

"No, Isaac, I don't consider you to be a drama queen. I gave it a lot of thought and I concluded that drama queens feed off of emotional chaos. The only way for them to maintain their high is to suck other people into their melodramas. From what I can see, your need for excitement doesn't require anyone else to divert their energy into your path. It seems to be about creating your own inner joy. I can't really relate to the route you take to get there, but I respect it . . . and maybe even admire it, a bit."

&)(&

"Why won't you tell me where we're going?" Ali asked as she climbed into the Firebird with Isaac.

"I have several reasons, actually. First, I want to find out if you like surprises. Second, I want to see how much you trust me. And third, I want to know if you can relax and have fun when you're not in control."

"I must say, I'm impressed by how much thought you've put into this date. Most of the guys I've gone out with haven't scrounged up enough creativity to think outside of the dinner-and-a-movie box."

Isaac was pleased with the compliment, and grinned.

"Maybe that's why *I'm* here sitting next to you and they're not?"

ଈ୦ଔ

A few minutes later, Ali burst out laughing when they pulled into the parking lot of Interbay Miniature Golf Course.

Still chuckling, she said, "Well this *is* a surprise! The man who loves skydiving, auto-racing, and downhill skiing is willing to spend an evening playing a game as tame as putt-putt golf!"

"Only with you, Ali. Only with you."

ଈ୦ଔ

As they exited the golf course, Isaac declared, "You're a hustler!"

""Who, me? No, I'm not! Besides, you're the one who thought up this little adventure. You're just sore because I beat the pants off you in both rounds."

"Exactly! How was I to know you're such a good golfer?"

"Oh, I think you might be a bit premature in lauding my golfing prowess based on a couple of rounds of miniature golf."

Isaac pulled the scorecards out of his back pocket and pretended to be checking the scores.

"You see?" he teased. "Here's where you really scored big. Likes surprises: 10; trusts Isaac: 8; has fun when not in control: 9."

"10, 8 and 9? Who were the judges on this? I want a recount! Why I didn't get a perfect score on all three?" Ali protested.

"One moment, please, while I confer with the other judges." Isaac turned his back and muttered as if arguing with himself. Then he turned to face her again and announced, "I'm sorry, but the judges' decisions are final. You only scored an 8 on trust issues because you hesitated when I refused to tell you where we were going on our date. And you scored a 9 on control issues because, well, you won, so you weren't really out of control. Still, those are pretty darned good scores. You should be proud of yourself!"

Ali took the scorecards from his hands, tore them up, and threw them in the air as she pulled Isaac close, wrapped her arms around him and whispered in his ear, "The only score I really care about, is how I score with you."

"Making the decision to have a child is momentous. It is to decide forever to have your heart go walking around outside your body."
~ Elizabeth Stone

Chapter 14
September 3, 2002

"I thought I'd seen every expression your face can make, but I don't recognize this one," said Ali as the nurse placed the fifteen-minute-old infant in her arms.

"That's because you've never seen me look at our newborn daughter before," Isaac replied. "It's awe. What you're seeing on my face is absolute and utter awe."

"She *is* amazing, isn't she?"

"She's more than amazing. She's breathtaking, she's perfect, she's incredible, and I can't believe she's ours. We did this! Us! Now I know why they call it 'the miracle of birth.' There's no way you and I could have created this life on our own."

"I feel the same way. There has to be a greater power at work here. We're so blessed."

"You know, Ali, after the miscarriage I wasn't sure I really wanted us to try again. It's not that I didn't want a kid, but you were so devastated and I felt completely shattered. Watching you go through that . . . and going through it myself . . . I thought, if this is how we feel after losing a nameless, faceless, eleven-week-old fetus, what would it be like to lose a child we'd come to know and love? Until then, I never really thought about what it must be like for a parent to lose a child."

Ali scoffed. "'Lose a child.' What a euphemism. It makes it sound like you just misplaced him and might find him again . . . as if there's hope of recovery."

"I guess that's just an example of the power of words. Somehow, it can be less painful to imagine someone you love being lost rather than dead."

"I had the same questions and reservations you did after our baby died, and I didn't really have any good answers until today. Isaac, I had no idea I could feel like this. The depth of the love I already feel for our daughter—it's just overwhelming. You feel it, too, don't you?"

"Oh, Ali, absolutely I do! The love and the joy I feel right now . . . that's what makes it worth the risk. I love you so much. I can't imagine a more perfect life than with you and Zoe."

Gazing down at the sweetness in her arms, Ali cooed, "Hello little Zoe. I think we picked the perfect name for you. It's Greek, for 'life.' That's what we see when we look at you— our life."

"The most important thing a father can do for his children is to love their mother." ~ *Theodore Hesburgh*

Chapter 15
August 30, 2008

"Ring around the rosie, pocket full of posies, ashes, ashes, we all fall down!"

Zoe squealed with delight as she and Isaac dropped to the floor. "I won, daddy! I won!"

"You sure did, Honey Bear . . . again!"

Ali felt her heart contract with intense joy as she looked up from the bunny-shaped cake she was frosting to watch her husband and daughter playing nearby.

Looking at the two of them, she thought to herself gratefully, *I'm living the life I imagined for myself, and it's everything I hoped it would be.*

"Daddy needs a little break, Pumpkin. You've worn me out!" Stooping down to whisper conspiratorially in Zoe's ear, he added, "You stay here and play while I sneak up on your mom and give her a big ole' kiss!"

Zoe crinkled her face, hiding her eyes beneath her hands and giggled in approval.

Isaac made a dramatic pretense of creeping up behind Ali just as she added the sixth and final candle to the cake. Placing his strong hands on her shoulders, he proceeded to massage her skillfully as he nuzzled her neck.

Melting under his masterful touch, Ali cooed, "Oh, I love when you do that. Sometimes I think it's the reason I married you." And turning to face him, she rewarded him with a passionate kiss.

With a deep sigh of satisfaction, he said softly, "This is heaven, right?"

"Oh, yes," Ali stopped to admire her own handiwork and melted backward into Isaac's embrace. "You ought to recognize it. We've been here for quite a while.

"You know, I can't tell which of you is more excited about her birthday," said Ali.

"Oh, I can tell you it's definitely me! You have to have lived a few years and have known some sadness before you can really appreciate this kind of happiness."

"Are you sure she's old enough to go to the speedway with us?" Ali still felt a little apprehensive.

"Ali, don't worry. You've been there enough times to know that there are lots of kids there even younger than Zoe. I think she's going to love it! She plays with my sprint car models all the time, and she's been around #76. She'll be fine."

"You're right. I'm being silly. Besides, I'm really looking forward to it, too. I always envied the families I've seen there. Now we'll be one of them. Mom, Dad, and Nathan are meeting us there at six-thirty. Chloe can't get there until closer to eight. I hope the traffic isn't too heavy. It is Labor Day weekend, after all."

ഇരുതു

As they drove up to the speedway, they were welcomed by the now-familiar sign, *Skagit Speedway ~ Where families come to have fun.* Everywhere she looked, Ali was reminded that this was more than just a tag line; it was obviously a mission that track owner, Steve Beitler, took very seriously. At just fourteen dollars for adults, ticket prices were a steal compared to the prices for other professional sports. And parking was free! You wouldn't find that in Seattle.

Zoe was fascinated by the sea of RVs and campers parked on the expansive grounds.

"As much as I enjoy coming to the races, I'm always a little amazed by the number of fans that show up for whole weekends, week after week throughout the season," said Ali. "How many campers do you think there are here?"

"I asked Steve about that a while back. He said the property is a hundred and thirty-four acres and on any given weekend there are usually four or five *hundred* campers and RVs. You might expect that it would be a big moneymaker for him, but he barely charges enough to cover his cost for removing the trash at the end of the weekend—and he's made some big improvements in the race track since he bought it in

2001. The speedway *is* a business, but Beitler's a race fan first and foremost. He's really committed to making this a place where families can come and enjoy themselves without going into hock. I think the main reason he's been so successful is that he just loves the sport. Any time you pour that much passion into something, you're bound to see amazing results."

��

"Two adults and one child, please," Isaac told the girl in the ticket booth.

"Kids under six get in free, you know," she responded.

Zoe jumped up and down excitedly, holding up fingers on both hands to show the ticket taker, "Today's my birthday! I'm six years old!"

"Oh! Excuse me for my mistake," the girl said apologetically to Zoe, with a wink to Isaac and Ali. "No more free passes for you, Missy!"

Isaac lifted Zoe up so she could survey the grounds from the security of his arms.

"Isaac, you might as well have the words 'Proud Papa' tattooed on your forehead!" Ali said.

"That's okay with me. I *am* a proud papa. I've been looking forward to bringing Zoe here for a long time and I want to show her off to all our friends. I think we should make the souvenir stand our first stop so we can get her some earplugs and sunglasses."

"Let's get her a hoodie, too. I was going to bring one from home, but I thought she'd like to pick one out with a Skagit Speedway design on it," said Ali.

"What do you think, Zoe, do you want to get a new sweatshirt?" Isaac asked.

Zoe's "Yes!" was punctuated with hand clapping.

Once they had her outfitted, Isaac turned his attention to Brady's Espresso stand. As they approached the booth, Dennis Brady greeted Isaac warmly.

"Ali, have you ever met Dennis? When he's not serving up the best espresso in Skagit County, he does all the electrical work here at the speedway."

"No, surprisingly, we've never met. Hi, Dennis, I'm Ali, and this is our daughter, Zoe."

"Today's my birthday! I'm six years old!"

"You are? No wonder you look so grown up!" Dennis said. Turning to Ali, he added, "Nice to finally meet you, Ali. I was beginning to think Isaac had made you up, but I guess he really does have a gorgeous wife and daughter."

"Flatterer." Ali blushed, and gave a sideways glance at Isaac, sending up a prayer of gratitude for her good fortune in sharing her life with this wonderful man whom she adored.

"What can I make for you?" Dennis offered.

"How about a caramel latte for me and a cherry Italian soda for Zoe?"

"Coming right up."

෨෬

As they entered the grandstand Zoe spotted the speedway mascot, Roscoe the Racin' Dog, coming toward them. At first, she hid her face in Isaac's chest, but Roscoe noticed and slowed his approach. With a few 'woofs' and waves of his paws, he quickly won her over.

The hungry trio happily followed Roscoe into the Speedway Café. Ali and Isaac watched with amusement as Zoe craned her neck to see the people leaving the counters with all kinds of delicious-looking food like burgers, chili dogs, nachos, and more. They knew she'd have a hard time deciding what to choose for her birthday dinner. In the end, the basic chicken strip basket won out.

෨෬

"Daddy, Daddy, when can I drive a racecar?

When she heard Zoe's excited question, Ali involuntarily gasped. She wanted her daughter to have fun and enjoy the races—but only as a spectator—not as a future driver.

As if reading her thoughts, Isaac turned to Ali and said, "Relax, Honey. She's only six years old. Chances are she'll outgrow any compulsion to race."

Ali looked her husband squarely in the eye and, with equal amounts of doubt, fear, and sarcasm in her voice, replied, "Uh-huh. Just like her father did."

Alice Ann Kuder

*"Some people come into our lives and quickly go.
Some stay for awhile and leave footprints on our hearts,
and we are never ever the same."* ~ *Flavia Weedn*

Chapter 16
December 1, 2012

Ali sat at her dining room table with twenty envelopes fanned out in front of her. Each one contained a handwritten letter to a "George" from her past. She had collectively dubbed them all George, in reference to the movie character who had inspired her to write the letters—George Bailey in, *It's a Wonderful Life.*

These amazing individuals had each played a pivotal role in her life, and she wanted to express her gratitude for their positive impact. She wanted them to know—in case they had ever doubted—that she was a better person and the world was a better place because of them.

Each of these twenty letters recalled special experiences and relationships. Janie embodied faith and acceptance. Cele demonstrated joy in serving others. Damon showed her the importance of taking responsibility for her own life choices. Ben exuded serenity. Don was a spiritual inspiration. Victoria offered unconditional love. Hilary gave her reason to hope. And her very own mother had modeled for Ali an attitude of gratitude—a quality that further inspired the trip she was about to take.

Ali had spent the last two days online trying to track down the whereabouts of her twenty Georges. She had lost touch with all but a handful and the rest were scattered across the country. Three had passed away. Two were in assisted living facilities. Two others seemed to have vanished. She considered hiring a private detective to try to find them, but that felt too invasive of their privacy. Perhaps they didn't want to be found.

☙❧

Google Damon James Ramey
"DAMON JAMES RAMEY" | Search, New York | Lackawanna
search.lackawannaonline.com/fast-elements.php?
Damon James Ramey, 62, of Lackawanna, NY, is expected to be charged with felony manslaughter Friday in the death of his mother, Margaret Ann Ramey, 87.

Damon Ramey is in prison for killing his mother? Ali was shocked! *It can't be the Damon Ramey I know. Maybe the name is more common than I realized.*

It never occurred to Ali that she might find one of her Georges in prison—especially a man who had been a moral and ethical icon in her life.

According to the newspaper accounts, Damon was found guilty of helping his mother end her life. He pled 'no contest' to second-degree manslaughter and was sentenced to ten years in prison. He was serving his sentence at Lincoln Correctional Facility in New York City.

Now, Ali wasn't sure whether or not she wanted to deliver the letter she'd written to Damon at all, let alone in person and in prison. Her Catholic upbringing had taught her that suicide was wrong in all circumstances, and she agreed with the teaching. Assisting another person to commit suicide was an even worse sin in her book.

Still, part of her felt she owed it to Damon to hear his side of the story. She just didn't know if she could listen without judging. And why should she? *Some things are black and white,* she told herself. *This is one of them. If he helped his mother commit suicide, he is exactly where he ought to be.*

Now that her travel plans were solidifying—with actual dates and destinations—Ali began to wonder, *can I really do this? Can I spend a year traveling around the country by myself showing up on the doorsteps of long-lost friends and mentors who might have no interest in a reunion? Just because these individuals were special to me doesn't necessarily mean that I was significant to them.*

The trip now seemed like a much more daunting undertaking than when she had first voiced it to Gwen. Nevertheless, she had already arranged the sabbatical with her bosses at PCC, so if she didn't follow through with this plan, what would she do with herself? No, there was no backing out now.

Pushing the letters to one side, she pulled out a road map of the United States, and began plotting her course using the addresses she had researched. With less than a month until Christmas, she decided to wait until the first of the year to start her trip. She wanted to be back home by early-to-mid-November, well before Thanksgiving, leaving about ten months for her travels. Having no expectation that she could deliver all twenty letters in that amount of time, she whittled the pile down to ten. She would contact those ten ahead of time so they were expecting her visit. The other ten she would take with her and see if time allowed her to make side trips to deliver them along the way.

Ali planned her stops so that she had no more than ten hours of driving time between destinations; usually closer to six or eight hours. Most of the towns where her Georges lived were within spitting distance of large cities, so she intended to check into B&Bs and visit all the tourist spots in each one. Allowing herself three to four weeks between stops would give her plenty of time to drive at a leisurely pace, spend either a few hours or a few days with each friend, and have time to see the local sights as well.

Her planned destinations included Clarkston, Washington; Kalispell, Montana; Lincoln, Nebraska; Dixon, Illinois; Xenia, Ohio; Louisville, Kentucky; DeLand, Florida; Atlanta, Georgia; Mobile, Alabama; Huntsville, Texas; Vernon, Texas; Albuquerque, New Mexico; Boulder City, Nevada; and Battle Mountain, Nevada.

She added stops to Yellowstone National Park and Mount Rushmore, since visits to both were on her bucket list. In all, she would drive approximately 7,600 miles across the United States and back. She trusted that the car would make the trip without breaking down. She hoped that she would, too.

"You're absolutely sure this is what you want to do?" Peggy asked her daughter.

"I'm sure. I'm a little scared, but I'm sure."

"I realize you're a grown woman, Ali, and capable of taking care of yourself, but it's a mother's prerogative to worry a bit. Especially when you tell me *you're* scared!"

"Yeah, I probably shouldn't have told you that, but it's a good kind of scared, Mom. It's the kind of scared you get when you know you have the chance to do something amazing if you just dare to leave your comfort zone."

"You're talking about the emotional challenge. I'm more concerned about your physical safety. What if you get lost or stranded . . . or in an accident?"

"I'm driving across the United States, Mom, not going on an African safari. My GPS will prevent me from getting lost, and I'll call AAA on my cell phone if I get stranded.

"It's that last possibility that's really on your mind though, isn't it, Mom? What if I get in an accident?"

"Of course it is. Can you blame me? If you're seriously injured—or worse—it could be hours before your dad and I are even notified, let alone how long it could take us to get to your side."

Ali took her mother's hand, stroked it gently, and spoke softly.

"I understand your concern, Mom, I really do, and I love you for it. Given how we lost Isaac and Zoe, it would be ridiculous if we *didn't* consider that awful possibility. I gave it some serious thought, and realized that I could get in a fatal accident leaving my own driveway. I can't stop living the way I want to on the off chance that something bad might happen."

"No, of course you can't, and I wouldn't want you to."

Attempting to restore their upbeat mood, Ali released her mother's hand and adopted a perkier tone.

"And don't forget that I'll be able to e-mail you regularly from my laptop and my tablet, so you'll be able to keep tabs on me that way. Heck, I'm so wired you'll barely notice I'm gone."

"Allow me one last nod to being silly and overprotective. I

have an offer for you to consider . . . something you might want you to take with you."

"I hope it's not a loaded revolver!" Ali said, half kidding.

"No, it's not, but that's not necessarily a bad idea. You wait here while I go get something out of the car."

Ali couldn't imagine what her mother had to give her, but if it would ease her mind . . .

A moment later, the door opened. Ali shrieked with surprise and delight.

"Tess!"

ഇന്ദ്ര

"Oh my God! Tess! You beautiful, beautiful girl!" Ali wrapped her arms around Tess before turning back to her mother.

"Mom, I can't believe you would really let me take Tess with me!"

"Your father suggested it. At first, I balked at the idea, but the more I thought about it, the more I realized it would make me feel much better about the whole thing. And I know you love her almost as much as I do."

"Oh, I do, I do. Tess and I have a great time together whenever you go away on vacation. Have you ever figured out what breeds she is?"

"No, you know she's a shelter dog, so your guess is as good as mine. I keep asking her, but she won't tell me . . . she's very closed mouthed about her heritage," Peggy said with a wink. "It's obvious she's part black lab, but who knows where she gets the curly tail from?"

"I just love the one-ear-up-one-ear-down thing she's got going on. It's very distinctive and cute as all get-out. And she's so calm and well-behaved that she really will make a great travel companion," Ali said.

"I think so, too," Peggy said. "She's old enough that she's happy to sleep most of the day, but she's spry enough that she'll pester you to take her on walks. Having her along will give you a good reason to get out of the car every few hours."

"It might make it a bit more difficult to find places to

stay," Ali admitted, "but there are more and more hotels and motels that allow pets. I'm sure I can find them online wherever I go.

"Mom, this really is a great idea. Thank you so much; you're the best."

"I wish I could go with you, but I know this is something you need to do by yourself. Taking Tess with you will be the next best thing."

"I have something I want to give you, too, Mom, though it pales in comparison to Tess.

"When I first had the idea of writing these letters, I started by making a list of all the people who are important to me—the people who've helped me become the person I am today. You and Dad, of course, topped the list. The very first letter I wrote was to you. Quite appropriately, I believe, I wrote it on Thanksgiving eve. I'm giving it to you now, but I'd prefer that you wait until you're alone to read it."

"That's because you know we would both be washed away in a flood of tears."

"Yep, that's a pretty predictable outcome. I think I'm going to mail letters to Dad, Nathan, and Chloe from the road. I feel as if I should give them to each of them personally, but my emotions are just too close to the surface right now, and it would demand more than I can afford to give at the moment. Will you please explain that to them for me after I leave?"

"Sure, Sweetheart, I can do that."

Ali embraced her mother tightly. "Thanks for understanding, Mom. I love you until forever."

"Until forever, Ali."

"How much more grievous are the consequences of anger than the causes of it." ~ Marcus Aurelius

Chapter 17
January 29, 2012

"April 5th?"

Ali shook her head back and forth. "I'll be in Italy."

Isaac searched his calendar for another possible date. "April 14th?"

"I can't say for sure if I'll be back by then."

"The 23rd?"

"There's an all-day manager's meeting scheduled for that day," Ali said apologetically.

"Ali, I don't see any other possible dates for us all to go to the Tulip Festival together. In the fifteen years we've been together, we've only missed the festival once, and that was before Zoe was born. She'll be really disappointed; *really* disappointed." Isaac's exasperation was beginning to show.

"I know, but it's not as if it's all my fault. Your race schedule interferes with our family time as much as my work schedule does."

"That's not true, and you know it," said Isaac. "Besides, that's only during the summer months and I don't have any control over the dates. You *do* have some control over your travel schedule."

"*Some* is right, but not much. Why do you always make it sound as if I purposely plan to mess up our family time? I'm so tired of being cast as the villain. Stop trying to make me feel guilty about being good at my job," Ali protested.

"It's not being *good* at your job that's the problem, it's being *gone* for your job that's the problem. My God, the Tulip Festival is two months away and your calendar is already full! You travel more every year and I'm tired of taking up the slack here at home. Zoe is almost ten years old now. She needs her mother. If I thought she only needed one parent, I'd ask for a divorce." Isaac's voice was rising with each new allegation.

"Is that what you want? Do you want a divorce?

Sometimes I think you want me out of the way so there's no one to prevent you from sucking Zoe into your thrill-seeking pastimes." The tone of Ali's voice matched Isaac's note for note, becoming shriller and louder with each question and accusation.

"I know you, Isaac. I know you can hardly wait until she's old enough to jump out of planes with you. You've already got her climbing the rock walls at REI and the Fun Center. It won't be long before she's begging to climb a real mountain with you."

"And what's wrong with that? Why is it wrong for Zoe to crave some adventure? It's never hurt me!" Isaac challenged.

"There's nothing wrong with wanting adventure, but it's our job as her parents to make sure that she stays safe and doesn't take unnecessary risks."

"We've always disagreed, Ali, on the definition of 'unnecessary' risk. I say that taking risks is what makes life worth living. You've always been satisfied to be an observer, getting your thrills vicariously—usually through me! You want to keep Zoe in a corner and pack her with cotton so she never gets so much as a scratch!" Isaac was waving his arms for emphasis by this time. The scorn in his words was almost palpable.

Ali inhaled sharply and was about to retaliate with more angry accusations when she looked Isaac squarely in the eye and fell silent for fear of what she saw there. It wasn't a fear of any physical threat. Isaac had never, and would never lift a hand in anger; she felt certain of that. Rather, it was fear of the disconnection she sensed between them that made her stop. Her sudden silence gave Isaac a chance to pull back and collect himself as well.

How had they come to this point? This was a familiar argument. *Why did it seem so much uglier and more serious this time?*

Finally, Ali looked at her watch and announced matter-of-factly, "I have to go."

"I know," Isaac said flatly. "What time is your flight?"

"Seven forty-three."

"Do you need a ride to the airport?"

"No. A coworker is picking me up."

Their conversation was now devoid of emotion.

"You realize we haven't resolved anything?" Isaac said.

Looking downtrodden and feeling dispirited, she confirmed his question with a nod of her head as she left the room.

The word "divorce" still hung in the air, as if it had been hoisted up a flagpole in the middle of the room and left flapping in the wind.

Chapter 18

1 January 2013—9 a.m.

A new day, a new year, a new adventure—no, make that a new reality. I woke up this morning with a now-familiar thought in my head . . . what the hell am I doing? This morning, I'm meeting Elaine for brunch at Salty's. This afternoon, I finish packing, and tomorrow I leave for my 10-month solo road trip as a self-appointed mail carrier. I hope I don't get sued by the postal union.

Aside from Mom, Elaine will be the first George to receive my hand delivery. I can't decide whether to ask her to read it when I give it to her, or later, when she's alone. I always feel a similar conundrum when I give someone a birthday gift. It's hard to stay quiet while they open it—and nerve-racking to watch their facial expression, especially since they know you're watching them. Come to think of it, gift-giving in general, is an emotionally risky business—and I'm about to embark on a gift-giving spree! No wonder I'm anxious!

Suddenly, I'm grateful that I haven't told any of my Georges about the letters. All they know is that I've invited myself for a visit to reminisce and catch up. Maybe what I should do is to stealthily leave each letter behind as I say good-bye. I'll have to think about this.

There I go on one of my famous journal tangents. Sometimes I'm fascinated by how my own mind works. It seems like I come up with my best solutions and most creative ideas when I don't directly concentrate on the problem. Like just now. I didn't even realize that my plan was missing an important step until I started journaling about it.

I'm off to meet Elaine. More later.

ഇൗൣ

Elaine lived in West Seattle, about twenty miles east of Ali's home in Issaquah. And although she and Ali didn't see each other often, they were Facebook friends and ran into each other occasionally. Knowing that Elaine loved breakfast food, but was not fond of rising early, Ali decided to treat her friend to the fabled Sunday brunch at Salty's restaurant on Alki Beach. The food was great, the view of downtown across Elliott Bay was outstanding, and guests were encouraged to sit and linger as long as they liked. It provided the perfect atmosphere and opportunity for Ali to deliver the letter and express her gratitude.

ഇൗൣ

"Another mimosa?" Ali offered.

"Why not? We're in no hurry, are we?"

"Oh, good." Along with the fresh drink, Ali handed Elaine the letter she pulled from her purse. "Here's something I want to give you."

"Really? It's not a subpoena is it? Because I hate when friends take me to brunch and then hand me a subpoena . . . it really spoils the mood."

"Very funny," Ali said dryly. "No, it's much more personal than that."

As Elaine took the letter from the envelope and began to read, she commented with surprise, "It's addressed to both Martha and me!"

"Yes, when I originally wrote the letter, I had hopes of getting the three of us together for a little reunion. When that turned out to be impractical, I just planned separate visits; I didn't see any point in revising the letter."

Elaine looked at the letter and then at Ali. "Should I read it now or later?"

"It's up to you, but I'll tell you what it's about. It says that I'm grateful for your presence in my life and the role you've played in making me who I am. It says that I believe I'm a better person because of you. Elaine, if there ever comes a time when you doubt that you have made a difference in this world, pull out this letter and read it again."

Elaine stared at her friend in silence for a few seconds. Then she reached over and hugged Ali, and whispered in her ear, "I feel the same way."

გ◌ლ

Dear Martha and Elaine,

The two of you were in my life for such a short time—just that one summer when we worked together at YMCA Camp Seymour—but I gained so much from our friendships. I look back on that as the summer that I learned how to let go and have fun.

I never went to summer camp as a kid. I remember hearing the stories my grade school classmates told and the camp songs they sang. I was jealous, but the idea of going to overnight camp scared the heck out of me. So I don't know what possessed me to apply for a job at a summer camp when I was 19. I remember seeing the advertisement posted on the jobs board at the community college, and going to ask my advisor about it. I'm not sure I had ever spent more than a single night away from home at that point in my life, but I was very ready to spread my wings and experience some independence. I remember that summer more vividly than any other single

Alice Ann Kuder

summer of my life. It changed me in very fundamental ways.

I was hired as the camp secretary; essentially an office assistant to the camp director. My job was to schedule activities, assign campers to cabins, run the camp store, etc. Being an innately organized person, I was well qualified for the job and thrilled to get it. Looking back, I'm guessing there probably weren't a lot of other applicants. Most would see the job as dull, boring, and generally devoid of the fun usually associated with camp life.

You were the arts & crafts director that summer, Elaine. You got to plan and teach all kinds of fun projects to the kids.

Martha, your title was activities director, but you were really second in command to the camp director. You were responsible for planning everything from the daily schedule to the songs and skits for the nightly campfire show. You did a great job, too.

Since we were considered program staff, and were generally older and more mature than the counselors—theoretically, at least— we didn't have to stay in cabins with the campers. The three of us got to share staff quarters in the administration building with other program staff. Remember Cathy, the aquatics director? She always reminded me of Mary Lou Retton. And Dave and Gail, the co-boating directors; they seemed to have such a great relationship—I envied them. And the cooks . . . I can't believe I can't remember their names! They were such a kick! The whole experience was like taking part in a three-month long slumber party!

I really liked my job. I was proud of how smoothly the camp office ran under my direction. You all knew you could depend on me to be efficient and effective, which made your jobs easier. But it didn't take you long to peg me as a bit of a stick in the mud—which I was. It wasn't because I didn't <u>want</u> to have fun, it was because I was always afraid of embarrassing myself by saying or doing something stupid. I soon discovered that saying and doing stupid things could be incredibly liberating!

You could easily have judged me as being hopelessly serious and intense, but instead you drew me out by including me in those great pillow fights, water balloon wars, and midnight kitchen raids, not to mention singing, dancing, and general silliness. You helped me unearth the whimsical nature I hadn't dared let show—or even knew I had in me! You taught me that embarrassment is the byproduct of self-doubt. As I gained self-confidence, I stopped fearing embarrassment.

Under your tutelage I became a leader of songs, a teller of stories, a lighter of fires, a hunter of imaginary lions, and even a chartreuse buzzard! When I think of all the joy I would have missed if we had never met, I understand why the two of you hold such a special place in my heart.

May you both know joy until forever,

Ali

৪৩৪৪

Alice Ann Kuder

A Google search found Martha on LinkedIn.com, which revealed that she was now living on the east side of the Cascade Mountains near the Idaho border in Clarkston, Washington. The six-hour drive would provide a gentle beginning to Ali's road trip.

"The only thing we have to fear is fear itself."
~ Franklin D. Roosevelt

Chapter 19

1 January, 2013—3 p.m.

I'm back from my brunch with Elaine. It was so great to see her. She's such a special and talented woman with an easy laugh and positive outlook. I wish our lives intersected more frequently.

As wonderful as my time with Elaine was, I'm still daunted by this trip. Nevertheless, I feel like this is something I need to do . . . something I am meant to do. Part of me thinks that writing the letters was enough. Why do I feel the need to deliver them in person? Then there's another part of me that senses that I have more to learn from these wonderful people—or maybe from the trip itself? I don't know. I guess I'll find out. Whatever I learn, I'm trusting that it will be worth the time and effort, worth nearly a year of my life.

One of my concerns is that I'll be spending so much time alone . . . alone with my thoughts. Am I really prepared to live without diversions, like my job and my friends? Sometimes I think the distractions of work and social obligations are the only things that kept me sane this past year. Now I'm purposely eliminating them from my daily life. Yikes! Can I really do this? Am I up to this?

Dr. Bolles seems to think I am. I've learned so much from her during my therapy sessions. In many ways, I feel stronger and more capable than I did before Isaac and Zoe died. Given a choice, it's not a price I would have been willing to pay, of course, but I'm grateful for this greater self-confidence.

I guess the only way to find out if I can do this is to try. Of course, Yoda would say, "Do, or do not. There is no try." How strange that I thought of that quote. I've never been a big *Star Wars* fan; that was Isaac and Zoe's department.

Packing for this trip has been a real eye-opener. There is so much about daily living that I take for granted because I have a safe, comfortable home. The daily routines that I enjoy seem <u>anything</u> <u>but</u> routine now that I'm leaving home behind for a long while.

In trying to keep my baggage down to a reasonable amount, I've had to think twice about everything I thought was essential for daily living.

First, there's the question of 'beauty' products, as the marketers call them. Do I even need to bring them? Of course I want to be clean and generally well-groomed, but do I want to bother putting on make-up every morning? Especially on those days that I'll be doing nothing but driving and stopping for an occasional meal at roadside diners filled with people I'll never see again? How vain am I? It really makes me wonder if I wear make-up and dress nicely more for myself, or for others?

I felt a similar quandary when deciding about jewelry—earrings, necklaces, rings—and other accessories. How many pairs of shoes should I bring? How many coats? Belts? Purses? When I look at what I 've packed compared to what I'm leaving behind, it makes me wonder why I have *all that stuff in the first place? Why do I feel like I need it? I really want to examine this more when I get back from this trip. Maybe it's time to 'downsize' my life.*

I suspect that this trip will shine a pretty bright spotlight on that question.

ഇന്ദ

Wednesday, Jan. 2, 2013

FB post: *I'm off!* ☺

ഇന്ദ

The odometer read 087014. Just as her dad had taught her, Ali jotted down the reading on the SUV so she could calculate the miles-per-gallon after she filled up the gas tank.

She wished she could have taken her Jeep Cherokee on this cross-country trip, but it had over two hundred thousand miles on it and it was just too small for both her and Tess, and all their paraphernalia.

She had considered leasing a car, but in the end, she opted to take Isaac's 2011 Ford Escape. It was newer, the perfect size, and she liked that it was a hybrid; it really was ideal for this type of trip. Besides, she would otherwise have felt obligated to sell it rather than let it sit in the garage for another year, and she just couldn't face that yet. It was difficult enough, emotionally, to clear his belongings out of the car. When she found his soft, leather racing bag in the back, she broke into tears. Clutching it to her chest, she hugged it for the longest time, as if it were a baby. She couldn't bring herself to open it so she stashed it in the bedroom closet, vowing to deal with it later.

ഇന്ദ

Ali was glad she had decided to take Isaac's SUV. Driving

his car made it seem almost as if he'd be traveling with her. And in addition to the fuel economy, the Escape had a good safety record. More than once, she'd wondered if Isaac or Zoe, or both, might still be alive if they had been in the SUV instead of the Corvette. She didn't like to dwell on questions like that; they only fueled her grief. "What-if's" could drive a person crazy.

As she pulled out of her neighborhood gas station and headed for I-90, Ali mentally reviewed the checklist she had just ticked off on her smartphone. It had been eleven months since the accident, but she still felt mentally sluggish much of the time.

Dr. Bolles assured her this was a normal reaction to such a significant loss and that she shouldn't expect her former intellectual acuity to return to one hundred percent anytime soon. Even so, she hated feeling less than sharp, and viewed it as one more example of collateral damage. The organizer app Evernote had proved to be invaluable for planning the trip.

Peering through the spotless windshield, Ali gave thanks for the uncharacteristically blue sky and bright sun. Uncharacteristic, that is for a January morning in Seattle. The theme song from the old TV show *Here Come the Brides* suddenly popped into her head and she sang happily:

"The bluest skies you've ever seen, in Seattle . . ."

She loved that song; it expressed perfectly her feelings about Seattle and the Pacific Northwest. "One good day here is worth two anywhere else," she often said. She was looking forward to traveling across so much of the American landscape that she'd never seen, but knowing that she would be coming back here—coming home—gave her the courage and serenity she needed to make the journey.

Stepping harder on the gas pedal, she merged onto I-90 heading to eastern Washington. Glancing at Tess in the rear view mirror, she said aloud, "Ready or not, here we go!"

"Remember that the most valuable antiques are dear old friends."
~ H. Jackson Brown, Jr.

Chapter 20
January 3, 2013

Ali was much relieved to hear the note of joyful surprise in Martha's voice when she called to invite herself for a visit. It gave her another reason to believe that this ten-month sojourn would be all she hoped for.

Now, with the help of a trusty GPS, a good set of winter tires, and her copilot Tess at her side, Ali found herself winding down the long driveway to Martha's vintage farmhouse on the outskirts of Clarkston. Four-foot snowdrifts lined both sides of the road. This was a familiar winter landscape for Martha, but not for Ali. Living in the Seattle area for the past twenty years, she was used to largely snowless winters, which suited her just fine. She really did love the white stuff, but she was happy to live in a place that it stayed in the mountains where it belonged; in less than a two-hour drive, she could visit it whenever she pleased.

When Martha opened the storm door to greet her old friend, Ali realized that they were just that . . . *old* friends, or at least old*er* friends. *Where had the years gone? Who had drawn these soft lines on their faces and the streaks of silver in Martha's once-raven hair?* No matter, for even if Martha's physical appearance was less familiar, her voice and her embrace were instantly identifiable.

Once they were curled up in front of the fireplace, nibbling on cheese and crackers and sipping hot tea, Ali asked Martha what had drawn her to Clarkston.

"Well, I worked at the Tacoma YMCA running various youth programs for several more years after our summer at Camp Seymour," Martha began. "I enjoyed the work, but I always felt that I was born to be a farmer."

"Really? You seem like such a social person. I'd think farm life would be too solitary for you."

"Yes and no. I do like being around people, and I also find

real contentment in spending time by myself. I get that when I'm out in the field or milking the cows. In this day and age, living on a farm isn't exactly *Little House on the Prairie*. If I crave company, the nearest town is only fifteen minutes away. Besides, I have cable TV, internet access and cell phone service, so it's not as if I'm cut off from the rest of the modern world."

"Did you ever get married?"

"Yeah, I did. I was married for eight years to a really good man. Dan worked for the American Red Cross as coordinator of the Preparedness Training for Youth program. We met when he came to make a presentation at the Y.

"We had a lot of things in common—and a couple of big differences. I wanted to live in the country; he wanted to live in the city. He wanted to have kids; I didn't. I like kids, I just never wanted to have any of my own. We thought we could make it work anyway, but in the end, the differences were just too much to overcome. When we divorced, I bought this farm and I've lived here by myself ever since."

"And what about him?"

"Dan married a really wonderful woman named Stella, who wanted to raise a family in the city. They live about a hundred miles north of here, in Spokane, with their three great kids. I'm genuinely happy for him. I'm happy for us both. We're still good friends. In fact, since I don't have any immediate family in the area, they always invite me to join them for the holidays. I go to their house every Thanksgiving and stay for the long weekend. Sometimes I spend Christmas with them, too.

Ali looked at her friend. "That's incredible."

"A lot of people seem to think that divorce equals failure. I don't feel that way. When Dan and I got married, we intended to be together for life. It didn't turn out that way, but neither of us feels like the marriage was a mistake. We had ten happy years together, counting the two before we got married, and then we realized that we couldn't both live the lives we wanted to live if we stayed together—so we gave ourselves permission to end the marriage without ending the relationship altogether."

"And now you're a farmer," Ali said with a smile.

"And now I'm a farmer."

"How did you choose Clarkston?"

"My college roommate grew up here. I spent spring break with her at her family's house one year and fell in love with the area. I never forgot how beautiful it was, so when I decided to buy a farm, this is the first place I looked for land. You're going to be in town for a couple of days, right? I'd love to show you around."

"I was hoping you'd say that," Ali said with a wink. "What's on the tour?"

"Oh, Ali, it's so beautiful here, it's nature at its best! Clarkston is in the Lewis-Clark Valley—named after the famous explorers—which is where the Snake River and the Clearwater rivers meet. Locals say the town sits 'at the confluence of the rivers.' I love that description. The word 'confluence' sounds so poetic and elegant.

"The town has grown some over the years, but the population is still just a little over seven thousand, and farming is still the main occupation. Tourism is big, too. Believe it or not, there are three big cruise ship lines that anchor tour boats at the Port of Clarkston, including American Cruise Lines, which operates a paddlewheel ship called *Queen of the West*. The cruise vessels bring in thousands of visitors every year between April and October. Man, are those ships impressive!

"So's Hell's Canyon. It's the deepest gorge in North America, so it creates some breathtaking scenic views from above and great whitewater rafting on the Snake River below.

"The climate here is wonderful, too. It's typically warm enough to do outdoor activities all year round."

"I know. It's great for the vineyards." Ali commented. "I don't think I told you that I'm a wine buyer for PCC Natural Markets. You've probably never heard of PCC on this side of the state, but it's well known in the Seattle area. It's a member-owned cooperative with nine stores; big enough to have some buying power, but not so big as to feel corporate."

"Well, that sounds like a fun job and a good place to work."

"It really is; I love it. Do you think we can fit in a visit to

Alice Ann Kuder

one or two of the local wineries while I'm here?"

"Of course we can! I know at least one—Basalt Cellars over on Port Drive—that welcomes visitors. I've heard they have an impressive tasting room. Maybe I'll learn a little something about wine. I'm pretty clueless when it comes to vino.

"So . . . that pretty much concludes your oral tour of my adopted hometown of Clarkston. The actual live tour should be a bit more stimulating. "

"Who knew there was so much to see and do here?" Ali said, with the slightest hint of amazement. Then, with eyes narrowed and her voice just above a conspiratorial whisper she said, "Now tell me about the *dark* side of Clarkston!"

"I'm sorry to disappoint you, Ali, but the only dark side of Clarkston that I know of comes at sundown, and the sunset that precedes it is simply spectacular most of the time.

"Speaking of sunset, it's almost that time now. It's pretty cold out, but would you like to get bundled up and go outside to watch the sun go down?"

"Only if we can sing *Taps* while it sets," Ali said, half-kidding.

"Just like we did every evening around the campfire at Camp Seymour?" said Martha, joining her laughter. "I think I remember the words. As I recall, neither of us has a great voice, but the sun won't hear us and the moon won't care."

Stepping out onto the front porch the two old friends huddled close together, with their arms draped over each other's shoulders, as they warbled, "Day is done, gone the sun, from the hills, from the lake, from the skies. All is well, safely rest, God is nigh."

Once their final notes faded, the women stood in admiring silence and watched Mother Nature show off. It was as if the Snake River was transformed into a golden ribbon of light by the setting sun before it disappeared from their sight altogether.

With a deep sigh of contentment, Ali reached into her coat pocket, pulled out the letter she had written for Martha, and handed it to her without comment.

"What's this? A bill for some past debt I've forgotten?"

Martha said jokingly.

"No. It's more like payment for a debt I owe you."

With that, Ali filled Martha in on the genesis of her road trip and the real reason for her visit. Then she sat down on the front steps, watching stars appear in the sky while giving Martha a chance to read the letter.

"I already delivered a copy to Elaine," Ali told her when she was done. "She asked me to give you a big, long hug from her, by the way."

The pair said good-bye to the night with hugs, laughter, and tears.

∞⃝

The next morning, at Martha's request, Ali pulled out her map of the United States and spread it out on the kitchen table. A bold, red line showed the route she intended to take in the coming months.

"You know, Martha, I was never very good at geography in grade school; I doubt I could even identify all fifty states. I've learned more while planning this trip than I did in sixteen-plus years of schooling!"

"I could say the same," Martha said, "but I don't think it's entirely our fault. I think the public education system in this country gives geography–especially *world* geography—a pretty short shrift. It's not the teachers' fault either. It's a sign of our ethnocentrism. We just don't put much importance on knowing about how and where people in other cultures live.

"I *do* know the geography of Europe pretty well," said Ali, "because I travel the wine regions there for my job."

"I guess we tend to learn about what really interests us." Martha said. "And it's not as if we have to stop learning once our formal education is over."

"So true. Now, back to my map.

"My next stop is Kalispell, Montana. It's a little over three hundred miles from here. I figure it should take me about six to eight hours, allowing for a couple of breaks for Tess and me."

"Isn't Whitefish Mountain Ski Resort somewhere around

there?" asked Martha.

"Yes, according to what I've read, it's at The Big Mountain, which is just west of Glacier National Park."

"Are you going to do some skiing while you're there?"

"Nooooo . . . Isaac was the skier. I love the snow, I just don't feel a need to go schussing down mountains. I might do a little snowshoeing though; that's more my speed."

"I'm sorry I never got to meet Isaac. From what you've told me, it sounds like he was quite a guy."

Ali felt her eyes begin to cloud and her throat to tighten. "That, he was. I'm sure you would have liked him. He taught me a lot about having fun, too, though I was no match for him in that regard. And you would have *loved* Zoe. She was . . . well, you've already heard me go on and on about her. Thank you, by the way, for making it so comfortable for me during my time here to talk about the two of them when I needed to, without feeling like I *had* to."

Giving Ali's arm a gentle squeeze, Martha reassured her, "Hey, that's what friends are for, right?"

Then, providing a segue to the less emotional topic of her travels, Martha asked, "So, who will you be visiting in Kalispell?"

"Maybe no one. I chose it because I need a stopover between here and Yellowstone, and Isaac's old college roommate lived there at one time. I haven't been able to find him online, though, so I thought I'd go and ask around. It's a fairly small town and if he's still there, I'm betting that someone at the ski resort will know him."

"So, from Kalispell you're heading off to Yellowstone National Park? In January?"

"Yeah, I know the timing isn't great in terms of weather, but I've always wanted to visit Yellowstone and I'll practically be passing right by. I have to spend the night somewhere, so why not there? I've always wanted to stay at Old Faithful Inn. Unfortunately, they don't allow dogs to stay at the inn, so I'll have to settle for one of their Snow Lodge cabins. And, hey, the park's not likely to be crowded this time of year, right?" Ali gave Martha a playful poke in the ribs.

"Good point. And after Yellowstone?"

"After Yellowstone, another non-George stop: Rapid City, South Dakota."

"Let me guess. Mount Rushmore?"

"Yep. That'll take care of another item on my bucket list."

"It's the friends you can call up at four a.m. that matter."
~ Marlene Dietrich

Chapter 21
February 8, 2012

"*Divorce?* She said she wants a divorce?" Jackie was caught off-guard.

"*Shhh*! Can you keep your voice down? I know we're in a public place, but I'd like this to be a private conversation," Isaac admonished his big sister mildly.

As they made their way to a table with their lattes, Jackie couldn't help but think how unusual it was for Isaac to be up this early. It was just past six a.m. and from the looks of him, he hadn't slept at all the night before.

"No, she didn't say she *wants* a divorce. At least, I don't think she did. I can't remember exactly who said what, but I think I was the first one to say the 'D' word," Isaac explained.

"Do *you* want a divorce?"

"No . . . I don't know . . . I don't think I do."

"Isaac, I'm stunned! You've mentioned that things have been a bit strained between you and Ali for the last several months, but you never let on that it was anything serious enough to start talking about divorce. You and I talk all the time. How could you not have said something before now?"

"I don't know. I guess I just thought things would blow over and get back to normal. Besides, I know I share a lot with you, but I've never confided details about the state of my marriage. That wouldn't be fair to Ali and it wouldn't be fair to you. Whatever problems Ali and I have, they're just between us. If we need outside help or advice, we'll get it from an unbiased professional."

"Okay. You're right. You know I love you and I want you to be happy, so I'll keep my nose out of it. I'm just a little confused. If you don't want to talk about it, why did you ask me to meet you here at this ungodly hour?"

"I don't know. I'm sorry. I guess I'm a little shell-shocked and I'm not thinking straight. Ali and I have had our share of arguments over the years, but neither of us has *ever* suggested the possibility of divorce before. Somehow, hearing it said aloud really brought me to my knees. It scared me, and I guess I needed to say that to someone. I shouldn't have put you in the middle."

"No, you shouldn't have. That probably sounds harsh, but even though I love you both, I can't pretend to be neutral. Ali's a good woman, a terrific mother, and a great sister-in-law, but you're my baby brother! How could I not take your side?"

"That's just it, Jackie, I don't want there to be any sides. There are no villains here. I'm not even sure what the problem is. As far as I know, there are no third parties involved. I've been faithful, and I'm pretty sure she has, too. I think it's just a build-up of all the little day-to-day annoyances. And some of the bigger annoyances, as well."

"Such as?" Jackie inwardly admonished herself for asking.

Isaac hesitated before answering. "Such as, Ali doesn't like my pastimes and I don't like her constant travel. That's all I'm going to say. Now let's change the subject."

"Can I just make one observation?" Jackie asked tenuously.

"As long as it's not trash talk about Ali. I won't listen to that."

"It's not. I just think this sounds like a *Seven Year Itch* kind of thing—times two, since you've been together more than twice that long."

"What do you mean?"

"Do you remember the movie with Marilyn Monroe? It's the one with the famous scene where she stands over a subway grate in that sexy white dress and wind from the passing train blows her skirt up around her waist. Well, the main storyline is about an average-Joe husband whose eye starts to stray after seven years of marriage. For a while, he fantasizes that Marilyn's character is wildly attracted to him and he has to resist the temptation to give in to her advances. Once he comes back to reality, he realizes what a good thing he's got with his wife and that he'd be stupid to let his delusion jeopardize their marriage.

"Maybe that's what's going on with you and Ali. Even if

there are no third parties involved, maybe you both just need to step back, look at what you've got, and decide if you want to recommit yourself to your marriage."

"Huh. You might be right. It certainly couldn't hurt to do a little emotional inventory. One thing's for sure: we seem to be reaching a turning point, and I don't want it to be a decision by default."

"I'm glad to hear you say that."

Then, in an attempt to lighten the mood a bit, she added, "One more thing, little brother. Next time you're feeling confessional, can you at least wait for the sun to come up?"

"See how nature—trees, flowers, grass—grows in silence; see the stars, the moon and the sun, how they move in silence. We need silence to be able to touch souls." ~ Mother Teresa

Chapter 22
January 6-19, 2013

Before turning onto US 93 for the final leg of her drive to Kalispell, Ali pulled over and set her GPS for 100 Main Street—the Kalispell Grand Hotel. She loved older, renovated hotels. Built in 1912, this one was one hundred-one years old and looked perfectly charming in the online photos. The website confirmed that it was smoke-free, pet-friendly, and located in the heart of downtown. Perfect!

As she'd predicted, it took her just under six hours to make the drive from Clarkston. The sun had already set, making it feel later than it was. *Why is traveling so exhausting,* Ali thought, *when it usually involves nothing more than sitting?* She was both tired and hungry, so finding a place to eat was her first priority.

Tomorrow she'd have time to do an easy walking tour of the city, providing that the weather cooperated. The forecast called for temperatures in the mid-thirties with perhaps a hint of snow—nothing she couldn't handle.

❧

"I noticed a place called Moose's Saloon about a block from here," Ali said to the hotel clerk. "Is the food there any good?"

"Well, I wouldn't describe it as gourmet, but if you're looking for someplace casual and fun, I think you'll like it. They make good pizza and sandwiches and they have a soup and salad bar, plus a nice variety of draft and bottled beer. If you want someplace a little more upscale, I recommend Jagz Restaurant on Highway 2. It's a fairly new steakhouse, and it's been getting good word of mouth. Then there's North Bay Grille, which is also a steak house and has live music. And

Charlie Wong's if you like Chinese. Lots of good options, really."

Tired as she was, the close proximity and casual atmosphere of Moose's Saloon won out. Pizza and beer hit the spot, while the salad bar let Ali feel as if she was eating somewhat healthily.

Now, back in her hotel room with Tess lying comfortably at her feet, Ali sat on the edge of the bed. Rather than turn on the TV, she let the silence envelop her. This was her third night on the road. Since she'd stayed with Martha the first two nights, it was the first she would spend alone. There was a time, she realized, when the silence might have been her undoing, but that wasn't the case tonight, and she knew why. It was because of Leslie.

Ali hadn't included Leslie in her original list of George letters because she didn't think she'd have the opportunity to deliver it to her personally. Now she decided that didn't really matter. She pulled the complimentary hotel stationery from the desk drawer and began to write.

5 January 2013

Dear Leslie,

You are, and have always been, my favorite troubadour.

It was my incredible good fortune to meet you early in your career when you were traveling from one small town to another—just you with your guitar—offering your concerts to church and community youth groups. I still remember how deeply affected I was the first time I heard you perform. I have lost count of the number of times your music and lyrics have brought tears to my eyes since then. Your earliest CDs—the ones that never made it to the charts—are still the ones I treasure most.

It seems ironic that you, a musician, are the

one who taught me to value silence.

Do you remember the concert you played for the Campus Christian Ministry crowd at Western in 1992? We'd met a couple of years earlier and kept in touch as I followed your concert schedule, occasionally getting the chance to attend your shows when you performed nearby. Then when I saw that you had three concerts scheduled in Bellingham over the course of a week, I invited you to stay at my apartment rather than in a motel. It was a win-win for us both: I got to spend some one-on-one time with you and you had the apartment to yourself all day while I was in class.

The first thing I noticed when I got home that evening was the wonderful aroma coming from the kitchen, where you were making dinner for the two of us. That was a fun surprise. Who knew you could cook?

The second thing I noticed was a tangible sense of peace. It took me a minute to realize that it wasn't just your presence, but the absence of noise that made it feel that way. Whenever I was alone in the apartment, I always had either the TV or the radio on in the background, even when I wasn't really listening. It wasn't a conscious choice on my part, just a habit. I thought that everyone did that, so it seemed odd to me that you apparently preferred the silence.

When I asked you about it, you explained that you found inspiration, as well as serenity, in the quiet. You said something like, "You can't sing one note while you're thinking of another."

That was the beginning of my love affair with silence. I broke my background-noise habit cold turkey. I discovered that silence not only made me

Alice Ann Kuder

feel more peaceful, it also made it easier to concentrate. Now, when I listen to music, I <u>listen</u> to the music. When I watch TV, I <u>watch</u> the program. If it's not worthy of my full attention, it's just noise.

But it was what you said next that really changed my thoughts about silence. You told me that it's in silence that we hear the voice of God. You said you used to be afraid to listen because you thought God would call attention to all your faults and failures. Instead, you discovered that God spoke only words of love and encouragement. It was you, yourself, who focused on your faults and failures. That's the beauty and the power of silent meditation, you said. Once we get over our fear, we experience God's unconditional love.

I wish I could say that since I last saw you, I have successfully incorporated silent meditation into my life on a daily basis. The truth is that my experience has been mixed. When I do manage to quiet myself and just listen, I feel the powerful benefits, but *every time* I sit down to meditate, I have to push through that fear first. Some days I succeed, some days I fail, but always, the opportunity and the invitation to hear the voice of God is there. The silence waits for me until I am ready to try again.

So, dear Leslie, this letter is to express my gratitude for helping me appreciate both music and silence. Now, more than ever, I recognize that lesson as an invaluable gift.

Your friend until forever,

Ali

Ali pulled out her laptop, tapped into the hotel's free Wi-Fi and did a web search to see if she could find an address for Leslie. They hadn't seen each other in years, but the last Ali had heard, she was touring full time with a band.

Bingo! Leslie was currently on tour, as a solo act, in Europe!

Good for her! Ali thought. *Bad for me. No chance I can catch her show anytime soon if she's traveling through Europe.*

Skeptical about her chances of getting the letter to Leslie while she was touring, Ali went online to see if she could track down a home address for her. When that failed, she searched for the address of Leslie's latest record producer. Success! Realizing that there was a good chance that the producer wouldn't be willing to act as a mail courier, Ali made a copy of the letter and tucked it into her suitcase for future delivery. *One way or another,* she thought to herself, *my words of gratitude will reach my friend.*

Holding that belief, Ali closed her eyes and imagined sending the missive out into the universe in care of a mystical messenger.

ഇരു

The next day, Ali drove to Whitefish Mountain Resort to ask around about Isaac's friend, Brian Prost. She hadn't had any luck trying to track him down via the internet, so she suspected that the chances of finding him were slim. But something was drawing her to the mountain. Maybe it was the fact that Isaac had skied there many times, and Brian would be another connection to him, however tenuous. As angry and unforgiving as Ali still felt toward Isaac much of the time, she found herself fighting fiercely to hold onto her memories of their life together.

ഇരു

Now that the holidays were over, the resort crowds had thinned, giving employees an opportunity to catch their collective breath.

Ali approached the woman behind the rental counter. "Excuse me, Brenda, is it?" Ali said with a nod to the woman's nametag. "Do you have just a minute to talk with me?"

Seeing that there was no one waiting in line, she smiled warmly at Ali and said, "Hi. Sure, I do. How can I help you?"

"I'm trying to find an old friend who used to frequent this resort. In fact, I think he might have been a ski instructor here a few years back. His name is Brian Prost."

Brenda paused and looked away, as if trying to recollect. "Gosh, that name sounds familiar. I've worked here quite a few years; there are so many employees that come and go. Brian Prost . . . Brian Prost. Let me think." She paused again. "Oh, yes! I remember Brian! In fact, I can't believe I forgot him at all. He was quite the handsome guy—lots of fun and a real charmer. Brian was a ski instructor here about ten years or so ago. He got his pilot's license and went to work for a charter service that specializes in transporting heli-skiers. He might still be piloting around here somewhere. There are at least a couple of charter services nearby.

"I remember he had a buddy who used to come here a lot, too. Another great guy. Everyone called him Iceberg, because he was so cool and fearless on the slopes. He was one of the original extreme skiers. I don't know what his real name was."

"Isaac." Ali said. "His name was Isaac Berg."

"Was that it? Well, I guess that explains the nickname. Do you know him, too?"

"Yes. He was my husband."

"Was?" Brenda grimaced. "Ohhh. Sorry. Divorced?"

"Widowed."

"Oh, now I *really* feel bad. I'm sorry I said anything."

"No, don't be. It's nice to meet people who knew and liked him. That's why I'm looking for Brian . . . to do a little reminiscing about Isaac."

"Are you staying here at the resort? Doing some skiing yourself?"

"No, I'm just here long enough to see if I can locate Brian. I'm not sure he knows that Isaac passed away."

Since there were still no other customers vying for her

attention, Brenda said, "If you don't mind waiting a couple of minutes, I'll be happy to write down the contact info for the local charter services for you. If Brian's still working for one of them, it shouldn't be hard to find him."

"That would be great. Thank you."

When Brenda ducked into the back room to get the information, Ali looked around the ski shop at the various displays of equipment and souvenirs. One display carousel had Christmas ornaments marked half off. Ali's throat tightened as she thought of the Christmas she had just celebrated—the first without Isaac and Zoe. She had done her best to kindle some Christmas spirit within herself, but had been minimally successful. She helped decorate the tree at her folks' house, but couldn't bring herself to put one up in her own home. Gwen brought her a miniature artificial tree with fiber optic lights in an attempt to help brighten the place. The next day, Ali put it back in the box and stored it away in the attic with the other Christmas decorations, promising herself that next year would be different.

Remembering that promise now, she fingered a beautiful, glass-blown ornament of a skier encapsulated in an iridescent ball. It reminded her of a very special snow globe that Isaac had given her, which was one of her most treasured keepsakes.

When Brenda came back out, Ali handed her the ornament and said, "Can you please wrap this very carefully? We've got a long way to travel together before we get home, and it could be a pretty bumpy ride."

₧⁗⁔

Ali struck out with the first charter service she contacted. When she called the second place, she reached a recording. The message said that although they were open for business, their office staff was on vacation following the busy holiday season, so there was no one available to take phone calls. "Please leave a message and someone will return your call as soon as we're able," the recording said. "Or, if you prefer, come by and visit us in person. See for yourself what heli-skiing is all about!"

Ali didn't really want to leave a message. She wondered if it would be worth her time to drive to the heliport. Ironically, heli-skiing was one of the pastimes that Isaac and Ali had quarreled about on more than one occasion. *She* viewed it as an expensive way to break your neck. *He* viewed it as a bargain at twice the price, to feel so close to being on the precipice of paradise.

"I just don't get it," Ali once confessed to Isaac. "What's so great about it? How can you feel anything other than complete and total, mind-numbing fear when you're cannonballing down a mountain, not knowing what unavoidable obstacle might pop up in front of you in the next split second?"

"It's not something I can explain, Ali. It's something you need to *feel*. Just the helicopter ride itself is an absolute thrill. A good pilot will scout a great line for you, then fly you over it so you get a prescient experience before your skis even touch the unbelievably pristine snow—snow that no one else has touched that day, if ever. Then, when I'm hovering over the drop site, the anticipation of the physical challenge starts to build in my gut. It's like I'm being heated from the inside out. I can actually *feel* the blood being pumped from my heart to every other part of my body. My adrenaline starts surging and my mind clears so that nothing else exists. I feel so incredibly and completely alive! It's me against the mountain, but it's also me *and* the mountain. In one sense, it's as if she's trying to buck me off. At the same time, I feel as if she's holding me close and trying to make me one with her."

"Yeah, it's that last part that concerns me. I don't want you to become part of the mountain! I want my man to be *separate* from the mountain," Ali declared.

"That's the difference between us, Ali. I think of it as *my* mountain, and you think of it as *the* mountain."

"I guess that *is* the difference. Luckily, it's a difference that makes me love you more, not less. You understand, don't you, that I just want you to be safe? I just want you here with me . . . always . . . 'to have and to hold' as the marriage vows say."

Isaac's voice took on a soft, almost reverent tone. He pulled her close and assured her, "I love you, too, Ali, and I have no intention of leaving you. Ever." Then he kissed her with an earnestness that made her feel certain of his love.

The argument was forgotten, but she couldn't help thinking to herself, *I still don't get it.*

∞∞

As long as I've come this far, I might as well drive a few more miles and see if anyone at this last charter service knows Brian, Ali decided.

Just as the phone message warned, there was no one in the office to talk with her, so she ventured out onto the service road leading to the helipad. The only person she could see was a mechanic who was apparently working on one of the helicopters.

"Hi," she said. "I'm sorry to interrupt you but I wonder if you can tell me if you know a man by the name of Brian Prost?"

"Brian? Sure, I knew him. He was a hell of a pilot."

"*Was?*"

"Yeah. Brian died about a year ago."

"Oh, I had no idea. Did he die on the mountain?"

"What? Oh, no! Nothing to do with flying or skiing. He had leukemia. He died three weeks after he was diagnosed. You know, everyone thinks this is such a dangerous sport, but very few people die on the mountain. It's the everyday things in life that get you, you know? Ironic, huh?"

"Yeah. Ironic," Ali whispered.

The next day, Ali checked into Whitefish ski resort and signed up for ten days of downhill ski lessons.

"A light shines in the darkness,
and the darkness shall not overcome it." ~ John 1:5

Chapter 23
January 20-February 2, 2013

The National Park Service website promised that Yellowstone National Park was, *"Open for visitors to enjoy year round. Make plans to enjoy scenery, wildlife watching, skiing, and snowshoeing throughout winter . . . amidst the natural wonders of Yellowstone."*

Further down the webpage was a paragraph assuring the public that Yellowstone was still operating at levels as high as in previous seasons. *In other words,* Ali thought, *the recession and the recent sequester haven't managed to degrade services at Yellowstone . . . at least not yet. Thank heavens for that.*

Ali was genuinely excited about visiting Yellowstone for the first time. She loved the serenity she always experienced amid the majestic trees of a forest. The idea that something so huge and strong grew from such a small seed—all by the grace of nature—gave her faith in her own ability to grow and thrive, even in difficult circumstances.

Fresh from her two weeks of ski lessons at Whitefish Resort, Ali had a new appreciation for winter recreation. She felt a twinge of guilt about all those years she had resisted Isaac's attempts to get her to try downhill skiing. She still wouldn't say that she loved the sport, but neither did she fear it anymore. The helicopter mechanic's comment about the relative dangers of day-to-day living versus those of extreme sports struck a chord in her. Both Isaac and Brian had spent endless hours enjoying physically risky pastimes, but in the end, they both died young from causes totally unrelated to those risks. She remembered all the conversations she'd with Isaac as he tried to explain how alive he felt when he was racing, skiing, mountain climbing and skydiving. The very thought of those activities still scared her senseless. She was so glad that Isaac had gone ahead and enjoyed them anyway. As young as he was when he died, no one could say he hadn't lived his forty-five years to the fullest. Even now that he was dead, he was still teaching Ali about life.

ℰℭ

As Ali was signing the register at Old Faithful Snow Lodge, she sensed someone approaching from behind and gasped when she felt masculine hands squeeze her shoulders. She instantly dropped the pen and turned around to find that it was her father. Surprised by her seemingly alarmed reaction, he stumbled backward a few steps.

"Ali, it's me! I'm so sorry. I just wanted to surprise you, not scare you. Are you okay?"

"Dad! What are you doing here? Oh, that didn't come out right. I mean, it's great to see you, but . . . but what are you doing here?"

"I came to spend some quality time with my daughter. I know you've been telling your mother and me that you're fine and the trip is going well, but according to your itinerary, you've been pretty much alone for the last couple of weeks and you aren't scheduled to visit a friend for almost another month. Your mom and I thought you might appreciate some company. She couldn't get away just now, but I could, and there's nowhere else I'd rather be. Is it okay with you that I came? Especially without consulting you?"

"Oh my gosh, Dad. Of course it's okay! You just surprised me, that's all."

"I'd say you seemed more shocked than surprised. I've never known you to be so jumpy."

"Yeah, that probably did seem a bit over the top, didn't it? It's just that . . . well, Isaac used to do that—come up from behind and squeeze my shoulders. I suppose there's no reason you would ever have picked up on that, even after all the years we were together because he mostly did it when we were alone. It was just his private, non-verbal way of saying 'I love you.'"

"Oh, Ali, I feel so stupid. You're right. I never consciously picked up on that, but maybe, without realizing it, I did. So when you felt me squeeze your shoulders . . . "

"Yes, I thought it was Isaac. Just for a split second, of

course, before rational thought kicked in. But my heart definitely skipped a beat or two."

Martin pulled his daughter close and hugged her. They stood in the lobby holding one another, rocking ever so slightly. After a while, Martin whispered in her ear, "I'm so, so sorry, Honey. I love you so much."

"I love you, too, Dad," she whispered back. "And I'm so grateful you're here."

Then, pulling away, she said, "And you're right. I have been sort of concerned about these next few weeks. I've truly been all right, but I do feel a touch of loneliness starting to settle in. Talking with ski instructors and food servers only carries you so far before you start to crave deeper conversations with people who really know and care about you. Tess is a wonderful companion, but talking with her is obviously a one-way conversation. Thank God for smartphones and Skype and the like, but still, nothing takes the place of honest-to-goodness, human contact with friends and family."

"Let's get checked in and call your mother," Martin said. "She'll want to know I arrived safely and that you didn't send me packing!"

&)(&

Yellowstone more than lived up to all Ali's expectations. Even though her recent downhill ski lessons at Whitefish had made her a passable skier, she still preferred the tranquility of snowshoeing. By her own estimation, she logged close to a hundred miles of snowshoeing through the park during her stay. While she liked the solitude it provided, she was happy that her dad accompanied her for at least half those miles.

Even though it was winter, there was still much in the park to see, explore, and learn. Old Faithful was fascinating, but Ali was more enraptured by the waterfalls. Nearly three hundred of them, each with a drop of at least fifteen feet, flowed year round. During the day, she and Martin hiked the historic trails, and visited several of the museums and archeological sites. In the evenings, they often enjoyed a glass of wine together, played cards, and shared conversations about life, love, and the pursuit of happiness. It was a special time for them both.

For some reason that she couldn't quite understand herself, Ali had not yet written a letter to her father. She hoped he hadn't noticed, but felt sure that he had, since she'd given her mother her letter weeks before.

Finally, as she and her dad were listening to a park ranger talk about forest fire management, something clicked and she knew exactly what she wanted to write to him.

₧₨

Dear Dad,

Here it is. I'm sure you've been wondering why you haven't received a letter from me before now. It certainly isn't because you are less important to me than those I wrote to earlier; quite the opposite. The simple truth is that on the several occasions I sat down to write this, I was overcome by a barrage of thoughts, memories, and emotions, and I couldn't seem to find the common thread. I needed to find that thread in order to weave a tapestry that could depict all the invaluable lessons you've taught me.

Did I ever tell you how I got started on this whole letter-writing project? It was Thanksgiving night at the cabin. I was watching It's a Wonderful Life for the umpteenth time, and even though I was missing Isaac and Zoe and you and Mom terribly, I really felt the truth of the title. It is a wonderful life.

At first, I felt a little guilty about having that thought so soon after losing my husband and daughter. Shouldn't I still be railing against my terrible loss? But then came the movie's closing scene where George is holding Zuzu in front of the

Christmas tree and she says, "Look, Daddy. Teacher says, 'Every time a bell rings, an angel gets his wings'." He assures her, with a knowing grin, that she's right.

As I watched that scene again, I could relate to the comfort, strength, and assurance that Zuzu was experiencing in her father's arms, because I have felt that from you throughout my life. You have taught me that life *is* wonderful. No matter the hardships, the losses, or the pain, life always regenerates itself. Things may not go as we wish, expect, or plan, but there is no event that totally fails to produce at least some positive result.

Nor is there such a thing as pure evil. God would not allow it. No matter how heinous the deed, no matter how heartless the action, no matter how devoid of redemption something might seem, the universe finds a way to bestow grace. You taught me that. Strange as it may seem, I was reminded of it by the park ranger we listened to yesterday. When she explained why the forest service no longer considers all forest fires to be detrimental—that some fires can actually be beneficial to the environment—I flashed back to times you pointed out the positive aspects of situations that seemed utterly devoid of goodness.

For example, when I was eight years old and my pet rabbit died. I was beside myself with grief, as any young child would be. You commiserated with me and let me cry and be sad for a few days. Then you took me to the animal shelter and showed me all the animals that were in need of homes. You told me I was very lucky to have had Snuggles to love and that I should always remember her, but her passing made room for *another pet to come into our home and share our love. That's the day we adopted Primer. What a great dog he was!*

As I got older, I recognized that you are always able to see the goodness that comes from things that others view as unredeemable. Tragedies, you taught me, often bring people together and inspire them to be more loving and caring toward one another, and to do greater good.

I recognized this in groups like Mothers Against Drunk Driving (MADD), which was born from the dedication of grieving parents; and the television show America's Most Wanted, which has helped to find thousands of abducted children. It was created by John Walsh after the tragic kidnapping and loss of his own son, Adam.

Eventually, I realized the implications of your point of view. Since every event produces some positive result and every person has some redeeming quality, then the blessings from any given situation will always eventually shine through . . . if I am willing to look for the good and acknowledge it.

Because of all I have learned from you, I know that there is no event I cannot emotionally survive, including this most agonizing loss, the death of my husband and child.

What more valuable lesson could you possibly teach me? I'm so fortunate and grateful to be your daughter.

All my love until forever,

Ali

Alice Ann Kuder

Ali slipped the letter under Martin's door and went to bed.

"It will never rain roses: when we want to have more roses, we must plant more roses." ~ George Eliot

Chapter 24

Sunday, Feb. 3, 2013

Abraham Lincoln has always been one of my heroes. If you asked me to name one historical figure I would most like to meet, it would be him.

When the movie *Lincoln* came out last year, I was first in line at the Cinerama on Fourth Avenue in downtown Seattle, dragging Isaac and Zoe along with me. (Well, maybe I wasn't actually the first in line, but I was pretty darned close.)

When I visited Washington, D.C., the Lincoln Memorial was on the top of my "must see" list of tourist attractions. So when I started planning this trip, I knew that I had to go to Mount Rushmore, even if it took me out of my way (which it didn't). Now, here I sit, gazing at his immense, twenty-foot-high visage, feeling the same sense of awe and admiration I always feel when contemplating the man history will never forget.

I realize I'm not alone in idolizing President Lincoln, but the connection I feel with him seems somehow otherworldly —as if I had known him personally and loved him as a friend. Maybe part of the reason is because several historians have included such intimate details about his personal demons, both mental and emotional. Much of it must be conjecture, given the limits of what researchers can uncover from an age when documentation was so limited, but a relatively consistent image does seem to emerge. Real or

Alice Ann Kuder

imagined (or a little of both), I find Lincoln, and the life he led, to be deeply inspirational, instructional, and worthy of my fascination.

It never occurred to me before, but now that I think of it, my brother, Nathan, shares many of Lincoln's admirable qualities. Both are kind, compassionate, strategic, forward-thinking men who inspire others to follow their lead. Both understand the powerful role that our thoughts play in shaping who we are and how we live out our lives.

With that thought in mind, Ali put away her journal, pulled out pen and paper from her suitcase and began to write the letter to Nathan that she been composing in her heart for some time.

℥℥

Dear Nathan,

"It matters not what price you've paid, you can't get gladness ready-made. To get the real and lasting kind, you have to grow it in your mind." Author unknown

Those words are from a poster you gave me when I was about 14 years old. You, Mom, and Chloe took a trip to the Ashland Shakespeare Festival in Oregon and I was upset that I didn't get to go along. I didn't see why it mattered that you were older and studying Shakespeare, and I didn't even know who Shakespeare was. When you got back, you gave me the poster as a consolation prize—or maybe it was a peace offering.

The poster itself was rather gaudy—neon pink and yellow—but even at that young age, I felt the profound truth behind those words. Believe it or not, I still have that poster all these years later and recently I even framed it! I often wonder if you knew that the hand of God was surely guiding you when you chose that particular gift for me. It might have been the first time I heard that sentiment from you, but it wasn't the last, and it has figuratively saved my life more than once.

We've never talked about this directly, so I'm not sure you know that I often felt very depressed when we were in high school. I think I hid it pretty well most of the time, but that's why I spent so much time alone in my room. Although it's hard for me to believe now, I confess that there were times when my emotional pain seemed so unbearable that I even thought about taking my own life.

Like most teenagers, I suppose, I was insecure about my looks and my personality. I believed that all the other girls in school were prettier and more popular than me, and I was convinced that the only reason anyone noticed me at all was because I was smart.

My self-esteem depended heavily on my academic success. As long as I had that going for me, I could usually convince myself that I was an okay person and life was worth living. But what I really wanted was to be popular. I told myself, "If I was popular, life would be easy and I would be happy all the time."

When I wasn't thinking that, I was thinking things like, "I'm so ugly. My nose is too big, my eyes are too squinty, and I'm too fat. I'll never have a boyfriend. I don't have any friends; no one likes me. Why would they? I'm dull and boring, and I always say and do the wrong things."

Alice Ann Kuder

Not only did I tell myself those things in my head, I wrote them down in my journal. Day after day, I filled my brain and those pages with negative messages about myself.

Here's the part you probably remember.

One day I picked up my journal and I could tell that someone had been reading it. I was furious! I ran through the house angrily accusing everyone of breaching my privacy, but no one would admit to it—which isn't surprising since you were probably all scared to death of me at that moment.

Later that night, you came to my room and confessed that you were the one who'd read it. I don't remember what excuse you gave, and your apology was pretty anemic, but that wasn't why you owned up. You wanted to talk to me about what I'd written.

I imagine that when you read my entries, you were expecting to find gossip about all the boys I liked or the kids I hated, but instead you read page after page about my self-loathing. Although you weren't my biggest fan—we had the same kind of love/hate relationship that most teenage siblings have—you were really disturbed by what you read on those pages.

I will never forget what you said to me next: "Why should anyone else like you? _You_ don't like you!"

At first, I was stunned, but it didn't take me long to defend my position by rattling off a list of all my faults. You were smart enough not to try to contradict me. Instead you went and got some paper and a pen. Then you handed me my journal, and said, "For the next ten minutes we are each going to make a list of everything that's _good_ about you."

You told me to include skills, physical and emotional characteristics, and natural abilities. At first, I couldn't think of anything at all positive about myself, but once I got started it became much easier. The list got pretty long and even impressive! I wrote down things like: courage, creativity, perseverance, beautiful hair, intelligence, musical ability, etc. When you showed me your list, I couldn't believe all the nice things _you_ had written. You even thought of some that I hadn't!

As we talked about the lists, you explained how our own thoughts can act as either a salve or a poison, and that my current thoughts were what motivational speaker Zig Ziglar called "stinkin' thinkin'." All the negative thoughts I was allowing to go through my head and all the self-criticisms I was writing on those pages were causing me tremendous pain. I was totally focused on my shortcomings and depicted my life as being much sadder than it was in reality. One negative thought attracted another, which attracted another, which attracted another. If I wanted to feel differently, you told me, I needed to replace those negative thoughts with positive thoughts.

Then you provided a very simple, concrete plan of action that you knew I could follow. "Every time you catch yourself thinking you're a loser, I want you to stop and repeat to yourself ten times: 'I am an awesome and lovable person.' Then go back and reread those lists we just made."

Although you didn't have a name for it, you were introducing me to the concept of

Alice Ann Kuder

affirmations.

Frankly, I don't know where, at such a young age, you got the wisdom you shared with me that day, or where I found the maturity to listen. In hindsight, I believe that the Holy Spirit was working through you. You were a prophet to me in the truest sense of the word—one who calls attention to things as they are and challenges us to see how they can be.

My depression didn't magically disappear after that, but I was amazed at how much better I felt whenever I replaced my negative thoughts with positive thoughts. Our discussion and the experience of using affirmations gave me a glimpse at the power of my mind to create and shape my own reality.

I know now that there was more than one cause for my depression. It was partly clinical, which I've since learned tends to run in families and can be helped by medication. The rest was a direct result of the negative self-talk I unwittingly nurtured in my head. No medication necessary to control that.

Your seemingly treacherous act of invading my privacy led to a life-changing lesson in self-love. Now I know that others can love me because I love myself.

And I love you until forever,

Ali

ജ∞ര

Ali felt both gratified and sentimental as she reread her letter to Nathan. Although it only touched on one aspect of everything that she so admired about him, she thought it honored him and their relationship.

Now how should I deliver it to him? She wondered. *I guess I will leave it to the good old U.S. Postal Service. If it was good enough for Lincoln . . .*

Ali crossed the lobby of the hotel. Just as she was about to ask the desk clerk where she could find a mailbox, she heard someone approaching from behind and felt two hands on her shoulders. She turned with a start, this time to find Nathan standing in front of her.

"Nathan! Oh my God! What are you doing here? This is like déjà vu all over again!"

"Hey, Ali Oop! It's so good to see you! I didn't mean to startle you." Nathan gave his sister a huge bear hug.

"It's great to see you, too, but you certainly gave me a start! Dad did the same thing to me at Yellowstone. Why is it that all the important men in my life feel the need to sneak up behind me and squeeze my shoulders? Oh, never mind, just answer my question. What are you doing here?" There was a note of suspicion in her voice.

"I missed you, I wanted to see Mount Rushmore, and I had some time off coming. When a perfect storm blows in, I find that it's best to pay attention. It's a round-trip ticket; if you don't want me here, I can get right back on the plane."

"Of course I want you here! Though I'm not sure I buy the bit about a ski instructor having time off in February, and it seems like a bit of a coincidence that you show up unannounced just days after Dad left. Is there a conspiracy going on in our family? Some sort of travel intervention?"

"Don't be paranoid," he admonished with a wink.

Taking hold of Ali's hands, Nathan took a step back and said, "You look good. I guess this trip is agreeing with you."

"You sound surprised. Did I look that bad before I left?"

"No, I wouldn't say you looked *bad*, but you did lose a lot of weight last year, and you didn't have many pounds to spare. At times, you were looking a bit pale, too. But the bloom seems to have returned to your cheeks."

"And what about my hair? It's a pretty different look for me, huh?" Ali prodded him for an opinion that she was a little afraid to hear.

"I like it." Nathan assured her.

Ali looked him in the eye and screwed up her face, giving him a second chance to be completely honest. "Are you sure?"

"Honestly, Ali, the color looks good. If you had asked me before you did it, I probably would have tried to discourage you, but letting your gray show is a brave choice and it's working for you. Personally, I've always liked the salt-and-pepper look and your gray is more like silver. It's very becoming. What made you decide to stop coloring it?"

"It was one part laziness and two parts curiosity. I don't know about men, but like a lot of women, I started coloring my hair before the gray really took hold, so I had no idea what I might look like if I stopped. I'm liking the salt-and-pepper, too. Now I say I have natural silver highlights!"

"I'm still not used to seeing you with such short hair. Are you planning to let it grow out again?"

"I haven't decided yet; Isaac liked it longer."

"Don't all men?" Nathan said, only half joking.

"After he died—when I was at my lowest point—it just didn't seem worth the trouble. Jane, my stylist, says that when a woman changes her hairstyle it usually signals some other significant event in her life. That was certainly true in my case."

"But the first time you cut it, it was still almost shoulder length. This is much more . . . dramatic."

"I suppose, but it's also more practical and convenient. It's hard enough to find a stylist you like on your home turf, but knowing I was going to be on the road for so long . . . I just couldn't imagine trusting my hair to someone I don't know. This way, I have several months before I really need to deal with it again."

"Good point. Well, like I said, I think it's quite attractive, but can I offer a little brotherly advice?"

"Sure. I can't promise I'll follow it, but go ahead," she said with a smirk.

"It's nothing earth-shattering, just passing along something Mom told me when I was in college and felt too poor to get my hair cut. She said, 'Don't neglect your personal appearance; it affects and *re*flects your self-esteem.'"

Ali smiled. "And we both know what a big role our thoughts play in creating our happiness. Sounds like good advice. I'll take it," she said with a playful poke to her big brother's ribs.

Painfully aware of the date—February 10th, 2013—Ali had been up since dawn, sitting in a hotel chair, staring out the window. She turned when she heard a soft knock at the door, but didn't get up at first.

After another slightly louder knock, she heard Nathan ask quietly, "Ali? Are you up?"

Still in her bathrobe, she drifted over to the door to let him in.

"Good morning," he said in a dulcet tone. Handing her a latte with a familiar logo on the cup, he stated the obvious. "I brought you some coffee."

"Good morning, Nathan. That's so thoughtful," she said. "Come on in."

"Is it really? A good morning, I mean." Nathan's voice was tinged with concern.

"Well," she said, "the sun came up again. That's always a good omen.

"Seriously, though, I'm okay," she assured him. "I suspected this day would be tough, but it is what it is . . . the one-year anniversary."

She wandered over to the window, and stood there staring at nothing in particular for a few moments, before commenting, "I've always thought it strange that anniversaries have such mental and emotional impact on people. I mean, if you think about it, they're pretty arbitrary. Why does the 365th day since they died feel any different than the 364th day or the 366th day?"

"I guess it must just fulfill some innate human need to mark time and commemorate significant events in our lives," Nathan said, feeling equally mystified.

"I guess so. It's easier for me to understand celebrating the anniversaries of happy occasions like birthdays. Why do you suppose we mark the anniversaries of sad things, too?"

"I don't have an answer for that, sis. I wish I did," Nathan said, then after a pause he pressed Ali further. "How are you *really* feeling? And please don't just say 'okay'."

Returning to the chair by the bed, Ali looked Nathan in the eye, but didn't say anything. He could see that she simply didn't have an answer, so he tried another approach.

"Do you know how you want to spend the day? I mean, do you want to spend it remembering, or would you rather try to put it out of your mind?"

"I've been asking myself those same questions, but I haven't come up with any answers." After another few moments of silence, she continued. "I'm feeling low . . . sad . . . a little depressed . . . but I don't *want* to feel that way. I realize it's not what Isaac and Zoe would want for me."

With that, Ali stood and squared her shoulders and said, "Let's do something active and fun—something we might all have done together if they were still alive."

"Are you open to suggestions?" Nathan asked.

"Of course. I can tell by the look in your eye that you already have something in mind. What is it?"

"You know me too well. I was talking to the concierge and he told me about a place called Flags and Wheels. Are you up for a little indoor racing?"

෯෬

Ali could hardly believe she'd let Nathan talk her into it, but he was right. Flags and Wheels, an indoor cart racing facility, was exactly the kind of place that Isaac and Zoe would have swooned over. It was also a good place for her to feel safe while trying another tamed-down version of an activity Isaac had enjoyed so much—racing.

"After all these years, I see that I was mistaken about Eve in the beginning; it is better to live outside the Garden with her than inside it without her." ~ Mark Twain, *The Diaries of Adam and Eve*

Chapter 25
February 8, 2012

As he drove away from Starbucks, Isaac had mixed feelings about having confided his marital problems to Jackie. On the one hand, he completely trusted Jackie and he did feel some relief after talking to her about it. On the other hand, he felt as if he'd betrayed Ali's confidence, and wondered if his confession would cause friction in the relationship the two women shared—yet another concern added to those already on his mind.

He felt the need to clear his mind and regain some perspective. Looking at his watch and noting the early hour, he winced, but pulled out his cell phone anyway, scrolled through his "favorites" and sent a text.

> **Need speed. Give me a push? 20 min?**

Barely a minute later, he got a reply.

> **Sure.**

&⊱⊰&

Isaac considered Skagit Speedway his home track, since it was just seventy-five miles from Seattle, but it was only open on the weekends, and only during the regular racing season, from April through September. Fortunately, Isaac had an alternative venue for days like this when he needed the peace of mind he got from racing.

Years earlier, he happened to strike up a race-day

conversation with Jay Hultberg, a farmer who was sitting next to him in the stands at the speedway. When they discovered that Jay's farm in Maple Valley was less than twelve miles from Isaac's house in Issaquah, Isaac invited Jay over to see his racecar. One thing led to another and soon the two men had an agreement. Jay had several acres of undeveloped, overgrown farmland that needed to be cleared of brush and tree stumps, and Isaac needed a place to run his sprint car when the speedway was closed. So Isaac agreed to provide the labor to clear the land in exchange for being allowed to use a small portion of it as a practice track where he could blow off steam whenever he liked. Of course, like all sprint cars, his required a push start, so he was somewhat at the mercy of others in that respect. This didn't bother Jay. He was a widower who generally stuck close to home. Truth be told, he got a kick out of jumping into his old Chevy truck with his yellow lab, Remington, and driving out to give Isaac a push start.

Eventually, word of the off-the-grid track got around and several local racing hobbyists offered to pay Jay for the privilege of using the track, so it became a small source of extra income for him, too. It was a win-win for everyone.

Today was one of those days when Isaac was particularly grateful that the farm was so close by and Jay was so readily available, especially at this early hour. He grabbed his racing bag, threw it in the trailer, and drove to the track with his racecar in tow to work out some of his tension.

⊱⊰

It was a particularly cold February morning. A hard freeze during the night had blanketed the field with frost so thick it looked like snow. The glistening landscape was a beautiful sight in the morning sun, and appeared mystical, if not downright magical. Isaac stopped for a moment to admire its beauty.

He emerged from his woolgathering when he heard the sound of Jay's truck making its way over the unpaved, rutted roadway.

"Mornin', Jay. Thanks for coming out on such short

notice. I wasn't sure you'd be up this early."

"Mornin'. Don't worry about me. Have you ever heard of a farmer who wasn't an early riser? You, on the other hand . . . I was surprised to hear from you so early. Or maybe it's late. From the looks of you, I'd say you never went to bed last night."

"You sweet talker, you. Do I really look that bad?"

"Friend, you look like you've been rode hard and put away wet."

When Isaac didn't respond right away, Jay let the silence stand for a minute, then said, "I know neither of us is the real chatty type, but if there's anything you want to get off your chest, I'm a pretty good listener."

"I appreciate the offer, but right now I really just want to get out on the track and feel some speed. That always clears my head. Can you help me get #76 off the trailer?"

"Sure, sure. Remington and I are looking forward to giving you a shove." Jay winked and poked Isaac in the ribs with an elbow.

Once both cars were in position, Jay called for Remington, but the dog was nowhere to be found. Jay wasn't concerned, since the lab knew every inch of the farm and never wandered beyond its borders.

Before getting back in the truck, he said, "The track still looks pretty frozen. You'd better go slow for a few laps until your tires can warm up the dirt."

"Yeah, I was thinking the same thing," said Isaac. "I'll take it easy."

"Do you want me to stick around for awhile in case you need another push?"

"No. I'm sure I'll be fine, and, no offense, but I need some time alone right now."

"No problem—but be careful what you wish for." Then he climbed back in the truck and waved, shouting, "Ready when you are."

With a push from Jay's Chevy, Isaac eased onto the track, trying to take it slow without stalling out.

After a few laps, Isaac felt the tension easing from his mind and body. The intense concentration required on the

Alice Ann Kuder

track somehow brought everything else in his life into focus, making him feel calmer and more capable of coping.

As he rounded turn three on lap ten, he caught a glimpse of something moving on the track about one hundred fifty feet ahead, but his mind couldn't process the image quickly enough to recognize what he saw. He thought it was an animal of some kind—a rabbit maybe? Whatever it was, he knew that if he hit it at this speed, the consequences would be dire for both of them. Instinctively, he swerved to avoid whatever it was . . . just a slight turn of the wheel. Ordinarily, such a negligible, evasive maneuver wouldn't have produced a significant effect, but that morning the ground was still unusually hard and slick. In his impatience to gain speed—and despite Jay's cautionary warning—Isaac hadn't allowed enough time for all the ice to melt. Coming into the shade of turn four, he hit a patch of black ice at the same time that he swerved to avoid the illusory animal. His overcorrection caused the car to spin out of control at breakneck speed. Suddenly airborne, he breached the straightaway between turns one and two and finally came to rest in the field about a hundred yards away.

&)(&

Although the car had stopped spinning, Isaac's body still felt as if it were in motion. His heart was racing and his mind was struggling to catch up and comprehend what had happened. He sat still for a minute, trying to put a name to what he was feeling. *It was fear!* He had so seldom experienced it, he didn't recognize it at first. He wasn't known as Iceberg for nothing.

He'd always been so cool and unflappable in the face of physical danger. *Why*, he wondered, *was he so frightened now? What was different? What had changed?*

With a flash of recognition, he knew the answer to his own question. Now he had more to lose. Namely, Ali and Zoe.

Though he always knew it was a possibility, the threat of losing his own life had never really fazed him before. The excitement had always been worth the risk. But just now, when he was spinning out of control, images of Ali and Zoe flooded his brain. The thought of losing them—of being lost to them—sent a wave of panic through him such as he'd never before experienced.

Still shaking and dazed, Isaac pulled himself up and out of the mangled car. He knew he was lucky to be alive, and suddenly wished he weren't alone. Just then, Remington came bounding up from out of nowhere with a dead rabbit in his mouth. Although he could have done without the gift the dog offered him, Isaac had rarely felt so grateful to see another living being.

Once his heart rate slowed, Isaac's first instinct was to call Ali, but his thinking was still muddled and he couldn't remember where his phone was. Besides, she was still out of the country on business and difficult to reach.

Instead, he staggered back to the Escape and lay down in the back seat, attempting to regain his composure. The urge to talk to Ali was almost overwhelming. He didn't want to tell her about the accident so much as he wanted to vanquish their emotional breach. *If I can't talk to her right now, I can at least write to her,* he thought. When he got up to search the cargo area of the SUV for his briefcase, he was surprised to find that he still felt weak in the knees. Steadying himself, he found the paper and pen he was looking for, crawled back into the car, and began to write.

February 8, 2012

Darling Ali,

It feels both strange and familiar to be writing you a letter. I wrote you so many when we were first together, even though we lived within ten miles of each other. I don't know why I stopped. That's probably common with young lovers. Even so, it's a shame.

Alice Ann Kuder

I've been thinking, recently, about those early days when we were falling in love. I want to remember what that was like and what brought us together in the first place.

I know that things have been strained between us for several months now. The fight we had before you left on this latest trip really shook me up. That's the closest we've come to addressing the tension, but still we skirted around it. This feels more serious to me than previous rough patches, though. Maybe it's because we *haven't* talked about it, so I can only guess what you're thinking and feeling, and that's scary. Maybe it would be better if we fought about it openly? Instead we've been letting our feelings fester slowly, building toward an emotional eruption that could mean the end of our marriage.

The way I see it, we've spent a lot of time and energy being mad at each other recently. It seems like I'm always angry about how often you travel for work, and you're always mad about my "dangerous" pastimes. And of course, we're both concerned about how those things affect Zoe.

After our last fight, I've been wondering if we would be happier apart. I imagine you've been asking yourself the same question. Since then I've been doing some soul searching, because I didn't want to have that conversation with you until I felt certain of my own answer.

After fifteen years together, we've both got long lists of each other's vices, warts, and weaknesses as well as each other's strengths, virtues, and beauty marks. I guess this is when we both pull out our emotional scales to see if the lists at least balance each other out.

Well, I've done that, and here's my conclusion.

Ali, you are one of the finest people I know. You have your share of shortcomings, but they could never outweigh your generous, loving nature and moral integrity.

Before I met you, I thought I knew what I wanted out of life. I wanted to get rich (and maybe famous) doing something I loved—driving a racecar for instance. I wanted a nice house, time to ski, race, skydive, and kick back with friends. Sure, I wanted someone to share it with, but basically it was all about me.

I met a couple of women along the way who could have helped me have all that, but when you and I started dating, my dreams changed. I understood that I could have and could be so much more with you than I could ever be by myself alone, or with those other women. You made me want to live for more than just myself.

I was attracted to you from the moment we

Alice Ann Kuder

met—I've told you that—but it wasn't love at first sight for me, and I believe that was a good thing. Love at first sight is just a romantic notion. I suspect it's more accurate to say that for a few lucky people, lust at first sight turns into love. Then over time, wishful thinking or selective memory re-labels the lust as love.

Like you, I had loved and lost before we met, so I wasn't foolish enough to mistake physical attraction for love. Love grows over time and it's not always easy to recognize the tipping point. In my case, I remember the exact moment when I knew I was in love with you.

It was the day we stumbled across the abandoned cabin on Mount Baker. We were in your Jeep and you were driving. We started up the mountain on the main road when you suddenly made a sharp turn onto a logging road that took us deep into the woods. When the road eventually became impassable, we got out and walked—somewhat aimlessly—just to see what we could see. It probably wasn't the smartest thing we've ever done . . . we could easily have gotten lost on the mountain. For some reason, neither of us seemed afraid of that. Soon we came to a scenic vista that amazed us both. We could see lakes, the Skagit River, and acres and acres of forest. It wasn't far from there that we found the cabin. As dirty, run down, and tiny as it was, I could tell that, in your eyes, it was perfection. We sat on the stoop, talking and holding hands for the longest time. Then you leaned over and rested your head on my shoulder and said, "I love this place. The forest gives me the peace and tranquility I crave, and the mountain peaks and whitewater rapids promise the thrills you covet." Then you kissed me; just a soft, chaste kiss on the lips. At that moment, I knew I never wanted to leave your side.

What I'm trying to say, my darling Ali, is that I love you deeply and forever. Whatever doubts may have managed to slither in through the back door of my unwary brain recently, disappeared as soon as I stared them down.

I know that my predilection for physical danger drives you crazy; I wish it didn't, but I have to acknowledge that it does. I need you to know that the love I feel for you is the only thing more powerful than the rush I feel when I jump from a plane, race around a track, dangle from a bungee or rappel down a mountain. The home that you and I and Zoe have built together is my true winner's circle.

There's another circle that's important to me, and I hope it still is to you. That's the circle of gold on my ring finger.

When we took our wedding vows, I knew exactly what I was saying and exactly what I was doing. I had no doubts then and I have no doubts now, that you are the woman I want to be with, today and forever. I realize that a ring is only a symbol—it's our actions that prove our love—but symbols are important, too, so recently I called our favorite jewelers, Margaret Ostling and Greg Brooks. I commissioned them to make you a new ring. Zoe and I are driving to Leavenworth to pick it up the day after tomorrow. I told Zoe it's a Valentine's Day gift, but really I had it made to reaffirm my love and re-dedicate myself to you and to our marriage. I hope you will accept it with as much joy as you accepted the first ring I gave you so many years ago.

You live in my heart, Ali. I hope I live in yours.

You have all my love, forever,

Isaac

☙ဎ☙

These thoughts and feelings had been doing battle in Isaac's mind and heart for several days. His conversation with Jackie and the scare from his narrowly-escaped injury accident had helped crystallize all he wanted to say and enabled him to get it down on paper. Gratified by the results, he stuffed the prose in his racing bag. Ali would be home the day after tomorrow. He couldn't wait to give her the ring and the letter and begin the next phase of their life together.

Meanwhile, he had to contend with his smashed up car and jangled nerves. Turning his attention to the dog, who had jumped into the back seat next to him, Isaac said, "Remington, old buddy, let's go visit our friend, Jay, and take advantage of the ear he offered to lend me."

"You can kid the world, but not your sister." ~ *Charlotte Gray*

Chapter 26
February 16-March 2, 2013

"Lincoln, Nebraska? Who do you know in Lincoln, Nebraska?" Chloe Skyped from her laptop to Ali's.

"Not a soul. I just needed to choose a stopover between Rapid City, South Dakota, and Dixon, Illinois, and when I looked at a map, Lincoln popped out at me," said Ali.

"Is it my imagination, or is there an unexpected theme developing for this trip? First Mount Rushmore and now Lincoln, Nebraska—and isn't there a monument to Lincoln in Dixon, too?"

Ali chuckled. "Yes, well, I don't remember issuing a formal invitation, but Abraham Lincoln *does* seem to have become my incorporeal traveling companion."

"Maybe he got cabin fever from hanging around the Lincoln bedroom all the time," Chloe teased. "Didn't you say he was in a dream you had a while back, too?"

"Uh-huh, he was one of the people at the Thanksgiving table. He's been in dreams of mine in the past, too. I told that to a therapist once; famous people frequently show up in my dreams. She said that's a bit unusual. When I told her about one dream involving Lincoln, she said, 'That sounds more like a memory than a dream.' We never explored that, but her comment and the concept obviously stuck with me."

"Do you believe in past lives?" Chloe asked.

"Not really—though I don't totally discount the possibility. I haven't spent much time thinking about it, probably because it conflicts with my beliefs about God and heaven and life after death. I don't have a burning need to figure it all out.

"Whatever the reason, I do feel a special affinity with Abraham Lincoln. Apparently, the universe thinks he has a lot to teach me, because it keeps throwing us together. I can't say that I see any strong parallels between our lives or personalities—I wish I did! He was such a brilliant and admirable man, and I've learned a lot just from reading about his life.

"It's pretty amazing how many 'quotable quotes' are attributed to him. One of my favorites is 'The best thing about the future is that it comes one day at a time.' That's certainly a truth I have clung to since Isaac and Zoe died."

"Okay, enough about Abe. How are *you* doing? You look good—or as good as anyone looks on Skype," said Chloe.

"I'm okay. It's hard to believe I've only been gone for six weeks."

"And even harder to believe you'll be gone another eight months! I really miss you, Ali Oop."

"I miss you too. If it weren't for technology, I think I'd feel pretty lost. I'm journaling a lot in the evenings, too.

"Valentine's Day was hard, and, of course the anniversary of the accident. Thank goodness Nathan was with me; that made it much easier. I was determined not to let the days surrounding it devolve into pity parties, so we concentrated on remembering the good things. One night, Nathan and I sat in front of a fire in the hotel lobby with a bottle of Isaac's favorite wine and a box of Ding Dongs—Zoe's favorite junk food—and told funny stories about her and her dad. It made me miss them more and miss them less, both at the same time."

Neither of them said anything for a few moments, then Chloe shifted the conversation to a lighter topic.

"How's Tess? Are you glad you took her along?"

"She's great. She's not much of a conversationalist, but she's good company anyway. And I doubt I'd be as vigilant about getting exercise if I didn't have her along to coax me into taking walks."

"Have you had any trouble finding pet-friendly places to stay?"

"Not as much as you might think. It's pretty easy to do internet searches for places that allow dogs, and there are usually several to choose from. I guess more and more people are traveling with pets these days."

"Where are you staying now?"

"I'm at The Rogers House B&B. It's right in the middle of

Alice Ann Kuder

the historic downtown district, just a few blocks from the capitol. I really love these old mansions. This one was built in 1914. You should see this room! They call it Doctor's Retreat. Here, I'll show you." Ali picked up the laptop and turned it slowly to pan around the room.

"Is that a four-poster bed?" asked Chloe.

"Yep. And there's a little sunroom that Tess has claimed for herself."

"How long do you think you'll stay in Lincoln? Is there much to do there in February?"

"I'm planning to stay a couple of weeks, since I don't need to be in Dixon until March 3rd. There seems to be plenty to see here. I'm told that the Art Deco capitol building is amazing and a 'must see.' Then there's the Larson Tractor Museum."

"Oh, for sure you wouldn't want to miss that!" Chloe laughed.

"I know it sounds kind of . . . um, unexciting, but Dad loves tractors so much that I think it'll be fun to find out about their evolution

"There's also the Museum of American Speed. The tagline is the 'world's largest collection of exotic racing engines and vintage speed equipment.' Who does *that* make you think of?"

"Ali, don't take this the wrong way, but I'd think you'd be grateful that you could skip that without Isaac around to drag you there."

"Yeah, you'd think. If he were here begging to go, I'd probably be rolling my eyes at the idea. Instead, his absence actually makes me want to see it more."

"I guess grief changes our perspective sometimes.

"What else is there to see and do in Lincoln? Are there memorials to your pal, Honest Abe, on every street corner?" Chloe asked.

"Frankly, when I was looking through a list of local attractions, I was surprised and a little disappointed to discover how few have anything at all to do with the president. I asked the hotel clerk about it and he gave me a pamphlet with some history about the city.

"It seems the city's original name was Lancaster. They changed it to Lincoln, but not because of any fondness for, or connection to the then-recently-assassinated president. Rather, it was part of a plan to *prevent* the city from becoming the state capitol. Local politicos knew there were still a lot of Confederate sympathizes in the region, so they figured the populace would balk at having anything—let alone the state capitol—named after the president. Obviously, they were wrong.

"That's probably more than you wanted to know, but I love that kind of trivia."

"You may not want to refer to it as trivia until you leave town—the locals might not appreciate it," Chloe teased.

❧❧

During the two weeks Ali was in Lincoln, she experienced a sliding scale of temperatures. On February 16th, the day she arrived, the temperature ranged from twelve degrees to forty degrees. The next day it went from a low of twenty degrees to a high of sixty-three degrees! On the morning of February 21st, she awoke to a snowstorm; the temperature stayed between twenty and twenty-four degrees the entire day.

Today, February 24th, the outdoor temperature was a pleasant forty-five degrees; a perfect morning to meander the cobblestone streets in the town's historic Haymarket District.

Having no schedule to keep, she wandered through the various specialty shops there, until a store called Bin 105 drew her in like a magnet. Billing itself as "Lincoln's newest quality wine shop," Ali, who was unable to completely separate herself from the work she loved, got into a lengthy discussion with the storeowner about their selection of terroir-driven wines made by independent producers.

Afterward, she stumbled upon a gift boutique called Abesque Variations. She was surprised to discover that besides cute knickknacks, the shop also offered professional voice and piano lessons! It took some persuasion, but Ali sweet-talked the manager into letting her play their antique, baby grand piano for a few minutes, just to ease her jones-ing.

Her fingers danced across the keys and music filled the shop. As she was playing, one of the customers mistook her for a professional pianist and commented to a clerk what an excellent idea it was for them to have hired her!

Ali's love for Haymarket spiked even higher when she popped into Dove Shannon Salon and Day Spa. There, she indulged herself with a pedicure, manicure and a facial. A little pampering was just what she needed to emerge feeling as if her caterpillar-self was truly a butterfly.

Returning to her room at The Rogers House, Ali felt content, if a bit tuckered out. The decaf latte she bought in the coffee shop down the street as a late afternoon treat, was a perfect accompaniment to the writing she intended to do. Now, she sat down at the small antique table in her room to compose the letter to Chloe that had been teasing her brain.

Dear Chloe,

Since our conversation earlier today, I've been thinking—again—about how much you mean to me and what a great sister you are. Like most siblings, we certainly had our share of fights when we were kids. I thought you were bossy, and you thought I was spoiled. As much as I love our brother, there's no denying the special relationship we have as sisters. Your love and support have been so incredibly and particularly invaluable to me since the accident.

Do you remember when we were kids and you found me crying in my room over my break-up with my first boyfriend, Matthew? I was in the seventh grade—still in the thick of adolescent angst—and I was absolutely devastated. I was sure that my life was over, that I was unlovable and would never find another boyfriend. At first, I didn't want to confide in you, because I was afraid you'd confirm all my fears. On this particular day, you were your best self—and my salvation.

At first, you just sat and listened to me while I cried and rambled on about my heartbreak. Matthew was such a great guy, I said, and I still loved him. I was sure that he broke up with me because I wasn't pretty enough or smart enough or funny enough.

Once I was exhausted from self-flagellation, you hugged me and empathized with me. I'd seen you go through break ups of your own, so I knew you could relate to what I was feeling. When I asked you how you had gotten over your heartbreaks, you told me that there are two critical ingredients to healing: the first is time, and the second is faith.

I wasn't surprised to hear you spout the old cliché, "Time heals all wounds", but I didn't know of any axioms about faith, and I didn't see how faith could be a cure for heartache.

You told me that, at the moment, I was in too much pain to think clearly. What I needed to do was try to believe it wouldn't kill me and just get through it one day at a time.

Then you admitted that time wouldn't do the whole trick. I needed to pay attention to the thoughts that were going through my head, you said, and start to turn them around, because they would all be negative at first.

You went on to warn me that I would likely tell myself that he was the only guy for me, no one else would ever love me, I'd never be happy without him, and a lot of other stupid stuff. It will all feel true, you said, but if I let myself believe it, it would take a lot longer to get over him.

"You've got to have faith that 'this, too, shall pass,'" you said.

Alice Ann Kuder

You encouraged me to find my faith by looking at my experiences. The sunrise, for example, should give me faith that the day ahead—as joyful or as painful or as it might be—will end and a new tomorrow will always come; the same with the seasons. No matter how harsh the winter is, spring always follows. That's just how life is. Nothing stays the same for very long. When you get hurt, you either die or you heal. Like the Kelly Clarkson song says, "What doesn't kill you makes you stronger."

Then you asked me to name some especially painful events from my past. Two things came immediately to mind. The first was when I broke my leg. The second was when my best friend, Melanie, betrayed me.

Together, you and I examined both events, looking for the unexpected good that came about as a result.

Breaking my leg made me appreciate my strong body and overall good health.

The falling out with Melanie taught me about the nature of friendships. I learned that friendships are precious gifts—even if they don't last forever.

Later, I examined other seeming tragedies from my relatively short past and discovered that each one had a silver lining. Each and every one. As a result, I came to agree with you that there is no such thing as an event that is totally bereft of some positive outcome. I suspect that you learned this from Dad, before passing it along to me.

As you predicted, I felt bad about the breakup with Matthew for quite a while, but our talk helped me believe that I would eventually get over it. *"You've got to have faith,"* you said to me. *And I do. I have faith—which has only gotten stronger over time—that life is good and all things happen as they should. I cling to that faith now, as I try to make sense of Isaac and Zoe's deaths.*

Thank you for encouraging me to nurture my faith.

I love you until forever,

Ali

She put down her pen and reread the letter. Finally, with warm feelings of self-satisfaction, sisterly love, and gratitude, she stuffed it in an envelope.

Just then, Tess, who had been napping at Ali's feet, suddenly sat to attention with her ears perked up full tilt. A moment later, Ali heard a knock on the door.

Baffled as to who it could be, Ali looked through the peephole and was equally astonished and thrilled to see Chloe standing in the hallway. She threw open the door, wrapped her sister in a tight hug and let out a squeal of pure delight as tears stung her eyes.

∾∾

"Skype just wasn't cutting it anymore," Chloe explained. "I decided I needed to see my baby sister in the flesh, so I convinced Roger that he could take care of the twins by himself for a couple of days, then drove to the airport and caught the first flight to Lincoln! I hope you're happy to see me?"

"Oh, Chloe, you know I am. I couldn't be happier!"

"I've gotta say, Ali, I'm impressed as all get-out by the fun you've been having on this road trip. It takes a special kind of . . . I don't know, self-confidence, I guess, for a person to be able to enjoy traveling alone. I really admire you."

"I don't know that there's anything particularly admirable

Alice Ann Kuder

about it," Ali said, "but I've certainly been enjoying myself. It feels different to be alone in unfamiliar places than it does to be alone at home. I can't quite explain it; it adds nuance to my grief. In some ways, I feel *more* connected to Isaac and Zoe out here on the road, rather than less."

Ali paused to consider her own words for a moment, then shook her head as if to dislodge the thoughts. "So, it sounds like my travel log has been so inspiring that you just had to come and experience some of the fun yourself, is that it?" she joked.

"That's part of it. Another part is that I noticed you only talk about going out during the day. What are you doing in the evenings? Are you just holing up in your hotel room?" Chloe asked.

"Pretty much." Ali didn't offer any explanation or excuse.

"Is that because you're not comfortable going out by yourself at night?"

"I guess it is. I never feel sorry for myself during the day, but those times when I've gone to dinner at a fancy restaurant or to a bar for a drink . . . I don't know, I just feel very conspicuous. I imagine that everyone in the place is looking at me and wondering why I'm alone. I realize that's silly. The reality is that most people are so caught up in their own life dramas they have little interest in the strangers around them. In fact, if I *wanted* to be noticed, I'd probably have to dance naked on a table top to get attention!"

"Yeah, I think that would do it!" Chloe said with a chuckle.

"It's really only the nights I spend in the non-George cities—and there are fewer of those coming up—that are a bit lonely. Some of my best times on the trip so far have been the evenings I've spent sitting around chatting and laughing with my friend, Martha—plus Dad and Nathan."

"Well, Ali Oop, put on your dancin' shoes, cuz your big sister is here and we're going out on the town! Watch out, Lincoln, the Benevento sisters are on the loose!"

&⟩⟨&

After consulting with Nora, the owner and hostess of Rogers House, Ali and Chloe decided on Barrymore's, a funky little lounge less than two miles from the inn. A quick online search seemed to confirm Nora's recommendation. Barrymore's opened in 1974, in what was originally the backstage area for the Rococo Theater, aka the old Stuart Theater. Reviewers lauded its cozy, fun atmosphere accentuated by cathedral ceilings, exposed brick walls, and suspended lighting.

"They weren't kidding when they said this place is 'out of the way' " Chloe remarked as they navigated their way down the alleyway between O and P Streets.

"I think the back alley entrance is kind of cool. We can pretend we're going to a speakeasy during Prohibition!" Ali whispered.

"Look at these old light boards and curtain pulleys!" Chloe pointed out as they went inside. "I love that they left those intact.

"The website says that Barrymore's specializes in martinis and cocktails and also has a great beer selection. They don't seem to have much of a wine list, though. Is that okay with you?" Chloe asked.

"Sure. I've got nothing against a good martini—especially when there's a piano to gather round."

As Chloe and Ali chatted with the bartender and ordered their drinks, a stunning, raven-haired woman dressed in a striking, cobalt-blue silk duster sat down at the piano and began to play softly.

"This must be the musician Nora was telling me about. She said that one of the regular piano players is a local woman by the name of Shari Harper, who writes a lot of her own music and lyrics. She suggested we request a song called "Waiting for the Rain."

"I don't think we'll have to; sounds like she's singing it now."

> *I know the early hours, they are familiar to me*
> *Guttered candles and a cup of tea.*
> *A thousand little troubles, a mantra … meditation*
> *Gently easing my anxiety.*

Alice Ann Kuder

The breezes through the window as the fog drifts off the ocean,
Ghostly vapors moving silently.
I am thinking of tomorrow, how to manage all the details,
Be the woman that I want to be.
Oh, I am waiting for the rain
Like a balm to my spirit let it wash me clean again.
Oh, open up the skies and then
Take away this pain,
Let me breathe again.
I am waiting for the rain.
Heavy clouds obscure the sunrise as anxiously I listen
For the soft familiar sound to fall.
This ancient wish for water felt deeply in my spirit
Healing, soothing, giving life to all.
I hear the world awaken the robins softly calling,
Rub the evening from my sleepy eyes.
The hissing of the tires… a gentle syncopation
As the water tumbles from the skies.
Oh, I am waiting for the rain
Like a balm to my spirit let it wash me clean again.
Oh, open up the skies and then
Take away this pain,
Let me breathe again.
I am waiting for the rain.

"What a wonderful melody," said Ali. "It has all the good qualities of a folk song without any melancholy or schmaltz."

"The lyrics are quite haunting, too. I love the imagery of the title," commented Chloe.

"Huh. Waiting for the rain," Ali mused. "Maybe that's what I've been doing without realizing it."

⁐⁐

As Shari finished her first set, Ali wistfully said to Chloe, "I really miss playing the piano. I spotted a baby grand in a local store the other day and practically started salivating! I talked the owner into letting me serenade her customers for a bit—shades of Nordstrom! But with the exception of that, I just haven't had the opportunity to play while I've been traveling."

"I hadn't thought of that. Your music has always been so important to you, too. You never seem happier than when you're sitting at a piano."

"You know me well," said Ali, getting up from her seat. "I'm going to go use the restroom. Will you order me another drink while I'm gone?"

"Sure. What would you like?"

"I'm feeling adventurous. Why don't you conspire with our server and surprise me with something avant-garde?"

When Ali returned a few minutes later, Chloe announced, "I have two surprises for you."

"Uh-oh," Ali said warily. "I assume the drink is one of the surprises. What's the other?"

"Well, I had a little discussion with the bar manager and Ms. Harper, and they both agreed that it would be more than okay for you to play a few songs."

"*What*? I haven't played in months and you want me to just saunter up to an unfamiliar piano and perform for a crowd of people that came here to listen to a professional? Are you crazy?!"

"Maybe—but that doesn't mean you shouldn't do it. You know you're more than capable of knocking the socks off these people, even though you haven't played for a while. *And*, you know you'd love it."

Ali paused for a minute, obviously giving the idea some serious consideration.

Finally, she said, "Okay. I'll play—on one condition."

"You have a condition? I finagle you a chance to play piano for a somewhat-captive audience and you want to negotiate a condition? I can't wait to hear this. What is it?"

"I'll play on the condition that you'll sing."

"Now who's crazy?"

"Oh, come on Chloe. You know you're every bit as accomplished a vocalist as I am a pianist. I always told you that you should sing professionally."

Now it was Chloe's turn to pause and consider her sister's challenge.

Alice Ann Kuder

"What the heck. I'd love it, you'd love it, and we're never likely to see these people again as long as we live. What have we got to lose? Let's do it!"

જીલ્સ

Having performed together for family, friends, and church congregations so often over the years, it wasn't difficult for Ali and Chloe to put together a quick set list of songs they knew would be familiar to the bar's patrons. For the next thirty minutes, they played and sang for a surprised and appreciative audience, earning several long and loud rounds of applause.

As the clapping faded at the end of their last song, Ali motioned for Chloe to lean down so she could whisper in her ear, "Now I have a surprise for you."

Then Ali addressed the crowd, saying, "We realize that none of you came here to hear us tonight, and we're really grateful that you've indulged our little attempt to claim our "fifteen-minutes". I'm going to stretch my luck just a little further by playing you an original song I've been composing for *years* and just recently finished. Unfortunately for you, I don't have nearly as good a voice as my sister has. Since she's never heard the song before, she can't sing it for you, so please bear with me.

"It's called "Lessons." "

Learnin' not to worry,
Finding inner peace,
Getting rid of all this jumble is my highest priority.
I'm taking all my little troubles
And chucking them into the sea.
Holding on to secrets that appealed to me
Made me feel kinda special, bolstered my superiority.
Thought I was foolin' everybody,
But I found the only fool was me.
It's been a long road, but I like the journey,
Watching where my mind goes
Bringing it all back to me.
Making life worth living

Sounds an easy thing.
Change they say is simple,
But oh the trouble it can bring.
All my good intentions fly away like a bird on the wing.
It's been a long road, but I like the journey,
Watching where my mind goes,
Bringing it all back to me
Holding on to secrets that appealed to me
Made me feel kinda special, bolstered my superiority.
Thought I was foolin' everybody,
But I found the only fool was me.
Thought I was foolin' everybody,
But I found the only fool was me.

The audience rewarded Ali's courage in sharing her music, with genuine and enthusiastic applause, which made her feel a smidgeon embarrassed at first. But seeing Chloe, Shari and appreciative strangers cheer her on, Ali also welcomed feelings of pride and gratitude. *Yes,* she thought, *I've learned a lot of lessons over the years. And I'm looking forward to meeting my next teacher.*

When they returned to their seats, Chloe leaned over to Ali and said, "That's not the song you played for the family last year in your living room, so you've obviously written more than one. Have you been harboring a latent talent all these years?"

"Oh, I don't know that I'd describe it as talent . . . well, maybe it is. I just know that every once in a while, a tune or some lyrics pop into my head, so I toss a little mental soil on them and see if they germinate. Most the time, they don't, but every once in a while . . . "

Chloe looked at her sister with even greater pride and awe than usual. Then she said, "What was the last line of that song you just sang?"

Ali laughed and sang, *"Thought I was foolin' everybody but I found the only fool was me."*

Alice Ann Kuder

"For it is in giving that we receive." ~ *St. Francis of Assisi*

Chapter 27
March 3-April 1, 2013

It had been hard to say good-bye to Chloe at the airport. They had such a memorable time together in Lincoln that Ali almost wished her sister could have accompanied her on the rest of her trip. But as nice as that might have been, traveling solo—not discounting Tess' presence—was a significant aspect of this journey, and one she was enjoying for the most part. Now she was back on the road again, heading for Dixon, Illinois, in the shadow of Chicago.

As Ali drove through the Dixon Veteran's Memorial Arch on the way into town, she tried to imagine what her former babysitter would look like after all these years. By Ali's calculations, Claire had been about sixteen when she was eight, so that would put Claire in her early-to-mid fifties now. *Whoa, where had all the years gone?* Ali wondered.

୫୭ଓଜ

Once they were comfortably seated in Claire's overstuffed armchairs, Ali asked, "How did you end up living in the Midwest after growing up in the Pacific Northwest?"

"I've asked myself that same question many times! No, I'm just kidding. My high school guidance counselor knew that I was interested in becoming a nurse and she thought I could benefit from getting away from home, so she encouraged me to apply for scholarships all over the country. I got a full ride to the School of Nursing at Saint Xavier University in Chicago. I fell in love with Chicago and I really didn't want to leave, so I started applying for jobs nearby. I was lucky enough to get hired at KSB Hospital here in Dixon, and I've been here ever since."

"What does KSB stand for?"

"Katherine Shaw Bethea. She was the wife of a local judge back in the late 1800s, but she died fairly young. Her dying wish was that a hospital be established in Dixon, so Judge Bethea donated land to the city for that purpose in her memory. It started with seventeen beds and now has nine facilities in the Sauk Valley. KSB is a terrific employer. I've been very happy there for all these years. And it's nice to know it sprang from a woman's vision for her community.

"And then there's my husband. He's a nurse at KSB, too. We met in 1989 and were married in 1991. As you can see from all the photos on the walls, we've got three great kids and two grandkids. I've got a good life; I'm very blessed.

"You know, when it comes down to it, Dixon's not really so different from Mount Vernon," Claire noted. "It's about the size now that Mount Vernon was when I was growing up there. They're both somewhat rural, but close to a big city, and they both have some agricultural heritage. The winters are a lot more severe here, of course, but you have to take the bad with the good, right?

"Now tell me about your life, Ali. What have you been up to since I last saw you? And what made you look me up after all these years?"

Since the pair hadn't kept in touch, Ali felt she needed to fill Claire in on the previous thirty years of her life before she could talk about Isaac and Zoe and the letters. By the time she finished her story the sun had set and they were both hungry.

"What's your favorite local restaurant? I'd like to take you out to dinner," Ali offered.

"I'd love that. Phillip is working tonight and frankly, I'm not a very good cook, so you're probably sparing yourself some indigestion.

"Let's see, I have a couple of favorites. If you like Italian, then I'd suggest Basil Tree Ristorante. If you're more of a meat and potatoes kind of gal, Galena's Steak House might be a better choice."

"You choose. I'm planning to stick around for a while, so whichever one we don't eat at tonight, we can hit in the next couple of days."

"I like that plan! And, Ali, I'm so glad you're here. You've grown up to be just the kind of wonderful person I thought you'd be."

"I could say the same of you," Ali said warmly.

As they left the house, Ali surreptitiously left her letter to Claire on the table in the foyer.

›❀‹

Dear Claire,

I remember so many special days spent in your care when I was a young girl. One of those days was in early December; I must have been about eight or nine years old. It was a parent-teacher conference day, so there was no school, but mom and dad still had to work. I was so excited when they said I'd get to spend the day with you instead of with Chloe or Nathan! I didn't really think of you as my baby-sitter, more as my friend.

Thanksgiving was behind us, and all I could think about was Santa Claus and all the things he'd bring me for Christmas! The first thing we did that morning was to sit down at our kitchen table to write my letter to Santa. In no time at all, I created a list of things I hoped to find under my tree on Christmas morning.

On the way to the post office, we stopped at a cash machine and you withdrew $50. "Now that you've thought about all the things you'd like to receive," you told me, "it's time to think about what you want to give."

Our next stop was Walmart. When we went into the store, you handed me the $50 and told me to spend it on canned food and toys to donate to the food bank and Toys for Tots. I had so much fun going down the aisles and choosing things to give away. I didn't fully understand what we were doing or why we were doing it, but I knew that it made me feel good. Later, after dropping off our donations, you took the time to answer my questions about the people I saw standing in line at the food bank and why we should help them.

The things we did that day, simple and unremarkable as they were, reinforced and built upon the values of giving and receiving that my parents had already taught me. My letter to Santa allowed me to feel excited about the things I wanted for myself, while our shopping trip showed me how good it felt to give to others—even people I didn't know. And our discussion helped me understand how little difference there was between us and the people who just needed a little extra help.

I wondered about the $50 you gave me to spend. I didn't know exactly how much my parents paid you for babysitting, but I knew it couldn't be nearly that much. When I asked you why you were giving away so much of your own money, you said that the more you gave away, the more you got back. Of course, it wasn't until many years later that I really began to understand what you meant.

I realize now that the things we did together that day illustrated your values and beliefs. Over and over again, you demonstrated to me the joy of giving and receiving. You helped me learn to look beyond myself and understand the interconnectedness of all humanity, not only with those we know and love, but also with those we haven't met—and perhaps never will.

I am a better person because of you. The world is a better place because of you. Please know this as truth and never doubt it.

Alice Ann Kuder

You have my respect and affection until forever,

Ali

ஐ০෨

The next day, the two women met up to tour the Next Picture Show Fine Arts Museum together.

Ali could tell by the look on Claire's face that she had found and read the letter.

"Ali, I can't tell you how touched I was by your letter. It was so unexpected and so appreciated. I babysat a lot of kids over the years, and until now, not one of them has ever looked me up, let alone said thank you.

"Of course, I didn't do it for the thanks. I was a teenager who needed to earn money, and babysitting was the only skill I had to offer. I did it because I got paid. It was a job. It's not as if I was doing it for selfless or humanitarian reasons. I don't know why you think you need to thank me."

"I'll tell you why," said Ali. "It's because you went way above and beyond what you needed to do to earn your money. You showed me that you cared about what kind of person I was and what kind of person I had the potential to become. You put thought and energy into being a good role model for me. That's not something that every babysitter does, and it's deserving of a show of appreciation. I suspect that caring that much is such a part of your nature that you don't realize how rare and valuable it is. Those same qualities probably drew you to the nursing profession, and I'm sure they make you an exceptional caretaker."

"I don't know what to say other than that I feel humbled by your assessment of my character and the impact I had on you. And Ali, seeing how you've turned out, I can honestly say it was all worth it."

"There is no surprise more magical than the surprise of being loved."
~ Charles Morgan

Chapter 28
February 10, 2012

"Dad, can we put the top down?" When Isaac was slow to answer, Zoe added, "Pleeeease?"

"Zoe, it's February 10th, and we're in Seattle, not Honolulu!"

"But the sun is out! This is the first time we've seen blue sky in months! I don't care if it's cold."

Neither did Isaac. He loved driving the Corvette with the top down, so his daughter didn't have to beg too hard to get him to oblige. Besides, she was right. It was a beautiful day, a perfect day, the kind of day that makes you glad to be alive. Unbeknownst to Ali, who was still away on her business trip, Isaac had taken their daughter out of school for the day—again—so she could go with him to Leavenworth to pick up the ring he had commissioned for Ali as a surprise.

With that mission accomplished, Isaac put the top down and eased onto the picturesque, rural highway.

"Are you hungry? I thought we could stop at Stevens Pass and have lunch with your Uncle Nathan."

"Yes! Yes! Yes! That would be so cool!" Zoe adored Nathan.

"I doubt he'll have much time to visit, but if we're lucky maybe we can catch him between sessions. I think he teaches a lot of private lessons on weekdays. I'd love to show him the ring."

80C8

Forty-five minutes later, Isaac, Zoe, and Nathan were enjoying lunch together at the Iron Goat Pizza Station.

Out of the blue, Zoe piped up. "Uncle Nathan, when are you going to get married?"

"Zoe! What kind of question is that?" her dad said with an

incredulous laugh.

"Well, I want to be a bridesmaid like a lot of my friends. Bridesmaids get to wear princess-y dresses and carry bouquets of flowers and stuff. Aunt Chloe's already married, so there's just Aunt Jackie and Uncle Nathan."

Nathan laughed and teased Zoe. "So, you think I ought to get married just so you can be a bridesmaid, huh?"

"Not *just* so I can be a bridesmaid. You should get married so you'll be happy."

"Oh, I see. And what makes you think I'm not happy now?"

Zoe furrowed her brow, contemplating the question. Unable to come up with an answer, she asked, "Are you?"

"Yeah, Nathan, are you?" Isaac chimed in with a smirk on his face.

"As a matter of fact, I am."

"Are you seeing anyone special?" Isaac asked.

"No, I'm not."

"You're happy being alone?" Zoe continued her quiz.

Nathan hesitated for a moment, trying to think of how he could explain his point of view in terms that a ten-year-old could understand. At the same time, he didn't want to talk down to her either.

"The thing is, Zoe, I've discovered that if you can't be happy by yourself, then you can't be happy with someone else. It's not fair to ask someone else to be responsible for your happiness; happiness has to come from inside you."

Nathan couldn't tell if Zoe understood what he was trying to say. She seemed satisfied with his answer and disinclined to pursue the conversation further, so he changed the subject. "I hear you're getting pretty good on your skateboard," he said.

With that opening, Zoe forgot all about weddings, and launched excitedly into a lengthy and animated description of the latest maneuvers she was learning.

∞∞

After a while, Nathan again addressed his niece. "Zoe, I need to talk to your dad alone for a few minutes. How would you like to go spend some time in the pro shop and pick out something you can talk me into buying for you?"

"Oh, boy! Okay!" And she was off.

"You know, Nathan, you could have been a bit more subtle," Isaac admonished him mildly. "She's ten years old now and she doesn't miss a trick. She's going to ask me what we talked about. So, what's up?"

"Well, Isaac, you can tell me it's none of my business, but . . ."

Isaac interrupted, "Since when have I ever asked you to butt out of anything? That's not the kind of friendship we have."

"This isn't about our friendship; it's about your marriage to my sister."

"Oh," Isaac faltered. "I guess you've picked up on the tension between Ali and me."

"Yeah, I have. You know I love you both and it concerns me. I know that your thrill-seeking nature has always been a bone of contention between the two of you, so I've gotta wonder if part of the trouble is Zoe's growing passion for physically risky pursuits? Skateboarding was your gateway drug, too, wasn't it?"

"Gateway drug!? I've never heard skateboarding called *that* before, but I suppose it's not totally inaccurate in my case.

"Okay, yeah," Isaac continued, "Ali and I have been going through some rough times for the last few months, and some of it has to do with her fear for my safety, and probably for Zoe's, but that's not a new issue for us. She knew when she married me—heck, she knew from the first day we met here at the Pass—that I'm an 'extreme sports' kind of guy, and I never led her to believe that was likely to change."

"But, Isaac, you know how Zoe idolizes you. You know that a kid that age wants to do everything her dad does. That's gotta scare the crap out of Ali."

"You're right, it does. And I've got to admit that I probably haven't discouraged Zoe as much as I should have because, frankly, it's pretty cool to have your kid want to be like you. It's a real stroke to the ego and that's not easy to give up. That doesn't mean I'm not just as concerned about Zoe's

Alice Ann Kuder

safety as Ali is. I've come to the conclusion that I need to have a serious talk with Zoe about this issue and then the three of us need to come up with a strategy for dealing with it that we can all live with, if you'll forgive the pun."

"Have you said any of this to Ali?"

"No, I haven't really been clear about it myself until just recently. And Ali has been traveling a lot for her job the last few months. That's another source of tension between us. I'm glad she's so successful and loves her job, but both Zoe and I would like her to be home more often. Talking on the phone and Skyping with an ocean between us just isn't the same as talking face to face.

"Nathan, I'm ready to start this discussion with Ali, but I'm a little scared that it took me too long to get here. We had another fight just before she left on this trip and the 'D' word got tossed around. We haven't had any significant conversations since then, and I'm afraid that when she gets back she might actually ask for a divorce."

"And what if she does? What will you say?"

"A couple of weeks ago, I might have said "yes", let's take some time apart. I'm glad, now, that neither of us was ready to ask that question, because I've come to my senses. I don't want a divorce. I don't even want a separation. Ali is the best thing that ever happened to me. When I thought about what it would be like to live without her, I realized that all over again.

"I guess, after fifteen years, it's easy to take each other for granted and wonder what else—or who else—is out there for you. The truth is, it just doesn't matter. Ali and I chose each other. We made promises to each other. We made a decision to live our lives together; our *entire* lives, not just a few years until we got tired of each other. That was my intention when we got married and that's my intention now. I hope she feels the same way."

"I'm glad to hear you say that, Isaac. I believe you mean it."

"You know, Nathan, I think marriage got really cheap for a while in this country. There were several generations that seemed to think spouses were disposable or interchangeable. I saw it with a lot of my parents' friends. If one person no longer felt the love, then they thought there was no reason to stay. But marriage is about love *and* respect. I've noticed that the marriages that last are the ones where respect is given equal weight to love. Feelings of love ebb and flow. Feelings of respect and commitment—and I believe that commitment comes from respect—are what span the breach.

"And as long as I'm on my soapbox, I'll add one more thing. In my mind, the thing that is nudging us back on the road to valuing marriage is that gay couples are finally being 'allowed' to marry in some states and countries, and hopefully soon here in Washington. I look forward to the day when our same-sex friends will finally be able to publicly affirm their commitment to one another. It's hard to believe they've ever been denied that legal right—just as hard as it is to believe that slavery was ever tolerated, or women and people of color were ever denied the right to vote. Anyway, it makes me realize how fortunate I am to have that commitment with Ali, and I don't want to screw it up!"

Nathan nodded in agreement. "So when are you going to talk to Ali, and how are you going to convince her that you're in this for the long haul?"

"Funny you should ask," Isaac said as he pulled out the newly-acquired ring. "She's due back from her business trip today. I'm planning on giving her this tonight and telling her everything I just told you."

Nathan let out a whistle at the sight of the ring. "Wow! That oughta convince her you're serious."

"Thanks for the impromptu rehearsal. I'm less nervous about it now. By the way," Isaac cautioned, "Zoe knows about the ring, but she just thinks it's a Valentine's gift. She probably picked up on the tension between her mom and me, but I don't think she has any idea we were so close to talking about divorce—and I don't want her to know. There ought to be some advantage to being young and innocent."

ଚଉଚ

Fifteen minutes later, Isaac and Zoe were back on the road, with the top still down.

Zoe opened the jewelry box she was fingering and peeked at the ring for the umpteenth time. "Mom is going to *love* the ring. I bet she'll think it's the best Valentine's gift ever."

"I hope so. You know, Zoe, I love your mother very much. Sometimes, when two people have been married for a while, like your mom and I have, it's easy to take each other for granted. I've been guilty of that lately, so I want to give her something special to let her know that I'm sorry and that I know how lucky I am to be married to her. I want this gift to reassure her that I'm in this for the long haul—I'm in it for life. You and your mom mean everything to me. You know that, don't you?"

"Yeah, Dad, I know it," Zoe punctuated her response by rolling her eyes. "Why did you go all the way to Leavenworth to have the ring made?"

"Well, you know the story of how we got engaged coming home from a trip to Leavenworth, right? I wanted to have this ring made by the same jeweler who made her engagement and wedding rings so they'd match. And I wanted you to see the town that's so special to your mom and me. We took you there a couple of times when you were little, but you were too young to remember. What did you think of it now?"

"It's pretty cool. I love that story; tell it again."

"Okay, well, we'd been dating for about a year. Your Uncle Nathan introduced us one day right there at Stevens Pass, and we both knew this was the real thing. But you know, real life isn't like the movies. A guy doesn't just pop the question unless he feels sure of the answer, and even then, he wants the formal proposal to be memorable. Friends and family are going to ask how you got engaged, so you want to have a good story to tell. It's a lot of pressure for a guy to come up with something romantic and original!

"So you know how much your mom and I both love the snow. Unfortunately, your mom isn't much of a downhill skier. She tried to learn once, but she just didn't enjoy it. She's always preferred the ski lodge to the ski slope.

"Anyway, I wanted to propose somewhere there was snow, but I knew I'd have a hard time convincing your mom to go on a ski weekend. So instead, I booked us tickets for a day excursion on the Snow Train to Leavenworth. I'd taken the trip on its inaugural run the year before, so I knew what to expect, but your mother didn't. She was pretty excited about it.

"The train left King Street Station around eight in the morning, which as you know is really early for a night owl like me. I was living with your Aunt Jackie on Beacon Hill at the time and your mom was living on Queen Anne, so she picked me up on the way to the station. Of course, she had to practically drag me out of bed, so we barely made it to the station on time. That didn't make her too happy, but the train ride was really relaxing and fun, so that turned her mood around really fast. We had breakfast on the train and toasted each other with mimosas while we watched the scenery get whiter and whiter.

"Your mom fell in love with Leavenworth from the moment we got there. Now that you've seen it, you know why. Somebody had a pretty great idea when they decided to make that little mountain town look like a Bavarian Village. And at Christmastime, with all the snow and the lights, it's really pretty dazzling."

"I want to see it! Can we go this Christmas? We could ride on the Snow Train!" Zoe suggested.

"I like that idea! I'll talk it over with your mom. Anyway, back to the story.

"We spent the afternoon doing all the typical touristy things. I'm not much of a shopper, but the day was about making your mom happy so I let her drag me through all the shops. She never suspected that I'd actually steered her to the goldsmith shop, Ostling and Brooks. I wanted to see if she liked their work as much as I did—and she did.

I'd met the owners, Margaret and Greg, at a street fair in Kirkland a couple of years earlier, way before I ever met your mom. I was so impressed by their really unique, custom designed jewelry that I kept their business card. When I decided to propose, I was totally intimidated by the thought of picking out an engagement ring, but I really wanted to surprise her, so I called Margaret and Greg to ask for advice. I told them how much your mom loved my grandmother's engagement ring. They suggested I send them a photo of it and let them design something similar, so that's what I did. It was still a risk, but they really came through and did an amazing job.

"Even though I felt sure your mom would think the ring was spectacular, I still wanted a special way to surprise her with it. Finally, I got an inspiration.

"All day long, while we were going from one gift shop to another, your mom kept stopping to *ooh* and *aah* at the snow globes that seemed to be in every window, including Ostling and Brooks'. Every time she picked one up and shook it, she would get this angelic 'little girl' look on her face as if she could feel magic inside. I'll tell you, if I hadn't already been in love with her, that look would have pushed me right over the edge.

"Then I had to figure out how to get away from your mom long enough to arrange the surprise, so I told her I wanted to shop for a new snowboard. Knowing she wouldn't want to come with me for that, I suggested she treat herself to a manicure at Shears. That's a little salon your mom and I had walked by earlier. It's tucked away off the main drag, so she wouldn't be likely to see where I really went.

"After I walked her back to Shears, I snuck back to the jewelry shop. I asked them to mount the ring inside a small snow globe and wrap it, upside down, in a box with Christmas paper. That night we had dinner on the train going home. After dessert I ordered a bottle of champagne, gave her the present, and told her it was a memento of the day. Because it was in the box upside down, when she opened it, she immediately turned it right side up. When the snow settled to the bottom she saw the ring. Her eyes opened so wide! A second later she started crying. Then I dropped to one knee in the classic pose and asked her to marry me."

Zoe finished the story with the familiar conclusion, "And everyone on the train started clapping and cheering!"

"That's right! So she had no choice but to say yes! Lucky for you, huh?" Isaac said.

The two of them fell into a happy silence, with silly grins on their faces, enjoying the afterglow of the story and the crisp, cool air rushing overhead.

Their reverie was interrupted by the sound of an incoming

text message on Isaac's phone.

"Dad! What happened to the family rule about turning off our cell phones when we're in the car? Don't you dare answer that."

"I'm sorry, Sweetie. The rule stands. I just forgot to turn my phone off this time."

They both remembered the day the rule was carved into stone. It was just the previous year, when the three of them were on their way to do some shopping at Issaquah's Gilman Village. Ali and Isaac had often argued about her inability to ignore her cell phone whenever it rang, beeped, or buzzed to announce a call, text, or e-mail. Her curiosity always won out and she would inevitably look at her phone, even if she was driving.

On that particular day, she did just that. But just as she looked at the screen, the car in front of them came to a sudden stop and Ali rear-ended them. Fortunately, they were in a heavy traffic area and only going about fifteen miles per hour, so no one was injured. Even so, the air bags deployed and there was some minor damage to both cars.

Isaac didn't have to say, "I told you so." Ali was mortified at having caused the accident and thankful that it wasn't more serious. Later that night, at the safety of their dinner table, the three of them agreed on the new rule. With cell phones turned off, there was no temptation to answer them.

With the buzz of his phone just then, the familiar urge to see the identity of the caller proved too strong to resist. He looked down and saw that it was a message from Ali.

> When will you be home? We need to talk.

The ominous tone of the message created a knot in his stomach.

A second later, he heard Zoe scream and looked up to discover that he had veered into the adjacent lane. A semi-truck was headed straight for them.

Alice Ann Kuder

"Never forget the three powerful resources you always have available to you: love, prayer, and forgiveness." ~ H. Jackson Brown, Jr.

Chapter 29
April 2-23, 2013

"I swear you're as excited as a kid in a candy store!" Elizabeth Berg observed as she made breakfast for Ali and herself.

"About going to the Kentucky Derby? You bet I am! I've wanted to go ever since I was a little girl. It took some careful planning on my part to make sure I'd be here for the month of April before heading to Kentucky in early May."

"Ali, I'm so grateful that you included us as a stop on your trip. I know you could just as easily have skipped right over Xenia and gone straight to Louisville."

"Elizabeth, I didn't even consider 'skipping over Xenia.' This trip gave me a perfect excuse to come and spend some extended time with you and Karl. I know you would have preferred to have Isaac and Zoe and me living closer to you all these years . . . we wished for that, too. It has to be even harder on you now that they're gone and you don't even have visits with them to look forward to. Isaac loved you both so much. *I* love you both so much. It's really comforting for me to spend some time here again, in the home where he grew up.

"I remember the first time he brought me here. He was so excited to have me meet you and show me around his hometown. If Ohio had mountains, I don't think he ever would have left!"

"It's nice for us to have you here, too. We don't get to see you nearly enough. I can't explain it, but somehow it feels like you brought Isaac and Zoe with you."

The two women sat in comfortable silence, lost in thought for a minute before Elizabeth decided to try to lighten the mood.

"Tell me how your trip is going. What are the best and worst things that have happened to you so far?"

Having finished their bacon and eggs, Ali poured them

each another cup of coffee and they moved into the family room to continue their conversation.

"The best and worst? Oh my gosh—that's an interesting question. I've been traveling for four months now, a lot has happened.

"Let's see. Well, it's not really a single event, but one of the most gratifying parts has been discovering that most people are really nice. I realize that probably shouldn't be a big revelation, but you know, we're bombarded with so much bad news all the time—stories of bad people doing bad things—that sometimes it's easy to forget that most people are really kind and well-intentioned.

"Do you remember what a news junkie I used to be? I could hardly wait for the morning paper. I was always tuning into the news on the TV, radio, and online, so afraid I might miss hearing about something important that was happening in the world. Have you noticed that I don't do that anymore?

"As a matter of fact, I have," Elizabeth admitted.

"Well, about a week after I started this trip, the radio in the Escape went out, which is something I didn't expect in a relatively new car. But anyway, since I was on the road, I couldn't easily find a place to have it fixed. The CD player was still working, so I was able to listen to music. After a couple of days, I realized that I didn't really miss hearing the news. In fact, I felt better when I *didn't* listen to it."

"Don't you want to know what's going on in the world?"

"I want to know about the good things, but that's not usually what gets reported. I decided that I don't need to hear about the latest mass murders, dirty politicians, or stock market nosedives. Taking in all that negative stuff day after day just made me feel worse about society; it didn't enhance my life at all. So I stopped watching and listening to the news. I've discovered that the news I need to hear, finds me. The universe always seems to find a way to make sure I know what I need to know, whether it's through Facebook posts, or conversations with people I meet along the way, or an occasional headline I glimpse when I pass by a newspaper vending machine."

"Well, I certainly respect your point of view, Sweetheart,

Alice Ann Kuder

but I've always prided myself on staying informed. I like knowing what's going on. If I didn't keep up on the news, I think I'd feel as if I was sticking my head in the sand," Elizabeth said.

"We might just have to agree to disagree on this, but I think you should try it. You might be surprised."

"So, have you had any really bad experiences on the road?" Elizabeth asked.

Ali inhaled deeply, held her breath for a moment, then exhaled quickly.

"Well, some days I've felt pretty lonely and depressed, which is no fun. I can't quite pinpoint what brings it on. I mean, it's a little bit about spending so much time alone, but for me, being alone and being lonely are really two different things. Loneliness comes from inside.

"One day, when I was particularly determined to host a pity party, I stopped at a little roadside café for lunch. The poor girl who waited on me—I think her name was Monica— when she asked me for my order, I just started crying and I couldn't stop. She was so taken aback; she didn't know what to do. I couldn't stop sobbing long enough to explain myself; not that I knew exactly why I was crying any more than she did. She was obviously busy with lots of other customers, but she stayed at my table for as long as she dared, handing me napkins in lieu of Kleenex. She even rubbed my back a bit, trying to comfort me. I didn't care that people were staring at me. It just felt so good to let it all out and not explain myself to anyone. Even so, I'm pretty embarrassed when I think back on the experience. I eventually pulled myself together and ordered something to go. Needless to say, I left Monica a *big* tip."

Both women chuckled.

"Then there was that one afternoon when I was driving through a particularly long, flat stretch of highway in Nebraska. I felt myself getting sleepy, so I pulled off to the side of the road to take a quick nap."

"Oh, Ali, that doesn't sound very safe. Everything must have turned out okay since you're here, but I'm afraid to hear what's coming next."

"It was pretty scary alright, but probably not in the way

you're imagining. Remember, I have Tess with me and she puts on a very convincing Cujo act whenever anyone approaches the car, so I felt pretty safe.

"When I woke up about thirty minutes later, Tess was whimpering to get out and relieve herself. Like I said, this was pretty much the middle of nowhere and there were very few cars on the road, so I opened the door and let her out without a leash. I was a little concerned that she might run onto the roadway if she saw something to chase, but I knew she wouldn't run away. Anyway, this was mid-February so it was plenty chilly, which was my excuse for staying in the car. Well, she was gone for five minutes or so before she finally came back. When I opened the door to let her in, she had a dead field mouse in her mouth!"

"Eeeew!" Elizabeth squirmed in her chair at the thought of it and Ali convulsed at the memory; both laughed.

"Poor Tess. She was so proud of herself. She couldn't figure out why I'd screamed and shoved her back out of the car. Now *that* was one of the worst things that's happened to me."

"Oh, good grief," said Elizabeth. "You're right. That's not at all how I thought that story was going to end. How funny!"

"Then, another bad experience was when I got food poisoning. I never did figure out exactly what it was I ate that was bad, but oh my gosh was I ever sick! I had to stop at the nearest motel I could find. I stayed there for two days until I recovered enough to get back on the road."

"Well if those are the worst things that happen to you on this trip, I'd say you will have fared very well."

୫୭ଓଷ

"What time does Jackie's flight come in, Mama Berg?"

"I can't remember exactly, but the info is on the fridge. I know it's really early—practically the crack of dawn, as I recall. Are you coming with us to pick her up?"

Ali grabbed the last of the grocery bags from the trunk of the Corolla and followed her mother-in-law into the house.

"I'd love to. I presume she's flying into Dayton

International?"

"Yes. It'll be so good to have her home for a few days. We haven't seen her since the funeral."

Elizabeth began putting away the groceries while Ali set about making lunch for the two of them.

Elizabeth's tone suddenly became wistful. "She and Isaac were so close, you know? More like best friends than brother and sister. She won't admit it, but I think she's been having a really hard time accepting his death."

"I think so, too," said Ali. "I remember Isaac telling me that one of the reasons he originally moved to Seattle was to live near Jackie. He always gave her a lot of credit for his success in the auto parts business, too. I think she loaned him some of the start-up money to buy Sterns', didn't she?"

"Yes, she did. She's such a savvy businesswoman, and she had complete faith in Isaac's ability to run a profitable business. She always teased him that he'd better learn to make a lot of money very quickly if he wanted to continue all his expensive pastimes. I'm sure that was a real motivator for him. I've got to admit, though, that his dad and I were both a little surprised at how quickly he was able to add locations and how lucrative a business it turned out to be."

"I know what you mean. He already owned three stores by the time we met. I think the two keys to his success were targeting a niche market of racecar owners, and then franchising the business. I never had aspirations to marry a rich man, but the money was certainly a blessing. For one thing, it allowed me to work for PCC doing a job I really love without worrying about needing to make more money. And I'm so grateful that he had the good sense to buy a life insurance policy, despite that fact that I found it rather morbid when he originally brought up the subject. If he hadn't, it would have been much more difficult for me to take so much time off work and finance this trip."

Before sitting down at the kitchen table, Elizabeth peeked into the living room to make sure her husband wasn't within earshot.

"Ali," she began quietly, "Jackie's not the only one having trouble accepting Isaac and Zoe's deaths. Karl has been having a real crisis of faith, and I don't know how to help him. Not that I've been having such an easy time of it myself, but I'm really worried about him."

"Oh, Mama Berg, I don't know what light I can shed on it. Acceptance has never been my strong suit, and losing Isaac and Zoe hasn't changed that. I've thought a lot about it and I just seem to come up with more questions. For one thing, I can't figure out whether acceptance is a gift we are given, or a lesson we learn. And why are we able to accept some things easily, but not others?"

"Yes, those questions have occurred to me, too. I also wonder about the difference between acceptance and plain old giving up. It seems like there are times when acceptance is a virtue and other times when it's a pretense for quitting."

"I guess when the thing you have to accept is death, there's just not a lot of choice," said Ali.

"I'm not so sure about that. On the surface, that seems to be true, but I don't think it is. When Karl and I first moved into this house, we had some elderly neighbors, Mr. and Mrs. Schwartz, who lived down the block. They were the nicest couple, both retired. They had several grown children and lots of grandkids. We'd often see them taking walks around the neighborhood, holding hands, obviously still in love even after fifty-plus years of marriage.

"One morning we heard the siren of an aid car and saw it pull up to their house. Mrs. Schwartz had had a heart attack and died en route to the hospital."

"Oh, how sad," said Ali.

"It really was. We all felt so bad for Mr. Schwartz. The neighbors really rallied round him and everyone was so glad he had his kids and grandkids to help him through his grief. But you know, even with all that he still had to live for, he just couldn't get over his loss. He passed away in his sleep three weeks after his wife died. No apparent cause."

"So are you saying you think he died of a broken heart?" asked Ali.

"Yes, I do. I'm sure he didn't make a conscious choice to stop living, but I suspect we have more control over these things than we'd like to think. Maybe refusing to live any longer without his wife, was his way of refusing to accept her death."

The two women sat in silence for a while, as they each wrestled with the questions they couldn't adequately answer.

Finally, Ali said, "There have certainly been times, since I lost Isaac and Zoe, that I felt like I didn't want to go on without them. I hesitate to say I was suicidal, because I never reached a point where I thought about *how* I would kill myself. Even so, the depression has been debilitating at times."

"Do you feel as if you've accepted their deaths now?" Elizabeth asked in a soft and tentative tone.

Ali didn't answer right away. "Well, I guess it's a matter of degrees. I don't feel like I've totally accepted it. I mean, I still use euphemisms like I just did instead of saying they died. Somehow it still feels so harsh and final to use words like 'dead' instead of things like 'lost' or 'passed away.'

"I miss them like crazy . . . sometimes so much that I get knots in my stomach. And of course, I still break down and cry now and then.

"At the same time, I *have* carried on with my life. This trip is proof of that. I can't quite imagine ever getting married again, but at least I can imagine being happy . . . or *happier*. I guess that shows a certain amount of acceptance, doesn't it? How about you? Do you feel like you've accepted their deaths?"

"Honestly? Some days, yes, and other days, no. Sometimes I choose to pretend that they aren't really gone. I feel happier that way. Friends tell me that's wrong—that I'm in denial and I have to accept reality. At first, I told myself they were right; after all, society consistently tells us that 'accepting reality' is the only right option for mature adults, doesn't it?

"Then I started asking myself: who gets to define reality? Is my reality the same as everyone else's? What about perception? How does that fit in with reality? Maybe I get to choose whatever reality makes me happy, so long as it doesn't hurt anyone else."

"Goodness," said Ali, "those are some pretty deep questions you're asking."

Elizabeth chuckled. "They really are, but you know me

well enough to know that I have neither the education nor the intellect to come up with any really satisfying answers."

"Oh, Elizabeth, don't put yourself down like that. You're an intelligent, compassionate, caring person; you don't need to be a world-class philosopher as well. Besides, I believe there's value in asking the questions, even if we aren't able to come up with definitive answers. Don't you?"

"I suppose so. But answers sure are nice."

∽◯∾

"Can you believe the temperature got up to eighty-one degrees yesterday and eighty-three today? Good grief! It's *April* 10th, not *July* 10th!" Ali said in disbelief as she and her in-laws deserted the dinner table in favor of the screen porch. Tess followed along behind and sprawled out on the cool floor.

"Just sit back and enjoy it," Karl advised. "Tomorrow it will probably be back in the sixties."

"Yes," Elizabeth agreed. "*Carpe diem!* I welcome any opportunity to sit on my porch swing with good company and a glass of wine after a nice dinner."

"You're right. This is pretty wonderful," said Ali. With that, the three of them sat quietly, each lost in their own thoughts.

After a while, Karl spoke up. "Ali, Elizabeth and I have a surprise for you."

Ali was intrigued. She couldn't imagine what the surprise might be or what had prompted it.

"Now, we love having you here, so we don't want you to get the wrong idea. We aren't trying to push you out the door," he prefaced.

"Oh, no," Ali said contritely, while scratching Tess' head. "A month was too long of a visit, wasn't it? I shouldn't have planned to stay here so long. I'm so sorry. You must be anxious to get your house back to yourselves."

"No, no, no," Karl shook his head and looked at his wife. "You see, Elizabeth, that's what I was afraid of. She thinks we're trying to get rid of her—that she's overstayed her welcome."

Alice Ann Kuder

"Well, you haven't even told her what we have in mind yet. She's jumping to conclusions.

"Ali, Papa and I . . . we've been trying for a while now to think of something special we could do for you. Something to show you how much we love you and how grateful we are to you for all the happiness you brought to our son's life. We know you miss him and Zoe as much as we do, but we understand that you need to get on with your life. You're too young to spend the rest of your life alone."

Karl spoke up again. "When we noticed that your itinerary for this trip didn't include any time in New York City, we thought that was a shame."

"Yes, you've always lamented about how every time you visit New York, it's for business so you don't get to see any of the sites," added Elizabeth.

" . . . so we bought you an airline ticket and booked you a hotel room in Manhattan for the last week of April," said Karl.

"Oh my gosh!" Ali gasped.

"We didn't want you to go alone, though, and The Big Apple isn't really our cup of tea, so we called Gwen and told her what we had in mind. She loved the idea. She said that's the beauty of having a job she can do from anywhere; it allows her to be spontaneous."

"You mean," said Ali, "Gwen's going to join me in New York?"

"Yes, Dear. You can leave Tess here with us. You fly out on April 23rd—that gives you another week here with us—and you fly back into Dayton on May 1st. So you'll have a day to rest up before you get back on the road and head off to Louisville for the

Kentucky Derby on May 4th," said Elizabeth.

Ali started to cry and ran into the house. Karl and Elizabeth looked at each other, perplexed over her reaction. A moment later, Ali reemerged from the house with a handful of Kleenex, blowing her nose and wiping away her tears.

"You dear, sweet, thoughtful, generous . . . how did I ever get so lucky as to marry into this family? Here you are, still grieving your own loss, and you're thinking of me. You are both just too wonderful.

"Doesn't it seem a little odd for me to go on a vacation while I'm on a road trip though?" Then, with a dismissive wave of her hand she said, "Oh, who cares? It sounds like heaven! I'll take your earlier advice, Mama Berg, and seize the day."

∞∞

Jackie had booked herself on a red-eye flight from Seattle, so Ali convinced her in-laws to let her pick their daughter up at the airport by herself. Better that Mama and Papa Berg welcome Jackie home after they enjoyed a full night's sleep.

Ali had noted a subtle coolness and distance between her and Jackie ever since the accident over a year ago. She assumed it was just Jackie's way of dealing with her grief, and that it would eventually fade. Hopefully, the George letter she'd written to Jackie would act as a balm and restore the warm relationship they had always enjoyed. Perhaps she'd give it to her once they got back to the house, if Jackie wasn't too exhausted.

∞∞

Dear Jackie,

Cliché as it may sound, the day I married Isaac, I feel like I gained a sister in you.

Isaac admired you tremendously and loved you so completely. He never stopped singing your praises. There was a time, when he and I were first dating, that I was actually a bit jealous of your relationship. The two of you had such a bond, even though, with your opposite strengths and abilities you could easily have become mean competitors. Instead, your mutual love and respect caused you to combine your strengths into one near-perfect whole. You complemented one another as siblings rarely do.

Over the years, you gave me many valuable

Alice Ann Kuder

insights into Isaac's personality. You helped me understand who he was and what he needed in order to be happy. In fact, you were able to articulate it better than he was (he was a typical man in that regard).

I remember when Zoe was born. Isaac and I were so happy and grateful that she was healthy, with all ten fingers and ten toes. I protested every time the nurses wanted to take her from my arms. Even though I was totally spent, I wanted nothing more than to feel her heart beat against my chest every minute for the rest of my life.

Isaac's impulses were totally different from mine. A few hours after she was born, he announced that he was going skydiving! I couldn't believe that he could leave us for a minute, let alone for the rest of the day. Where was the guy who had just been marveling at his newborn daughter's perfect nose?

I was furious and hurt and disappointed in him. I started second-guessing myself and him, wondering what kind of father he would be.

You walked into the room just after Isaac left, and I was so grateful to see you. If I hadn't been so physically and emotionally exhausted, I might have felt ashamed of myself for devolving into the lunatic you witnessed. Looking back, I'm amazed that you were able to understand a thing I was saying as I alternated between sobs and rants. I confided to you all my doubts, fears, and concerns about Isaac, Zoe, and me.

You remained remarkably calm and quiet until I eventually ran out of steam. After reassuring me that I would be a fine mother and Zoe was a fortunate baby, you addressed my anger at Isaac for his perceived indifference.

"The thing you have to understand about Isaac," you said, "is that physical activity helps him clear his head. When he starts feeling overwhelmed by emotions or events, he looks for a way to put on the brakes. He does that by putting himself in situations that require his complete and total attention, like skydiving. Somehow, it puts everything into perspective for him, and afterwards, he's able to deal with life again head-on. It may not make sense to you or me—and I'm not sure he realizes that's what he's doing—but it works for him. I've seen him do it time and time again. Haven't you?"

I realized that I had, but I hadn't made the connection before. I never let it bother me again.

I've also benefited from your presence in my life in ways that had nothing to do with Isaac. I'm most grateful for the lesson you taught me about the confluence of love and forgiveness.

Soon after you and I first met, you invited me to be your guest at the annual WestSide Baby Benefit Tea in West Seattle. As a table captain, you had invited a group of ten women to join you at the fundraiser. One of them was your dear friend, Katrina, who you introduced me to that day.

After that, and for the next several years, I ran into you and Katrina frequently at various events. Then one day I realized that I hadn't seen the two of you together for several months. When I asked you about her absence, you told me that she was in a serious relationship with a man who "kept her on a short leash." She was crazy in love with him and willingly did everything he asked of her, which included ditching all her old friends. Rather than telling you this face-to-face, she wrote you a letter explaining that Todd believed you were a bad influence on her. Per his wishes, Katrina was breaking off all contact with you, and no longer considered the two of you to be friends.

You were obviously devastated by her words and actions, and admitted to me that you felt rejected and betrayed. Katrina had been your close friend and confidante for years. To be cut off so suddenly and completely for no apparent reason seemed quite cruel and callous.

It must have been about five years later, at the 12th Annual WestSide Baby Tea, that Katrina suddenly reappeared! The two of you behaved as if the intervening years of silence had never happened, so I waited until later to ask you about the reunion.

The story, you said, was that you had happened upon a new boutique shoe shop in West Seattle and sat down to try on some shoes. You heard a sales clerk come up from behind and when you looked up, you realized it was Katrina. You were so surprised that your unthinking reaction was elation! If you had seen her through the store window first, giving you time to think, you told me, you probably would have turned and walked away, thwarting a reunion. Equally stunned, she was thrilled to see you, too.

The meeting could have become awkward very quickly if Katrina hadn't immediately hugged you and told you how glad she was to see you. Later, in a private conversation, she confessed her shame and humiliation at allowing Todd to *control her thoughts and actions for so long. She'd come to her senses and left him three years earlier, but she was too embarrassed to approach former friends and ask for the forgiveness she didn't feel she deserved.*

Everyone would have understood if you had rejected Katrina's explanation and apology, but you didn't. You welcomed her back into your life like the proverbial prodigal son. The love you felt for your friend, you told me, far outweighed the pain she had caused—and it had made forgiveness easy.

Easy? Forgiveness has never been easy for me, but through you, I learned that it is incredibly powerful and life-giving. Until recently, I had forgotten that lesson. Perhaps—by forgetting it—I have crippled myself unnecessarily by failing to forgive Isaac for perceived transgressions. So once again, I owe you a great deal.

By teaching me about the power of forgiveness, you may have returned my love to me; you may have given me back my Isaac. And even just that possibility is an incredible gift.

I am your loving sister and you are mine, until forever,

Ali

☙❧

Jackie chose to read the letter in Ali's presence. Afterward, she put it down on the coffee table that separated them and looked up with an expression that Ali couldn't quite fathom.

"Jackie? What's the matter? What's wrong?"

Jackie inhaled deeply, holding her breath for several beats before exhaling. Then, as if having come to a difficult decision, she said, "I'll tell you what's wrong. I probably should have told you months ago. I'm angry. I'm angry *at you*."

Ali's eyes grew wide, registering her surprise at Jackie's admission. Somewhat bewildered and at a loss for words, she responded meekly, "Okay . . . can you tell me why?"

"I'm angry at you because I think you made Isaac's last months on earth miserable. I hate that you constantly made him feel guilty about doing the things he loved, and that you were gone so often for work. I hate that he died doubting your love for him and wondering if your marriage would survive."

Ali's shoulders slumped and she sank back in her chair in stunned silence, as Jackie continued her vehement censure. Even though Ali realized it was all coming from Jackie's grief and frustration, it wounded her deeply. She didn't interrupt her sister-in-law because she knew Jackie needed to get it all out . . . and because she felt she deserved every punishing word.

She's right, Ali thought, *I did make Isaac's last months miserable by all my criticism and disapproval. He died doubting my love for him. For that matter, when he died I doubted my love for him. How could I have let that happen? Why did I let all my stupid, petty complaints get in the way of our happiness? Why did I let my work consume so much of my time? I don't blame her for being mad at me. I'm mad at me.*

When Jackie finally came to the end of her tirade, she looked at Ali coldly and said, "Well, I'll bet now you don't think I'm such a great role model for understanding and forgiveness, do you?"

"The final forming of a person's character lies in their own hands."
~ Anne Frank

Chapter 30
April 29, 2013

"Gwen, I can't tell you how thrilled I am that you were able to join me for this spur-of-the-moment vacation in New York," Ali said as together they negotiated a busy Fifth Avenue sidewalk. "As much as I've wanted an opportunity to play the tourist here, it's not a city I'd like to see alone. I'm pretty sure I'd be missing Isaac and Zoe much more if you weren't here."

"No need to thank me; it's been just as much fun for me as it has for you. I've been to New York a few times over the years, but so much is always changing here that it's a new experience every time. Plus, I've missed you something awful, so I jumped at the chance to come spend some time with you—especially in The Big Apple!"

Ali flipped through the pages of their dog-eared guidebook. "I think we've succeeded in hitting just about every tourist attraction there is, and then some. Broadway, Time Square, the Empire State Building, the Statue of Liberty . . . we've definitely made the most of every minute. And we still have two more days!"

Gwen put her hand to her stomach and said, "And can you believe all the fabulous restaurants? I'm sure I would have gained five pounds by now if it weren't for all the walking we've done. I love, love, love strolling through Central Park, don't you?"

Gwen noticed that Ali got quiet at the mention of Central Park.

"Whoa! That was a quick mood change. What's up?" Gwen asked.

"I forgot how well you can read my moods. Have I ever told you about Damon Ramey?"

"I seem to recall seeing that name on your original list of Georges, but I don't think you've ever told me any details. Who is he?"

With just a subtle nod of her head, Ali steered Gwen toward a sidewalk café where they could sit and savor a glass of wine before the happy hour crowds began to pour in.

Once they were seated, Ali continued. "Damon was a mentor of mine at the Skagit Valley YMCA. He gave me my first post-college job. I've always considered him to be a pillar of ethics and high moral standards."

"And?"

"And when I started searching the whereabouts of my various Georges, I discovered that he's in prison for helping his mother commit suicide. In fact, he's serving his sentence here in New York. And get this—the prison backs up to Central Park!

"I wrote him a George letter before I found all this out. Now, I don't know what to think. I'm finding it impossible not to judge him."

"Apparently, a jury of his peers did, too," Gwen said with a note of sarcasm. "Are you going to give him the letter?"

"I don't know. That's what's got me tied up in knots. One minute I think I should go see him, the next minute I don't. What do you think?"

"Well . . . I don't know. I can see why you're hesitating. I suppose it might be an easier decision if he were a friend rather than a former employer."

"Probably," Ali agreed. "When I finalized my road trip destinations back in December, I decided against visiting him. I didn't feel a need to go that far out of my way, but when Karl and Elizabeth surprised me with this trip to New York I began to reconsider. I mean, I'm right here in the same city he is; it would be so easy to see him."

"Maybe you should look at it from a future perspective. How do you think you will feel if you leave the city *without* seeing him and giving him a chance to tell you his story?"

"That's a good question. I guess I might feel like I let him down."

"Like *you* let *him* down? It seems to me that *he* let *you* down."

"I suppose, but I'll never know if I don't talk with him. I'm strongly opposed to assisted suicide; I don't really care to hear any arguments in favor of it. I really doubt that anything he could say would change my mind about the issue."

"Is that what you're afraid of? That he might convince you that what he did was justified?"

"I don't know. Maybe."

"Well, since you asked my opinion—sort of—I think you should go talk to him."

"Really? Why?"

"Because I think that if you don't, you'll always wonder how someone you respect—respected—so much could do something so out of character. I guess what I'm saying is that I think you should go see him for your own benefit, not necessarily for his. Does that make sense?"

"Actually, it does. I'm going to chew on it a bit longer, but I think you're right. If I'm still feeling this way tomorrow, I'll check on visiting hours and go see him before we leave on Wednesday."

℠℟™

When Ali walked up to the Lincoln Correctional Facility, she was taken aback by how "un-prison-like" it looked. Even though it was a minimum-security prison, she expected it to look more bleak and intimidating. It still seemed a bit incongruous to her that the building faced the north side of Central Park. That seemed like a luxury location that should be reserved for the never-incarcerated.

This made more sense when she learned that the 1914 facility was originally built as a branch of the Young Women's Hebrew Association. It served as a place where newly immigrated Jewish women could get assistance in acclimating to their new lives in America. It didn't come into use as a prison facility until 1976. *No wonder it seemed more pleasant than formidable*, she thought.

Now that she stood at the front entrance, the time for vacillation was over. She could either leave the letter for Damon at the front desk, or stay to visit and hand it to him in person. She chose the latter.

Dear Damon,

Is there anything as beneficial to one's personal and professional growth as a boss who is a good mentor? I certainly feel fortunate to have had that in you.

It's hard to believe that it's been more than 20 years since I worked for you at the Skagit Valley Family YMCA as a program director. Fresh out of college and ready to take on the world, I was a typical twenty-something adult, sure that I had all the answers and knew everything. The fact that I was highly capable and intelligent only added to my misguided sense of certainty.

You probably won't remember the incident I'm about to retell, but it had a profound effect on me, which is why I am writing this letter of appreciation.

My job was to propose and plan a slate of programs that would appeal to a teenage audience and get them involved with the Y. I supervised a team of two part-time employees and three volunteers who assisted me.

Our first two programs of the year went quite well. We reached ninety-five percent of our registration goals, and the kids gave us very positive feedback. The third program, however, was a complete flop. We only reached fifteen percent of our registration goal and had to cancel the event, costing us precious resources.

The day after the official cancelation, you called me into your office. I was sure you were going to chastise me and put me on notice that I'd better not have any more similar disasters.

Frankly, I wasn't used to failure and it didn't sit well with me. Sure enough, you asked me for an explanation of why the event foundered. I blamed it on my staff, on poor publicity, on wayward kids . . . anyone but me. Your tone and demeanor were calm and controlled. You weren't angry, you didn't scold, you weren't threatening, but each time I attempted to shift the blame, you brought it right back to me. Wasn't I supervising my staff? Yes. Didn't I approve the publicity plan? Yes. Didn't I understand the kids' needs? Yes. Then how, you asked, was the failure anyone else's responsibility?

Finally, I had to admit to us both that I was, in fact, ultimately responsible for the unsuccessful effort. Once I acknowledged it out loud, I was surprised to discover that I actually felt better! I felt stronger and prouder of myself than I had before the meeting began. You made me realize that dodging responsibility and placing blame are the acts of a coward. Taking personal responsibility for one's actions is a mark of strong character and moral integrity. Possessing those qualities is much more important than avoiding blame.

Even so, I steeled myself for the judgment and discipline I assumed would follow. Instead, you told me you were glad I failed. I was stunned!

You said that the fact I was so rarely unsuccessful was evidence that I set my goals too low and didn't take enough risks. I was too afraid of failure. You actually told me that in the future, you wanted me to set higher goals that were harder to achieve, even though I would have a higher rate of disappointments.

Alice Ann Kuder

Our whole conversation lasted about twenty minutes and has positively affected my entire life. I can't tell you the number of people who have escaped being blamed by me over the years because you called me on the carpet that day.

If you had handled that situation differently— with less patience and respect—it's unlikely I would have learned those valuable lessons.

You have my respect and appreciation until forever,

Ali Benevento Berg

∞∞

When Ali emerged from her visit with Damon, she felt grateful that she'd taken Gwen's advice and gone to see him.

Damon hadn't changed her stance on assisted suicide, but hearing about his experience enabled her to feel a degree of compassion and understanding that she had previously lacked. Ultimately, she came away feeling that he was still worthy of her respect and sympathy. Perhaps she would have made a different choice than he had; perhaps not. Unless she was unfortunate enough to be put to the same test, she would never know. She was convinced that Damon had done the best he could under the circumstances, and that's all anyone could ask.

Chapter 31
February 10, 2012

> When will you be home? We need to talk.

Pacing nervously around the family room with her phone in hand, Ali hesitated before hitting "Send." Maybe a text message wasn't the best way to resume such a serious conversation, but she hadn't been able to stop thinking about the argument they'd had just before she left on her business trip twelve days earlier. It probably wouldn't be hard for Isaac to guess what she wanted to talk about, but surely asking to talk was better than coming right out and saying, "Do you want a divorce?"

She had arrived home less than twenty minutes ago, not knowing if Isaac would be there to greet her or not. Finding an empty house, her heart sank. Their communication while she'd been away had consisted mostly of terse phone conversations and brief, impersonal e-mails, most of which centered around Zoe. She couldn't remember any other time in their relationship when simply talking to each other had required such effort or felt so joyless.

Truth be told, Ali wasn't sure what she wanted from Isaac, but she knew she didn't want this emotional chasm. There was still so much love between the two of them, if only they could figure out what was preventing them from feeling it. She wasn't ready to give up on their marriage, and she hoped that he wasn't either. Fearful as she was of the possible answer, it was time to put the question of divorce on the table. The anticipation of such a discussion made her stomach muscles tighten.

Like most couples, she and Isaac had encountered difficult times in their marriage before and gotten past them. *Why,* she wondered, *did this time feel so different?* She searched her memory for clues. She couldn't identify a day when normal everyday annoyances had begun to feel like unendurable irritants.

Maybe journaling would help. She knew from experience that train-of-thought writing—or free-style rambling as she liked to call it—sometimes revealed truths from within her subconscious that might otherwise have remained hidden.

Besides, she was feeling a bit jet-lagged from her travels, and journaling always helped her unwind.

10 February

How did we get here? When did we stop paying attention to our marriage . . . and to each other? Is this the life we want? It seems like it should be. We are so blessed. We have a beautiful daughter whom we both love and adore. We have good jobs, a comfortable home, money in the bank, wonderful friends and family, outside interests. What more could we want?

Maybe it's just normal to stop and question things every once in a while. It's so easy to take life for granted . . . to take people for granted. Isaac and I have succeeded in building the life we said we wanted. We should be happy. Is this what happy feels like? That's a stupid question, of course it isn't.

Maybe we need new dreams and new mountains to climb. OMG! I can't believe I used that analogy! Isaac's mountain climbing is one of the things that makes me UNhappy. I do nothing but worry when he goes on one of his "adventures." I imagine him hurt and alone—or worse—at the bottom of a ravine. I don't understand the attraction. I never have and probably never will. It seems so unfair that so many of the activities he loves, energize him and drain me. I wish I could share his love of all-

things-dangerous, but I just can't. He says I worry too much. I say he takes too many chances.

We have always recognized this difference between us, but maybe we overestimated our ability to work around it. Maybe our "love conquers all" mentality was wishful thinking. It's possible that our arrogance might be the cause of our downfall.

Why, after fifteen years, though, does this issue suddenly seem to have gained so much significance? What's changed?

Feeling frustrated that she had so many more questions than answers, Ali put down her pen and headed toward the kitchen. There, she opened a bottle of Petite Sirah, poured herself a glass, and took it with her to the master bedroom. Perhaps the wine and a long, hot bath would provide the relaxation that eluded her. A few minutes later, she gratefully sank into the tub and allowed her mind to drift.

Sure enough, not twenty minutes later as she was relaxing in the tub, her eyes flew open wide.

Oh my God! I know what changed! We had Zoe! We became parents. I didn't make the connection until now because it's been 10 years since she was born. But now she's getting old enough to decide what's fun and what's not, and I'm terrified that she'll take after her father! It's one thing to worry about Isaac getting injured, but if Zoe follows in her father's footsteps and starts racing cars and jumping out of airplanes . . . I don't know if I can hold up under that kind of stress.

Her thoughts continued to fly. *Is that why I'm so angry with Isaac all the time? Is it because I'm afraid he will entice her to join him in his thrill seeking? Am I delusional enough to think that distancing myself from him will somehow keep Zoe safe?*

Anxious to capture these new insights, Ali got up from the bath, put on her robe and pulled out her journal once again. Just then her phone alerted her that she had a new text message. Expecting that it would be from Isaac, she was both disappointed and relieved to see that it was from her office at PCC instead. They were sorry to disturb her so soon after returning from her trip, the text said, but the wine manager at the Greenlake store was just taken away in an ambulance with probable appendicitis! There was a big wine shipment due in anytime, and no one was available to take over his shift. Could she possibly come and help?

She stared at the long message for a minute, then took a deep breath and exhaled slowly before wearily texting back that she would be there within the hour.

"A teacher affects eternity;
he can never tell where his influence stops."
~ Henry Adams

Chapter 32
May 2-30, 2013

Orb, Oxbow, Palace Malice. *One thing is for certain in horse racing*, Ali thought, *you can't predict a winner by the horse's name alone.* Even so, she loved it when the odds-on favorite had a name she connected with. She supposed that she ought to care more about which horse won, but really, she just loved watching the cadre of equines run.

Ali had been looking forward to these next two minutes for nearly forty years. Ever since she watched her first Kentucky Derby on TV as a child, she had dreamed of being there in person. Now that dream had come true. She was about to experience the Derby's reputation as "the most exciting two minutes in sports."

I can't believe that after all these years, I'm here! She thought to herself. *I'm actually sitting in the stands at Churchill Downs, about to witness the Kentucky Derby! I'd give anything to have Isaac and Zoe here—more than just in spirit—but even so, I feel as giddy as a schoolgirl!*

Everything was just as she had imagined it—except for the rain. She was really hoping for a gloriously sunny spring day, but she mused that in the end, the rain would make for better storytelling.

While she was still pinching herself, the starting bell rang, bringing her out of her reverie and into the present moment.

Keeping with tradition, the announcer sang out, "THEY'RE OFF, in The Kentucky Derby!

His narration of the race was classic. "*Java's War* was off to a slow beginning. A good start for *Verrazano* and *Falling Sky*. *Falling Sky* is the early leader. And now, *Itsmyluckyday*. And coming through on the inside is . . . *Orrrrrrbbb*, is coming with giant strides in the center of the track! And here comes *Orb* on the outside now, to take the lead as they come down to the sixteen pole. It is *Orb* in front from *Normandy Invasion*, *Mylute*,

Alice Ann Kuder

and *Golden Soul*, between horses, down to the wire … *ORB HAS WON THE KENTUCKY DERBY* for Shug McGaughey!"

Two minutes and .289 seconds, and it was over. Two minutes and .289 seconds that Ali would never forget.

଼୦ଔ

It was a happy coincidence that one of Ali's Georges lived in Louisville.

Ali had taken piano lessons from. Marilyn Andouille for six years as a youth, and loved every minute of every lesson. Each session began with a cup of tea, a cookie, and a question. The kind of tea and the kind of cookie varied—green tea, white tea, or chamomile tea; madeleines, sugar wafers, or chocolate chip—but the question never did.

"How was your week?" Mrs. Andouille always inquired with sincere interest. Ali eventually noticed how much calmer she felt and how much better she played after updating Mrs. Andouille on how she was feeling about her life at that moment in time.

଼୦ଔ

It's difficult for a twelve-year-old to accurately assess the age of most adults. Looking back, Ali estimated that Mrs. Andouille was probably in her early to mid fifties when they began working together. Since Ali was now forty-three, that would make Mrs. Andouille in her early to mid eighties. Although it wasn't easy tracking her down after all these years, Ali felt very strongly about finding her teacher to tell her what an important and positive influence she'd been. Even though Mrs. Andouille hadn't been a traditional classroom teacher, she was symbolic for Ali, of all the wonderful teachers she had had in her lifetime, as well as her own mother's dedication to the profession.

"Teachers aren't paid *nearly* enough," was a chorus Ali was known for singing, especially when it came time to pass school levies. She always voted "yes".

Locating the current whereabouts of a retired person proved more difficult than finding someone who was actively employed. At first, her search seemed doomed. Then, she remembered that Mrs. Andouille had a son named Alexander. She found him living in Louisville. He had convinced his mother to move there as well, a dozen years earlier.

When signs of dementia became evident, making it unsafe for her to live alone, Alexander moved his mother to the best assisted-care facility he could find in Louisville.

Ali contacted Alexander back in December, and was very happy when he encouraged her to come and visit his mother.

"Teaching piano was as essential to my mom's happiness as air was to breathing," he said, "and every one of her students was special to her. That's why she never took on more than a dozen students at a time and insisted on one-hour lessons, even though she only charged for forty-five minutes. I know she would be thrilled to have you visit. Please come."

Ali was a little surprised, as she rang Alexander's doorbell, to realize how excited she was to see Mrs. Andouille again. Alexander had warned her that his mother's health was in flux. Ali hoped he was right in believing that her former teacher would remember and be glad to see her.

"Alexander, hi. I'm Ali Berg."

"Of course, welcome! Please come in."

After exchanging pleasantries over a cup of tea and cookies—*it must be a family trait*, Ali mused—Alexander told Ali that he had some bad news.

"Mom passed away quite suddenly, almost three weeks ago," he said. "Please forgive me for not notifying you before you got here. It just didn't seem right to tell you the news over the phone while you were on the road."

Ali was crestfallen. She felt herself slump in her chair as a deep, mournful sigh escaped from deep inside her. Everything about this leg of her trip had seemed so fortuitous. To have come so far, both geographically and emotionally, only to find she was three weeks too late, made her incredibly sad and disappointed. Neither of them knew what to say, so they sat

Alice Ann Kuder

together in silence for a while, gazing into their teacups, looking for solace.

Finally, Ali reached into her purse and pulled out the letter she had written to her teacher. After giving Alexander a brief explanation of the purpose for her visit, she handed him the letter.

"I'd like you to have this," she said. "You may appreciate it almost as much as I hope she would have."

"I'm honored to accept it. If you don't mind, I'll read it later when I'm alone.

"Ali," he continued, "I hope you don't feel like your visit is wasted. When I told Mom you were coming to see her, she lit up like a Christmas tree. You know, dementia affects short-term memory, and many times leaves long-term memory practically unscathed. She remembered you vividly. The anticipation of your visit alone made her very happy. So, you see, your actions and intentions added significant joy to her last few months. That's an amazing gift!

"I don't know what your beliefs are about an afterlife," he continued, "but I can't help thinking that Mom got your letter, even if you didn't get to hand it to her in person before she died."

Ali nodded her head in gratitude for his kind words and dabbed at her tears with the tissue he handed her.

"Can I ask you a question?" said Alexander.

"Of course," said Ali.

"I don't want you to think that Mom gave up all your secrets, but . . . can you still fart at will?"

Alexander's outrageous question made them both laugh until their sides hurt. It was an incredibly effective way to insert humor into a conversation that had gotten way too intense.

"Oh, it feels so good to laugh," Ali confessed. "Sometimes I forget it's okay to laugh even when I'm sad. Thanks for the reminder."

"I think Mom would say that it's not only okay, it's mandatory," said Alexander. "She loved to laugh."

"In answer to your question . . ." Ali grinned, shifted in her chair and demonstrated that yes, she could.

Dear Mrs. Andouille,

I realize you would probably prefer that I call you Marilyn at this stage of our lives, but for all those years when you were my piano teacher, you were Mrs. Andouille to me, and I am happy to continue to pay you that respect.

I remember the day my mother and I went to your house to meet you and discuss the possibility of having me take lessons—I was twelve years old. While the two of you discussed the business end of matters, I succumbed to the seemingly palpable, magnetic attraction of the grand piano that graced your living room. Circling it with reverence, I admired the deep, dark cherry finish and peered into its belly at the strings and hammers. The fallboard was down so I couldn't see the keys, but oh, how I longed to play them.

I wasn't scheduled to take my first lesson until the following week, but you suggested that Mom leave us alone to get acquainted.

You could tell how smitten I was with your piano, so you invited me to sit and play anything I liked while you went to the kitchen to make us some tea.

I was nervous about playing such a fine instrument—afraid that it would tattle on my lack of skill—but the lure was too strong to resist. I imagine you were probably taking the opportunity to listen from the kitchen rather than standing over me as I played for you for the first time.

For the next twenty or thirty minutes, we sat in your living room drinking tea—that made me

Alice Ann Kuder

feel so grown up—and discussing everything under the sun. You asked me about my goals for taking lessons; what level of skill did I want to achieve? We both knew that I was starting lessons too late in life for me to have a career as a concert pianist, but I remember feeling that if that had been my objective, you would not have discouraged me. In fact, I remember feeling that you truly cared about everything I had to say on any subject, which is not necessarily an experience that every young person has around adults.

Each week, before we started our lesson, you took time to ask me how I was doing. Not just in terms of my practicing, but with whatever was going on in my life. Sometimes, if life seemed particularly hard—as it often does to an adolescent—I would ramble on and on. You always gave me your undivided attention and listened carefully, no matter how incoherent I might be. I always felt so much better afterward. Whether or not it was your intention, I'm sure I was better able to concentrate on my lesson after relieving myself of the day's emotional baggage. It must have been a good two years or more before I identified the pattern in our little preambles. First, you asked me how I was, in a way that invited a real response. Second, you listened without interruption. Third, you neither judged me, nor offered any advice. You didn't try to solve my problems. You just listened and cared.

It occurs to me that you taught me about music in much the same way. You told me to only play music that I cared about. Then to listen— really listen—to the music as I played it, to hear what it had to tell me.

"Imagine that the music has a life of its own and you are in a relationship with it," you said. I will never forget that.

For all those years, I thought you were teaching me to play, but you were really teaching me to listen. I am proud to say that it is a lesson I learned well—not perfectly—but well. I'm grateful for my memories of all the times I asked my darling daughter Zoe how she was doing and then really listened to her answer.

I owe that to you. That, and so much more.

You have my gratitude until forever,

Ali

"Unexpected kindness is the most powerful, least costly, and most underrated agent of human change." ~ Bob Kerrey

Chapter 33
May 31-June 15, 2013

Atlanta	9
Macon	92

Oh, thank goodness; just nine miles to go, Ali thought, sighing with relief and squirming in the driver's seat. She was coming to the end of a long day of driving—over four hundred miles. She'd left Louisville early that morning, after spending the entire month of May exploring the surrounding Kentucky countryside. She spent a good amount of time riding, visiting several local stables and watching a number of local horse show competitions. She hadn't taken the time to do that since she was a young girl.

೮೧೧೩

The outside temperature as they traveled south along I-75 had reached the low eighties according to the gauge in the Escape. Thankfully, the air conditioning kept Ali and Tess at a comfortable sixty-five degrees. They'd stopped for lunch in Nashville, which only left her wishing she could have spent some significant time in that city. Although she wasn't a big fan of country-western music, she would have loved to see the Grand Ole Opry, among other local tourist attractions. Unfortunately, she was already feeling exhausted and looking forward to checking into the luxurious St. Regis Atlanta for her two-week stay in that city, so she pressed on.

Now it was close to five o'clock, and although the sun

wouldn't set until almost nine, Ali considered the day to be nearly over.

Just as she was imagining herself relaxing in a cool, comfortable restaurant, enjoying a steak dinner with a glass of wine, she heard a loud *pop* and felt the steering wheel pull sharply to the left.

No, no, no, no! I can't have a flat tire! She thought as she pulled over to the side of the road, shaking her head in frustration and cursing her bad luck. These were brand new, top-of-the-line tires, she'd had installed just before she left home. How could she have a flat?

Ali hesitated before abandoning the cool interior of the car, knowing she'd be assaulted by a blast of hot, humid air the moment she opened the car door. Necessity and her curiosity won out, however, and she got out to examine the tire. Not one, but two nails had penetrated the rubber! She didn't remember seeing anything on the roadway, but there they were.

With a heavy sigh, she thought, *this is why I joined AAA.* Climbing back into the car, she reached for her purse to get her cell phone. As she rifled through her handbag she was reminded of how—in direct defiance of female stereotype—she hated purses. For one thing, they were always either too small or too large. For another, they either had so many pockets that she couldn't remember what she put where, or they had no pockets, so everything got jumbled up together in a dark, bottomless pit.

Feeling more irritable by the minute—thanks to the heat and her exhaustion—she dumped the contents of her purse onto the car seat. Meanwhile, noticing that the car had stopped, Tess woke from her nap and looked at Ali with eager anticipation, tail wagging excitedly. *She* was more than ready to exit the car.

"*Yes, yes, Tess. Wait just a minute until I call AAA and get someone out here to help us.*"

Continuing to sift through the contents of her purse, what had been a feeling of irritation began to morph into panic. *Where's my phone? I CAN'T FIND MY PHONE!*" She shouted out loud. Her uncharacteristic outburst startled Tess to

Alice Ann Kuder

attention.

Attempting to avoid the hysteria she felt coming on, Ali tried to concentrate. Where could it be? When had she used it last? Then she remembered. After checking her e-mail, she'd set it on the counter in the bathroom at the restaurant in Nashville . . . and obviously left it there.

Now what was she going to do? There was no spare tire. She remembered the dealer's explanation when they bought the car, that manufacturers had stopped including spares in order to increase storage space and improve gas mileage. The can of Fix-a-Flat she carried wasn't recommended for this type of flat.

She decided against walking the nine miles into town. Although she had plenty of bottled water, she didn't think either she or Tess would fare well in the heat.

I guess I'll just have to flag down a passing car and ask for help, she reasoned, *or wait for a Georgia State Patrol car to come by.*

Thirty minutes later, neither plan had panned out. Cars kept whizzing by; no one stopped. No state troopers came by, either. Another thirty minutes passed, and still no luck. Now Ali was tired, hungry, hot, and sweating. Her mood turned foul as she mentally castigated all the selfish, uncaring people who obviously couldn't be bothered to stop and help her.

Feeling as if she just couldn't take it anymore, she started to cry. Sensing her person's distress, Tess nuzzled up to Ali, trying her best to provide some comfort. Distracted by her wordless commiseration with the dog, Ali didn't notice the tow truck pull up behind them. A minute later, she was startled to hear someone rapping on her window.

There stood a young woman dressed in mechanic's overalls with a patch on the pocket that read "Ron's Emergency Road Service."

As Ali rolled down her window, the young woman said with a melodic Southern drawl, "Hi. I'm Lindsay. I'm told you need some help."

"Oh, am I glad to see you! Yes! I definitely need some help. I picked up a couple of nails in my tire."

Surveying the damage, Lindsay said, "Ouch! You sure did. I can't fix it here, but I can tow you into town."

"That would be so great. I assume you'll take a credit card?"

"Of course we take credit cards, but yours is no good."

When she heard that, Ali's mouth dropped open. "What do you mean, mine's no good? I've got great credit, but I can pay cash if you get me to an ATM."

"Your cash is no good either."

Now Ali was really stunned . . . and puzzled. "What? How can my cash be no good? Why did you stop to help me if you don't think I'm able to pay you?"

"I didn't just happen to stop," Lindsay explained. "We got a call from one of our regular customers who saw you were stranded. He couldn't stop to help you himself at the time, so he asked us to send a tow truck out as soon as possible. He also suggested that I be the one to come because you might be frightened if a man showed up out of nowhere."

"Wow. And here I was feeling sorry for myself, and being angry at the world. Wait a minute. That still doesn't explain why you won't take my credit card or my cash. How am I supposed to pay you?"

"You aren't. He was afraid you might not be able to afford the tow service, so he gave us his credit card number and said to send him the bill."

"You're kidding? You have *got* to be kidding. What an incredibly kind and generous thing to do! Can I get his name and address from you so I can thank him and reimburse him?"

"Sorry, ma'am, but he gave us strict instructions that we're not to give you any information that might help you identify him. He said he wants to remain anonymous. I'm not going to betray his confidence, but I'll tell you, I know this guy and he would love it if you pay it forward."

With tears clouding her eyes, Ali vowed to herself to do just that.

෨෬

Despite the happy outcome to Ali's roadside mishap, by the time she reached Atlanta and the St. Regis she was totally spent. Exhausted as she was, however, she felt uneasy about being without her mobile phone so she asked the hotel clerk to help her arrange for a replacement as soon as possible. *Concierge service is one advantage of staying at a luxury hotel,* she thought. And she whispered a prayer of gratitude that Zoe had taught her to always back up her contacts and photos online so they would be easily retrievable in case her phone was ever lost or stolen. *I'm still benefitting from your loving care for me, you darling girl.*

Atlanta was one of the few big city, non-George destinations on her route. It was a place she had always wanted to visit, thanks to her fascination with the movie *Gone With the Wind.* She knew it was silly to harbor such a romantic image of the city, based on a fictitious depiction that wasn't even current day, but she did. She couldn't help it. Whenever anyone said "Atlanta," in her head, she heard the name being spoken in Vivian Leigh's sweet Southern drawl—which was, of course, also fictitious.

Now, here she was in a luxury hotel in this historic city with two weeks to do every touristy thing she desired. She had already created a tentative itinerary for herself. No one, she was told by friends, should go to Atlanta without seeing the Botanical Gardens, the recently-restored Fox Theater, and the Martin Luther King, Jr. National Historic Site.

The bellhop stopped the luggage cart outside her sixteenth-floor room at the end of the hall. Feeling quite pampered, Ali handed him her key card and waited for him to show her through the door. Tess followed politely behind, as she had been trained to do, then proceeded to explore the cool quarters with enthusiasm. Ali glanced appreciatively around the spacious room with its floor to ceiling windows and Juliette balcony and was very happy she had decided to indulge herself.

After tipping the bellhop generously and listening for the door to shut behind him, Ali eyed the king bed. Afraid that if she stretched out on it now she might not get up again until the next morning, she instead pulled out her laptop. Thanks to the complimentary Wi-Fi connection, she was quickly online searching to see what special events might be happening in the city during her intended stay.

Hmmm. There was something called the Mud Crusade happening the next day. It was billed as "an intense obstacle course 5K mud race" designed to "test your mental and physical limits to see how far you can push them." Isaac would have loved it. Ali would pass . . . *though I wouldn't mind seeing a few of the muscular and muddied male participants when they finished the course.* This last thought caught her off guard. It seemed like a long time since she had had any objectifying thoughts involving men. She supposed it was about time.

While they were talking earlier, the concierge suggested she purchase an Atlanta CityPASS—a discount card that would get her into five of the main tourist attractions, including Zoo Atlanta, the CNN Studio Tour and the World of Coca-Cola. That sounded more like her speed than did a mud run.

While online, she checked her e-mail and caught up with some of her friends on Facebook. *And maybe,* she thought, *today is the day to do that Google search I've been thinking about.*

෨൬

Sure enough, Google gave up "Eric Wicks" as currently living in Beaverton, Oregon, a suburb of Portland. *Portland? All this time, he was as close as that? Good grief!* She thought, *Portland is only a hundred and ninety miles south of Seattle, just three hours driving time!*

Of all the Georges on Ali's list, Eric was the person she was most nervous about contacting. She hadn't tried to find him until now, and she was already six months into her road trip. Why? She wasn't sure. Maybe it was because there had been an element of romance with him. Fantasized romance to be sure—and all on her part—but romance nevertheless.

The movie *When Harry Met Sally* was a box office hit the year Ali met Eric. Ali's physical attraction to Eric made her join the debate about the film's central question of whether men and women can ever really be "just friends." She felt sure that it was a non-issue for Eric. He was totally and publicly committed to his fiancé, Nancy, and never gave Ali a reason to think that he considered her to be anything more than a friend. In the end, her unrelenting attraction was probably the real reason Ali let the friendship go. As much as she valued the relationship, it just took too much energy to constantly suppress her desire for it to be more.

Now that so many years had passed, her memories of their friendship were warm and fond. She hoped he would be open to reconnecting—but what if he wasn't? What if she called him up—SURPRISE!—and he was obviously unenthused, or worse, merely polite? Ouch! That would hurt.

Ali decided to try a safer approach that required less vulnerability on her part. She would reach out to him online. Sure enough, Eric had both Facebook and LinkedIn accounts. LinkedIn seemed too business-like, so she sent him a friend request through Facebook.

"Here goes nothing," she said to herself as she clicked on Add Friend

She was a bit shocked and a great deal relieved when just a few minutes later, she received an acceptance notification! She opened the notice but there wasn't any personal note attached. *How*, she wondered, *should I interpret that? Was this just a perfunctory acceptance? Does he typically befriend anyone who asks?*

Now it seemed as if the ball was right back in her court. It was up to her to start a conversation about why she had contacted him out of the clear blue after all this time. Before she did that, she decided to dig around his personal timeline to see what information she could glean about his life.

The first surprise was that he was single. The second surprise was that he had two children, an eight-year-old girl and an eleven-year-old boy. Where was Nancy? She couldn't believe that they would have divorced. Both Eric and Nancy had been very vocal about their belief that marriage was "till death do us part."

As Ali continued scrolling back through Eric's timeline she noticed that among the various causes he supported, several were related to the eradication of pancreatic cancer. Sure enough, she soon came upon the announcement of Nancy's death five years earlier. Nancy was just thirty-six when she was diagnosed with pancreatic cancer, and succumbed to it seven months later. Their daughter was just four years old at the time; their son was seven.

Pancreatic cancer? Ali thought. *Until Steve Jobs' death, I'd rarely heard anything about it. I'll bet it's because pancreatic cancer isn't as*

"sexy" as breast cancer or as provocative as lung cancer. Come to think of it, I don't even know what function the pancreas serves!

She typed "pancreatic cancer" in her browser, clicked the entry from the *American Cancer Society: Cancer Facts & Figures*, and started reading:

- *The pancreas is a gland located deep in the abdomen between the stomach and the spine (backbone). It is about six inches long and less than two inches wide.*

- *The pancreas is really two separate glands inside the same organ. The exocrine gland makes enzymes to break down fats and proteins in foods so the body can use them. The endocrine gland makes hormones (such as insulin) that help balance the amount of sugar in the blood.*

- *Pancreatic cancer is the fourth leading cause of cancer-related death in the United States.*

- *Ninety percent of people suffering from pancreatic cancer are fifty-five years of age and older.*

- *Pancreatic cancer has the highest mortality rate of all major cancers. Ninety-four percent of pancreatic cancer patients will die within five years of diagnosis—only six percent will survive more than five years. The average life expectancy after diagnosis is just three to six months.*

- *Pancreatic cancer is one of the few cancers for which survival has not improved substantially in nearly forty years.*

- *Pancreatic cancer may cause only vague symptoms that could indicate many different conditions within the abdomen or gastrointestinal tract. Symptoms include pain (usually abdominal or back pain), weight loss, jaundice (yellowing of the skin and eyes), loss of appetite, nausea, changes in stool, and diabetes.*

- *Treatment options for pancreatic cancer are limited. Surgical removal of the tumor is possible in less than twenty percent of patients diagnosed with pancreatic cancer. Chemotherapy or chemotherapy together with radiation is typically offered to patients whose tumors cannot be removed surgically.*

Alice Ann Kuder

- *Pancreatic cancer is a leading cause of cancer death largely because there are no detection tools to diagnose the disease in its early stages when surgical removal of the tumor is still possible.*

According to these very sobering facts, Nancy was unusually young to develop this particular type of cancer.

So, Eric had been a widower for the past five years. Ali could only try to imagine the kind of inner strength it must take for him to raise two young children while mourning the loss of his soul mate.

ഇൽൽ

Ali was relaxing at Erica's Sidewalk Café on Baker Street in downtown Atlanta after an enjoyable day of sightseeing when her cell phone rang.

"Ali? Is this Ali Benevento?"

Even after all these years, Eric's voice was immediately familiar to Ali, but she didn't let on at first.

"Yes, this is Ali Benevento Berg."

"Ali, this is Eric Wicks. I hope you don't mind that I'm calling. After I got your friend request on Facebook, I had the strongest urge to talk to you, so I tracked down your cell phone number . . . which wasn't easy, by the way."

"Eric, I don't mind at all. It's good to hear your voice. How are you?"

Ali hoped this meant she would have a reason to circle one last stop on her road map.

And she had another letter to write.

"Even the smallest act of caring for another person is like a drop of water—it will make ripples throughout the entire pond."
~ *Jessy and Bryan Matteo*

Chapter 34
February 10, 2013

"Stevens Pass is an awesome ski area. It's on the crest of the Cascades and it's only a two-hour drive from Seattle. It's got more than seventeen miles of groomed cross-country ski trails, which is great for beginners like you. If you ever switch to downhill skiing, Stevens is primo for that, too. Night skiing there is a blast!"

That's what the sales associate at REI had told Curtis, and so after picking up a set of cross-country skis at the famed outdoor outfitter, today he intended to find out for himself.

Curtis was new to the sport, also known as Nordic skiing, and he purposefully chose to avoid the weekend crowds on his first time out. If he was going to embarrass himself, he preferred to do it in front of as few people as possible. He supposed that the more prudent course of action would have been to rent ski equipment until he was sure he liked the sport, but the money from his early tax return had been burning a hole in his pocket, so he decided to go for it and get his own gear.

The day before marked the fifth day in a row for measurable snowfall on the pass, bringing the snowpack up to a generous one hundred twenty-two inches. The forecast was for clear skies with the temperature threatening to reach into the mid-forties—not ideal ski conditions he'd been told—but Curtis decided to take his chances. It wasn't often that he could get a weekday off from his job at Theo Chocolate in Seattle's trendy Fremont neighborhood, and he didn't want to waste it.

Twenty-eight and single, Curtis also hoped to meet some young, attractive women today. He wasn't very good at approaching the ladies, but he hoped the ski lesson he'd signed up for would provide a natural conversation starter. Failing

Alice Ann Kuder

that, there was always the resort lodge. In the movies, ski lodges were depicted as cozy, relaxing places full of friendly-looking people chatting in front of a fireplace. Never having been in one, he wondered if that image matched reality.

He considered coaxing his younger brother into coming with him, but then dismissed the idea. His brother was six foot two, lean, and blonde with movie-star-like features. Curtis decided he didn't need that kind of competition today. It would be difficult enough to attract women when simply staying upright was likely to be a challenge.

He reached the Nordic Center by 9:15 in the morning, giving him plenty of time to get the lay of the land before the 10 o'clock beginner's class. Already hungry, he pulled out the apples and cheese he brought with him for a snack, as he wandered over to the resort directory map. He wanted to scope out the restaurants in case he met someone he wanted to invite to lunch. He was impressed by the number there were to choose from, including The Foggy Goggle, The Iron Goat Pizza Station, The Bull's Tooth Pub and Eatery, The Cascadian and several more. He made a mental note of The Iron Goat Pizza Station as a likely choice. Everyone likes pizza, he reasoned, and a full-service restaurant gives more time for conversation than a counter-service place. Then again, a pub might offer a more promising ambience.

With a solid game plan in his back pocket, Curtis headed back to his car to get his ski equipment, then over to the main lodge to join the class for his first lesson.

80CR

Three hours later, he was sitting at the bar in the Bull's Tooth Pub with the cute brunette from his class. Apparently, he hadn't made too big a fool of himself during the lesson, because she agreed to join him for lunch and now they were exchanging phone numbers. Yes, this day was going very well, and it was only half over.

Feeling quite pleased with himself, he slid behind the wheel of his car and pulled out onto Highway 2, heading west back to Seattle.

As he descended the pass, the snow that had been lightly falling at the higher elevation started to fade away, revealing a clear blue sky. By the time he passed through the town of Skykomish, a couple of miles down the highway, the roads were still wet, but mostly cleared of snow, and traffic was light. *Now this is just like in the movies,* Curtis thought, picturing himself in a long shot, enjoying a scenic drive on a curvy mountain highway.

Feeling happy and carefree, Curtis had his window rolled down and the radio turned up. His reverie was disturbed, however, when he heard a loud but indistinct noise. *Thunder?* he thought. No, it was more like an explosion. He turned down the radio, but didn't hear anything more. Then, as he rounded a curve in the road, he saw the source of the noise. It was a car accident, less than half a mile ahead. From what he could see, a semi-trailer truck had collided head-on with a Corvette. The tractor-trailer had jack-knifed across both lanes and what was left of the Corvette was wedged under the semi's front bumper. Debris from the car was strewn hundreds of feet in every direction. Curtis couldn't see the driver or any passengers. The driver of the semi stumbled out of the cab of his truck, obviously quite dazed.

Frightened and shocked by the scene in front of him, Curtis immediately pulled off to the side of the road, scrambled to find his cell phone, and dialed 911 as he whispered a prayer for whoever was in the car. Surely they would not survive.

∞∞

Within five minutes, state troopers arrived on the scene, followed by an ambulance. Five minutes after that, a medevac helicopter circled overhead, ready to transport victims to Harborview Medical Center in Seattle.

It flew away with no additional passengers.

As the officer interviewed him about what he had witnessed, Curtis could see the driver of the semi-trailer sobbing uncontrollably as the paramedics tried to both comfort him and assess his condition. He didn't seem to be

Alice Ann Kuder

seriously injured physically, but Curtis wondered if the man would ever recover psychologically from the horror of what he had experienced here today.

઼ଓଚ

There wasn't much that Curtis could tell the investigating officer. He hadn't seen the accident, only the aftermath. Still, after the officer thanked him for his help and told him he could leave, Curtis couldn't bring himself to just get in his car and drive away. He felt strangely light-headed and agitated, as if he had been in the accident himself. It didn't seem prudent to get behind the wheel feeling as he did, so he decided to leave his car on the side of the highway and take a walk down the road. By now, there were dozens of cars in line, waiting for the state patrol to open the highway again so they could pass.

Once his head felt clearer, Curtis turned around and walked back toward his car. Along the way, he noticed a small, elegant box on the side of the road. It looked strangely out of place amid the other debris. Picking it up, he noted the imprint "Ostling & Brooks." For some reason that he would never understand himself, he climbed back into his car, impulsively tossed the unopened box into his glove compartment, and drove away.

*"I slept and I dreamed that life is all joy. I woke and I saw that life
is all service. I served and I saw that service is joy."*
~ Kahlil Gibran

Chapter 35
June 16-30

"Going once. Going twice. Sold for $500!"

Ali walked into the Alliance Community Center on an eighty-two-degree June night, just as the auctioneer pounded his gavel. He had just awarded the most sought-after item of the night—twelve dozen chocolate chip cookies. These were not just any cookies. These were Sister Cele's homemade chocolate chip cookies—one dozen each month for a year.

Ali was not surprised to find her old friend and spiritual inspiration, Cele Bachman, spending a Saturday night at a community auction. Nor was she surprised that Cele's infamous baked goods commanded top dollar. As sublime as her cookies were, however, Ali had no doubt that the real reason Cele's donation was bid up so high was because of the esteem with which she was regarded. Not only did the top bidder win twelve platefuls of freshly baked heaven, they also got the pleasure of Cele's company when she hand-delivered them each month. To know her was to love her and desire to be in her presence.

The two women had met in the Bellingham, Washington, years before, but now Cele was living in DeLand, Florida— nicknamed the Athens of Florida—caring for the elderly nuns in her community. Ali and Cele had kept in loose touch over the years, with Christmas cards, birthday cards, and well-intentioned promises to get together. They had the kind of friendship that didn't depend upon frequent visits. When they did see each other, the reunion was always easy and comfortable, like slipping into a favorite pair of soft leather loafers.

Ali stood in the shadows for a while, watching her friend greet person after person with genuine delight, as if each was a long lost relative. Soon Ali's desire to claim her own hug overcame her patience, so she crossed the auditorium and tapped Cele on the shoulder. True to her nature, Cele's face revealed authentic joy when she turned and saw Ali.

"Ali! You're here!" Cele exclaimed as she embraced her old friend. "How was the drive? Are you terribly exhausted?"

It was after 9 p.m. and Ali had been driving all day.

"The trip has been incredible. I'm so glad to be here with you, and I don't mind admitting that yes, I am dog-tired."

"Well, then, let me take you home and get you settled into my guest room. It seems like ages since I last saw you. I've managed to keep my whole day free tomorrow, so we'll have plenty of time to visit after you get a good night's sleep."

"Speaking of being dog-tired, I think I forgot to tell you that I have a traveling companion. Come out to my car and meet Tess."

ഏറ

The next morning, Ali woke to the smell of coffee and bacon. She followed her nose to the kitchen where Cele was serving up breakfast. Tess was already enjoying a bowl of kibble.

Cele greeted her with a smile. "I hope you like scrambled eggs and toast, because that's about the only thing I know how to cook. You can't believe how excited I was when I discovered that you can cook bacon in the microwave! I never could fry it on the stovetop without burning it beyond recognition. Even friends who claimed they like their bacon crispy wouldn't eat mine."

"I do seem to recall the day I discovered that the recipe for your famously delicious chocolate chip cookies is the *only* one in your recipe box!"

"What recipe box?" Cele asked, as both women laughed.

ഏറ

After a long catching-up session over a leisurely breakfast, the pair planned the rest of their day.

"Since you've never been to DeLand before, I thought you

might like a tour of the area," Cele offered.

"I really would. The only thing I know about DeLand is that it's supposed to be a nice place to retire."

"Not just a nice place, but one of the *top* retirement destinations in the entire country according to an article in *Where to Retire Magazine*!"

"Are you telling me there is an entire monthly magazine dedicated to the topic of 'where to retire'?" Ali asked in mock amazement.

"You'd better believe it. Retirement is big business. There's more to DeLand than just retirement living, though. The city has an interesting history in that the founder, Henry A. DeLand, actually had a vision and a plan for the city from the very start. He quite intentionally modeled it after the ancient Greek city of Athens. He wanted a city named after him that would be the cultural, educational, and spiritual fulcrum for this part of Florida. And Mr. DeLand wanted the city to be aesthetically pleasing as well."

"So, do you think he was successful?"

"To a large degree, yes, I do. The city is home to Stetson University, which furthers the educational goal. The Museum of Florida Art, the African-American Museum of the Arts, and the Florida Museum for Women Artists all vouch for the intrinsic cultural value of artwork. Then there's the Sculpture Walk, which makes art available in public places, *and* DeLand hosts two major outdoor art festivals each year, featuring literally hundreds of artists from around the country. Add in the Athens Theater, which is a beautiful example of Italian Renaissance architecture, and you have a pretty convincing argument for a citywide commitment to honoring the arts.

"Is that all there is to do in DeLand?" Ali teased. "Seriously, though, that's an impressive legacy. I'm sure Henry DeLand is smiling down on the city with great pride from his perch behind the Pearly Gates."

∽✧⌁

The pair had a wonderful time experiencing the city together, and Ali realized how much she missed her old friend.

The next time Cele went to bake cookies, she found Ali's letter taped to her cookie sheet.

Dear Cele,

I have decided to petition the Holy Father to name you Patron Saint of Chocolate Chip Cookies, because I'm pretty sure yours have been the source of at least a few miracles.

As far as I know, there have not been any actual polls conducted, but I suspect that the common chocolate chip cookie is easily America's all-time favorite. Having perfected the recipe, however, you have elevated it to the equivalent of manna from heaven. Over the years the cookies you so lovingly prepare and generously give away have warmed hearts, vanquished tears, broadened smiles, and expanded waistlines.

Why, you might wonder, am I carrying on so about your cookies? Well, I'm using the cookies as a metaphor because I want to express my esteem for you and I have a hunch you will be more comfortable accepting praise for your cookies.

Like your cookies, you are unpretentious yet extraordinary, and always a welcome sight.

I don't recall when we first met, but I do remember that we got to know each other when we were both volunteering for the Bellingham Food Bank. I was in my last year of college at WWU, and ready to play Nurse Nightingale to all of society's ills. I took on what I considered to be the heavy lifting of running the food bank, such as recruiting and scheduling volunteers, arranging food pick-ups, organizing fundraiser events, etc. I was very efficient and effective at those essential organizational tasks, but I felt somewhat disconnected from the people we served. Then one day, I came out of the back office to get a cup of coffee and overheard a conversation you were having with one of the guests, punctuated with your familiar laughter. I don't remember what was said, but I do remember your demeanor and the way our guest responded to you. I'm sure she felt what I observed, which was a singular degree of attention and respect. I realized that although I was ensuring that bodies got fed, you were seeing to it that souls got fed as well. It reminded me of a lyric from the song "Bread and Roses" sung by Judy Collins: "Hearts starve as well as bodies; Give us bread, but give us roses."

Since that day, I have been in awe of your character. You embody so many of the positive traits to which I aspire. Day-to-day and moment-to-moment, you exhibit uncommon levels of acceptance, gratitude, and humility in your interactions with everyone you encounter. It seems to me that serving others only makes you a stronger and happier person.

We all know people who seem to suck the air from a room, depriving others of oxygen. You breathe it back in. When you enter a room, you imbue it with a sense of calmness and balance. You are like a gentle breeze that wafts through a field of wheat, creating beautiful ripples without harming the grain.

I have watched you over the years, offering yourself in one form of ministry or another. You never complain, you never criticize, you never fail to recognize the blessings of your circumstances.

If I were a sculptor, I would carve a statue of

Alice Ann Kuder

you with open hands, palms reaching skyward to offer up whatever you have and accept whatever God chooses to give you.

You epitomize one of my favorite quotes from Maya Angelou: "I've learned that people will forget what you said, people will forget what you did, but people will never forget how you made them feel."

Throughout the days, months, and years of our friendship, you have always made me feel valued and appreciated. I hope this letter does the same for you.

Until forever,

Ali

"Hope is the dream of a waking man." ~ *Aristotle*

Chapter 36
July 1-15, 2013

Mobile, Alabama, wasn't a city that Ali had ever imagined visiting. It's not that she'd purposely steered clear of it, she'd just never had a reason to consider it before. She realized that she knew nothing about it, really, other than the tales of racial strife back in the sixties, which had undoubtedly skewed her perception. She was about to find out what the city was really like, as she delivered a letter to another of her Georges, Rochelle Bremmer.

❧❧

Ali arrived in Mobile on July 1st, anxious to escape the ninety-one degree heat and check into The Kate Shepard House in midtown Mobile—another wonderfully unique, vintage home, transformed into an inn. Earlier, when scouting pet-friendly B&Bs online, she saw the photograph of The Kate Shepard House owners, Bill and Wendy James, posed with their Chow Chow, Koa Bear. *If this place isn't pet-friendly,* she thought, *no place is.*

Originally built in 1897, it was incredibly ornate, as befits a Queen Anne style Victorian home. Ali knew she was likely to spend several hours happily examining all the intricate features. Then, there was the added bonus of a treasure trove of historical documents that the James's had discovered in the attic when they purchased the home. Most were dated from the 1800s, and the collection included rare Civil War documents. All were on display in the library for guests to peruse at their leisure.

When she drove up, Ali saw that the inn was surrounded by magnificent Magnolia trees, which she would later learn were over one hundred years old. And she could see Koa Bear, along with a couple of unidentified canine friends, looking out the window, ready to greet her and Tess. She also noticed a nearby street sign pointing the way to the Old Dauphin Way Historic District she had read about online and confirming that the inn was well located for sightseeing.

When Ali asked Bill and Wendy for suggestions about "must see" sights, they told her that the Bellingrath Gardens were absolutely breathtaking. And no visitor, they said, should pass up the opportunity to tour the USS Alabama, the keystone of Mobile's one hundred seventy-five acre Battleship Memorial Park.

As interesting as these attractions sounded, they would all have to wait until Ali had a chance to visit with her old friend, Rochelle.

∽◌◌∾

"Ali! You made it!" Rochelle said as she ushered her friend through the door of her screened porch.

"I sure did, safe and sound. Could you please turn down the heat and humidity a little, though?" Ali teased.

"Hmmm. It's early afternoon in July in Mobile, Alabama. I'll see what I can do. I'm on a first-name basis with Jesus, but I try not to bother him with the little stuff."

Rochelle hugged her long-lost friend and then pointed toward the porch swing where Ali happily took a seat.

"Now, if you offer me a mint julep, my fantasy about lazy southern afternoons will be complete," Ali said. "I have no idea what's in a mint julep, but they must be good."

"Sorry, I'm fresh out of julep. How about some sweet tea with a little mint or lemon instead? That's a traditional southern beverage, too."

"Sounds perfect! I'll try the mint, please."

A few minutes later, Rochelle emerged from the house with two glasses of sweet tea and a three-year-old holding onto her skirt.

"Ali, I would like you to meet Leann. Leann, this is my friend, Ali."

A minute later, Rochelle's mother-in-law came out from inside the house. After a quick introduction, she made her apologies for having to rush off.

The next two hours flew by as the women filled each other in on the events of the years since they had last been together.

During a break in the conversation, Rochelle observed, "It looks to me like someone is ready for her nap."

"Do you mean me, or Leann?" Ali said as Leann rubbed her eyes and yawned.

Rochelle chuckled, "I meant Leann, but I wouldn't mind one myself."

Ali lit up, as if with a great idea. "Why don't you?"

"Why don't I what?"

"Why don't you go in and take a nap? It'll be my gift to you, assuming it's okay with you that I stick around for a couple more hours? I'll be happy to stand guard in case Leann wakes up before you do."

"Sweet Lord, I can't remember the last time I got to take a nap in the middle of the day. That sounds like a little slice of heaven! But I can't leave my guest to fend for herself! Won't you be bored?"

"Not at all. I've got my laptop with me, and a good book. It'll be nice for me, too."

"In that case, I've offered you your last out. I gratefully accept . . . as long as you agree to stay for supper. Terrance should be home around 5:30. I can't wait for you to meet him."

⊰⊱

Rochelle was a terrific cook. She whipped up a traditional southern meal while she and Ali visited some more. Just as they were setting the table, Rochelle's husband, Terrance, walked in the door. Once the introductions were done, they all sat down and enjoyed the fruits—and fried chicken, and collard greens—of Rochelle's labor.

As she was leaving to go back to Kate Shepard House, Ali turned to Rochelle and said, "I can't imagine a more perfect day. I hope I'll get to see a lot more of you while I'm in town.

"By the way, I left a little something for you on the night stand in Leann's room when I said good-night to her. I hope it makes you smile."

Dear Rochelle,

Of all the people I know, you may be the most courageous, and my greatest source of hope.

I remember the day we met. It was my first day on the job at the West Seattle PCC. We were both in our early twenties. You had been working there for a couple of years as a checker and I had just been promoted and transferred from the Greenlake store. I was so nervous . . . both about the transfer and the promotion. As I was about to begin my shift, you pulled me aside and said, 'Welcome aboard. You're gonna love it here.'

Those few, simple words sounded like both a promise and a prediction to me, and you seemed to make it your personal mission to see to it that they came true. As far as I was concerned, our fate as friends was sealed then and there.

As I got to know you over the next few months, I realized how little we had in common and discovered that it didn't matter one bit. You were raised in the deep South; I was raised in the Pacific Northwest. You came from an urban-dwelling family of seven; I came from a suburban family of five. You were raised Baptist; I was raised Catholic. You were married; I was single. The list of contrasts went on and on.

Certainly, our experiences play a strong part in shaping and defining us. They are not, however, the last word in forming our character. Character, I believe, comes from within us. And it was your strength of character that drew me to you.

That became really clear to me when you confided in me about your husband's gambling addiction.

He was a good man, you said, and you loved him beyond all reason. His addiction hadn't surfaced until after you'd married. Now it was slowly and relentlessly eroding your chances of building the life you wanted to have together. But hope dies slowly, you told me, especially when you love and believe in someone. You had already spent years hoping that Clayton would change . . . that he would somehow beat his addiction and return to being the man you married. Instead, his uncontrollable gambling got you deeper and deeper in debt. You had no hope of buying a home because your credit rating was so poor. You owed back rent and feared that you'd both end up living in your car. Your job at PCC and the benefits it provided were your best chance at salvation.

Knowing how much you and Clayton both loved and wanted children, I wondered why you hadn't started a family. You said that your last hope of convincing Clayton to get help was to refuse to bring children into the marriage until he got his problem under control. Even that threat wasn't effective. Still, you just couldn't give up hope that he would change. Hope, which had appeared to be a lifeboat, was instead creating an undertow, ensuring that you would eventually drown. As your friend, it was a very painful process to watch.

As if your life wasn't difficult enough already, that's when you slipped on the ice in front of your home and fell. Fortunately, you had excellent

Alice Ann Kuder

health insurance through PCC, but the medical bills weren't your main concern once the doctors told you your prognosis. The damage to your spine had paralyzed you. The doctors said there was very little hope that you would ever walk again.

You refused to accept their medical conclusions. "There's always hope," you said. "Hope is the first step toward faith, and faith makes all things possible. I could see that you believed what you were saying. So much so, that you made me believe it, too. I listened to the doctors and I read the statistics that formed the basis for their prognosis. Then, I looked in your eyes and I knew they were wrong; just as you knew it.

Two years later you walked down the aisle ahead of me as my bridesmaid. That tiny seed of hope that you nurtured within yourself eventually culminated in what some might call a miracle.

Later, you told me that the lengthy recovery time after your accident had brought about another unexpected and positive miracle of its own. It gave you the perspective you needed to honestly evaluate your life. You realized that it was time to give up the illusion that Clayton would change, and you left your marriage.

It was only after you moved to Mobile, and we lost touch, that I realized how much I'd learned from you about the role that hope plays in our lives. It seems to me that hope is a double-edged sword that one must wield with care. In your relationship with Clayton, holding onto hope became a destructive force, yet in your recovery from the accident, holding onto it was your saving *grace. That's quite a paradox. I find myself trying to understand the nuances of hope, and how it figures into in my own life and healing.*

It's so wonderful to know that you are happy, healthy, and enjoying life as a wife and mother. You deserve every moment of happiness you can squeeze out of the new life you've built for yourself.

Thank you for showing me that having the courage to hope can bring about miracles.

Your friend until forever,

Ali

ଈଓଔ

Later that week, Rochelle and Ali dropped Leann off at her grandmother's house for a visit while they strolled through the Old Dauphin Way Historic District. Rochelle loved window-shopping. Having Ali along for company was a special bonus.

Ali was telling Rochelle all about her flat tire episode when suddenly, she stopped short. They were standing in front of the Crescent Theater on Dauphin Street where a line was forming for the next showing of *Superman Man of Steel.*

Ali had an idea. She turned to Rochelle and said, "I hear this is a fabulous movie theater. Do you want to go in and see the movie?"

Screwing up her face, Rochelle looked at Ali and said, "Not really. Do you?"

"No, not me either," Ali said, then paused. "I know this probably seems strange, but will you please wait here while I talk to the ticket taker for a minute?"

"You're right. That does seem strange since we're not going to see the movie, but sure, I'll wait."

Ali waited in the short line, walked up to the ticket booth, pulled out her credit card and handed it to the ticket taker. A minute later, she was back with Rochelle and they continued down the street with no particular destination in mind.

The ticket taker called out, "Next!"

Two teenagers stepped up to the window and were handed tickets.

With a shocked look on their faces, one of them said, "But we haven't paid you yet!"

"You don't need to," said the ticket taker. "The woman who just left paid for ten general admission tickets and said to give them to the next ten people in line. You're numbers one and two. Enjoy the movie!"

"When a tree falls it resounds with a thundering crash; and yet a whole forest grows in silence." ~ *Jocelyn Murray*

Chapter 37
February 10, 2012

Ali had barely arrived at the Greenlake store when her cell phone rang on that February afternoon. Her phone didn't identify the caller, so she hesitated before answering—she guessed it was probably a wine rep hoping to sell her their latest vintage. As a wine buyer, she fielded several such calls each week. But this time, the caller wasn't a salesperson—it was Officer Charles Braden from the office of the Washington State Patrol.

Officer Braden had been on the job for nine years. Of all the duties he performed, this was by far the worst. There was simply no good way to inform someone that their loved one had been killed. He had witnessed every conceivable reaction from denial to disbelief, and from silence to screaming. There was no way to predict how an individual would behave when given such horrific news, and there was no single response he could offer that was guaranteed to provide comfort.

When the officer identified himself, Ali was suddenly gripped by fear. Her stomach convulsed even before he told her about the car accident near Stevens Pass. Two of the victims—*victims*, that word sent an immediate wave of panic through Ali's mind and body—had been identified as Isaac and Zoe Berg. The information the state trooper found in Isaac's wallet listed Ali as their emergency contact.

For the next few minutes Ali struggled to make sense of what Officer Braden was saying. He had to be mistaken. For one thing, this was a school day. Zoe should be getting on the school bus to come home right about now. Yes, Isaac sometimes took Fridays off, but what would he and Zoe be doing near Stevens Pass? Officer Baden had to be mistaken. But he wasn't.

₮℞

Over the next few days, Ali got answers to some of her questions. Others remained a mystery. The most puzzling of all was why Isaac and Zoe were on that road at all? The officer said they had spent time in Leavenworth that morning and were apparently headed back home, but the purpose of their brief visit was still an enigma. Why would they drive from Seattle to Leavenworth and back again in a single day?

ॐ

Ali couldn't bear to see the aftermath of the crash, even in police photos. Officers told her the impact was head-on and that wreckage was strewn along the highway for hundreds of yards. Isaac and Zoe were dead when officers arrived at the scene, apparently killed on impact. Ali found comfort—minimal as it was—in knowing that they didn't suffer.

The driver of the semi survived physically, but his emotional state was by all accounts, shattered. Being cleared of responsibility for the fatal crash did little to ease his torment. He told the officers that the driver of the car seemed to be looking down at the time he veered into oncoming traffic. The police investigation confirmed that Isaac had been using his cell phone just before impact. This created yet another riddle for Ali, because of their sacrosanct family rule about abstaining from cell phone use while driving. She might have been able to understand his transgression if he had been traveling alone, but it was incomprehensible to her that he would have answered a text with their daughter sitting right next to him in the car.

Chapter 38
August 15-September 5, 2013

When originally plotting her cross-country course, Ali purposely avoided most of the larger cities in favor of smaller towns because she wanted to return home having experienced "true Americana." She wasn't afraid to abandon the major highways in order to take Robert Frost's lead and explore the roads less traveled by. And rather than just flit through these cities, she planned to spend an average of two weeks in each one. Friends warned her that she may die of boredom along the way. What, they wondered, would she find to do in these little burgs where she knew no one?

Ferreting out historical Bed and Breakfast inns in the cities along her route became an obsession for Ali. Sometimes she had to grease a palm or two to get owners to allow Tess to stay, but having her dedicated canine companion was well worth it. Typically, the B&B owners delighted in telling Ali all about the history of their city and loved helping her create an itinerary for her stay.

As she headed west from Mobile, her latest find was the Walnut Grove Bed and Breakfast in Vernon, Texas, one of several non-George stops on her road trip. Owners John and Jean Moore had restored the house and then opened it as a Bed and Breakfast in 2005—one hundred years after it was originally built. And, it really was nestled in a grove of walnut trees.

Ali and Tess stayed in the Countryside Room, which was decorated in a hunting and fishing motif. Ali couldn't decide which antique furnishing she coveted most. If it weren't August, the rocking chair might have had a slight edge over the brass bedframe only because of its position in front of the wood burning fireplace.

At least one handmade quilt graced each guest room. Many of the designs were incredibly intricate, and the colors ran the gamut from subtle to bold. The quilts made Ali wish the weather were cooler so she could snuggle up beneath one. But even without the coziness of a quilt, she and Tess both slept soundly in their well-appointed accommodations at the Walnut Grove.

৪০৩

After two weeks in the relative calm of Vernon, Ali was ready to experience the much faster pace of life in Albuquerque, New Mexico. She arrived on the evening of August 15th, anxious to reunite with her childhood friend, Janie Hargrove. They hadn't seen each other since their graduation from Mount Vernon High School. Unbeknownst to either of them, the two had lived less than twenty miles from one another much of their adult lives. It was thanks to the powerful tentacles of Facebook—*after* Janie had moved fourteen hundred miles away—that they reconnected all these years later.

After hugs and a few tears, Janie led Ali out onto the patio so they could enjoy the evening air while they got caught up and planned their time together. "So, what would you like to see first?" Janie asked, referring to the list of Albuquerque attractions she had compiled for Ali.

"Old Town Plaza looks like it has a little of everything."

"Good choice. I never get tired of going there. We can start at its heart, with a visit to San Felipe de Neri Church!

৪০৩

The next morning, Ali and Janie arrived at the two-hundred-twenty-year-old church just as the daily Spanish Mass was letting out.

"Are you interested in hearing about the church's history?" Janie asked.

"Of course," Ali answered honestly.

"Good, because I like telling it!"

The two slipped into the church, and took a seat in a back pew as they continued to chat.

"San Felipe is the oldest operating Spanish mission church

on the North American continent. It was established by a Franciscan priest and about thirty families from nearby Bernalillo way back in 1703. The original name was San Francisco Xavier, but it got changed by the Duke of Alburquerque. Albuquerque, by the way, was spelled Alburquerque back then. Someone wisely vanquished the extra "r" at some point . . . not that it's much easier to spell, even without it!"

"Albuquerque had a Duke?"

"Oh, yes. From the Spanish conquest and all that. The city was named after him. That's where Albuquerque gets the nickname 'The Duke City.' I'm not sure when the last Duke disappeared from the picture.

"Anyway, the original church building was destroyed by heavy rains in 1792, and rebuilt in 1793. The "new" walls are five feet thick—they weren't taking any chances. Over the years, they've remodeled and enlarged the buildings. The towers, for instance, were added around the time of the Civil War. For the most part, though, they've retained the character, and certainly the purpose."

Ali got up and wandered around the mission, admiring the simple, traditional architecture, statues of the saints, Stations of the Cross, and general ornamentation.

When she returned to where Janie was sitting, she changed the direction of their conversation.

"What made you decide to move to the Southwest, Janie? It's a pretty drastic change from the Pacific Northwest."

"That was the point. After Peter died in the car wreck, Rob and I and our other kids—Quincy and Avery—drifted for quite a while. That's the best way I can think of to describe it. Or maybe 'drowning' is a better word. Yes, we were drowning. Drowning in a sea of 'what now?'

"We each dealt with the loss in our own way, but I think it's fair to say that life seemed pretty surreal to all of us. Well, you know how it feels."

"Yeah, I do. 'Surreal' is a pretty accurate description of my experience, too," Ali agreed.

"We were living in Kirkland at the time. Rob and I had just started a new import-export business about five months before

Alice Ann Kuder

the accident. It was a big financial risk for both of us to leave our old jobs with their steady incomes, but it required very little start-up capital. Of course, any new business needs an incredible amount of time, love, and attention to get off the ground. I think we had a pretty solid business plan, including savings in the bank to tide us over until it started generating a profit. We were really excited about it and the outlook was very promising.

"Then, when the car accident happened and Peter died . . . well, it just knocked the wind out of our sails. It was as if all the energy we were devoting to getting the business up and running got sucked up in a vortex of emotions that threatened our very survival. Just getting through one day to another took all the strength we had. There was nothing left to devote to the business, and within a few months, it failed. Or more accurately, we failed to keep it going. It just didn't feel as important as dealing with our grief.

"About that time, Rob got a call from a headhunter who was looking for someone with his skills and experience for a high-paying position with Management Recruiters of Albuquerque. The funny thing is, Rob had gotten similar calls over the years for even better jobs, and we never seriously considered any of them because we didn't want to move.

"This time, we gave it some real thought. That's when we sat down as a family and discussed our options.

"At first, the kids were against it. They didn't want to leave their friends and have to start at a new school, which was understandable and not at all surprising. We promised the kids that we wouldn't make the move if they were strongly against it, so we dropped the subject.

"A couple of days later at the dinner table, Quincy, our oldest, put down her fork and said she'd like to talk some more about moving. After *lots* more discussion, we all agreed that a fresh start in new surroundings might be just what we needed. From there, things just started to fall into place. We moved to Albuquerque three months later."

"It seems like it was a good decision for you."

"It really was. It wasn't easy, of course, but it got us out of survival mode and into . . . well, I don't know what kind of mode it got us into, but it forced us to focus and redirect our energy in a positive way."

Ali reached over and gave Janie a long hug.

Sensing that it was time to shift to a more upbeat line of conversation, Ali said, "I don't know about you, but I'm hungry. Where do you suggest we go for lunch?"

"Saggios is my favorite pizzeria in all of Albuquerque. The food is fantastic and the atmosphere is hip and party-like. Of course, the décor might make you think you're on an acid trip, but that just adds to the fun. *And*, it's family-owned and operated." Janie loved turning visitors on to truly unique, local businesses.

"Sounds good to me. Is it close by?" asked Ali.

"Very. It's in the UNM District. We can work off our lunch afterwards with a walking tour of the campus."

"UNM?" Ali asked.

"Sorry, the University of New Mexico," Janie clarified.

"Oh, of course. What about seeing the rest of Old Town?"

"You're going to be here for two weeks, right? We'll save it for another day. Tomorrow, I thought we'd go tour Casa Rondena Winery."

"You read my mind."

❧

"Here's the thermostat that controls the air conditioning in this room. Sorry we don't have a separate guest bathroom. The kids are pretty considerate about getting in and out when we have company, though. Here are clean towels for you. Feel free to sleep in or get up early. We're flexible around here, especially in the summer.

"I think that's about it," she said with a smile. "Sleep well so we can play hard tomorrow!"

"Thanks for offering to let Tess and me stay here with you for a few days," Ali said, gratefully. It's a nice change from hotels and inns—even the nice ones we've been fortunate enough to stay in. Sometimes I miss a real home.

Ali took hold of her friend's hand and said, "Janie, before you go off to bed, I have something I want to give you."

"You do? I can't imagine what."

Ali turned to get the envelope out of her suitcase and handed it to Janie.

"It's just a letter I wrote to you a few months ago, thanking you for being such a good friend. Even though we lost touch for a lot of years, I consider you to be a very special . . . a very *inspirational* person. I'm grateful for all you've taught me about life and death and love and acceptance. That's the real reason for my visit. I wanted to go on record as someone who recognizes and appreciates what a remarkable person you are."

Janie didn't say anything at first. As she took the letter, Ali thought she detected the glint of tears.

Finally, Janie chuckled softly and said, "Ali, I appreciate all the compliments, but I would have let you stay here for free anyway."

 හ◌ශ

Dear Janie,

Can it really be twenty-five years since I last saw you? How is it then, that I can still see your smiling face and hear your easy laughter as clearly as if we had just left each others' company? When I think of all the other people I have known <u>and forgotten</u> in those same twenty-five years, I remember you because of the aura of joy you generate.

I'm not sure how to explain that without making you sound like some sort of perfect angel, which would be quite unfair to you. Surely it can't be difficult for an angel to be joyful, can it? It's much more of an accomplishment for us humans, and you are wonderfully human. As I recall from our grade school days, you were more impish than angelic! Angels (I suspect) are rather boring. Imps are much more fun.

We must have been about 9 when we met. My parents had just made the painful decision (for financial reasons) to take me out of Catholic school and enroll me in public school. I was timid and frightened and felt like an outsider. I expected my new classmates to reject me, and many of them did. Then there were those special few (you, Carol, Kari) who accepted me immediately and offered your friendship without hesitation. To a 9-year-old, that kind of acceptance was a lifeline. I'm sure that experience made me a much more compassionate and empathetic person than I might otherwise have been. Over the years I have tried to pay forward the kindness you extended to me.

That's one aspect of acceptance I experienced from you. Now, all these years later, you are teaching me another lesson in acceptance. If there is one thing I never wanted to share with you or anyone, it's the experience of losing a child. I know that your precious boy, Peter, died in a car accident a few years ago. I lost my daughter, Zoe, the same way a little over a year ago. Although you and I weren't part of each other's lives when your son died, I find hope in seeing the acceptance you have achieved over time.

Surely there is no greater pain a person can be expected to endure than to outlive their own child. The very notion makes one want to storm heaven's gate and demand the undoing of such a terrible wrong.

I have always regarded acceptance as being a virtue, a quality to be desired and nurtured. When Zoe and Isaac died, well-meaning friends told me I would learn to accept it in time. How I

Alice Ann Kuder

hated hearing that! Suddenly, acceptance felt like a bad thing. It felt like giving up and giving in. Accepting their deaths seemed like the equivalent of saying it was okay that they were gone. As irrational as I knew it was, I felt that if I refused to accept this tragedy, then God might somehow relent and send them back to me. God would <u>have</u> to send them back to me.

I didn't want any part of acceptance. Acceptance was not an option to consider, let alone something to be sought after.

I am so grateful that you called me when you heard about my loss. I went to a survivor group after the accident, and it helped a bit, but there was something profound about sharing the experience with someone I knew when we were both children ourselves. I can't really explain that either, but I feel it. You told me I would survive this. I must confess that I didn't believe you. I didn't <u>want</u> to believe you, but I knew you were telling me the truth.

Now that some time has passed and I have begun to heal, I am struck by the relationship between faith and acceptance. It seems to me that if they are not actually one and the same, then surely faith is the midwife of acceptance.

I realize that some parents literally do *not* survive the death of a child. Some are so overcome by despair that they are not able to give their faith time to emerge and evolve into acceptance. I am thankful that you and I were not among them.

I have never thought of myself as possessing great faith, but Jesus assured us that even faith "the size of a mustard seed" is sufficient. I suspect I am living proof of that.

Seeing your faith and your acceptance was a gift to me. You made me believe I could get there, too. I want you to know that and to feel that.

I will be grateful for your loving lessons in acceptance . . .

Until forever,

Ali

೧೧೧

"It's so great that you came to Albuquerque in August when the weather is really at its best," Janie said.

"It was a fortunate coincidence," replied Ali. "Like I told you, I knew nothing about Albuquerque—or the Southwest for that matter—before this. I had the impression it was all endless desert with year-round sweltering heat! When my plans put me here in New Mexico in August, I was afraid it would be too hot to enjoy. The July monsoon rains you describe were a surprise, too. I heard there was a flash flood warning the day I drove into town, but apparently it was a false alarm. And I was shocked to hear that you get snow in the winter and the temperature gets down to zero!"

"All true, however, today should be a perfect day to tour the winery. It's such a beautiful place and *really* popular for weddings. In fact, they have three separate spaces on the grounds that they use for events; I've been to weddings in all three and I can't decide which I like the best.

"Their wine club hosts some really nice events, too. I realize, though, that you've toured wineries and vineyards all over Europe for your job. I hope this won't pale in comparison."

As they approached the hacienda style building with its distinctive green tile roof, Ali assured her, "If the architecture alone is any indication, I can already tell that it won't disappoint."

Janie's prediction for perfect weather proved true. In Camelot-like fashion, it rained the night before. Now a cooling breeze complimented the eighty-five degree temperature for their stroll among the grapevines. The pleasant setting gave Janie the courage to broach the subject of Ali's loss.

"Ali, we've talked about me and my family and how Peter's death affected us. How are you holding up under the weight of your loss? I can't imagine how different it would have been for me if I had lost Rob at the same time . . . especially if Peter had been my only child."

Ali took a deep breath and held it for a moment before exhaling slowly. When she didn't say anything, Janie reached over and grasped her friend's hand as they continued walking together in silence.

"I don't know quite how to answer your question, Janie. I'm sure you know the feeling. I've been through so many different phases and moods over the past year and a half. Right now—today—I feel pretty strong. The trip has definitely been a positive experience for me. I guess, in a way, it's similar to your moving to a new city, just not as permanent. I've gained some much-needed perspective by traveling to unfamiliar places, and staying in each one for a couple of weeks was surprisingly restful. Having Tess along has been a godsend; she's such a comfort. People who don't have pets just don't know how much love they're denying themselves."

"I couldn't agree more. I never really wanted a pet, but Quincy started asking for a dog as soon as she could pronounce the word. We didn't give in until we moved here. Now, I can't image life without our little wire-haired terrier, Homer."

Noticing how Ali had shifted the direction of the conversation, Janie decided not to press her friend to talk about her heartache any further.

Even with the breeze, the heat of the afternoon sun began getting as intense as the discussion had been, so the women turned around and headed to the tasting room.

ৠ০ৎ

The two friends bellied up to the bar, anxious to try the wares. Ali first sampled the 2008 Meritage, reading the description aloud to Janie. "This classic Bordeaux-style wine is a blend of forty-eight percent Merlot, thirty percent Cabernet Franc, twenty percent Cabernet Sauvignon and two percent Petit Verdot. Complex with a lingering finish, the Meritage Red shows flavors of vanilla, currant, blackberry, and chocolate."

"Sounds delish, but I tend to prefer white wines, so I'm starting with the 2012 Viognier." Janie picked up the bottle and attempted to take on the tone of a stuffy sommelier as she read aloud, "'A dry white wine with dense flavors of pineapple and honey, Viognier is the perfect expression of the Southwestern high-desert growing region showing its rich mouth feel and crispy acidity.'" Chuckling, the friends clinked glasses and sipped appreciatively.

After sampling the winery's 2009 Cabernet Franc, 2006 Animante, and 2009, 1629, Ali pronounced herself quite impressed and gave the winery high marks.

ৠ০ৎ

"Janie, I'm so impressed by all that Albuquerque has to offer! I'm having a ball!"

"I'm enjoying every minute of it, too. You know how it is. Sometimes you take for granted all the fun stuff in your own backyard and only make time to see it when guests come to town. What's been your favorite thing so far?"

"Oh, don't make me choose! I couldn't spend enough time in Old Town, but I really got a kick out of the balloon museum—I'd love to come back when the International Balloon Festival is going on, and maybe even go for a ride. And of course, the winery was awesome, even if it was a bit of a busman's holiday.

"Then again, we aren't even halfway through the BioPark yet, and I'm loving it. Somebody had a great idea with this train system. Zoe would have absolutely adored touring the zoo aboard a train."

Alice Ann Kuder

"So would Peter. What is it about trains that's so appealing?"

"I don't know. There's something very romantic about them, though. I don't think I've ever met anyone who didn't like the idea of traveling by train."

Ali suddenly got quiet for a moment before turning to face her friend. "Janie, this may seem like a strange question, but mentioning the kids just now made me think of it. Have you ever noticed that there's no name for people like us?"

"People like us?" Janie asked.

"Uh-huh. Parents who've buried a child. I mean, people refer to me as a 'widow' because my spouse died, which is accurate—but that's not all I am. I find it strange that there's no equivalent term to describe my 'status'—for lack of a better word—as a parent who has survived her child."

"Surprisingly enough, now that you mention it, that never occurred to me. It does seem kind of odd. I wonder if other cultures have a word for it?"

"That's a good question," said Ali.

"You've obviously given this some thought. Do you have any theories about why it's not in our English lexicon?" Janie asked.

"Actually, I do. I suspect it's because no one wants to think about the possibility of it happening to *them*. Once you name something, it becomes more real. I suppose that subconsciously, we think that if we don't put a name to the experience of outliving our child, it won't happen to us."

"If only that were the case," Janie said wistfully. "You know, I'll bet that at least some of the Native American tribes have a term for it."

"You're probably right. I don't know much about their languages, but if, the movie *Dances with Wolves* was at all true-to-life, their monikers seem pretty descriptive."

"If they do have a name for it," Janie said, "it's probably something like 'better her than me'."

∞⊗

Returning from an early morning walk together with Tess

and Homer, Janie and Ali poured themselves tall glasses of iced tea and sauntered onto the patio. Bypassing the unlit beehive-shaped kiva fireplace, they sank gratefully into their favorite lounge chairs.

"I must say, Janie, these past ten days here in Albuquerque have been some of the most relaxing and *exhausting* of my entire road trip! I'm so lucky and grateful that you've been able—and *willing*—to spend so much time with me. By the way, remind me to thank Rob and your kids for sharing you with me. Getting to know them just a little bit, and getting to know you all over again . . . well, it makes me regret that we ever lost touch. Let's not let it happen again."

"I feel the same way, Ali. It's been a real treat. I guess one of the benefits of getting older is learning to recognize what's really important in life, and spending time with friends certainly ranks very near the top of the list. You know, though, as much as we've seen and done, there's at least one more place I wish I could take you while you're in Albuquerque," Janie said.

"Really? I can't imagine what's left!"

"Sandia Amphitheater."

"Oh. I've heard of it. It's supposed to be an exceptional concert hall."

"It really is. Rob and I have seen a number of big-name performers there. Donna Summer, Elton John and James Taylor, were some of our favorites. It's a fabulous open-air venue with a really cozy, casual feel to it, unlike a lot of stadium-style concert halls. And the stage is flanked by these huge fountains with pastel-colored lights that shine from their bases into the star-pocked night sky. When the breeze catches the mist and sends it into the stands, the sensation is just heavenly; especially at the end of a hot summer day."

"It sounds amazing! No wonder the amphitheater was on the 'not-to-be-missed' list you made for me," Ali said coyly. "In fact, you were so convincing that I was determined to see a concert there, so I conspired with Rob and bought five tickets to the Keith Urban/Little Big Town/Dustin Lynch show on August 28th. I don't suppose you'd like to go?"

"Oh my God! You're kidding? Rob was supposed to buy us tickets, but he said they were all sold out before he could get them."

"Yeah, sorry about getting your husband to lie to you, but I really wanted it to be a surprise. I also had him check your calendar to make sure you didn't have anything scheduled that night. But I figured that even if you did schedule something later, chances were good that you'd be willing to cancel whatever it was."

"You say you bought five tickets?"

"Of course. You, me, Rob, Quincy, and Avery. You don't think I'd leave your kids out, do you?"

"Ali, if you tell anyone I said this, I'll deny it, but you just bumped my mother from the top of my 'best-guest-ever' list."

Chapter 39
October 1-30, 2013

On the one hand, the five hundred seventy-six miles between Battle Mountain, Nevada, and Beaverton, Oregon seemed interminably long to Ali. On the other hand, they seemed to fly by; probably because her emotions were equally polarized. She felt both dread and excitement at the prospect of seeing Eric again after all these years.

Beaverton was the final destination on her ten-month road trip, a destination that hadn't been part of her original plan. She and Eric had only committed to having dinner together— one dinner—and yet her travel calendar placed her in Beaverton for the entire month of October! Of course, Beaverton was really just a suburb of Portland. She had made short visits to the city on various occasions over the years, but never really taken time to explore. *There must be plenty to do and see in a city the size of Portland,* she reasoned. *And if not, it's just a hundred and eighty-eight miles from there to Issaquah. I can just go home earlier than planned.*

Ali had taken several different tacks in delivering her letters to her various Georges. The methods she chose were determined by the uniqueness of each relationship. Once she met up with a George, she simply waited for inspiration, never knowing how she was going to accomplish delivery until she did it. Some, she had handed over in person. Others, she had left behind as a surprise to be discovered after her departure. Her letter to Eric was the only one she chose to send by way of "snail mail" before their reunion took place. Somehow, his seemed more intimate than most of the other letters, and she was afraid that if she didn't send it ahead of time, she would chicken out. So she entrusted the task to the United States Postal Service.

☙❧

Alice Ann Kuder

Dear Eric,

"Joy is like the rain . . ."

That's the refrain from the song you were playing the first time I heard you singing in Red Square at Western. I don't remember the rest of the lyrics, but that phrase spoke to me then, and still does today. I wonder if you realize what a powerful experience those morning sing-a-longs were for me and for so many others?

Do you remember the day we met? I do. I had been stopping by the fountain to join the singing every morning for months. I found it so uplifting that I often showed up even on the days I didn't have a class nearby.

I will confess to you now that I had a little crush on you. Maybe it was your music, maybe it was the atmosphere you created, or maybe it was just that I thought you were so darn cute. Whatever the reasons, I finally got up the courage to introduce myself and thank you for the mini worship service you led. I was afraid that you might be annoyed by my presumption. I never expected that you would receive me so warmly, let alone invite me to join you for coffee. It was obvious that you were being friendly, not flirtatious, which brought an end to my little fantasy, but it was a beginning to a precious friendship—a friendship I regret having let slip away.

College life is such a unique and illusory experience. It's an opportunity for pushing boundaries, challenging assumptions, and making judgments. It's a time when our idealism is maximized, tested, and juxtaposed with the temptations of real life. Will we always live up to *our highest and best intentions or will we come up (at least) a bit short of where we would like to land? For the philosophers among us, those years are a heady and transcendent joyride. I felt privileged to travel part of that road alongside you.*

You were, for me, both a teacher and a fellow student, but your most significant role in my life was as a spiritual instigator and rabble-rouser.

Without minimizing the divinity of Jesus Christ, you introduced me to the sacredness of other great teachers such as Buddha, Muhammad, Krishna, and many others.

Socrates said, "The unexamined life is not worth living." Elton Trueblood's variation postulates, "the unexamined faith is not worth having." You taught me the truth of that statement.

You mercilessly interrogated me about what I believed and why I believed it, peppering me with questions that stirred my soul and forced me to examine my faith.

With your help and encouragement, I took an unflinching look at what I was taught to believe, versus what I knew in my heart to be true. I discovered some conflicts that disturbed me and some congruities that pleased me. In the end, my self-scrutiny left me with a faith that has guided and sustained me through some terrible storms and enables me to find joy in God's continuous graciousness.

They say that each person who comes into our life fulfills a specific purpose; some stay for a day, some for a season, some for a lifetime. I had hoped our friendship would be for a lifetime, but I'm

Alice Ann Kuder

grateful for the season we had. It was one that shaped and fashioned who I am today . . . a person of faith who wants to love again.

I hope you are open to the possibility of experiencing another season together.

With gratitude, respect and affection until forever,

Ali

"Joy is Like the Rain"

I saw raindrops on my window. Joy is like the rain.
Laughter runs across my pane, slips away and comes again.
Joy is like the rain.
I saw clouds upon a mountain. Joy is like a cloud.
Sometimes silver, sometimes gray, always sun not far away.
Joy is like a cloud.
I saw Christ in wind and thunder. Joy is tried by storm.
Christ asleep within my boat, whipped by wind, yet still afloat.
Joy is tried by storm.
I saw raindrops on a river. Joy is like the rain.
Bit by bit the river grows, 'til all at once it overflows.
Joy is like the rain.

Words and music by Miriam Therese Winter.
(c) copyright Medical Mission Sisters 1965. Used with permission.

Since I Last Saw You

Chapter 40
October 30, 2013

Following a hearty breakfast at Biscuits Cafe, Ali waved good-bye to Eric and pulled out onto SW Baseline Road. It was 9:38 a.m. Once she merged onto I-5, after ten months, seventy-six hundred miles, and eighteen cities, she'd be just three hours from coming full circle. She would be home.

"Home" had taken on a whole new meaning since she began this journey. Remembering the fears and misgivings that threatened to derail the trip before it even started, she felt gratified to know that she had made the right decision. There was not one day or one mile that she regretted having traveled. Experiencing a transient lifestyle, so distinct from anything she had ever known, had given her life more context. It also deepened her appreciation for the blessings she'd previously taken for granted.

During her travels she'd seen and met people from all walks of life and various economic circumstances. While she was fortunate enough to be assured of affording a safe, clean place to stay each night, she saw homeless men and women on the streets in every city she visited. She knew that many of them were hungry as well. This knowledge was driven home by a roadside billboard she'd seen while traveling through the "breadbasket" of America. It read: *1 in 6 Americans faces hunger.*

Never having known hunger herself, it was nonetheless an issue that had always caused Ali considerable unease. Growing up on the berry farm, her parents always stressed that food should never be wasted. The Beneventos regularly allocated a significant portion of their annual crops to local food banks, and not just those berries that weren't pretty enough to please the general public.

The year she volunteered at the Bellingham Food Bank was a deeply satisfying experience, which made her realize that she was seeing just the tip of an iceberg. Since then, she'd always meant to do more—donate more food, more money, more time—but never seemed to get around to it. Knowing she wasn't alone in her neglect did little to assuage her ongoing feelings that she was sinning by omission.

୨୦୯୧

Despite persistent requests from her family and Gwen, Ali refused to disclose her ETA. She knew they would want to be at the house to welcome her home, and it was important to her that she experience the emotions of returning home without distraction or obligation. She just couldn't predict how she'd feel. She turned the final corner and looked down the familiar street. There it was, just as she'd left it; the home she'd shared with Isaac and Zoe for so many years.

Now, as she pulled up into the driveway, a torrent of memories and emotions washed over her. She remembered the first time she and Isaac saw the house, in 1999, as well as the day they brought Zoe home from the hospital. They designed the paddock in back when she bought Palermo. This was where they weathered the Hanukkah Eve windstorm in 2006, and the week of record-breaking, one-hundred-plus degree weather in the summer of 2009.

So much life had happened in this house. *Could I be happy here again without Zoe and Isaac, or should I find a new home?* She didn't know.

As soon as she walked in the front door, she had her answer. If there were ghosts here, they were Caspers. It was as if the air was perfumed and the walls were frescoed in cherished memories; she sensed only love and comfort.

Putting down her suitcases, Ali walked over to the piano, sat down, and raised the fallboard. Without thinking, she began to play the melody she had played for her parents and siblings nearly two years earlier in the very same room.

During her ten months on the road, bits and pieces of lyrics occasionally came to her and she logged them in her journal when they did. Now she began to wonder if all the words and phrases might be ready to come together, so she went to get her journals and a pad of paper. Sitting down at her kitchen table, she began leafing through her logs and extracting the notes that once seemed random but which now appeared to be bona fide lyrics. When she had finished, she stared at the paper as if it were an unexpected love letter. Tears stung her eyes and she whispered, "This is for you, my loves."

Then she returned to the piano and began to play and sing:

Since I last saw you, lessons have been learned.
Since I last saw you, life has taken many turns.
And the pleasure in remembering the time we shared
The laughter rings so true
Since I last saw you.
Since I last saw you, the scenery has changed.
Leaves have fallen, but my heart remains the same.
And the smile your memory can place upon my face
Gives me a better view,
Since I last saw you.
Ours was a treasure out of time.
New every day whether rain or shine.
Soft with the green of spring upon the land.
The music filled our nights, and
The flames of friendship fanned.
Since I last saw you, the simple things remain.
A truth for each new day, laughter and the pain.
And the memory of our journey helps to keep me strong.
It warms me through and through,
Since I last saw you.
And the memory of our journey helps to keep me strong.
It warms me through and through,
Since I last saw you.

෨෬

Relieved to find that she still felt at home in her own house, Ali called Gwen and invited her to come over, then set about the task of unpacking.

Ali felt a certain amount of pride and satisfaction at having returned home with not much more baggage than she'd had when she'd packed for the trip. It hadn't been as hard as she thought to resist buying things while she was on the road.

She'd gotten used to traveling light, and discovered that she quite liked it. She had to admit, however, that she was sick and tired of every item of clothing she'd been wearing all those months. *Goodwill, here I come*, she said out loud on behalf of her travel wardrobe.

Ali came out of the garage with several empty boxes just as Gwen arrived on her doorstep carrying two bags full of groceries.

"Welcome home, stranger! I thought you might be hungry and I knew there was no food in the house."

"Oh, you're a lifesaver! But first, put down those bags and give me a big hug! It's *sooo* good to see you!" Ali said with great sincerity.

"And it's *sooo* good to have you home!"

"By the way," Ali said, "thanks for keeping a eye on the house for me all these months."

"You're welcome. I didn't mind at all. It made me feel as if I was playing some small part in helping you on your journey. And Ali, I hope you have taken the time to congratulate yourself. You really did an amazing thing."

"Thanks, Gwen. I guess I did, didn't I? I remember how scared I was when I left, but when I faced it just one day at a time . . . not so much." She smiled broadly and noted her feeling of self-satisfaction.

∞∞

"That was a great lunch; simple and satisfying," said Ali. "It made me feel quite European."

"Bread, cheese, fresh fruit, and wine. What more could you want?" Gwen said with a shrug of her shoulders. "So now that our tummies are full and we're caught up on all the gossip, shall I help you unpack?"

"Actually, I'm pretty much done with that. I didn't have all that much to unpack, and I'm giving away a lot of the clothes I took with me. Frankly, I never want to see most of that stuff ever again," Ali said with a laugh.

"Is that what the boxes are for?"

"Yeah. I thought that as long as I'm putting together a

donation box, maybe it's a good time to go through Isaac's things, too. I couldn't bring myself to do it before, but I think I'm ready now."

"What about Zoe's things?"

"I don't think I'm *that* strong yet. Let's see how this goes first," Ali said cautiously.

∞∞

When Ali opened the bedroom closet door, the first thing that caught her eye was Isaac's racing bag. She flashed back to the memory of her mini-meltdown when she'd found it in the Escape back in January.

"What's that?" asked Gwen.

"It's Isaac's racing bag. It's sort of a combination duffle bag and treasure chest. Every racecar driver has one. They use them to carry everything from practical things like extra goggles to sentimental stuff like talismans. Isaac always used to say you never really knew a man until you saw what he kept in his racing bag."

"What did Isaac keep in *his* bag?"

"Well, I have to admit, I don't know. I knew it was practically sacred, so I never looked inside and he never offered to show me."

"Are you going to open it now?"

"I guess I have to. I can't very well send it to Goodwill without unpacking it."

"I hope you're ready for what you might find."

"I hope so, too," Ali said with obvious trepidation.

When she unzipped the bag, out fell the envelope addressed to her in Isaac's handwriting.

The two women looked at one another without saying a word. Slowly, Ali sat down on the bed and tentatively fingered the envelope. Finally, she lifted the unsealed flap, took out the letter and read:

February 8, 2012

Darling Ali,

It feels both strange and familiar to be writing you a letter . . .

∞∞

Gwen watched Ali's face for clues as to what the letter might contain. Her imagination was conjuring up all sorts of possibilities—some good, some not so good. She was concerned for her friend, but all she could do was stand by and be ready to either pick up the pieces or join in a celebration.

Ali started to cry softly as she continued reading. Looking for a tangible way to help, Gwen searched for a box of Kleenex. Finding one on the nightstand, she handed Ali a tissue and sat on the bed next to her.

At last Ali finished reading and looked up at Gwen, still crying.

"Oh, Gwen. He still loved me. This is a letter he wrote to me dated two days before the crash. He says he's sorry for his part in the troubles we'd been having and he wants to re-commit to our marriage. Despite everything, he still loved me."

Gwen let out a sigh of relief and reached over to hold Ali as they both cried.

"All this time, I've been wondering if our marriage would have survived. Jackie accused me of making his last months miserable, and I was afraid she was right. I've been feeling so much guilt. This letter answers so many questions. Oh, my God. It's such a blessing!

"Would it be okay if I read it?"

"Yes! I *want* you to read it."

It took Gwen several minutes to read the lengthy, handwritten letter and to begin to digest its contents. Finally, she looked at Ali and asked, "What happened to this ring he talks about? Did you ever get it?"

"No, I didn't. This is the first I've heard of it. What do you suppose happened to it?"

"I can't imagine. Maybe a call to the jewelers will shed

some light on it."

Greg and Margaret were devastated when they got the call from Ali telling them about the crash that took Isaac and Zoe's lives. If it had made the local news at the time, they'd missed it. The week leading up to Valentine's Day was always one of the busiest of the year for them. They barely had time to eat and sleep, let alone watch the news or read the paper.

"Frankly, Ali, Margaret and I were a little surprised that we didn't hear from Isaac after he gave you the ring," Greg said. "We didn't know him all that well, but he was so excited that we thought maybe he'd call to tell us your reaction."

"Well, Greg, that's the thing. He never got the chance to give me the ring. In fact, I didn't even know it existed until today. I was hoping you knew something about what happened to it. Apparently, you don't."

"Gosh, Ali, I'm sorry to disappoint you. I have no idea what happened to the ring after he picked it up that day."

"He must have had it in the car with him. Maybe the state patrol or the towing company might know something?"

"Maybe. It seems unlikely that they wouldn't have made the connection and given it to me, or at least returned it to you—your store's name must have been on the box."

Ali paused for a moment, then asked, "Greg, what did it look like? Can you describe it to me?"

"We've designed a lot of rings since then, but I remember this one well because he ordered it to match your wedding set. And even though yours wasn't one of the most expensive sets Margaret ever designed, I always thought it was one of the most spectacular.

"Anyway, this was what jewelers call a wrap ring. Just like your wedding ring, it had a crested row of black diamonds with a contrasting row of white diamonds set in a white gold band. I'm afraid I've never been very good at describing rings, but we take photos of everything we design. I could upload a digital copy and send you a link to our cloud if you'd like."

"I'd like that very much, Greg."

Alice Ann Kuder

"Ali, let me just say again how sorry I am for your loss. Your daughter was a lovely young woman and Isaac was a good man. They obviously loved you very much. I hope you take some comfort in knowing that."

"I do, Greg. I do."

"The supreme happiness of life is the conviction that we are loved."
~ Victor Hugo

Chapter 41
November 6, 2013

Ali expected that once she got back from her sojourn, she'd somehow settle into a new normal—though she had little idea of what that would look like. What she hadn't counted on was finding the letter from Isaac, and how it would change her whole perspective.

Even a week afterward, she was still sorting through the thoughts and emotions his letter had stirred up. *Thank goodness I have Dr. Bolles, Gwen, and my family for emotional support.* She was grateful that her parents had offered to let Tess stay with her in Issaquah for at least a couple more weeks; the house would seem awfully empty without her. Pretty soon the three of them would have a difficult decision to make together regarding Tess' future. Ali would hate to give her up, but she couldn't blame her parents for wanting her back. Too bad Tess couldn't cast a vote.

Maybe I should adopt a dog of my own? She thought. *Raising a puppy is a lot of work, but it might be good for me to have another living being to think about and care for. Or I could adopt an older dog that needs a good home; God knows the shelters are full of them.*

Ali looked up from her morning coffee when she heard the familiar rattle of the mailbox. Even though the mail rarely brought anything but bills and marketing promotions these days, she always got just a tiny bit excited when it arrived. She supposed it went back to the days of her childhood when it was much more common to get handwritten letters every once in a while.

Today her optimism was rewarded. Sorting through the contents of her mailbox, she found an envelope addressed to her in unfamiliar handwriting.

4 November 2013

Dear Mrs. Berg,

My name is Curtis Vinson. We've never met, but it's possible that you may have heard my name. I'm the person who first called 911 from the scene of the accident that so tragically took the lives of your husband and daughter almost two years ago.

I thought about contacting you at the time, but I didn't want to intrude on your grief. Now that some time has passed, I wonder if you would be willing to meet with me?

If so, I can be reached at 206-805-8102 or curtis@curtisvinson.me.

Respectfully,

Curtis Vinson

Ali thought her heart might leap out of her chest! Here was someone with new information about the last day of Isaac and Zoe's lives; someone who had actually been there. She immediately picked up the phone and called the number.

∞∞∞

Ali didn't know what to expect when she opened the front door. The man standing in front of her was young and unremarkable in appearance, but to her, he looked like a dream come true. If she had had a red carpet and rose petals at her disposal, she would happily have thrown them down before him as she ushered him into her home.

Curtis, on the other hand, hadn't anticipated Ali's enthusiastic welcome. The two of them had talked only briefly on the phone when they set up this meeting. He felt somewhat guilty and ashamed that he hadn't reached out to her before now. He was also a bit apprehensive about how she might react when she discovered that he had kept the ring from her all this time.

"Mr. Vinson. Hi, I'm Ali Berg—I guess that's obvious, isn't it? Welcome. Please come in."

"It's so nice to meet you, Mrs. Berg. Please, call me Curtis."

"Of course. And please call me Ali. I so appreciate your agreeing to come the same day I got your letter. I realize that Issaquah probably isn't familiar territory to you, and it gets dark so early this time of year. People who live in Seattle proper seem to think this is the end of the earth, even though it's less than twenty miles from downtown.

"Oh, dear. I'm rambling, aren't I? I guess I'm a bit nervous," Ali admitted.

Leading him into the family room, Ali motioned toward Gwen and Nathan, who stood to greet Curtis. "I hope you don't mind that I invited my good friend, Gwen, and my brother, Nathan, to join us? I knew they'd be as anxious to meet you and hear what you have to say as I am. Besides, I want to remember everything you have to say, and three memories are better than one."

"I don't mind at all," he said, not quite sincerely. He hadn't counted on having to explain his actions to anyone other than Ali.

"Please sit down. Can I get you something to drink? A glass of wine, perhaps?"

Without waiting for an answer, Ali went to the kitchen to get beverages and the plate of hors d'oeuvres she had prepared earlier. She knew that playing hostess would help to expend some of her nervous energy.

Once everyone was seated and comfortable, Ali said, "Curtis, what can you tell us about that day?"

Not knowing what Ali did or didn't know about his involvement, Curtis decided it was probably best to begin at the beginning.

"As you probably know, I didn't actually witness the crash, but I rounded the curve just after it happened. I immediately called 911," he said, then paused. "But it was pretty clear that there was nothing else I could do to help your husband and daughter. I'm so sorry."

He went on to describe the arrival of the first responders and their admirable work to contain the scene once they determined that Isaac and Zoe hadn't survived.

"I remember seeing the Corvette pass by just as I pulled onto the highway. The top was down and your husband and daughter were laughing. They looked really happy. I remember feeling a little jealous.

"I wish there was more that I could tell you."

Ali's eyes were wet as she reached for a tissue. Even so, Curtis thought her expression looked serene—even happy.

Sensing that Ali was choked up and unable to respond as she'd like, Gwen spoke up.

"Curtis, you may never know how much this little bit of added information means to Ali. We're grateful that you came forward to share it."

Nathan nodded in agreement.

"There's another reason I asked to meet with you," Curtis said, inhaling deeply. "I have something to give you— something I found that day that I think must belong to you."

The three of them looked at Curtis quizzically, unable to imagine what he could mean.

Curtis reached in his jacket pocket, pulled out the jewelry box, and handed it to Ali.

Nathan was the first to clue in. "Oh, my God. It must be the ring!"

It took a moment for his declaration to register with Ali. Then her eyes opened wide. She flipped up the lid on the box and stared at the contents, at once stunned and amazed.

Still unable to speak, Ali verbally stumbled, trying to formulate the right question.

"But how . . . where . . . I don't understand—how did you end up with this?"

This was the moment Curtis had been dreading. How could he explain why he had the ring and why he hadn't returned it sooner?

"The short answer is that I found it on the side of the road after the accident."

"And the long answer?" Nathan asked.

Curtis hesitated, then asked, "Did the state patrol show you photos of the crash site?"

Ali closed her eyes and shook her head from side to side. "They asked me if I wanted to see them, but I said 'no.' I didn't see what good it would do, and I didn't want those images in my head."

"That was probably a wise decision," Curtis said, before continuing with his story.

"I don't mean to make this about me—I really don't—but I had never experienced anything like that before, and I'm still . . . it's one thing to see it on the news and a whole other thing to be there in person.

"After talking to the officers for their investigation and seeing the emergency medical crew remove the . . . well, I felt as if the wind had been knocked out of me. I could barely see straight, let alone think straight.

"I couldn't just drive off like nothing had happened. I couldn't just go home and forget all about it. Even if I'd wanted to, I couldn't have. The wreckage was scattered all across the roadway and the police had to photograph and document every little piece of debris so they could determine the cause of the accident and hopefully clear the truck driver of wrongdoing.

"So, while I was waiting around for the officers to finish their investigation, I decided to walk down the road to try and clear my head.

"On the way back to my car I saw this perfect little box in the ditch beside the road—I don't know why it caught my eye—but I picked it up and put it in my glove compartment without even looking inside. I never showed it to the police. I never told anyone about it. I just kept it. I can't explain why because I don't understand it myself.

"By the time I got home, several hours later, I was still feeling shaken and muddled and I'd forgotten all about the box. It was almost a year later when I happened across it again while I was searching for something else in my glove compartment. When I finally opened the box, I felt even worse, because it's obviously quite personal and quite valuable."

No one spoke for a minute. Then Gwen asked, "You said you didn't remember you had it for nearly a year, but it's been almost two years since the accident."

"So you're wondering why I didn't return it sooner? It was

selfish on my part, I suppose. I felt guilty and ashamed and I didn't relish the idea of having to try to explain my actions to you. I stashed the box away again and tried to forget about it. I wasn't successful, so here I am.

"Can you forgive me?"

The expression on Ali's face as Curtis told his story had been unreadable—at least to him. He could only describe it as soft and mercifully devoid of anger.

In a dulcet tone, she said, "Curtis, I've never been in your position and you've never been in mine. I don't believe you had any malicious intent so I don't see that there's anything to forgive. Thank you for helping me understand your point of view. Now let me return the favor.

"When a loved one dies in this kind of circumstance, those of us who are left behind wish for one thing more than any other—to go back. Go back and sift through the refuse to see what can be salvaged. Go back and see what we could have done differently that might have saved us all from this incomprehensible outcome.

"What you've shared with me today fed that desire in a way that no one else could have. You were there. That fact alone . . . well, it makes you special to me.

"I'm grateful, of course, that you found and returned the ring, but I didn't even know of its existence until a week ago. Just to know that Isaac and Zoe were laughing and happy when you saw them—shortly before they died—that's worth ten diamond rings to me."

§◎◈

As they walked Curtis to the door, Nathan put a hand on his shoulder and said, "Listen. We realize it couldn't have been easy for you to come here this evening. Try to let go of the guilt and shame you talked about. We all know you did the best you could under really difficult circumstances. And it was enough. We're truly grateful to you."

Curtis stood silent and motionless, searching the faces that surrounded him. When he turned back to Nathan and looked him in the eye, he could see his sincerity. He felt grateful and humbled by the compassion these relative strangers offered him when they could easily have treated him with much less understanding. At a loss for words, he simply said, "Thank you," and walked to his car with tears in his eyes.

೫০೪

After Curtis, and then Gwen, left, Nathan and Ali sat down by the fire and shared another glass of wine.

"Ali," Nathan began, "there's something I need to tell you."

"Oh, please, Nathan. Haven't we had quite enough disclosure for one evening?"

"Maybe, but this is related to the ring so it seems like a good time to fess up."

"Fess up? What could you possibly have to confess?"

"I knew about the ring, and I didn't tell you."

"What do you mean you 'knew about the ring'? You knew of its existence before I found Isaac's letter last week?"

"Yes."

"How? How did you know about it? And why didn't you tell me?"

"Well, you already know that Isaac and Zoe stopped and had lunch with me at the Pass the day they died."

"Yes, you told me about that."

"I told you some, but not all about it. After we finished our lunch, I sent Zoe off to the pro shop so I could talk with Isaac alone. I could tell that you and Isaac were both unhappy, so I played the 'big brother' card and asked him what he was going to do about it.

"That's when he pulled out the ring and told me pretty much what he wrote to you in the letter. He said he was going to give it to you that night and do his best to convince you that he loved you and wanted to stay in the marriage. He didn't tell me he'd written you a letter."

Ali didn't know what to say. Once she gathered her thoughts, she asked, "You told me about the conversation. Why didn't you tell me about the ring?"

"It was a judgment call; apparently a bad one. At first, I

       Alice Ann Kuder

just forgot about it. Then, I realized that no one else had mentioned it. I couldn't figure out what had happened to it. I called the state patrol and the towing company, but no one had seen it. I didn't call the jewelers because I knew Isaac had already picked it up. I came to the conclusion that it had been stolen, so I didn't see the point in telling you about it. I thought it would just add to your grief."

Ali's voice took on a mildly angry tone.

"Nathan, you're my brother and I know you love me, but you're right. You made a *bad call.*

"All this time I've been doubting how Isaac felt about me and our marriage at the time he died. Despite your attempts to reassure me that he loved me—I mean, *what else* are you going to say? I've felt guilty and ashamed and angry because so much was unsettled between Isaac and me. This ring is evidence—no, it's more than that, it's *proof*—that he still loved me. You should have told me. You should have found a way to convince me."

Nathan knew she was right and he felt awful about it. He looked at her sheepishly and—hoping to make her smile—said, "All's well that ends well?"

"Forgiveness is unlocking the door to set someone free and realizing you were the prisoner." ~ Max Lucado

Chapter 42
November 7, 2013

The events of the past week had stirred up a myriad of strong emotions within Ali, and she was having trouble sorting them all out.

So much had happened since she returned home just seven days ago. The letter from Isaac, the meeting with Curtis and the appearance of the ring as well as the conversation with Nathan last night . . . she couldn't seem to focus long enough on her feelings about any one event to reach clarity.

There was something else vying for attention in her subconscious as well, but she couldn't quite put her finger on it.

She was grateful that Nathan had offered to stay the night. Knowing Ali so well, he correctly guessed that she'd need to talk some more about the surprises of the previous evening. She'd taken in a lot of information and needed time to digest it all.

Ali recognized the now-familiar feeling of an emotional tornado gaining momentum within her and knew she needed help to clear her head. Journaling sometimes did the trick, but another way to relieve this kind of emotional pressure was to saddle up Palermo and go for a ride. Just then, Nathan came down the stairs, dressed in running clothes.

"Nathan, can I persuade you to go riding with me instead of jogging? I think it would do me a lot of good to take Palermo out on the trail, and I'd love your company."

"Sure, but won't the two of us be a bit of a heavy load for him?" he joked.

"Very funny, Smarty Pants. Fortunately, we're . . . I mean, *I'm* boarding the neighbor girl's mare while she's away for a few days. I know she'd appreciate it if we could give her some exercise. Are you game?"

Forty-five minutes later, Ali and her brother had saddled up and were galloping alongside one another on a well-worn horse path in the nearby woods. Even after all these years of riding, the sensation of sitting astride a horse, especially her Palermo, always relaxed her and made Ali feel grounded in a way that nothing else did. She could almost feel her thoughts sorting themselves out, as if she were organizing a file cabinet in her mind.

As they slowed the horses to a canter and then to a trot, Ali suddenly knew what it was that had been bothering her. She reined Palermo in and turned to her brother.

"Nathan, why did you tell Curtis, 'You did the best you could?'"

"Why? I thought my meaning was pretty clear."

"Not to me. I've never cared for that saying. It always sounds to me like an excuse, a way to relieve someone of responsibility for not having made better choices.

"How can you tell whether or not someone really did the best they could? It's rare that a person has no options in any given situation. Usually, we can identify two or more possible choices, and sometimes we just make bad choices."

Nathan paused for a moment, then asked, "So, you think that if a person has multiple options and chooses to act on one that the rest of us would judge as being the wrong choice, that means he didn't do the best he could?"

"Well, yes, I guess that's what I'm saying. I take it you don't agree?"

"No, I don't. I understand the logic in your thinking, but we're not Vulcans. We don't use logic as the only yardstick for human choices.

"The way I see it," he continued, "'She did the best she could' is more or less the equivalent of, 'The mind is willing, but the flesh is weak.' Sometimes we're simply helpless against our own humanity."

"I don't think I buy that," Ali protested mildly.

"Think of it this way: every decision we make—every action we take—has two components to it. I think of them as spirit and energy. Or, maybe 'intention' is more accurate than 'spirit.' Sometimes, we have *both* the intention *and* the energy to choose and act on our best option. But sometimes, for whatever reason, we only have the intention. We honestly lack the energy.

"I believe," Nathan continued, "it's one of life's great paradoxes that each and every person does the best they can at every given moment of their life. They may want to do better, they may even believe they *could* do better, but the fact is that it's not possible to be better than we are in the present moment. That's where the paradox comes in. Even if a person weighs two choices, believing that one is the way he *should* or *would* go if only she were a better person, and instead chooses the opposite, *that* is the best she could do at the time. She genuinely lacked the strength and the stamina to act out the better option."

"Wow. That's some pretty heady stuff you're spouting there. When did you become such a philosopher?" Ali teased.

Nathan chuckled. "I understand your skepticism. I've seldom been accused of producing pearls of wisdom, but I really am more than just a pretty face."

Now it was Ali's turn to chuckle. "Everyone does the best they can, huh? You make a pretty convincing argument; I might have to re-evaluate my stance on that," Ali conceded.

୧୭୧୧

The horseback ride had gone a long way toward calming Ali's internal turbulence, yet she still had an overabundance of emotional energy, so when they got back to her house, she decided to resume the task of sorting through Isaac's belongings. Nathan offered to help but understood when Ali said she really preferred to do it alone. He assigned himself the task of loading the boxes into the car and hauling them to the second-hand store.

Later that afternoon, Gwen arrived bearing fresh Chinook salmon she'd bought at Pike Place Fish Market that morning. Although it was early November, the weather was still mild enough that they were able to grill the salmon on the outdoor grill. Nathan tossed together a green salad while Ali opened a bottle of Elk Cove Winery's 2009 Pinot Noir. It was a classic Northwest feast.

Both Gwen and Nathan stayed until late into the evening, unwilling to leave until they felt sure that Ali was at peace with all that had happened recently. Now that they had gone home, Ali poured herself another glass of wine and sank into a hot bath before collapsing into bed. Even though it was only a few minutes after 9 o'clock, she felt sure she would be asleep within minutes.

As she drifted off to sleep she swore she could hear a choir of people from her past faintly repeating, "He did the best he could."

ଛୁଓଡ଼

At 2:13 a.m., Ali awoke with a start and sat straight up in her bed.

"*He did the best he could.*" Both in her wakefulness and in her sleep, it seemed to Ali as if those words kept returning to her the way a merry-go-round pony appears, disappears, and then reappears again. This time around, Isaac was riding that pony.

Suddenly she understood what she now thought should have been so obvious to her all along. *Isaac did the best he could.*

Wanting desperately to capture this powerful truth before it disappeared in the fog of semi-consciousness, she reached for a pen and her journal and began to write:

7 November

I have been so angry with Isaac for so long that I couldn't see what was right in front of me, what should have been so obvious. Our marriage, his parenting, the accident—he did the best he could—every single day. And so did I.

He didn't take up risky pastimes to annoy me or cause me grief; that's just who he was. Zoe didn't idolize her dad to scare me. I didn't go on work trips to avoid spending time with my family. We were all doing the best we could to create a life together, and for the most part, it was a wonderful life. How could I be angry with them? It's not their fault that they died. It's not anyone's fault. I guess I just needed someone to blame, and the cell phone made Isaac an easy scapegoat.

As her anger melted, she fell back asleep, having no premonition of the darkness the morning would bring.

৪১৫৪

Ali awoke with the dawn, as she always liked to do. She rolled over in bed to discover that her journal was still next to her; she must have fallen back asleep with it still in her hand. As she reread the entry from the night before, she felt a lightness of heart that had been so rare in the past two years that it felt foreign. Letting go of her anger initiated a spiritual shift she could only describe as rapturous.

Ali lay in bed trying to mentally adjust to her new emotional reality. Yes, it felt freeing to forgive Isaac. Surely now she would be able to move on with her life in a way that she hadn't been able to before.

Why, then, couldn't she get out of bed?

Alice Ann Kuder

"When you forgive, you in no way change the past—but you sure do change the future." ~ Bernard Meltzer

Chapter 43
November 8, 2013

There were few things in life that Ali abhorred more than vomiting.

She remembered vividly the confusion and terror she felt the first time she got the stomach flu. She was four years old and had recently graduated from a crib to sleeping in a big girl's bed just like her sister, Chloe.

She felt fine when she went to bed that night, but a few hours later she woke up feeling very strange. Frightened, she called out for her mother. Chloe, who was sleeping in her own bed just a few feet away, was awakened by Ali's cries first.

"What's the matter?" she asked her little sister groggily.

"My stomach feels all wiggly."

"Wiggly? What do you . . ." Before Chloe could finish her question she heard the distinct sound of vomit splattering on the floor in the darkened room, followed closely by its nauseating odor. She was relieved when she heard their mother coming down the hall to the rescue.

Ali was crying now and feeling close to panic. She reached for her mother and asked with alarm, "Mommy, what's happening to me?"

∞∞

It's not easy to explain the stomach flu to a young child. It's not much easier to explain the effects of delayed grief to an adult. Somehow, the two felt very similar to Ali.

Like the temporary relief one feels after vomiting, the tremendous relief she felt from releasing her long-and-closely-held anger was short-lived. In its place appeared a terrifying and overwhelming sense of grief that threatened to create an emotional sinkhole. She felt sure that it would swallow her whole.

It wasn't a completely unfamiliar feeling. She remembered feeling this way those first few days after the accident. Then, as now, she felt an unbearable sadness and awareness of what she had lost. Now, it was as if one giant boulder had been lifted from her shoulders, only to be replaced by another on her chest.

Cognizant of the shallowness of her own breathing, and frightened by the threat of despair, she puzzled over the cause of her emotional paralysis. *Where did this come from?* She wondered. *And why now?*

Recognizing that she needed help, she reached over to the nightstand, picked up the phone and hit Speed Dial #1. When she heard the open line, it was all she could do to keep herself from wailing, "Mom, what's happening to me?"

ⅮⅯ

An hour later, Peggy was sitting on the edge of her daughter's bed, holding her hand and wiping the tears from Ali's eyes.

"I don't get it, Mom. Why am I suddenly crumbling like this? It's been nearly *two years*. I've been doing fine. For God's sake, I just spent ten months traveling across the country by myself!"

"Ali, Honey, I can't tell you why this is happening to you now, but I suspected it would hit you sooner or later."

"It? What do you mean by 'it'?"

"Grief."

"Grief?" Ali repeated with incredulity. There was anger in her raised voice now. "You don't think I've been grieving these past two years?"

"Yes, of course you have been, Sweetheart, but . . ."

"But, what?"

"But, I don't think you've let yourself follow it all the way to the bottom. I think maybe you tried to take a shortcut and now you're paying the price," said her mother.

Ali responded with indignation. "Shortcut? What shortcut? How can you say that to me? You've seen me try to come to grips with my loss. You've seen me struggle to put my life back together."

"Ali, I'm not criticizing you," Peggy said softly, in an attempt to soothe her daughter. "I'm not saying that you haven't been in pain. God knows it tears me up inside to watch you suffering.

"Do you remember that a few days after the funeral, I gave you a book titled *How to Survive the Loss of a Love?* It's just a thin little volume with a mix of poetry, affirmations, and suggestions for how to recover from emotional hurts."

"I remember the book," Ali said in a somewhat calmer voice.

"Well, although it doesn't actually name her as an inspiration, it certainly brings to mind Elizabeth Kubler-Ross' work describing the five stages of death and dying. Did you read the book?" her mother asked.

"I started to read it, but I don't think I finished it. I remember that each page felt so emotionally charged. Sometimes I could only read a couple of pages before it got too painful to continue.

"The poems, in particular, were very poignant. It was as if the author was reading my mind; like she was giving voice to all my painful thoughts and feelings. At several points, it got so intense that I finally had to stop reading. Like I said, I don't think I ever finished it."

"Do you remember where you stopped?" Peggy asked.

"No, I don't. It seems like that was a lifetime ago. I'm sure I still have it somewhere, though."

"Do you think you could find it?"

∞⊙∞

Fifteen minutes later, Ali came out of her bedroom with the book in hand.

"I see there's still a bookmark in place," said Peggy.

"It's divided into four sections," said Ali. "The Loss; Surviving; Healing; and Growing. It looks like I stopped partway through the section on healing, right when it starts talking about anger." Ali paused and looked at her mother. "But you already knew that, didn't you, Mom?"

"Oh, I can't say I *knew* it, but it doesn't surprise me."

"Because . . . ?" Ali encouraged her mother to say more.

"Because when I first read the book myself, after your grandmother died, I was able to gauge where I was in the healing process by where I was in the book. If I tried to read pages that addressed a stage beyond where I was emotionally, it became too difficult to read, and I had to put it down for a while.

"Tell me this, Ali, if you were to pick this book up again today, where would you start reading?"

"Well, after the epiphany I had last night, I'd probably pick up where I left off and read what it says about healing and anger."

"What's the next section about?" Peggy asked.

"Growing."

"As I recall, Kubler-Ross cautions against the idea that grief is a linear process that's identical for everyone. She observed that most people experience all five stages—but not necessarily in the same order—and there's no standard time frame for each stage. One person might stay in the bargaining stage, for example, for several days and another person for just a few hours."

"And you think I've been stuck in the anger stage, don't you, Mom?"

"Don't *you*?" Peggy asked.

"Before last night, I would have said 'no'."

"And today?"

"Today," admitted Ali, "I'd have to say, yes. But why did I get stuck there for so long?"

"Well, do you like the way you're feeling today?"

"God, no! Yesterday, even though I was still angry, I felt more in control and in less pain."

"That's because anger often makes us feel powerful. It's such an intense emotion that when we let ourselves feel it, it blocks out almost everything else—even pain.

"I think," Peggy continued, "that you've been hanging onto your anger because it was easier and less painful than feeling grief. It was a way to delay letting go until you were really ready."

Alice Ann Kuder

"But I didn't consciously hold onto my anger. I thought I *had* let go. I thought I had grieved the loss of Isaac and Zoe."

"I'm sure you had, to a certain degree," Peggy tried to reassure her daughter. "As I said before, grief isn't a linear process. We don't just start with step one, complete it, then move on to step two, and so on. I've come to think of it as more of a spiral that starts out broad at the bottom and gets narrower as we travel up. You know, like the abstract drawings of a Christmas tree. Anyway, we travel up and around the spiral spectrum, continually repeating the pattern. Each time we go through a stage again, the spiral narrows and feels less intense until we eventually reach the tip. There's no telling how long it will take us to make it to the top of the spiral. Every journey is unique.

"Ali, Honey, we all know that you're doing the best you can." The irony of her mother's statement, coming so closely on the heels of her discussion with Nathan, was not lost on Ali.

"Mom, I'm so grateful that you came over, and I don't want you to think I'm tossing you out, but if you'll excuse me, there's one more letter I need to write."

> *"Any fool can know; the point is to understand."*
> ~ *Albert Einstein*

Chapter 44
November 8, 2013

Dear Isaac,

How do I begin this long-overdue letter? I'll start with a memory.

I still remember our first touch. Most people dwell on the significance of their first kiss, but the first time you touched me was even more meaningful and electric.

It was the day we met. You, Nathan, Chloe, and I were sitting at a table at the Iron Goat having lunch when you accidentally kicked me under the table. Most people would have been unnecessarily apologetic. You said nothing. You simply looked me in the eye and smiled. We hadn't spoken a word to each other yet, but you were utterly comfortable with our unintentional contact. It felt to me like both an invitation and a promise.

I remember our last touch, as well, because it was right after our fight and just before I left for the airport. We didn't kiss good-bye—we were both still too angry. Just as I was about to go out the door, you grabbed my hand, squeezed it and looked me in the eye, as if to assure me that our anger was temporary, and our love was constant. I squeezed your hand right back in silent agreement. It was sweeter than a kiss could ever have been.

Isaac, I'm ashamed that it took me so long to come to grips with my anger. I couldn't get past

Alice Ann Kuder

all that I've lost and I blamed you for taking it all away. One minute I had a husband, a daughter, and a plan for the future. The next minute, it was all gone. You were gone, and I missed you so terribly . . . _miss_ you so terribly. Now I understand that I was using the anger to protect myself from the pain. I know you understand that, too, and I know you forgive me.

There's something else you'll be glad to hear.

I get it. I finally get it.

Remember all those times I asked you to explain your attraction to your daredevil pastimes, and I just didn't get it? Well, now I do.

All my life, I let my fear of physical injury override my desire to experience the ecstasy that you felt commonly. You tried and tried to pry my fingers off the safety bar of life, but my grasp was firm. If you hadn't respectfully disregarded my constant yellow flags, you would have missed out on so much bliss in your too-short lifetime, and it would have been my fault. I finally understand that extreme sports were your portal to extreme life. I thank God you didn't let me squelch your constant pursuit—and achievement—of maximum joy.

Tomorrow would have been our fifteenth wedding anniversary. Unlike the stereotypical husband, in all our years together you never once forgot my birthday, Valentine's, Day or our anniversary; never once. It wasn't until recently that I got your very last Valentine's gift to me. Your letter and the ring enabled me to finally cast out all my anger, fear, doubt, and shame. All that's left is the love; always, the love.

It's because of that love—yours and Zoe's—that

I want to live again and love again. It's a tribute to you both that I want desperately to experience that bliss anew. How could I not?

You said in your letter that you hope you live in my heart. Isaac, you are the very beating of my heart, and you will be,

Until forever,

Your Ali

Alice Ann Kuder

Chapter 45
November 2, 2013

If it's true that "It takes a village to raise a child," then it seems only right that the villagers should gather to celebrate their success, Ali thought as she drew up her Thanksgiving Celebration invitations.

> *Because you have significantly contributed to the joy of my life's journey, you are invited to attend my Family-of-Choice Thanksgiving Celebration*

Dear Friend,

In the nearly two years since Isaac and Zoe's deaths, I've been forced—or rather, I've had the opportunity—to re-evaluate my life; where I've been, where I am and where I'm going. Much of this introspection included taking stock of the people and events that have shaped me. I now understand that I truly am the resultant handiwork of a village, and you are one of the villagers.

I was fortunate enough to spend much of this year traveling across the country renewing a few of the friendships that have blessed my life, but there are so many more people I want to thank, you included. You are one of the many special people that I'd like to bring together and introduce to one another. Just imagine being in a room full of people you *know* to be capable of changing your life for the better!

Of course, what I learned during my travels is that this is true of the people in any room you enter, whether it's a roadside café in Belgrade, Montana; a Laundromat in Folkston, Georgia; or a gas station in Marianna, Florida.

Last year, I spent Thanksgiving—the first without Isaac and Zoe—by myself. Not because I didn't have anyone to spend it with, but because I felt the need for some solitude. This year, I feel the need and desire for just the opposite. I have so much to be thankful for, and I want to spend the holiday surrounded by as many friends and family as possible, so I've reserved a banquet hall near my home in Issaquah for the occasion.

I realize that Thanksgiving is a holiday rife with family traditions and I want to add to that rather than distract from it, so this celebration will be on the Saturday of Thanksgiving weekend.

My first thought was to have it catered, but I realized that a potluck is more symbolically appropriate, because each person brings something different and unique to the mix.

Also in keeping with the spirit of the holiday, there will be a barrel available to collect canned food donations, which will benefit our local food bank.

I sincerely hope you will come, and bring along one or more of the villagers from your own life.

෨෬

Alice Ann Kuder

Ali shivered as she came back in the house from retrieving the mail. *It's the middle of November,* she thought to herself. *Time to stop pretending I can go outside without putting on a coat.*

"That's a sizable stack of mail you have there. Are any of them responses to your invitation?" Gwen asked as she refreshed the hot tea in Peggy's cup, as well as Ali's and her own.

Ali plopped down on her living room sofa next to her mother and began rifling through the mail. "I've heard from quite a few people—more than I expected, actually. You know how hard it is to get RSVPs from people these days."

"How many invitations did you send out?" Peggy asked.

"I sent a couple dozen paper invitations to the people I have street addresses for and another couple dozen e-vites to the ones I have only e-mail addresses for. Then, I also posted it on Facebook, with privacy settings set to "Friends only," of course. Altogether, I'm not sure how many people I invited. I've heard back from about twenty people so far. Not all of them are coming, of course, but a number of people wrote to say that they love the idea and were happy to be invited. A couple of them who couldn't make it even asked if I intend to do it again next year!"

"Well, do you?" her mother asked.

"I don't know. I haven't thought that far ahead. Who knows what this next year will bring? I've learned the truth of the adage, 'We make plans, and God laughs'!"

"So true," said Gwen, as all three women chuckled. "Who's coming so far?"

"Mostly the people who live fairly close by: Jessica, Ryan, and Carter; Barb and Carle; Earl, Al, and Derik; Evie, Shari, and Robert; Laurie and Coleen. A few long-distance surprises, too. Marilyn is flying in from New York, provided the weather cooperates. John and Nancy are going to make it a road trip, driving in from Ohio, believe it or not, with their kids Rachel, Kevin, and Michelle."

"Who's sent their regrets?" Peggy asked.

"Nadine and Daniel can't make it. Josh and Lindsay will be out of the country. Sharon and Margey are probably going to be in Arizona."

"I know that all these people are special to you or you wouldn't have invited them, but is there anyone you were especially hoping to see that isn't coming?"

"Well, I'm really disappointed that Martha can't come, but at least I got to see her on my road trip. And Renate can't make it. Or Eric."

"Eric?" Peggy questioned. "Do I know Eric?"

"No, Mom, I don't think you do," Ali replied with as much nonchalance as she could muster.

"He's a guy she had a crush on in college," Gwen offered up.

Ali cast an annoyed look at her friend. Despite their close and loving relationship, Ali hadn't confided in her mother about Eric or the time they had spent together during her month in Portland. After all, what could she say? They were friends, that's all. Having a few meals together, meeting his kids and going to a couple of movies didn't constitute a "relationship" in the romantic sense of the word . . . *did it?*

"I don't think you've ever told me about him," said Peggy.

"There's really nothing to tell. We reconnected on Facebook in early June when I was staying in Atlanta. Then, about a month later—it must have been in mid-July, because I was visiting Rochelle in Mobile—he called and asked if I'd like to stop and visit on the last leg of my trip. He lives just outside of Portland and I had to pass through there on my way home anyway, so I thought, *why not?"*

"I see," said Peggy, exchanging a surreptitious, knowing look with Gwen.

Ali continued, "It was really good to see him again. Neither of us *looks* the same as we did back then, but it was a surprisingly comfortable reunion after so many years."

Recalling their conversation of over a year ago, Gwen asked, "Didn't you say he married his college sweetheart?"

"Uh-huh. They had two kids who are now about nine and twelve."

"Had?"

"He's a widower now. Nancy died of pancreatic cancer about five years ago."

"Oh, that's a shame. You're both so young to have lost

spouses," Peggy said. "What an unfortunate thing to have in common."

"We didn't spend much time talking about it, but I must admit that it created a different kind of connection than I feel with . . . well, with most people."

Hoping to distract her mother and her friend from this topic of conversation, Ali got up from the sofa and went to the kitchen. When she returned with a basket of fruit and the teapot, it was obvious that her attempt had been in vain.

"So you had a nice, long visit with Eric?" Gwen asked.

"You know I did. You've already heard all about it. Stop trying to stir up the pot."

Turning to her mother, she said, "He's a nice guy, Mom, you'd like him."

Taking the hint that her friend wasn't likely to divulge much more information, Gwen stood up and said, "Well, ladies, I hate to go, but sometimes I actually do have to work. Those bills just aren't going to pay themselves."

After saying good-bye to Gwen, mother and daughter sat back down in front of the fireplace to finish their tea and resume their lazy morning visit.

Sensing that her mother might be feeling a teensy bit shut out, Ali somewhat grudgingly returned to the topic of Eric.

"Mom, I'm sorry I didn't mention Eric to you before. I wasn't trying to hide anything; it just feels kind of . . . I don't know . . . kind of weird to even *think* about the possibility of romance, let alone talk to *you* about it."

"I understand, Sweetheart. Some things are easier—and more appropriate—to talk about with friends than with your mother. But I won't pretend that I'm not dying to hear about him!"

"Well, I think you pretty much got the gist of it. I met Eric when I was at Western. I had a big crush on him and we became friends, but he was already deeply committed to his high school sweetheart and never gave me a second look in a romantic way."

"Hmm. Well, time and circumstances have a way of altering our perspective." Then she asked tentatively, "Are you still attracted to him? Did you get any inkling that *he* might see *you* differently now? "

"Now, Mom, don't start encouraging my imagination. It's embarrassing enough to swoon over a guy when you're young, let alone after you've been married, had a kid, and are pushing middle age."

"So you *did* get the feeling he might be interested?"

Ali hesitated before continuing. "Well, it's really nothing he said or did . . . nothing specific or concrete." She paused again. Peggy wisely decided not to interrupt the silence.

After a while, Ali continued, slowly and quietly. "Something *was* different. I just can't put my finger on it. Like I said before, it was just so comfortable, so easy and relaxed. And I think . . . it seemed as if he looked at me differently than he did back then . . . more intently."

Ali was quiet and distant again; then she suddenly came back to earth. Her voice took on a clipped, breezy tone.

"But . . . I probably imagined the whole thing. He's not coming for Thanksgiving—something about his kids needing to see their grandparents—chances are that I won't see him for another twenty years, except on Facebook."

With that, Ali abruptly changed the subject. "Good grief! We've had so much tea that I'm about to float away! I'm going to use the bathroom. Then maybe we can decide on what to have for lunch."

Peggy could tell that her daughter wouldn't be coaxed into saying anything more for the time being, but she felt sure she hadn't heard the last about Eric Wicks.

Chapter 46
November 30, 2013

Ali felt a twinge of trepidation as she stood outside the door of the empty banquet hall. *What if no one comes?* Even though over thirty people had said "yes" to the invitation, she couldn't help but worry that the attendance would be disappointing. Worse yet, what if those who did show up didn't enjoy themselves?

Determined to dislodge her baseless thoughts of self-doubt, she stepped inside and was immediately mollified by the magic her mother had worked. Peggy had lent her special Thanksgiving touch to make the space feel homey and intimate by bringing in overstuffed chairs and sofas, plants, rugs, and lights. She'd even rented three electric fireplaces with convincingly real-looking flames. An elegant banquet table stood in the center of the room with the Benevento's rustic horn of plenty spilling its contents from one end of the table to the other.

Several display easels supporting large pin boards were set up around the perimeter of the room. Ali hoped each one would soon be covered with photographs—large and small, color, and black and white, dog-eared and pristine—of deceased loved ones that guests wished to honor and remember. Three tables stood ready to display framed photographs as well, with those of Isaac and Zoe front and center.

₮›кг

By 2 p.m. it was apparent that all of Ali's fears were unjustified. The room was brimming with people who were obviously delighted to be there. When the onslaught of arrivals slowed to a trickle, Ali slipped into the kitchen to help Peggy and Gwen organize the potluck offerings and coordinate the meal.

Peggy gave her daughter a big hug and said, "You must be thrilled with this turnout, Darling! It looks like an even bigger crowd than you expected!"

"It is." Ali acknowledged gratefully. "There are even some people who initially said they couldn't come, then changed their plans so they could be here!"

"Really?" said Gwen. "Like who?"

"Rebecca drove down from Bellingham. Mike and Elizabeth came up from Centralia. And I got a call from Mark Cadungug who lives down in Portland. He wasn't able to come but wanted to call and say Happy Thanksgiving."

"And didn't I see Susan Schuster and Nolan Shafer from Silver Star Stables in the crowd?" Peggy asked.

"Yes," said Ali. "I'm really looking forward to visiting with them. It's going to be a challenge to get in face time with everyone."

"Anyone else unexpectedly come or call? From Portland perhaps?" Gwen asked coyly.

Despite Ali's smirk, Gwen thought she sensed a bit of disappointment in her friend's demeanor when she said, "No. No one else from Portland."

Peggy looked at Gwen, then at Ali, remembering their conversation earlier that month about Eric. Choosing to let the moment pass, she instead commented, "It's a good thing we decided to make it a potluck, otherwise I'd be concerned about having enough food. Instead, we'll probably have trouble making sure none of it gets wasted."

The women all looked at each other and said in unison, "Nickelsville," referring to the camp for the homeless, in Seattle's Central District.

₭₭₭

Ali was chatting with some of her guests when she looked up and saw her sister-in-law come through the door. This was the first time she'd seen Jackie since their conversation in Xenia; a conversation that had seemed more like a berating to Ali. The resultant tension remained unresolved. She experienced a momentary, involuntary shiver of dread as Jackie approached her from across the room, but then she could see that Jackie's demeanor and the expression on her face were soft and conciliatory. The anxious feeling immediately subsided, replaced by memories of all the years of loving friendship they'd shared.

Both women stretched their arms open wide and hugged each other with genuine joy.

Without loosening her embrace, Ali said, "Jackie, I'm so glad you came."

"Are you really? After the dreadful things I said to you the last time we saw each other?"

Ali didn't say anything, and only hugged Jackie tighter.

Finally, Jackie stepped back, keeping hold of Ali's hands.

"Listen, I know this isn't the time or the place for a lengthy apology, but I want you to know how sorry I am for coming down on you so hard that day. I can't say I didn't mean most of the things I said, but I am embarrassed by the way I handled it. I let all those thoughts and feelings mingle with my grief to the point that they festered and grew all out of proportion. If I had only told you what I was feeling sooner, well . . ."

"Jackie, you did the best you could, didn't you?"

"I guess I did. I just wish I'd handled it differently. You were a wonderful, loving wife to Isaac, and a great mother to Zoe, and I regret anything I said or did that made you doubt that for even a second."

"Fortunately for us both," said Ali, "I've learned about forgiveness from a master—you."

୫୦୯୫

Despite the fact that many of the guests were strangers to one another, everyone seemed to be mingling with ease. A pleasant buzz of conversation, punctuated by frequent laughter, filled the air.

The serving tables overflowed with food. The turkey and ham Peggy and Ali provided were flanked by every imaginable side dish. No doubt each guest brought their favorite.

Martin and Chloe circulated around the room keeping

glasses filled with wine and sparkling cider.

Ali eventually made her way to the head of the table. Tapping her goblet with her spoon, she asked for her guests' attention and invited them to gather round.

As she surveyed the expansive banquet table and looked around the crowded room, Ali's eyes began to water and her throat to swell. *I feel so blessed and gratified by the presence of all these amazing individuals,* she thought. *If only Isaac and Zoe could be here.*

She stood for a moment in silence, attempting to control her emotions.

Finally, she began, "My heart is so full at this moment. Looking at all of you, I know that this is what Thanksgiving is all about. Who cares what the first Thanksgiving was really like? What counts is how we celebrate it now. To be in the presence of people you love and admire . . . what could be more . . . it's just so . . . I guess I should have hired a speechwriter; I'm obviously having trouble expressing myself." Her guests laughed with her.

"As you all know . . . well, maybe not all of you; there are some friends of friends here today. Anyway, my husband, Isaac, and my daughter, Zoe, were killed in an auto accident about a year and a half ago . . . twenty-one months ago. Zoe was my—*our*—only child. And, Isaac was my only husband." More tittering from the crowd. "Thanks for rewarding my attempt to add a little levity there. The point is, my life changed suddenly and drastically in so many ways. Some would say I lost my family. I'll admit it felt that way at first, and sometimes it still does. But I found my family, too.

"In the end, it's the love we give and receive that outlives us and makes our mark on the world. We're all the descendants of love, and that makes us all family. Thank you, for being here today and for being my family."

The sounds of clapping and cheering filled the air as Ali's guests expressed their agreement.

"Before I let you get back to celebrating, I want to invite you to participate in one more Benevento family tradition. Many of you probably already observe the Thanksgiving custom of having each person at the table say something they are thankful for. Back in 1978, the year of the big Thanksgiving

Day storm, my family added a nuance to that tradition. In addition to naming some*thing* we are grateful for, we also say the name of some*one* not present who we *wish* could be with us. It may be a person who has died or who, for some other reason, just can't be here in person. It's a way of expressing our gratitude for those special people in absentia, who love, and have loved us."

With that, Ali raised her glass and said, "Happy Thanksgiving, Zoe and Isaac." Silently, she added, "and Eric."

Following her lead, Peggy stepped forward, raised her glass and said, "Happy Thanksgiving, Grammy Marge!"

One by one, every person in the room followed suit.

After everyone had spoken the name of a loved one, Ali once again addressed the group. "The party is just getting started. Stay as late as you like, but when you do leave, please take a box of stationery with you from the table by the door. The letters I wrote and delivered this past year changed my life, and I want to encourage you to write letters of your own to people who might be surprised to discover how much they matter to you.

"Now, please raise your glasses one last time and join me in acknowledging our blessings and saluting one another. Cheers!"

As the sound of clinking glasses once again rang out, Ali sensed someone approaching from behind her and felt two strong hands rest on her shoulders. Feeling her heart begin to race, she turned to find Eric standing there, smiling at her.

Ali's Itinerary

From:	Dates:	To:	Miles	Hours
Issaquah, WA	Jan. 2	Clarkston	290	6
Clarkston, WA	Jan. 3-5	Kalispell	330	6
Kalispell, MT	Jan 6-19	Yellowstone	420	7
Yellowstone Nat'l Park	Jan. 20-Feb. 2	Rapid City	564	9
Rapid City, SD	Feb. 3-15	Lincoln	520	8.5
Lincoln, NE	Feb. 16-March 2	Dixon	424	7.5
Dixon, IL	March 3-April 1	Xenia	397	6.5
Xenia, OH	April 2-April 23	New York	Flight	Flight
New York, NY	April 23-May 1	Xenia	Flight	Flight
Xenia, OH	May 2	Louisville	154	2.5
Louisville, KY	May 2-30	Atlanta	422	7.5
Atlanta, GA	May 31–June 15	DeLand	425	7.5
DeLand, FL	June 16–June 30	Mobile	480	8
Mobile, AL	July 1–July 15	Huntsville	513	9
Huntsville, TX	July 16–July 30	Vernon	358	5.5
Vernon, TX	Aug. 1–Aug. 15	Albuquerque	460	7
Albuquerque, NM	Aug. 15–Sept. 5	Boulder City	575	8.5
Boulder City, NV	Sept. 5–Sept. 15	Battle Mtn.	503	8.5
Battle Mountain, NV	Sept. 16–Sept. 30	Beaverton	576	9.5
Beaverton, OR	Oct. 1-Oct. 30	Issaquah	188	3
	Totals:		**7,599**	**127**

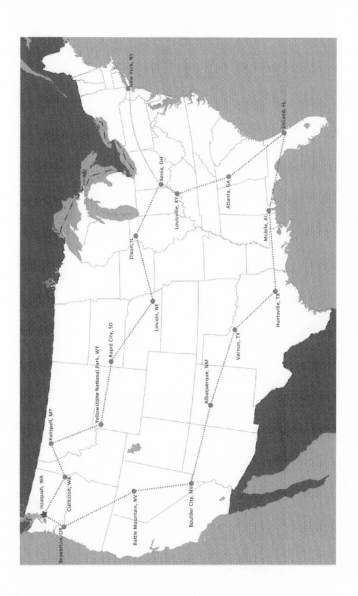

Since I Last Saw You

Acknowledgements

Writing can be a very solitary undertaking, but that has not been my experience in composing this novel. I am overcome with gratitude to the many individuals—friends, acquaintances and strangers—who generously agreed to assist me in bringing this book to fruition. Some provided expert information, others shared their very personal experiences, and still others were sources of inspiration and encouragement.

The collaboration has been nearly as gratifying as the writing itself.

Here, in alphabetical order, are the names of (most of) the villagers it took to write this book:

Laurie Aull, for being an avid reader and critiquing an early draft
Steve Beitler, for introducing me to the world of sprint car racing
Lori, Michael, Avery and Quincy Bento, for embracing me
Jody Bento, for facilitating her husband's trip down memory lane
Mark Bonne, for giving me insider information about life in Lincoln, NE
Greg Brooks, for acquainting me with Leavenworth businesses
Lauren Bruns, for sharing her expertise in horsemanship
Linnea Bruns, for giving me an Issaquah resident's perspective
Dave Correia, for sharing his knowledge of, and passion for skydiving
Josie Czeskleba, for introducing me to Zoe and giving her a face
Julie Dahlem, for never doubting I could achieve this goal
William Dahlem, for pointing Curtis in the right direction
Rick Donker, for sharing his childhood memories of Mount Vernon
Susan Dunn, for reading early drafts and always believing in me
Paul Gates, for cluing me in on being a "wine guy" at PCC
Barb Joseph, for lending her artistry to create a Berg family portrait
Debbie Kerns, for giving Ali a broad smile and a captivating countenance
Marilyn Kielbasa, for being a friend and a real-life Mrs. Andouille
Sara Kirschenman, for teaching me the ABCs of caring for a horse
Shari Kruse, for enthusiastically agreeing to share her musical talent
Donald Lawn, for kindly showing me the way as a fellow first-time author

Nick Musser, for introducing Isaac and me to heli-skiing

Keniai Neuman, for early enthusiasm and a teenage point of view

Helen Nolan Shafer, for eloquently expressing a young girl's love of horses

Kelly Nolan Shafer, for never tiring of hearing about my latest project

Margaret Ostling, for her skillful and creative jewelry designs

Wander Pedersen, for her early interest, enthusiasm and hostessing

Kevin Porter, for graciously allowing me to audit his static line class

Cynthia Reid, for allowing me to use her cabin as a writer's retreat house

Jani Riffe, for answering my endless questions and sharing Peter's story

Peter Riffe, for being such a powerfully enduring spirit

Dale Ross, for being the embodiment of Isaac

Danielle Schindler-Cheung, for reading my first draft between contractions

Coleen Small, for her blind faith and ever-positive outlook

David Bryan Smith, for cheering on and sharing the writer's dream

John Sterns, for his eagle-eye editorial assistance

Jim Sutton, for facilitating my reintroduction to skydiving

Tess, for accompanying me on my own life journey

Yessika Yoncee, for being a great neighbor and a skilled PhotoShopper

I also want to publically laud the efforts and accomplishments of my editors, **Kathy Mulady and Karalynn Ott.** This being my first novel, I was tempted to forego the services of a professional editor. Now, that notion seems foolish and incomprehensible to me. They both worked extremely hard, and showed an exceptional amount of dedication to helping me perfect my prose.

Karalynn displayed great diplomacy and skill in massaging my first draft into a viable end product.

Kathy, in addition to her invaluable technical expertise, expressed an enthusiasm for this story that enabled me to believe in myself and in it.

Bibliography

Books:
Adler, Rabbi Morris. *May I Have a Word With You?* Crown Publishers, 1967. Reprinted from B'nai B'rith International.

Colgrove, Melba; Harold H. Bloomfield; and Peter McWilliams. *How to Survive the Loss of a Love.* New York: Bantam Books, 1976.

Davis Kasl, Charlotte. *Finding Joy: 101 Ways to Free Your Spirit and Dance with Life.* Edited by Janet Goldstein. New York: HarperCollins, 1994.

Hicks, Esther and Jerry. *Ask and It Is Given: Learning to Manifest Your Desires.* Editorial supervision by Jill Kramer. Carlsbad, CA: Hay House, 2004.

Motion Picture:
What the Bleep Do We Know? Captured Light and Lord of the Wind Films, LLC, 2004.

Music:
"Amazing Grace." Circa 1876. Public domain.

"Joy is Like the Rain." Words and music by Miriam Therese Winter. © copyright: Medical Mission Sisters, 1965. Used with permission.

Kruse, Shari. "Lessons." Words and music by Shari Kruse. © copyright 2013. Used with permission.

Kruse, Shari. "Since." Words and music by Shari Kruse. © copyright 2013. Used with permission.

Kruse, Shari. "Waiting for the Rain." Words and music by Shari Kruse. © copyright 2013. Used with permission.

Kruse, Shari. "Thanksgiving Song." Words and music by Shari Kruse. © copyright 2013. Used with permission.

Original songs written and performed by Shari Kruse can be found at: https://soundcloud.com/aak

About the Author

In my heart-of-hearts, I am a teacher. Unfortunately, I don't possess the temperament to be happy or successful teaching in a traditional classroom setting, so I have always found other ways to fulfill my perceived vocation. For many years, I developed and presented workshops on topics as varied as personal budgeting, leadership development and catechism.

Someone once pointed out to me that storytelling is the most powerful and well-received form of teaching. That's one reason that Jesus, among other great teachers, used it so liberally and to such effect.

Since that time, I have dreamed of coming up with an entertaining and inspiring story that would allow me to share some of the life lessons I've learned. In particular, I wanted to tell a story that would elucidate the role of gratitude in creating and living a joyful life. *Since I Last Saw You* is the result of that desire.

Thanksgiving—the most underappreciated holiday on the American calendar, in my opinion—seemed like a perfect backdrop for such a tale, and is featured prominently in my novel. It's my hope and my dream that *Since I Last Saw You* becomes a holiday tradition— a story that readers will want to revisit year after year and share with their families— much in the way that watching *It's a Wonderful Life* is for me.